M000314667

TENTYRIAN
LEGACY

ELISE WALTERS

TENTYRIAN LEGACY

ELISE WALTERS

PERMUTED PLATINUM

TENTYRIAN LEGACY

ISBN (hardcover): 978-1-61868-210-9
ISBN (eBook): 978-1-61868-211-6

Published by Permuted Press
109 International Drive, Suite 300
Franklin, TN 37067

Cover art by Conzpiracy Digital.

Follow us online:

Web: http://www.PermutedPress.com

Facebook: http://www.facebook.com/PermutedPress

Twitter: @PermutedPress

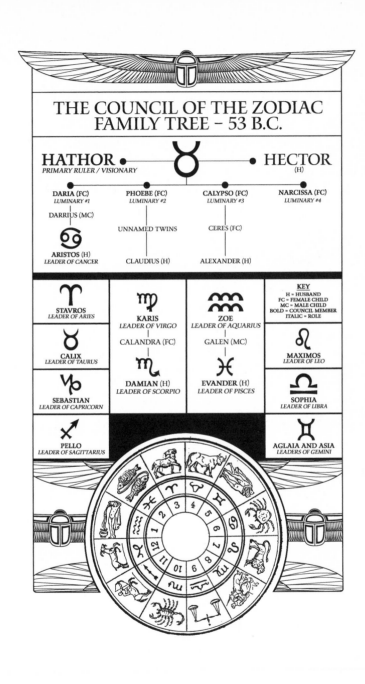

THE COUNCIL OF THE ZODIAC
FAMILY TREE – 53 B.C.

HATHOR ●———♉———● **HECTOR**
PRIMARY RULER / VISIONARY (H)

DARIA (FC)	**PHOEBE** (FC)	**CALYPSO** (FC)	**NARCISSA** (FC)
LUMINARY #1	*LUMINARY #2*	*LUMINARY #3*	*LUMINARY #4*

DARRIUS (MC)

UNNAMED TWINS   CERES (FC)

♋

ARISTOS (H)
LEADER OF CANCER

CLAUDIUS (H)   ALEXANDER (H)

♈	♍	♒	**KEY**
STAVROS *LEADER OF ARIES*	**KARIS** *LEADER OF VIRGO*	**ZOE** *LEADER OF AQUARIUS*	H = HUSBAND FC = FEMALE CHILD MC = MALE CHILD BOLD = COUNCIL MEMBER ITALIC = ROLE

CALANDRA (FC)   GALEN (MC)

♉	♏	♓	♌
CALIX *LEADER OF TAURUS*	**DAMIAN** (H) *LEADER OF SCORPIO*	**EVANDER** (H) *LEADER OF PISCES*	**MAXIMOS** *LEADER OF LEO*

♑			♎
SEBASTIAN *LEADER OF CAPRICORN*			**SOPHIA** *LEADER OF LIBRA*

♐			♊
PELLO *LEADER OF SAGITTARIUS*			**AGLAIA AND ASIA** *LEADERS OF GEMINI*

For my husband
— your love and encouragement
made this book happen.
And for my brother, who inspires me
— and doesn't laugh at my vampires.

TABLE OF CONTENTS

PART I

PROLOGUE

53 BC, AUGUST
TENTYRIS, EGYPT
THE ROYAL VILLA

The ivory comb slipped quietly through her raven hair. Her scalp tingled from Hita's washing, and her skin glowed with balanos oil. Mixed with extract of lotus, myrrh, and cinnamon, the oil infused Hathor's body and bath chamber with the essence of her power. She knew she would need every ounce of it tonight. Temporary reprieve from company, except from Hita's, was welcome. The aching in her temples was reduced to a dull throb. Fortunately, the warm bath in the marble basin made her feel almost whole.

"My lady, you look radiant," Hita praised.

"Thank you. Your hands have worked wonders. I feel much better," answered Hathor absently. Her mind was elsewhere.

"You should rest more," Hita chastised. Hathor secretly loved how Hita clucked at her like a mother hen—despite the fact that Hathor had walked the Earth almost four times as long as her.

"Oh Hita, there will be plenty of time to rest when I'm dead, which may be soon enough. I will wear the violet stola tonight," Hathor said without pause.

Never one to make jokes, Hita knew Hathor meant every word of what she said. Hita crossed the stone floor to the ebony chest where the ceremonial robes were stored. Before she unlatched the lid of the intricately carved chest, she ran her hand over the zodiac symbol emblazed on top and said a silent prayer to Bes. If any god could protect her mistress, it would be Bes with his arsenal of swords and knives.

"Hita, my stola," Hathor snapped. "We don't have much time."

"My apologies, my lady. It is here."

Hita lifted the silk garment out of the chest and gave it a light shake. After slipping the rich fabric of the long robe onto her mistress, Hita straightened the linen tunic underneath with a firm tug. Her hands had gone through these same motions for almost half a century, just like her mother before her. The love and duty Hita felt for Hathor weighed on her. How many more years would there be? She knew Hathor was uneasy.

"I will wear my gold belt and bracelets," said Hathor.

"Just a minute, my lady—I asked Selene to polish them." Hita walked briskly to the door to call for the young maid, only to find her patiently waiting outside with the jewelry.

"Why didn't you come in, Selene? Our lady has places to be," asked Hita.

"I'm sorry," replied Selene with downcast eyes. "I was afraid to interrupt."

"No matter, run along now," Hita said kindly.

Ever since Selene joined the villa staff a year ago, Hita encouraged her to be more confident, with little result. However, Hita understood. Working for the Tentyrian royal family could be an intimidating task.

The belt clasped together by two snakes' heads soon encircled Hathor's small waist, and her gold bracelets gripped each pale wrist like manacles of strength. The zodiac pendant that never left her neck draped gracefully between her porcelain breasts—loosely shrouded by her vibrant garb. She reached up to the pendant and traced the embossing with her fingers, each touch a reminder of her responsibility.

"No palla, makeup, or hair intricacies tonight. I will go like this," said Hathor.

"But the embroidered palla with gold completes your outfit. Perhaps some ochre for your lips?" Hita fluttered about Hathor in her last-minute attempts to ensure her mistress looked perfect, although little was needed to enhance the already flawless Hathor.

"No. Tonight is not about pomp and circumstance. It is about reality. Please hand me my sistrum," Hathor commanded.

"As you wish."

Hathor slipped on her leather sandals, and with her favored ceremonial instrument in hand, she looked briefly at herself in the polished copper Hita held for her. The eyes that looked back were filled with knowing.

"Are my daughters ready?" Hathor asked.

"Yes. The Royal Luminaries are waiting for you in the temple, along with the rest of the Council."

It was time to make the announcement.

CHAPTER 1: POOLSIDE

2001 AD, MARCH
NEW CANAAN, CONNECTICUT
THE PARKER ESTATE

Her head hurt. In fact, it always hurt. Codeine, Imitrex, calcium channel blockers, you name it; she had taken it to etase her headaches. At fifteen, Arianna Elizabeth Parker had tried almost every therapy available to treat her diagnosed cluster headaches and schizophrenia. But they never seemed to make a dent in the pain that pummeled her head or the voices that drowned out her thoughts.

Fortunately, Ari—as she preferred to be called—mastered the art of making it appear as if she took her medication. She knew it didn't work, so why take the pills that made her feel like a zombie and more of a freak, she rationalized. Under the watchful eye of her overbearing housekeeper Irena, who executed her parents' orders with unparalleled Russian efficiency, Ari would put the pills under her tongue, after which she would skillfully spit them into the toilet, but not before Irena (aka the Iron Curtain) made her "wash them down" with a glass of orange juice. It was fresh squeezed and organic, of course.

Ari could barely remember when she'd eaten something that was not healthy for her. The Parker house was gluten-free, sugar-free, and low-fat 24/7. Even the few times Ari went to birthday parties as a child, she had shown up with her own lunch bag complete with a slice of tofu birthday cake for her enjoyment. It was humiliating. Usually she didn't stay long, and everyone ignored her. But Laura Delia's birthday party had been different, she remembered. Laura lived down the street, and Ari viewed the invitation as a token gesture for the homeschooled neighbor girl. She was excited, nevertheless.

It was a rare instance when Ari was even allowed to leave the grounds of the Parker residence. School was out of the question, so she had a string of private instructors instead. Aside from her black Labrador retriever, Beau, Ari had no friends. The teachers, her doctors, and even her parents came and went. At the tender age of seven, Laura's birthday was a welcome escape, despite her mother's insistence that it would likely be a "mediocre" affair. Since Ari's parents believed she was taking her medication and her episodes were in-check, she was allowed to go . . . just barely.

Ari remembered she wore her patent leather party shoes with frilly socks to the party. Roger, the driver who always smelled of Altoids and cheap cologne, dropped her off. Ari entered the front door of the charming Georgian brick home and was immediately overwhelmed by the high-pitched buzzing that filled her ears. Ari fought back against the sounds in her head that threatened to crush her. She was determined to be there, and Ari knew she could do it if she stayed focused.

Ari navigated her way through the sea of girls to hand Laura her present. She didn't know what it was but hoped the Iron Curtain had the good sense to get the Barbie she'd pleaded for. Laura graciously accepted the gift and took Ari's hand. She led her to the kitchen where Laura's mom, Mrs. Delia, was putting the finishing touches on the cake—a pink-frosted concoction with white roses and plastic ballet dancers.

"Ari, hello there, darling!" Mrs. Delia greeted her. "I haven't seen you since your parents' Christmas cocktail party, and that was a year ago. My how you've grown, and aren't you as beautiful as ever! Where is your tiara? Laura, be a love and get Ari her tiara. We only allow princesses in this house." Ari stood there speechless. The warmth and genuine pleasure around her took her off guard. This was the opposite of her home.

Laura handed Ari a sparkling sequin crown, the same as those that graced all the little girls' heads at the party. It was one of the most beautiful things she had ever seen. Ari placed it carefully on her hair, mindful not to muss the tight French braid the Iron Curtain crafted that morning with her shriveled hands.

"Laura, has your father finished setting up the games?" asked Mrs. Delia. "Why don't you show the girls where we've set up Pin the Bow on the Ballerina?"

"Come on, Ari," said Laura cheerfully as she held out her hand. But before Ari could grab it, Mrs. Delia said, "Ari, you stay here with me for a second. Laura, why don't you get the girls started?" Ari's heart sank. They probably wanted her to stay in the kitchen in case she scared the other children. But at least she had a tiara, thought Ari practically. She could play princess with Beau later.

Ari waited for Mrs. Delia to instruct her where to sit, but instead Mrs. Delia flashed a mischievous smile before she lifted Ari up to a kitchen-counter stool. "Now, I know you have your own lunch and snacks to eat; your housekeeper called me twice to remind me. But I think we both know that you'd prefer something else." With a twinkle in her eye, Mrs. Delia filled a flowered birthday party plate with three hot dogs and almost half a bag of puffy Cheetos. "I won't tell if you won't," she said.

The birthday party was magical. Ari played with the other children and won a purse full of plastic jewelry. She managed to keep the voices primarily at bay by focusing on the activities. There were no episodes. When she returned home that evening, she wanted to vomit all the food and birthday cake she had gorged herself on. But she held it together. She could be a normal kid, she told herself.

Ari remembered that day had taken its toll as the sounds in her head were at a fevered pitch. The Iron Curtain started Ari's bath and stripped off her gingham party dress. Ari couldn't speak as she climbed into the Japanese soaking tub that was almost as deep as she was tall. As soon as her head slipped beneath the surface, the buzz and voices quieted. If only every day was like this, she had thought, or if at least she had been born a mermaid princess. That way she could stay under the water forever and never have to hear the voices that haunted her. Irena pulled Ari from the bath that night and put her to bed. She passed out and afterward slept for two days straight.

But that was almost eight years ago. Ari was no more a mermaid princess than she was that idyllic seven-year-old. Older and wiser, she knew she'd never be normal; she had come to terms with that. Howard, her physics teacher, had just left. The rest of the afternoon was hers. Yet it always was hard to relax after her lessons with him. Howard gave her the creeps. A lecherous feeling came over her during today's lecture of quantum control and the cooling and trapping of atoms. She ignored the buzzing and unintelligible whispers in her ears, like she always did, but today it was more difficult than usual.

Needing to wash away the feelings she felt helpless to control, Ari decided it was time for a swim. She meticulously reorganized her textbooks and papers before she turned the library lights off and dashed up to her bedroom—her place of escape. Walking into her room felt like walking into a cloud. The shades of cream and gray were a mature color palette, but the soothing effect was what Ari loved. Since she spent the majority of her life in her room, alone, Ari was given free rein to decorate as she wanted.

From the scalloped pillowcases with embroidered taupe edges to the Scandinavian armoire that elegantly hid her plasma TV screen, Ari chose every element of her room with the details in mind. It was her domain, so she was expected to keep it scrupulously ordered. If not, Irena was instructed to tell Ari's parents immediately, resulting in one or more of her limited privileges taken away.

Most teenage girls' bedroom walls had posters of their favorite movie stars or bands. At least that's what they looked like on TV to Ari. Her walls were painted in Farrow & Ball's "No. 203 Tallow" and were hung with a few carefully chosen landscapes she had purchased at auction from Sotheby's online. Her walk-in closet didn't have an article of clothing out of place. Wooden hangers, almost exactly one inch apart, were hung with an array of J.Crew and Ralph Lauren clothing also purchased online. Ari knew her parents had their flaws, but their gift to her of financial freedom, in the form of a Platinum American Express card and Mac laptop computer when she was thirteen, wasn't one of them. However, with the few freedoms she did have, she knew not to abuse them. After all, they were easily taken away.

Ari put on her turquoise bikini, the one she hoped she would wear on vacation with her parents last spring. But they didn't take her to Bermuda. They never did. She was told the potential for her having an episode was too risky between the airport lines and travel logistics. So she stopped asking to go. But she always held out hope she'd be included . . .

Ari stared at herself critically in the full-length mirror of her closet. Too tall, too lanky, she reflected. She had yet to develop the curves of her equally tall mother, who was renowned for her beauty. In time, she hoped she would look like her mom, but she vowed to never be like her. Frustrated with what she felt was a lacking appearance of boring brown shoulder-length hair and too sharp of facial features, Ari turned away from the mirror and gave a whistle.

Beau came bounding down the hall and skidded to a stop at Ari's bare feet. He planted slobbery kisses all over her legs. The adorable Labrador was truly a girl's best friend. After grabbing a monogrammed towel, Ari led Beau to the indoor pool adjacent to the conservatory.

Although spring was around the corner, winter's chill had not lifted, making it impossible to swim outside.

The Parker mansion was vast. The Iron Curtain was in the east wing of the house instructing the maids, once again, on how to polish the floor to her standards. In the west wing, Ari and Beau proceeded to the pool unnoticed. Ari loved her home, from the grand colonial façade to the rooms that seemed to ramble one after another. Her parents had spent close to four years renovating it before she was born. They turned the 1872 mansion into the epitome of New England elegance. However, while their home was picture perfect on the outside, the lives within were far from it.

Today, Ari's mother was likely at a ladies lunch, maybe even one to raise money for the causes that were "so dear to her heart because of Arianna." Ari had heard that one too many times to count. The irony certainly wasn't lost on her. Gloria Parker would rather attend charity events for schizophrenia and raise money for research than spend five minutes alone with her own daughter. Ari's father on the other hand was probably at work. It was Saturday.

Ari wondered what Laura Delia was doing today. Occasionally, she saw her jogging on the road wearing her "New Canaan High School Track" sweatshirt. She had seen pictures of Laura and the NCHS track team in the paper. They were Fairfield County champions and were going to the state championship meet in a couple of months. Laura probably had a great social life and a boyfriend, Ari thought wistfully. She opened the French doors to the pool and strode over to the chaise lounge to spread out her towel. Ari picked up Beau's rubber ball from the wicker basket of toys and tossed it in the pool. With a splash, Beau hit the water in fast pursuit.

Ball retrieved, Beau pulled himself out of the water and shook off the droplets clinging to his glossy coat onto Ari. "Well thank you for that!" she exclaimed. Laughing, Ari grabbed the ball and tossed it back into the pool. Just then, she realized that the buzzing in her head had grown louder and the whispers had started again. When she turned to reach for her towel on the lounge, she saw Howard. He was standing in the door watching her.

"Howard, what are you doing here?" asked Ari, surprised. She wrapped the towel around her self-consciously. Modesty had been in-grained in her, and she certainly didn't like Howard's eyes roving over her body.

"I forgot to leave a study guide I wanted you to complete before Tuesday. When I came back to give it to you, you weren't in the library.

I heard some splashing so I came to the pool," he said.

"Great. Thanks. I'll work on it later tonight." Ari took the guide from him quickly and stepped back closer to Beau, who was waiting patiently for the next toss.

"Are you out here all alone?" Howard asked. He decided to remove himself from the doorway and walked over to the lounge chair.

"I've got Beau, and Irena is around here somewhere," said Ari nonchalantly. The back of her neck tingled, and the throbbing in her head became a fierce pulse. Making himself comfortable in the chair, Howard relaxed into it and kicked off his Converse sneakers. With his vintage T-shirt under his tweed blazer, he had a hipster geek look about him that didn't quite fit, like he was trying to be eighteen when he really was thirty.

Howard had received his doctorate in physics from Dartmouth and was one of the university's youngest PhD graduates. But rather than becoming a university professor, Howard had decided to become a teacher and tutor to the wealthy. It certainly paid better. Several New Canaan and Greenwich families used him to further propel their young's trajectory toward success. Not that Ari needed to be propelled. She excelled in academics and her extracurriculars, despite her illness.

When Ari was three, she was labeled "asocial." She shunned company and would rarely speak, often screaming when strangers, or even her own parents, approached her. It was clear to the doctors that Ari didn't want to form connections with those around her. But that wasn't entirely true. Ari wanted to; it just hurt. Ari's quiet and nearly silent demeanor, consequently, turned her into an acute listener and learner. When Ari would have been in second grade, she was at a sixth grade reading level. When she should have been a beginner in Spanish, she was fluent.

From fencing to swimming, Ari was also skilled physically. This was highly unusual in someone with her condition, as many schizophrenics had cognitive impairments. But Ari had no physical handicaps. Her handicap, however, was perceived to be in her brain. It had been explained to her when she was little that parts of her brain just weren't like other people's. And it was because of those parts she had terrible headaches and often heard things that weren't there. Being isolated in the house helped, as it muted the pain and generally kept the voices quiet. But as soon as she was in the company of others, a wave of noise would hit her and she'd feel like she was drowning.

Ari reached a turning point in her illness when she was around six and realized that her parents and doctors couldn't help her. It was an epiphany she had after Irena had insisted on taking her food shopping. The new maids had just been fired, and there was no one to watch Ari at home. So Irena took Ari with her. The grocery store trip resulted in a horrific episode and another fruitless attempt by her doctors to try a new medication combination. Not surprisingly, it didn't work. From then on, Ari decided that she would have to start pretending she was better. She'd stop saying she heard voices, and she'd try harder to be around people. Her parents thought the change in Ari was due to the new medication. But it was really Ari's resolve. Because of it, Ari was rewarded with Beau.

Despite Ari's success academically and the perceived improvement in her condition, her parents lived in constant fear she would relapse. Ari couldn't completely hide the pain of her headaches and her obvious preference to be alone. She still became exhausted after a day of coming into contact with more than four or five people. Ari had no siblings, friends, or peers. And as her parents' only child, they continued to view her as the daughter that never quite lived up to their expectations.

As Howard lounged in the chair, Ari knew she needed to be polite. If she was rude, her mother would find out, and those expectations would become even further from being met.

"Do you have other lessons to give today, Howard?" Ari asked conversationally, hoping he would get the hint and leave. She hated how he asked her to call him Howard, instead of Professor Watkins.

"Hmm, nope. You're my only one," he answered with a smile. "You must get lonely . . . A beautiful girl like you should have friends or a boyfriend to keep her company, especially on a Saturday." Gross. He was coming on to her.

"I need to go take my afternoon pills before I forget. I'll walk you out," she said quickly.

Howard grabbed her slim wrist and yanked Ari down to the chair so that she was sitting sideways on his lap. "Ari, I can make sure you aren't lonely," he said. Ari instinctively slapped Howard across the face with an open palm. She had seen it done on General Hospital and was surprised she actually did it. However, Howard hardly looked discouraged. He looked excited. One of his arms circled firmly around her bare waist.

"Howard, you have the wrong idea. I'm still in high school. You're my teacher." Ari tried to stand up, but his arm held her in place.

"You aren't in high school. You are a homeschooled mental case," he sneered.

"I think you should leave. Irena will be here any minute," Ari said while struggling to stand.

"You should be grateful I've even taken an interest in you, Ari," Howard taunted as he held her. "For someone so smart, you are incredibly inexperienced. I bet you've never been kissed. It's a shame. You have an amazing body." Howard's free hand grazed her neck and moved down to her left shoulder blade. She couldn't believe this was happening. His fingers suddenly pulled the bow of her halter bikini. She grabbed it immediately to keep it from falling off.

"Whoops. My fingers slipped," Howard teased. She had enough. She may have been sheltered, but she'd seen enough Lifetime TV to imagine where this situation could take her. Howard maneuvered her in his lap so that her back was to him. Ari knew she could scream, but she wasn't sure if Irena or the maids would hear her in time, as they were at the opposite side of the house. Instead, Ari whipped her head back and heard a sickening crunch as the back of her head connected with his nose.

"What the fuck!" screamed Howard, blood gushing from his nose. "You bitch." Howard's excitement was gone. Beau had been sitting patiently, waiting for Ari to get up and throw the ball. But as soon as Ari delivered her blow, Beau's patient pant turned into a growl. The affable Lab's protective instincts kicked in, and he lunged for Howard's leg. Beau clamped down on his right calf.

Howard yelled, "Get him off! Get him off!" With his left leg, Howard kicked Beau. The impact was so hard, Ari was sure he'd broken some of Beau's ribs. Without thinking twice, Ari kicked Howard in the groin with all the force she could muster and punched him under the chin. His jaw clacked together, and he crumpled onto the flagstone floor. Beau, meanwhile, held tight to Howard's calf.

"Don't you ever hurt my dog, you bastard! I'll kill you!" Ari straddled Howard, punching him repeatedly. She was seeing red—Howard hurt the one thing that loved her unconditionally. By this point, Irena had come to the pool to investigate the commotion and was shocked to find Ari delivering punches like a hoodlum in a street alley.

"Jesus, Mary, and Joseph. Arianna Elizabeth, get off of him right now! Oh my God, he is unconscious. Carla!" shrilled Irena. "Call 911!" Irena yanked Ari off of Howard. "What have you done, young lady?" Ari had no response. All she could think was how pathetic Howard looked in his bloody Beatles T-shirt and puke-colored blazer.

One of the maids, Carla, soon appeared. Flabbergasted, she looked from Ari to Irena, confused as to what she should do. Irena's bark at her to get moving interrupted her bewilderment, and she ran for the phone. Ari called to Beau and at the sound of her command, he released his grip. Her poor pup, he needed medical attention before that bastard Howard. It was then that Ari realized her bathing suit top was undone. Embarrassed, she quickly tied it. She would not cry, she resolved.

The paramedics and police arrived on the scene. Howard was taken away on a stretcher with a brace around his neck. Ari was told her mother was on her way home. At Ari's insistence, Roger the driver took Beau to the veterinary clinic downtown for X-rays. Unfortunately, Ari had to remain for questioning. The paramedics tried to get her to go to the hospital, but she adamantly refused. Ari assured them there was no need for a rape kit and that she wasn't injured.

After the EMT examined Ari and it was clear all she had were some bruised knuckles, she was turned over to Officer Lefkowitz. Wrapped in her towel, Ari sat patiently in a rocker by the pool while the middle-aged officer took out his notepad and recorded the basic details about the incident—names, ages, and such. She focused on the notepad, silently counting her exhales. All the activity around her caused her head to spin. Although Officer Lefkowitz didn't notice, she was struggling to focus her mind.

"So, Arianna, how did this happen?" asked the paunchy officer. He had a kind enough face, she thought. Ari took a deep breath.

She said calmly, "I was here at the pool when Howard showed up. It was after our lesson. He said he forgot to give me some homework. Next thing I knew, he pulled me onto his lap and tried to take off my bathing suit. I told him to leave, but he didn't listen. So I hit him and my dog bit him."

"And has Mr. Watkins ever acted like this before? Made any advances previously?" asked the officer.

"No, but he always kind of . . . weirded me out," she replied hesitantly.

"I know this may make you feel uncomfortable, but I have to ask. Other than undoing your top, did he touch you at all anywhere else?"

"Gross. No. He is a creep, but no. He's never touched me other than what he tried to do today."

"Okay, good. Now how often do you see Mr. Watkins?"

"He teaches me physics every Tuesday and Saturday."

"So you don't go to school?"

"No, I'm homeschooled."

"And do you enjoy it?"

"It's okay. I can't go to school because of my illness."

Before he could ask her to explain, she quickly interjected, "I just get headaches . . . a lot." Ari left out the schizophrenia part. She knew as soon as she told him, he'd think she was crazy. Everyone did.

"Well this is an unfortunate incident," said Lefkowitz. "But the important thing is that you are safe. Now that we have your statement, my partner will speak with Mr. Watkins. We just heard back from the EMTs and he likely has a concussion and a broken jaw and nose. He'll need a few stitches for his leg and a rabies . . ." But before he could finish his sentence, a high-pitched trill interrupted him.

"Oh my God! Where is Arianna! Irena! There is blood on this floor! Is my daughter all right?" The hysterical voice, followed by the fast click of heels, could only belong to one person—her mother.

Officer Lefkowitz stood to brief Gloria Parker, a thin woman who was a good five inches taller than his modest stature of five foot four. Lefkowitz didn't get a word out before the strikingly beautiful woman's own interrogation began.

"Irena, what happened? Why are there policemen in this house and why is there blood on my floor? What happened? Someone tell me now!" Gloria's impatient hands gestured wildly. Meanwhile, her auburn hair remained perfectly in place within its elegant chignon.

Irena, who had been directing the various officers about the house and ordering the maids back to work, stopped what she was doing and turned her full attention to Gloria. "Mrs. Parker, there was an incident with Arianna and her physics teacher. She has not been hurt. Mr. Watkins is at the hospital now."

"What kind of incident? Did he slip and fall? I just don't understand . . . Did Arianna take her medication this afternoon?" asked Gloria, with more than a hint of suspicion creeping into her voice.

"She was scheduled to take her afternoon pills right around the time this happened," answered Irena as she gestured obviously to the blood on the floor and Ari.

"Arianna Elizabeth, did you hurt Howard?" asked her mother accusingly.

"No! He attacked me. I was just playing with Beau and he tried to take my clothes off!" Ari exclaimed defensively.

Ari wrapped her arms tighter around herself and continued to count her breathing. She was white as a sheet. Gloria's arms crossed over her mink coat while her Roman nose remained held high. Lefkowitz was confused by the mother-daughter exchange. Any other mother would have embraced her daughter, telling her it was going to be all right. Any other mother would have demanded the arrest of the man who attacked her child. Not this mother. There were no tears. No hugs.

"Officer, what's your name? Have you spoken with Howard yet? How seriously injured is he?" asked Gloria impatiently.

"It's Officer Lefkowitz, ma'am. And my partner is talking to him right now. He has some serious injuries, but he is lucid and able to provide a statement."

"This whole situation is unseemly," said Gloria, exasperated. "Undoubtedly it will be in the Advertiser tomorrow. How embarrassing." Of course, she would be concerned over what their neighbors and friends would think if they saw this in the town paper, thought Ari.

"Mrs. Parker, it does seem that based on your daughter's account, her teacher tried to molest her," said Lefkowitz.

With a sniff and raised chin, her mother said, "Indeed. Officer Lefkowitz, please let me know what your partner finds out. You may speak with me in my office afterwards. Irena, please make sure that Arianna takes her medication, gets cleaned up, and goes to bed. She looks like she is going to pass out."

"I need to wait to see if Beau is all right, Mother," said Ari.

"No excuses," Gloria replied coldly. "Irena will bring dinner to you in your room. When Beau returns, I'll have Roger bring him up to you. You're lucky I even let you keep that dog. Irena, show Officer Lefkowitz to my office when he is done here." Gloria then turned on her heel and flounced away. Lefkowitz looked at the teenage girl, who rose slowly from the chair. She did look like she was going to faint, but her facial expression was not one of fragility; it was of anger. She left the pool without a word as the housekeeper followed behind.

An hour later, Lefkowitz was sitting in an uncomfortable antique chair that probably cost as much as six months of his salary. He surveyed Gloria's office with a mixture of curiosity and reverence. Decorated in a combination of English traditional and chic contemporary, the room was a testament to fine taste. Unfortunately, he left a boot print on the Oriental rug. He hoped she wouldn't notice. The fire was lit in the fireplace that Gloria had started with a click of a manicured finger.

Now that she had a few minutes to compose herself, Gloria appeared calm and as sweet as honey. She sat demurely behind her Lucite desk, her lips freshly appliquéd with a soft rose color. Gloria offered Lefkowitz a nonfat soy latte, but he declined. Dunkin' Donuts regular coffee was more his speed.

"Officer Lefkowitz, I first want to apologize," said Gloria warmly. "I know the New Canaan police have much better things to do than come out here on a weekend." Actually, they didn't. Aside from the occasional speeding ticket and illicit teenage party, New Canaan was a sleepy little town. Crime was practically unheard of.

New Canaan was the location of choice for New England's and the nation's wealthiest. Ranked number one in the US for the highest median income, its sprawling mansions were spread acres apart and were separated by stone walls and electric gates. New Canaan was a country paradise, especially for New York's investment bankers, brokers, lawyers, even the occasional rock star. The day Officer Lefkowitz could afford to live there would be the day he won the lottery and his ex-wife wanted him back.

"Not to worry, ma'am, it's our job. I just feel sorry for your daughter. But she's a tough one. No tears there."

"Yes, well Arianna is very strong willed. She is also a very sick girl. Unfortunately, she suffers from schizophrenia and very severe headaches that have forced her to remain confined to this house for most of her life. Her father and I have spent hundreds of thousands of dollars treating her condition, which has been quite the cross to bear. Arianna has a very strict treatment regimen that, if not followed, can have terrible results. Over the past few years, her episodes have mostly stopped, thanks to the medication. But I fear she may have experienced one again today."

"Why do you think that, Mrs. Parker?" he asked quizzically.

"You should know that Arianna hears voices in her head. She says she doesn't know what they say. Most of the time, it sounds like a low hum for her. When she becomes agitated and is around too many people, the humming and voices get louder. With the onset of an episode, the voices overwhelm her, and her reactions can range from passing out to screaming and even hitting. In one of her episodes, when she was six, she began screaming at the Food Emporium, knocked down four food displays, and broke Irena's hand and nose when she tried to remove Arianna from the grocery store."

"It sounds like a bad temper tantrum," said Lefkowitz.

"Officer, it's much more than a temper tantrum. Afterwards, Arianna is usually so exhausted she can sleep for days. Her headaches will set in and she needs to remain in a quiet, dark room to limit the pain. It has been terrible for our family."

"I can't imagine," said Lefkowitz sympathetically.

"Well, most people can't. What did Howard say about the incident?"

"I want to first advise that in he-said she-said situations, it is often very difficult to determine the truth," Lefkowitz replied. "Unfortunately, there is no eyewitness; this situation could become difficult if either party decides to press charges. Of course, we respect that Arianna may be a victim, and we will uphold the law should you decide to take legal action."

"Officer, what did he say?" Gloria demanded. Her demeanor had evidently cooled.

"He said that Arianna invited him to the pool and tried to seduce him. Then she suddenly had an unexplained outburst and began punching him, saying she would kill him." Gloria's face was expressionless. Lefkowitz wondered what she was like at poker. "Mrs. Parker, these are serious accusations, but to be honest, he could be lying. He doesn't have any priors or a history of deviant behavior, but this could be the first time. For now, Mr. Watkins will be in the hospital for a couple of days. He has not yet indicated if he wishes to press charges. He did request that he speak with you, though. I personally would not recommend that. I am advising you to take some time and talk to your daughter. Maybe talk to a counselor. Think about if you want to file charges against him. Luckily, Arianna has no injuries, other than some swelling in her hands."

"No. No charges. We will handle this matter quietly. I will speak with Howard directly. Again, thanks so very much for coming all the way out here. I hope we have not inconvenienced the department."

"Not at all. It's our job, as I said. I know you are trying to protect Arianna, but Mrs. Parker, you should take some time and think about it. If Mr. Watkins really did do this, he'll probably do it again."

"Thank you for your time, Officer. I will show you out myself." With a gracious smile, Gloria ushered Officer Lefkowitz to the black and white marble foyer and shut the thick walnut door behind him as he exited. Gloria breathed a sigh of relief. She needed to call Walter immediately. Arianna's father would not be happy. He rarely ever was.

Gloria went back to her office and picked up the old-fashioned rotary phone and dialed her husband's office. "Hello," answered Walter gruffly. He hated being interrupted, especially when he was working on a difficult case. Gloria could just imagine him, sitting behind his desk littered with files and leftover takeout containers. She told him no more takeout. His cholesterol was out of control. He had gained at least twenty pounds since she'd married him. Not to mention his once full head of hair was almost gone. Years ago, she'd fancied him a Clark Gable—Clark Bar was more like it now.

Walter had called in his "A team" over the weekend to strategize on a high-profile case in which they were tasked with defending an accused money launderer. They had lost an important appeal, and if their next move wasn't planned just right, they would lose the case. Walter Albright Parker did occasionally defend the innocent. And those he defended who weren't innocent, which was most of the time, paid a pretty penny for Walter's services and subsequently funded Gloria's shopping habits. Unfortunately, Walter's stress level was already high, and this news wouldn't help . . .

"Walter, I need you to come home early tonight. We have a problem," said Gloria quickly.

"What is it, Gloria? I'm busy," replied Walter tersely.

"Walter, I came home today to find that Arianna had beaten her physics teacher unconscious by the pool. They are saying he will need to have his jaw wired shut."

"That doesn't sound like her. Gloria, what happened? And make it quick."

"She told the police that Howard attacked her and tried to take her clothes off. But I know she didn't take her medication this afternoon . . . and Howard is saying she attacked him . . ."

"Jesus, the police came? Did he say he wants to press charges?"

"Not yet. But he told the officer that he'd like to speak with us."

"Everyone has a price," responded Walter flatly. He certainly knew better than anyone. "Is Arianna hurt?" he asked.

"No. She's fine. I'm concerned about what we should do with her, though. What if this happens again? Maybe it's time we send her away. We have talked about Silver Hill. And it's close enough that we can visit. Maybe they can reach her. I certainly can't. She flat-out denied she was responsible. I just don't believe it."

"Gloria, she hasn't done something like that in at least nine years."

"Walter, our daughter is a diagnosed schizophrenic with a history of violent episodes. Anything is possible."

"Maybe . . . but we need to handle this out of court and without the police. I for one don't want our names anywhere near the police blotter. It's not good for our reputation or my firm."

"I agree," answered Gloria with relief in her voice.

"The best way to do that," said Walter, "is to ensure no charges are filed and that this doesn't reach the media. I'm sure Howard has some student loans and the officer who came to our house today has a mortgage to pay."

"Yes, but Walter, what do we do with her?"

"Gloria, you are her mother. Figure it out. I have to go."

"Fine. I'll see you later tonight. Dinner is at seven-thirty." With a curt good-bye, Gloria hung up the phone. Not a surprise, thought Gloria. Walter always left the parenting to her. It was time to send Arianna away, she determined. Arianna was a quiet teenager yes, but the stress of worrying about her health or if another episode would occur was like a shadow that constantly followed Gloria around.

Gloria was not the maternal type. In fact, she hadn't wanted children to begin with. She would have been happy playing the trophy wife, but Walter wanted a son. Arianna was the disappointing result. Maybe if she were born normal, things would be different. Maybe if Arianna were even affectionate toward her, Gloria wouldn't be sitting here pondering their relationship or lack thereof. Whenever she saw mothers and daughters embrace or appear as if they were in each other's confidences, Gloria didn't understand it. Even as a small child, Arianna had demonstrated that she didn't want to be around Gloria. While Arianna's condition had improved in the last few years, they still never had a connection, and Gloria wasn't going to try building one now.

Her daughter was impeccably polite—manners were certainly drilled. But Arianna always had a way of seeming detached. The doctor said it was because of her schizophrenia, but Gloria couldn't help but feel that sometimes Arianna just didn't like her. There were times when she would catch her daughter looking at her with those piercing green eyes and she could sense . . . judgment.

Gloria had risen to the occasion, hadn't she? She became an advocate for her daughter's illness and raised tens of thousands of dollars. Arianna had everything that she could possibly want. Beautiful clothes, a beautiful home—she never wanted for anything. "I am a good mother, damn it!" Gloria said to the flames in the fireplace. She glanced at the antique grandfather clock in the corner of the room. It was almost five o'clock—too late to call Silver Hill. It would have to wait until Monday. It was time to dress for dinner.

CHAPTER 2:
THE COUNCIL

53 BC, AUGUST
TENTYRIS, EGYPT
TEMPLE OF HATHOR

Hathor entered her temple with bodyguards Argus and Cadmus trailing in her wake. As they passed into the central chapel, the walls seemed to watch in anticipation. The carved reliefs, highlighted by the glow of torch light, showed Ptolemy VIII and his brethren dancing with offerings in her honor. The walls were laughing now. The Ptolemies had long been allies, but now they were quickly becoming enemies. The current reigning king, Ptolemy XII "Auletes," was back from his exile in Rome, and his fear of growing factions was increasing. Egyptian unrest was palpable.

Cries for shelter and food fell on deaf ears, and the angry protests outside Auletes' palace walls raged on. If it weren't for the Gabiniani mercenaries stationed throughout Alexandria to uphold his and ultimately Rome's authority, the palace would surely be stormed in a matter of days. Hathor thanked the gods Tentyris was at least nine days' distance from Alexandria and the bulk of the unrest.

The Egyptian people had watched for decades as their Hellenistic puppet king recklessly emptied their coffers for his master—Rome. The tipping point was near. However, Auletes' suspicions and mistrust were misdirected at Tentyris. Tentyris, home to Hathor and her people, was not the enemy. The Egyptian people that Auletes conveniently ignored and Rome were.

As Hathor approached the main chamber that was covered in a ceiling of stars, she saw her daughters and trusted advisors waiting in the ceremonial circle. They were the Council of the Zodiac. Stationed at the edges of the circle's quadrants were her four daughters—the Royal Luminaries. It made Hathor's breath catch looking at them. All Tentyrians were blessed with unusual beauty and youth. After coming of age, they never appeared a day older than twenty-five. Yet no one surpassed her daughters' magnificence.

From their delicate faces to their tall stature and matching violet robes, they looked so much like her it was like looking at herself. Their angular features, like the rest of their kind, echoed a blending of Greek and Macedonian ancestry. With the unique pale skin tone of all Tentyrians, their looks contrasted sharply with that of the Egyptians' golden brown.

Her daughters' waist-length hair, each possessing its own unique shade, hung freely down their backs, which were held straight in anticipation of the night's meeting. Interspersed evenly among her daughters was the rest of the Zodiac Council. The thirteen leaders stood patiently in their blue pallas, embroidered with the symbols of their Covens.

"Greetings. Blessed be," Hathor said. With the shake of her sistrum and the loud clank that followed, the Council sat in unison on their stone benches that lined the circumference of the room. Standing in the center, Hathor addressed them. "Thank you for joining me tonight on such short notice. I know many of you just returned from Alexandria a few hours ago. However, this meeting could not wait. I wish to be frank. I have had a vision that will affect the future of Tentyris." Heavy silence filled the room. "Although I am the clan's Visionary, you all know my prophecies are never absolute. The world is a collection of possibilities that can shift easily with one small action. However, I have foreseen my own death. I suspect that our dear friend Auletes is in the midst of crafting my demise as we speak. That is, if he can tear himself away from his goblet of wine and precious flute to devise a strategy. Even so, in less than one year's time, I may no longer be here," said Hathor. The Council appeared uneasy.

She continued: "Precautions have been put in place, and the Tentyrian Guard has been increased throughout the complex and outside the walls. At almost all times I will have Hita, Argus, and Cadmus with me. Daughters, as the clan's Luminaries and second in command, you as well are to have guards with you. You all are to ensure your Guardians keep a close eye on the children. Coven leaders, I am leaving you to discern the level of protection you wish to employ for your people. I know all of you are already well equipped, but of course you are welcome to utilize the Tentyrian Guard as well."

"Hathor, we hardly need protection. It is the humans who do," said Calix flippantly. Calix was the Coven leader of Taurus. "Taurus can take care of itself."

"Indeed it can, Calix, as can all of the Covens," replied Hathor, "but it never hurts to take precautions. Even we can die. The real purpose of tonight, however, is to discuss the implications of my vision and the next steps for Tentyris."

"Mother, are you sure it is Auletes plotting your death and not the Egyptian rebels that killed father?" asked Narcissa. Hathor turned to her daughter's worried face. Narcissa, the youngest and Fourth Luminary, was a gifted healer and skilled botanist. However, she had much to learn about the art of deception.

"It is likely he orchestrated your father's death," Hathor said, "and he will ultimately be responsible for mine. In my vision this morning, I saw beneath his feigned sympathy for Hector's murder and felt his true anger at Tentyris. He suspects that we are more powerful than we let on, although he doesn't understand what that power originates from. Our Tentyrian Guard doesn't come close to rivaling his army in size. But he knows just a handful of our Guard are capable of subduing up to fifty Egyptian rebels, as occurred in the brief skirmish last month. He also wants our wealth—all of it. In my vision, I saw a blade dispatched by one of his mercenaries cutting across my sleeping throat. It leads me to believe Auletes no longer thinks we are just a religious community of priests and priestesses skilled in healing. Our warriors, advancements in medicine, and kind treatment of the Egyptian people undermine his authority. We've done our best to not get involved in his politics, and we quell any talk of our powers or riches. But our presence itself is the problem. As long as our numbers grow and we continue to thrive, we will be a threat. In the last 128 years, our Covens have doubled. The sheer concentration of intelligence and resources we have is what he wants to stamp out. And he doesn't even know the extent of our true power . . . yet."

Maximos, leader of the Leo Coven and Hathor's most faithful advisor, stood and addressed the seventeen stoic faces. "We've been anticipating this day. We spoke of it when we first established Tentyris and have spoke of it at every Council meeting since. We knew our payments of grain and gold, above and beyond what would be expected from a small 'religious community' such as ours, would one day no longer satisfy the Ptolemies and Rome. Our relations with Auletes have been tenuous, at best, even with Hathor's and the Luminaries' diplomacy. If Auletes is responsible for Hector's murder and if he is planning Hathor's, he seeks to destroy us all."

"It is true, Maximos," said Hathor. "Rome's greed has grown, and Auletes feels his kingdom slipping away again. He does not want to lose it as he did several years ago. He thinks eliminating the Tentyrian leader will further strengthen his hold on the Egyptians and line his pocket with gold. Unfortunately, as I have seen, he thought ordering the assassination of my beloved Hector would achieve that." Deep sadness washed over the Visionary Queen's face. It had only been one full moon since her husband's ashes were released to the north winds of the Nile. Hathor still couldn't understand why she didn't see his death coming.

Every morning before dawn, Hector had surveyed the Tentyrian lands and visited with the Egyptians who were paid, fed, and sheltered for their labors. He'd loved riding through the miles of Tentyrian barley fields and fruit orchards, while admiring the glow behind Tentyris as the sun rose and cast its rays on the sprawling complex. He used to marvel at how the stone temples sparkled and Tentyris came alive with activity. Even watching the Egyptians come out of their whitewashed mud-brick homes near the outskirts of the complex to greet the day and begin their labors had been joyous to Hector.

The Tentyrians would also emerge from their own simple but expansive limestone villas to begin their days alongside the Egyptians. They oversaw the Egyptian farmers, builders, merchants, and servants that worked within their small city. Many Tentyrians were also healers and spent their days solving the ailments of the Egyptian people at the Sanatorium. Next to the Sacred Lake, the Sanatorium of Tentyris functioned as a healing center and hospital. With the Tentyrians and Egyptians working together in harmony, the day's activities flowed efficiently and their community prospered.

Hector would often ride over to the Sanatorium and Sacred Lake after his morning's survey. He loved to check on the status of the Egyptian pilgrims, many of whom had traveled to Tentyris over several days, seeking the Tentyrian healing talents and waters. Tentyris was Hector's pride and joy. From the lush gardens where lotus bloomed in abundance to the efficient training grounds and stables where the Tentyrian Guard honed their skills, Tentyris was an oasis where his kind had managed to create a haven. That haven was built under the guise of a religious community that had been revered by the Egyptians for over a century.

But by noon one fateful day, Hector hadn't arrived at the Sanatorium or the Sacred Lake. In fact, he never arrived at all. The Guard found his decapitated body five miles outside of the gate. It wasn't clear if Hector's killers had lured him outside of the complex and then killed him or if he was murdered within and his body and severed head were dumped outside. The Egyptian laborers and all Tentyrians were thoroughly interviewed and their deepest secrets analyzed. But no one saw or heard what happened to Hector.

Ten days later, an emissary from Alexandria arrived with a letter from Auletes. Six men confessed to killing Hector. They were apparently part of an Egyptian rebel group that had been wreaking havoc in Lower Egypt, hoping to undermine the Ptolemaic throne. They were subsequently captured in an assassination attempt of Auletes, and not long after, they confessed their involvement in Hector's murder. Hector's death was the first of a Zodiac Council and royal family member in Tentyrian history. That history, while still young, was swiftly becoming uprooted from its Egyptian soil.

"Of course, Auletes would think a simple female couldn't rule on her own, so he killed our father," surmised Phoebe sadly. Phoebe was Hathor's second oldest daughter, the clan's Second Luminary, and a skilled manipulator of energy and light. "Auletes has never been a smart man. His own daughter may have his own kingdom one day, if Rome doesn't get it first."

Sophia, Coven leader of Libra and master interpreter of Tentyrian law due to her patient wisdom, spoke next. "We've all suspected it wasn't the Egyptian rebels that ambushed Hector. Although we delve out punishment when warranted, we treat all Egyptians with the utmost fairness. The raid on Tentyris two months ago is a prime example. When the rebels from Alexandria realized their fighting was fruitless, we could have put the survivors to death. But we didn't. Instead, we offered them jobs with our building and farming crews. We offered them the opportunities that Auletes denied them. Their actions were reprehensible, thinking they could steal from our peaceful community and get away with it. However, how we handled their crimes should be proof enough that the rebels would be in debt to us. Until now, we haven't had proof it wasn't the Egyptian rebels that killed Hector. But not only does your vision confirm it, Hathor, now we also have the results of our investigation to share. Daria can elaborate . . ." The Council turned its expectant eyes to Hathor's oldest daughter, the First Luminary.

Daria was the clan's most gifted mind reader. No one in Tentyrian history had demonstrated the skill she possessed in seeing others' thoughts. As a rule, though, Daria was prevented from mind tapping the other Council members. Each possessed their own unique mental blocks they had cultivated through years of practice, including Daria, to prevent any form of mind control. Mind blocks among the Council were a necessary precaution to keep the governing body of Tentyris objective. The members of the Council, as well as all Tentyrians, had varying degrees of power ranging from telekinesis to telepathy. What separated the Council from the rest of the Tentyrian population, though, was their ability to "shift" or move from one location to another with just a thought. Only nineteen people had ever shown the skill—and they all comprised the Council of the Zodiac. However, since Hector's death, they were now a council of eighteen.

Daria had just shifted from Alexandria with her husband, Aristos, Coven leader of Cancer and fellow Council members Sophia, Sebastian, and Pello. Sebastian was the Coven leader of Capricorn and Pello of Sagittarius. Together, they sought interviews with the men who confessed to killing Hector.

"After Pello bribed the jail guards, I read the rebel prisoners' minds, and the confessions are a sham," said Daria firmly. "The men agreed to admit to killing Hector and to planning an assassination attempt on Auletes. Their wives received eight hundred tetradrachm in exchange. They knew that exchange would result in their own deaths . . . but for them, it was worth it. The deal would ensure their families' well-beings, which the men could better ensure dead than alive." Most Egyptians lived in abject poverty; eight hundred tetradrachm would be a windfall for anyone.

"We know that the man the 'rebels' accepted the terms from had his identity concealed. They never saw his face nor learned his name," said Sebastian. While the Capricorn leader had some basic telepathic skills, they weren't effective enough for frequent use. Sebastian's real strength was in his natural power of persuasion and intellect. "We suspect it was Aulus Gabinius who may have orchestrated the cover-up under Auletes' direction. But when we requested an audience at the palace to confirm it, we were denied entrance every day for the last two weeks. We were given the message that Auletes was tending to important political matters but that he conveyed his sincerest condolences."

"It would have taken at least thirty mortal men to subdue Hector. Six would barely draw blood," said Aristos. As leader of Hathor's Cancer Coven, head of the Tentyrian Guard, and beloved son-in-law, he knew firsthand the manpower it would take to stop the virtually unstoppable Hector. "Auletes had the quantity and quality of merce-naries to ambush Hector and effectively coerce the men to confess."

"Auletes is a pig. Mother, with your and the Council's permission, I could enter the palace and slit his throat. No one would ever know who it was," said Calypso vehemently. Calypso was the Third Luminary, and with the right level of concentration she could make herself invisible. The apple of her father's eye and third eldest daughter, Calypso took Hector's death the hardest.

"Calypso, while I appreciate your talents, that is not the way of our kind," said Hathor gently.

"It isn't the way of our kind, Hathor, but now we know it must have been Auletes," said Stavros, Coven leader of Aries and the most out-spoken proponent of increased power for Tentyris. "Your vision practically confirms it. Aristos is right: Auletes had the resources to deploy a force of Gabiniani that could kill Hector. We need to make a stand! We have the power, and it's time we use it. For too long we've played by mortal rules. Yes, we've made a life for our kind here—but at what cost? Certainly Hector's. It is time we remind ourselves that we are not their equals; we are their betters. In fact, should we be so inclined, we could wipe out the feeble humans throughout Egypt in a matter of months."

"Stavros, we are not animals!" retorted Hathor. "We are Tentyrian. Need I remind you, it is those feeble humans that keep us alive? Without their blood, we wouldn't be here. We know that we aren't that much different from them. It is only by some random deviation in our makeup, which even we don't fully understand yet, that separates us. We were born from humans, and with the exception of the second and third generations, which some of you here have borne, we are the first and only of our kind. Who is to say that our unique race will even continue? When I accepted the role as queen and Visionary for our clan, I agreed to put the interests of our people first. Don't think for a second I don't want revenge for Hector's death. He was my best friend and father to my children. But my recognition that Tentyris must continue enables my restraint. You should find your own, Stavros."

With an impassive face, Stavros took his seat.

"As Maximos has said, we've known this day would come. If Auletes succeeds in killing me," continued Hathor, "he will dismantle our people. Yes, we can fight back, but it is not worth the exposure and bloodshed."

"Ah, but the bloodshed would be delicious," sniggered Calix. Laughter followed from the Gemini Coven leaders, Aglaia and Asia.

The twin sisters, with a knack for manipulating fire, ruled their Coven jointly.

"Shut your mouth, Calix. Your words are an embarrassment to all Tentyrians!" said Narcissa angrily. Narcissa had come to loathe Calix not long after she came of age. Her mother never understood why, as she always thought Narcissa considered herself quite in love with him. She recalled the days when Narcissa would dance around the villa, singing his praises. But something changed five summers ago. Maybe she had seen beneath his charm—so powerful it could alter the memories of the weak.

Hathor slammed her sistrum into her palm with a loud clash. "Your attempt at humor is not appreciated, Calix," she said.

Undisturbed by Hathor's obvious displeasure, Calix replied nonchalantly, "This situation may not be humorous, but I agree with Stavros. Why are we so concerned about causing a little upset? It would be liberating."

"Yes," replied Hathor with an edge in her voice. "Liberating for how long? You have not seen the visions I have. I have seen a time when we are hunted for our powers, the secrets that lie in our blood, and for what we ultimately will be seen as and called—vampires."

"Stavros and I don't mind the label. It is you that do, Hathor," said Calix.

"It is not just Hathor that minds," spoke Evander, the leader of Pisces. Now married to Zoe, leader of Aquarius, their two Covens had merged into one, and together they governed with the same honor and love they bestowed on each other. Their son, Galen, was nine years old. "I believe I speak for the majority of the clan when I say that we know what we are and what we are not. We are Tentyrian first and foremost. The stories of vampires are dramatizations about killers. And we aren't that. We take what blood we need to survive. When we feed, we always ensure that our hosts are unharmed and have no recollection. We honor the Code."

Zoe held her husband's hand and said in earnest, "If we were to fight, reveal our powers and what we truly are—just imagine what those stories will become. The few humans outside of Tentyris who know what we are capable of have spread rumors like wildfire. Thankfully, we have the ability to wipe those memories and quell the talk. But we all know we can't stop them forever. In the last five years, more than a few scarce whispers have reached Auletes' ear, which has likely spurred his interest in destroying us. Everything that we stand for and the Code that we've pledged to follow over one hundred years ago will be for naught should we choose to fight. We don't want to live in fear that our children will be hunted. A sentiment I'm sure you all can relate to."

Many of the Zodiac Council members were mothers and fathers. Safely under the watchful eyes of their Guardians and Covens, their children remained blissfully unaware of the changes to come. Daria looked to Aristos as she thought of their ten-year-old son, Darrius. They'd left him just an hour ago, wrestling with his Guardian Ammon. Eager to be the honored fighter like his father, Darrius rarely put down his play sword and shield. It was a constant struggle to keep him out of a scrape and in clean clothes. Thankfully, like all Tentyrian children, he had a Guardian to help keep tabs on him. Her little boy was quickly becoming a warrior, though Daria prayed he would never need to be one.

Phoebe thought of her twin babies, tucked snugly in their cradles at home, while their doting father, Claudius, rocked them. Their Guardian, Tale, was undoubtedly hovering. Tale wouldn't leave the twins' side for more than a minute, should they want for anything. As a Luminary and wife to a former mortal, Phoebe understood both sides of the coin. She and her husband's love surpassed their physical differences. After much deliberation, Phoebe changed Claudius at his request. It was not a decision to be made lightly; it was physically painful, arduous, and required unanimous agreement by the Council.

Phoebe knew the potential dangers Tentyris faced by making a stand. She also knew there was potential for them to continue to coexist peacefully with humans. After all, they weren't that much different. The question was—could they continue to coexist by remaining in Tentyris? In her heart, she knew it was not to be.

Calypso imagined her five-year-old daughter, Ceres, probably playing in her makeup by now, waiting for Calypso to come home. Ceres was Calypso's crown jewel, and while she would do anything to protect her, the pain of losing Hector slaked her thirst for revenge. She needed time to think and consult with Alexander. Her husband always knew how to calm her with reason. And lately she felt like she was losing her ability to think rationally. Being married to a Luminary wasn't easy, but Alexander took it in stride. Alexander was second-generation Tentyrian like her. Their ten-year marriage was just the beginning of what they planned for as eternity.

Narcissa, the Fourth Luminary, wasn't married, but she cared for her little nieces and nephews like they were her own. Her sisters and mother were her best friends, the Council of the Zodiac her family. She couldn't imagine a world where they weren't together or where

Tentyris didn't exist. Yet she knew they would not be safe if they stayed.

Damian and Karis looked at each other knowingly as they sat on their shared stone bench. Married for twenty years, the Scorpio and Virgo leaders governed a blended Coven that their four-year-old daughter, Calandra, happily knew as her family and protectors. To put their daughter in danger was their greatest fear. However, they wanted her to grow up in their homeland.

"Evander and Zoe, would you rather we do nothing?" said Stavros to the Pisces and Aquarius Coven leaders.

"We don't believe aggression is the answer," retorted Evander.

Damian rose to Stavros' side and asked, "What do you all propose then?"

"We propose we leave," responded Zoe with resoluteness.

"I can't support that decision when I know we have no reason to," challenged Stavros. "Who here feels this way? Let us take an informal vote. Say aye if you believe we should leave." Seven ayes followed. "Calix, Aglaia, Asia, Damian, Karis, and Calypso, I see that you don't support abandoning Tentyris, along with me. To the rest of you, why are you so quick to fold? By the gods' good graces we are basically immortal. Yet you want to flee in fear of the mortals? The mortals who are thankless for all that we have done for them?"

Daria stood to face Stavros. The same zodiac pendant that hung on a gold chain around her neck, as it did from her sisters' and mother's, twinkled in defiance.

"Stavros, it is true that if it weren't for our presence, there would surely be thousands more poverty-stricken Egyptians," said Daria. "All of our laborers are well taken care of. Not to mention we're the only legitimate source of medical help throughout the Sixth Nome. And while we may not always receive the thanks we deserve, their blood gives us life. That life coexists in a balance with the humans. If we overturn that balance, the outcome may not be in our favor . . . as my mother has already seen."

Stavros' ice-blue eyes turned directly to Hathor as he addressed the Council. "Hathor has said it herself. Her visions and the future are not absolute. They are also not as dependable as they once were now, are they?" Hathor held her anger. It hurt to hear Stavros' dig at her recent inability to call her sight to her. But it was true. A prevailing weakness plagued her, and more often than not, she had headaches rather than visions.

Her headaches were not the same as those she had experienced when first finding her sight, or even those she knew Daria and the other telepaths often experienced due to the energies they were so sensitive to. It was something more. Hathor knew deep down that she was dying. It was a miracle she was able to put together the fragments of her recent vision to finally see Auletes' involvement in Hector's death and predict her own demise.

"If I may interrupt," said Aglaia lightly. "I hardly think Stavros is saying we abandon the Code, overturn the Ptolemaic dynasty, and appoint ourselves leaders." Hathor, meanwhile, wasn't so sure that Stavros wasn't thinking that. Aglaia continued: "My twin and I are in agreement that the balance needs to be reset, which doesn't need to involve us leaving Tentyris."

"Yes. But what does 'resetting' it mean to us and our Covens?" asked Hathor.

"It means revenge for father," said Calypso.

"It means freedom from pacifying an incompetent king," Calix answered.

"It means unleashing our real power and for once being who we are!" proclaimed Stavros.

"It means showing that we are superior," intoned Maximos.

Hathor was taken aback by Maximos' bold statement. It was unlike him to tout the superiority of Tentyrians over humans. She could understand that grief was dictating Calypso's emotions. She could even understand Stavros and Calix—they had always wanted more freedom. But Maximos believed in and deeply respected the Code, which he helped craft. Why the sudden change of heart?

Maximos continued: "Showing that we are superior means being superior in mind, body, and spirit. If that is what we are, as Stavros believes, our kind can thrive anywhere. This has been our home for over a century. But why hold onto something that is crumbling? We know this land is on the verge of revolution. If we fight now and take down Auletes openly, there will surely be many more battles to come. We have been given the gift of eternity. Let us use that gift. Unlike the humans, we are not burdened by geographies or most mortal dangers. Our time at Tentyris is done. Let us move on."

Hathor breathed a sigh of relief. The split second she had doubted Maximos had shaken her. She knew she would die. And when that happened, she would especially need him to help her daughters carry on the Tentyrian legacy and keep the Council of the Zodiac together. It was just over thirty years ago, right before Narcissa's birth, when she'd had a vision of Maximos protecting the generations of Luminaries to come. And he would be around when it came time to stop "the Event."

"Before we submit to a formal Council vote regarding whether we should stay or leave, I wish to speak in further detail about our relocation," said Hathor. "When we first discussed finding an alternate home for our kind, we agreed to appropriate funds yearly to the effort and inevitable reconstruction. I started using those funds about twelve years ago. The location was found and construction is near completion."

Hathor saw the surprise on many of the Council members' faces. "Only Maximos, Aristos, Pello, and the Luminaries have known about the project," said Hathor. But before she could finish, Stavros interrupted.

"Hathor, why would you not consult and gain consensus from the rest of us?" Anger rolled off Stavros in waves, despite his calm exterior, making Karis' mind swim. Her empathic abilities made her highly sensitive to emotions around her. Easing her discomfort, the Virgo Coven leader modified her breathing and strengthened her mental barrier.

"That is why we are here," said Stavros, "to provide counsel and equitable representation amongst the Covens. It is within your right as queen but in opposition to all of your past policies. The Tentyrian relocation should be a democratic vote amongst the Council. Yet you've already made the decision yourself."

"Typical," Hathor heard Aglaia mutter.

"Yes, I have made that decision, as was my right as queen and Primary Ruler, with the consent of all four Luminaries," said Hathor fiercely. "I did what I thought was right as your leader. Many years ago, I had a vision of an isolated mountain that would become a safe haven to our kind. After that, I sent out numerous expeditions to find it. And as much as I wanted to garner consent from you all to build once the mountain was found, I saw that agreement would never happen. You all would inevitably argue over the timing and location—saying that it was premature. So I initiated the project with the Luminaries' approval, which again, I'll remind you, is within my power."

In the pit of her stomach, Hathor felt the guilt of not sharing the relocation plans with all of the Council members. But the vision she had . . . had been haunting. It wasn't just that the Council would ultimately argue and never agree on a location. She saw that if she involved them all, it would cause a rift in the Council of the Zodiac and break it apart. Her visions didn't reveal to her all the intricacies of an event, but she knew that if she chose to involve all of the Coven leaders, their Council would split in two. She hoped her actions would circumvent that fate. But Hathor knew better than anyone—you can never really escape fate.

"This may come as a surprise," said Hathor, "but I do not believe our entire clan should relocate together. History often repeats itself. I don't want us to move only to find us threatened again. While there is strength in numbers, our race as a whole has grown too large to remain unified in one place. It is amazing that Tentyris has existed for this long without the outside humans understanding what we are and what we can do. Granted, we have gone to great lengths to achieve that. I have thought long and hard, and I am recommending that your respective Covens relocate permanently to places of your own choosing."

Murmurs of confusion bounced off the temple walls.

"I don't understand. You said that construction is almost done?" said Sebastian. "What is the purpose of this mountain then?"

"When the mountain was found, we began building into it to construct a new complex. Its secluded location and vast deposits of monazite and bastnäsite make it ideal. From these minerals, we can produce lanthanum ore, which you all know as the energy source we have developed here in Tentyris. However, as I alluded to, the complex is not designed to permanently house our entire clan of six hundred plus. As part of my vision, I saw this sanctuary in the mountainside as a capital and central location for us to govern. If necessary, it could serve as a temporary refuge for our kind . . . I didn't and don't expect you all to want to live there permanently with your Covens. It is important you know I was not trying to take your autonomy away when I didn't consult with you all regarding my vision and the building of this new complex. All of you are capable and powerful leaders; hence you are the Council of the Zodiac. You have your own interests and those of your Covens to look after. That is why I am suggesting you relocate to where you see fit."

Hathor hoped the olive branch of independence she was extending would ameliorate any anger, especially from Stavros. Their friendship had long been strained, and she worried he was no longer her ally.

"There is more than enough money and resources for each Coven to have a significant appropriation," explained Hathor. "Funding should not be a concern. I know this announcement was unexpected, and for that I apologize. I hoped that it would be some time before we needed to discuss this. But I think this strategy is in the best interests of your Covens. It will preserve the safety and longevity of all Tentyrians."

"What about the Luminaries, Hathor? Where will they go?" asked Sophia.

"I have discussed it with them, and they will relocate to the new sanctuary with me," said Hathor, "along with their families' Guardians, servants, and the Tentyrian Guard. However, it appears Calypso may be having second thoughts . . . Aristos' Coven will also reside there. As Daria's husband, they are sharing in the decision to relocate the Cancer Coven. We can accommodate additional Covens, if you wish. However, I have expressed my concerns regarding that issue. You should know the location of the new complex and its surrounding conditions are, in short, challenging." Nodding to Maximos, he continued for Hathor.

"The mountain is located over four thousand miles away, requiring us to traverse many seas and miles of land. With our powers and resources, we can get there far more easily than any human, without the dangers. And as Council members, we can shift there in a matter of minutes. However, it is still far from our current homeland and very different. An ice sheet predominantly covers the land. The land is generally inhospitable, with summertime temperatures rarely reaching above the freezing mark. Wintertime temperatures are hostile, and the territory is shrouded in snow. The mountain itself is the closest peak to what we know as the Northern Pole. Most of you are familiar with the properties of snow and ice. Essentially frozen water, they can cause hypothermic reactions in humans and Tentyrians who have not yet come of age. As adult Tentyrian bodies don't feel external temperatures, we won't be affected. But nevertheless, it is not a warm or thriving environment for humans or animals. There are almost no humans there, except for a few tribes of people who are indigenous to the area."

"But what will be the blood source if the humans are so scarce?" asked Damian.

"It will require a modification in diet," answered Daria. "Many of us already drink animal blood in addition to human. This new area has animals, though different from what we have seen and domesticated here in Tentyris. But based on our expeditions, their blood is compatible with our digestive systems. Feeding primarily off of animals is for our own benefit. Suspicions amongst the humans as to what we are will be minimized. And although our access to human blood will be limited, the isolation will work in our favor. Humans are unlikely to find the complex, even thousands of years from now. It is hidden deeply within the mountain and is situated in an area that is almost impossible to access."

"I don't understand what is remotely appealing about this. This place has temperatures that can barely support life, and it's almost at the opposite end of the Earth. Not to mention you are planning on drinking animal blood? That's just unnatural," protested Stavros.

"The appeal is in the anonymity," Daria replied curtly. "It is not for our entire clan to live there. This place is to serve as a safety net. It is about establishing a safe place for our people that humans will never find. This new sanctuary will be the point of governance for Tentyrians and the location of our yearly Council meetings. Mother, my sisters, and I can travel to and from the various Covens quite easily when our counsel is necessary. In the event that emergency meetings or governance sessions require the presence of all Council members, we can convene at the new sanctuary on an ad hoc basis."

"Isn't this an overreaction?" asked Damian. "Only Hector has died, and we are capable of fighting back."

"It's about being proactive and putting measures in place to protect ourselves. There will be a time when we are at war. The longer we can stave that off the better," resolved Hathor.

Sophia addressed the group next. "I understand Hathor's motivations, and it's important we all remember that her visions have rarely led us astray. She speaks what she sees as truth. I am confident the Luminaries and Hathor can oversee the Covens from the new complex. It is a rare instance, anyway, when they all are needed to weigh in on regular Coven proceedings. As far as I can see, this changes nothing about the Code. It can and should still be followed. Our governing structure will remain intact. The only difference is that we all won't be living in the same ten-mile radius."

Sebastian trusted Sophia's word implicitly—the Libra Coven leader was all that was reason and truth. He secretly wished, though, that she could set aside the rational for the emotional and realize how much he loved her. Being separated from Sophia would be difficult. But Sebastian understood that leaving Tentyris was for the best. However, the logistics of the mountain for the royal family, their humans, and the Tentyrian Guard were nothing short of daunting.

"Granted you all can probably live off the animal blood alone," said Sebastian, "but we still supplement our diets with human food. Plus the Tentyrians who are not of age and the human Guardians and servants require grains, meats, vegetables, and fruits. How can you obtain that easily? The humans and your own children who have not yet turned can't possibly survive in so difficult an environment. They need heat, light, and nourishment . . ."

"You bring up an excellent point, Sebastian," said Hathor in a conciliatory tone. She needed as much support as possible. "With Phoebe's skills and Pello's engineering, we've found a way to manipulate the mineral deposits in the mountain to produce lanthanum ore in mass to create the necessary energy. There are now lanthanum processors built within the core of the complex that supply endless amounts of heat and energy. We've also been able to create a self-sustaining farm inside of the mountain. As you all know, we've been experimenting with energy lamps and new agricultural processes for many years. Our technology is years ahead of the humans. The supply of lanthanum found in the mountain, after being processed, has enabled Phoebe to create energy orbs that mimic solar light to make crops grow. The entire complex is illuminated by these orbs, which can darken accordingly for sleep cycles. In total, approximately four square miles have been carved out of the inside of the mountain. The farm grows from nutrient-rich soil that has been crushed from mountain rock. Water is brought into the mountain from aqueducts that filter fresh water when it is available and salt water from the surrounding fjord when the mountain air is too dry to produce snow. The fjord also contains a bountiful supply of fish, which can be used for food."

"This construction is a technological wonder," said Aristos. "I've seen it myself. The years of work will soon pay off. There are approximately ten more months of construction. Our Tentyrian builders skilled in telekinesis have worked tirelessly under Pello's direction to carve out this refuge. Along with them, Hathor, Maximos, the Luminaries, and I have routinely visited to help with the construction. If all goes according to plan, you will see the splendor at our next yearly Council meeting."

"The new complex is impenetrable," said Pello confidently. Pello, leader of the Sagittarius Coven, could transform matter into rock and, conversely, break and carve it easily with the power of his mind. Pello was the primary engineer behind the new sanctuary and was responsible for the building of Tentyris itself. "The depth of the rock will protect this new complex for generations. Although the mountain is unremarkable from the outside, the structures within have the same beauty, design, and comforts of what we are used to here," said Pello with pride.

"I'm sure I speak for many of us when I say that I am disappointed I was not included in this decision," said Karis with palpable hurt in her voice. "But I am not questioning your judgment, Hathor. The new sanctuary sounds wonderful." After hearing the rationale, Karis and Damian both agreed to support the relocation. "Damian and I will be there at the Rising of Sirius for our next Council meeting. But what is the complex called?" asked Karis.

"We thought 'Sanctum' made sense," said Narcissa. "It is, after all, designed to be a sanctuary for our people."

"But Calypso, it appears you've changed your mind," pointed out Stavros. Throughout the debate, Calypso listened with furrowed brow and obvious discontent.

"I won't leave Tentyris without avenging my father's death. I, however, will leave when that is accomplished," she replied firmly.

"Your own mother said that is not the way of our kind," answered Stavros.

"It is also not the way of our kind to not implement swift justice and action," retorted Calypso. "I will only leave Tentyris under the condition that Auletes dies."

Hathor knew she needed to tread lightly. To not have Calypso's support would mean she'd only have the Luminary vote of three. Based on the Code, she would need unanimous agreement from her daughters to relocate the heart of their Council. The Coven leaders were advisors and needed for democratic votes when Hathor and her daughters wished it. However, at the end of the day, the real power of the Zodiac was between Hathor and her kin.

A lot had changed since mother and daughters agreed to build the new complex twelve years ago. Since then, their people had grown. Egypt was on the brink of war. Hector was dead. And Hathor knew she was next. With her death on the horizon, Hathor couldn't allow Calypso to remain in Tentyris. Her four daughters needed to be together, not just to protect each other but to protect the future. Hathor would have to compromise.

"Auletes will die prior to us leaving for the Sanctum," answered Hathor. "It will need to appear as an illness. We will not kill him openly and allow his death to be traced back to us. Calypso, I know you wish to dispense his punishment, so I will leave it to you. But mind me, Auletes will not die until our preparations for leaving are finalized. Now, let us take a formal vote amongst the entire Council regarding our plan of action," said Hathor. "The relocation of the Luminaries, me, and Aristos' Coven will happen with or without the vote of the Coven leaders. However, the eleven remaining Covens' decision to stay in Tentyris remains in the balance. You will need at least seven votes to decide one way or the other. Who votes the Covens stay?"

Stavros, Calix, Aglaia, and Asia said aye. Karis and Damian changed their minds, along with Calypso, giving the majority to those who wished to disband from Tentyris.

"Then it is done," Hathor said decisively, with a hint of sadness in her voice. "We will leave in ten months' time. Now, for the remaining

Covens, you must decide where you will go. You all have traveled the world, and many of you already have small enclaves set up in various regions. Ultimately, you will make the best choices for your Covens. You don't need me to remind you that this may be the most important decision you will make as leaders. If you need more time, and if ten months is not enough, you are welcome to reside at the Sanctum in the interim. You will not be staying in Tentyris, though. We shall abandon the city and leave it to the Egyptians. They will carry on with the bounty we'll leave behind with our temples, homes, and fields. Who knows, maybe they'll even commemorate our kind—one day."

CHAPTER 3:
TREATMENT

Ari had been at Silver Hill a week. The doctors ran their tests, only to reveal that Ari's "episode" with Howard was likely the result of her not taking her medication. This was a natural conclusion considering she had been throwing out her pills for years. Ari was unusual in that her brain scans were atypical of a schizophrenic. Rather than demonstrating a loss in gray matter, which her doctors expected to occur when she was first diagnosed and then increase through her teen years, her brain scan revealed no degeneration. This finding was consistent with what doctors' saw in her scans previous, but it continued to boggle them.

What they did find different this time was an enlargement of Ari's corpus callosum. The corpus callosum, located centrally in the brain, was the neural bridge that connected the two hemispheres of the brain to each other. The enlargement wasn't dangerous, as it didn't look like it was the result of abnormal blood swelling or cancerous cells. And it was possible that it had been there since childhood—but they were just seeing it now. It had been at least five years since Ari's last scan, and imaging technology had improved significantly.

The doctors couldn't attribute her condition to her unusual corpus callosum, but they resolved that it was worth exploring. At least one doctor in particular did. Dr. Aman Raad saw Ari's brain scan by chance. He was a neurologist new to Silver Hill, and his pioneering research made him well respected in the psychiatric community. Raad had accepted a position at Silver Hill, as he'd wanted to move away from the demands of a daily operating schedule. In his role at the facility—Connecticut's best treatment hospital for psychiatric disorders and addictions—Raad had reviewed neurological scans of patients and assisted in appropriate treatment plans.

Dr. Raad had been taking his first in-depth tour of the Silver Hill lab when he saw Ari's scan on the light box. He immediately pointed out the abnormal thickness of the neural bridge and requested Ari's file. Dr. Wilson, Ari's primary doctor and director at the hospital, agreed it was an interesting find but remained convinced her previous diagnoses remained accurate. After all, Ari's medication worked before to treat her schizophrenia and cluster headaches. It was her not taking the medication, as indicated by the toxicology reports, that was the catalyst for her episode.

Ari hated Silver Hill. The mental noise she experienced was excruciating. With patients, nurses, orderlies, and doctors surrounding her, the voices in her head increased tenfold. Not even the walls of her private room could keep them out. On top of it, Ari was pumped full of drugs, and she felt like she was sleepwalking while a constant buzzing played over loud speakers. She felt numb as she went through the motions of answering the doctors' questions and interacting in her group sessions. It was a constant struggle to stay focused and to not give in to the hysteria that was building in her mind.

Ari felt sad for the people around her. In many instances, they were worse off than she. There was one woman who used to be the perfect housewife—that was until the stress of four children and a cheating husband sent her into a spiral of depression and an unsuccessful suicide attempt. There was one boy in her therapy group, not much older than her, who suffered from an oxycodone addiction. And then there was her lunch companion who saved her a seat every day. He was around thirty and had Tourette's syndrome, in addition to an imaginary friend. Ari was amongst a bunch of misfits—even she didn't belong.

Surprisingly, Silver Hill was beautiful. It had acres of rolling lawns, gardens, and trees. The rooms and hallways were immaculate, and the staff was pleasantly mannered. But the environment was choking Ari. With every day that passed, she felt she was one step closer to losing touch with reality.

Ari refused to speak about what happened with her physics teacher to the doctors. In the days leading up to her parents bringing her to Silver Hill, she tried desperately to explain what happened. But her father wasn't around to explain it to and her mother simply didn't believe her. In her mandatory therapy session with her parents and doctor on her first day, they discussed her as if she weren't even in the room. She was invisible. The truth was irrelevant.

Ari was feeling that invisibility again as she sat in another session with her parents and Dr. Wilson.

"Arianna, now that you have had time to reflect on what has happened, do you understand how important it is that you take your medication?" said the tight-faced doctor as he pushed his rimless glasses further up the bridge of his nose. He waited expectantly for Ari to answer.

"I understand that to you I am a lab rat. And to my parents I am a problem," she replied bluntly. Ari heard her mother gasp at her uncharacteristically bold words, but it didn't stop her. "The medication I have taken on and off for over ten years doesn't work. So no, I don't understand!"

Ari could see her father's eyes fixated on the black and white clock that hung beneath the crown molding. He was probably counting the seconds until he could get back to the office. Her mother, on the other hand, was fuming.

"After everything we have done for you, Arianna! How can you not understand? And where are your manners? Please apologize to Dr. Wilson," scolded Gloria.

"No, I will not apologize," Ari replied defiantly.

"If I may interrupt," said Dr. Wilson. "Arianna, I sense that you are angry. Can you tell us why?" he asked.

She stared at his white coat embroidered with his name. The prefix "Dr." gave him all the power that mattered. He could keep her there forever. She should have controlled her temper, she silently chastised herself. If she had any hope of leaving, she would need to appease them.

"Dr. Wilson," she said apologetically, "I'm sorry. I'm not angry. I'm just tired. I feel upset because no one will tell me how much longer I am staying here." Ari was ashamed at how pathetic her voice sounded.

"I need to speak with your parents about that, but before I do, would you like to stay here, Arianna?" Dr. Wilson asked. She could almost see the dollar signs in his eyes.

"No," she replied. "I want to get back to my dog and my life." Whatever sad life she had, Ari thought.

"Arianna, you can't get back to your life until you realize how important it is that you take your medication and come to terms with your anger at your illness. You said yourself that you don't think your medication works and that you are a 'lab rat,'" said the doctor. "Can you tell us more about that?"

What else was there to tell? Breathe, breathe, breathe, she chanted silently.

"Dr. Wilson, I'm not angry about my illness. I accept it. I just want to go home. I'll take my medication. I promise." Ari felt the hard shell she put around her begin to crack. She knew she sounded desperate—but she couldn't take it much longer. The knot in her throat was rising and threatened to burst into a sob.

"I misspoke, Dr. Wilson. Sometimes it feels like the medication doesn't work. I am feeling much better, though, since I got here," she lied. "And it's just that I'm undergoing so many tests all the time. Can't you understand that I'm tired of it? I've been poked and prodded with needles and machines since I was little."

"I hear how you feel, Arianna. I'd like to talk more about this. I think we can make some real progress together," answered Dr. Wilson like a robot reading a script. The lack of feeling made Ari wanted to slap him. The doctor then turned to her parents and asked them if they could speak privately.

"Arianna, we are going to go back to my office. You are welcome to stay here or return to your suite," said Dr. Wilson. She knew they were going to decide her fate, which was clearly out of her hands.

"I think I'd like to go for a walk outside," said Ari in a detached voice. The inevitable outcome was sealed.

"We'll have things wrapped up in forty minutes or so. I'll send a nurse to get you. Please stay on the main pavilion," replied Dr. Wilson as he escorted her parents out. Ari stared after them as they walked down the hall to Dr. Wilson's office. They didn't even say good-bye. No, "We'll see you in a few, sweetheart." Ari left the therapy room that was wallpapered with peach floral. She expected some people found the walls soothing. She found them disgusting. In fact, the whole situation she was in disgusted her.

Ari pushed open the doors to the pavilion with a frustrated shove. It was warmer now, but April's showers left the beautiful grounds looking soggy and muddy. A few patients strolled about, and a small group played croquet. Ari looked for a place to be alone. She sat on an iron bench next to the fountain of stone water nymphs. She hoped no one would talk to her. She would normally find the fountain beautiful as the nymphs embraced each other and water spouted from the urns they held. But today, she felt too jaded.

As water from the fountain flowed into the waiting pool of koi carp, Ari felt hot tears trickle down her cheeks. She had never felt more alone. It was as if she really were crazy. If she were to scream at the top of her lungs, no one would really hear her. That pervert Howard probably had a fat check in his pocket, while she was stuck in a hospital filled with anorexic, drug-dependent, and mental people. What upset her most was that her parents repeatedly ignored her explanation of what happened. They just wanted it to go away, like her.

In that moment, Ari determined to cut her parents out of her life. She would never forgive them. It was true she never liked them, but up until now, they were tangentially part of her life. She tried to be a part of the family and at times even wanted to. Ari had even accepted their obvious lack of love because she believed she was to blame. Not anymore.

While Ari was resolving her hatred, her parents and Dr. Wilson discussed her situation. As Dr. Wilson was explaining the benefits of the Transitional Living program—where Ari could live at Silver Hill on an extended basis—a knock interrupted their conversation.

"Excuse me, Dr. Wilson. I knew you were meeting with Arianna Parker's parents today, and I wanted to introduce myself." It was Dr. Raad. The golden-skinned doctor in his early fifties ignored the obvious look of displeasure on Dr. Wilson's face. He strode in confidently and extended his hand to Gloria and Walter.

"It's a pleasure to meet you both," Dr. Raad said. "I apologize for interrupting, but I wanted to offer my opinion on your daughter's case."

"Well thank you, Dr. Raad. We were just discussing next steps regarding her treatment. We were talking about enrolling her in the Transitional Living program," Gloria replied, flashing a demure smile. It wasn't beyond her to flirt with a handsome doctor.

"Dr. Raad is the neurologist who reviewed Arianna's brain scans," said Dr. Wilson begrudgingly. He hoped to have Ari's admission forms signed and twelve months of treatment fees on his desk by the end of their meeting, which Dr. Raad was apparently determined to derail. A wrinkle creased Dr. Raad's forehead when Gloria mentioned the program.

"That's very surprising," said Dr. Raad. "I've been over Arianna's file thoroughly, and I would think so intense a treatment program would be unnecessary. With the exception of her recent mishap, Arianna appears stable and quite bright. A permanent living situation here seems needless. Her IQ tests indicate she is already capable of learning at college-level curricula, and her interview transcripts show her ability to empathize and communicate clearly. I think it would be a grave mistake to keep Arianna here when we risk derailing her schoolwork and isolating her further. My understanding from the nurses and her group therapy counselor is that in the short week since she arrived, Arianna has become more withdrawn and deeply unhappy. I would like to interview Arianna in person. However, my access to her has been . . . let's say . . . limited."

The two doctors eyed each other with contempt. Dr. Wilson wouldn't allow Dr. Raad to see Ari personally and even forbade him from joining the meeting with her parents. But Raad was not going to let Wilson subject a patient to an endless treatment program that would likely do nothing. Raad needed more time to analyze Ari's case and what was happening with her neural bridge. It could be the key to making her better.

"Mr. and Mrs. Parker, it is entirely possible that Arianna is not schizophrenic, despite her symptoms," Dr. Raad said plainly. Dr. Wilson looked apoplectic while the Parkers looked confused.

"But what about her medication?" asked Gloria. "It has worked in the past. Not to mention we've taken her to almost every doctor and specialist in the country who have given the same diagnoses. What has changed?"

"I've found something unique about a part of Arianna's brain that is enlarged. I don't want you to be alarmed; it isn't putting her health in jeopardy. But it's possible it's linked to her condition. If I can have time with her to conduct some tests, I'll be able to take a closer look."

"Well that's not a problem with us. You can have all the time with her you need. We are enrolling her here on a semi-permanent basis," said Gloria breezily.

"I don't think you understand me, Mrs. Parker," said Raad. "Keeping her here isn't going to help. She should be at home where she is happy. If she can come back here, let's say once a week, I'll be able to perform the tests I need. I can even make house calls, provided that I don't need my lab equipment. As of right now, I can say confidently that there is no treatment program at Silver Hill that will make her better. In time we may find some remedies, maybe, but keeping her here while we figure that out will be counterintuitive to our goals."

"Yes, but Dr. Raad, she could be a danger to herself or others. You know her teacher was just released from the hospital!" said Gloria with a dramatic huff.

"I believe that situation was a fluke," said Raad reassuringly. Raad could tell the mother was going to push back on him; the father was barely listening while he checked his BlackBerry.

Wilson knew he needed to jump in. If he let Arianna Parker out that door, it was $250,000 gone.

"I for one think Arianna should stay here," Dr. Wilson interrupted. "Dr. Raad is new to Silver Hill and our methods. He doesn't yet fully understand how our well-rounded program can benefit Arianna, as we discussed previously. As far as her schooling, we have tutors here, and she can receive the necessary instruction so her progress will not be interrupted."

Gloria looked satisfied. Raad would have to appeal to the father if he had any hopes of doing what was best for this girl. He'd appeal to his wallet.

"Mr. Parker," Raad barked. Walter looked startled at being addressed so harshly. He had been deep in thought about his current case. This appointment, like all the others Gloria ever scheduled, was an inconvenience to him.

"I want to be frank with you," Raad continued. "The cost of keeping Arianna at Silver Hill will run you at least $250,000. The tutors here I'm confident are not up to par with what Arianna needs. That will cost you an extra $25,000, at least. Plus tack on another $30,000 for her room and board fees, you are looking at spending around $300,000 this year just to keep your daughter five miles from your home when I am telling you she does not pose a threat to herself or others. Does that math make sense to you?"

Walter tapped his fingers together as he thought about it. He'd told Gloria to handle the situation, and clearly she hadn't. She assured him that all the doctors recommended Arianna stay at Silver Hill, that she would be safer, that they could make some additional strides in treating her schizophrenia. But what he was hearing was that the expense, which certainly wasn't minimal, was needless. Gloria could be so incompetent sometimes. They obviously didn't need to keep Arianna here. The other downside to having her at Silver Hill was that he'd have to visit.

"Then it is settled," said Walter. "Arianna will come back home. Dr. Raad, you may examine Arianna further and conduct the tests you need. Please work with Dr. Wilson and my wife to schedule them accordingly. If you can find a better solution to the medication she is on, great. If not, you tried."

"But Walter," protested Gloria, "this is not what we discussed!"

Walter gave her a piercing look and replied, "It's not, but you are not being practical. And I'm not wasting money on something that is senseless. We will pay for whatever tests and treatments that result from Dr. Raad's analyses. But $300,000 to keep her here for no reason is not going to happen. End of story, Gloria. Even I have my limits. Now, I need to get back to the office." Walter was done with the conversation. He stood up, kissed his wife on the cheek, and shook the doctors' hands.

Gloria was clearly embarrassed by Walter's abrupt departure. But she would have to do as Walter mandated. He controlled the purse strings.

"So when should I bring Arianna back?" asked Gloria dejectedly.

"I can come to you," said Dr. Raad. "My first session with her will be informal, just a conversation, really. Does next Thursday work, let's say 2:00 p.m.?"

"Yes. I'll have my housekeeper contact you with directions to the house."

"Mrs. Parker, I'll discuss the costs with Dr. Raad and get back to you and your husband," said Dr. Wilson, whose face was beet red. There was still an opportunity to make money from this, but Dr. Raad was on thin ice. Wilson was going to have a word with the board immediately.

"I'll go collect Arianna then," replied Gloria flatly.

Raad privately marveled at her reaction. What kind of mother was this woman who would happily pass her child off to an institution just because she didn't want to be bothered anymore? He'd certainly seen his fair share of child neglect growing up in a slum of Iran. But these people were wealthy. What was their excuse?

From what Raad read in Ari's file and from what he found out from the other patients and nurses, Ari was polite and quiet. She rarely spoke, which wasn't a surprise with all the medication she was now taking. But she never demonstrated violent or hysterical tendencies. She was kind to the other patients. And she was also borderline genius. This was definitely going to be an interesting case study . . .

After their good-byes, Gloria found Ari outside by the fountain. When she was told she was going home, Ari was elated. She would get to see Beau, sleep in her own bed, and even eat Irena's gluten-free pancakes. But the reaction she shared with her mother was one of impassivity. She would hate her forever. Ari didn't know what convinced her parents to let her go home, but God was she thankful.

"Although you are going home, Arianna, you will still need to undergo additional tests and treatment once a week," said Gloria snidely. "You have your first appointment on Thursday with a doctor. And you are to behave yourself and do as you are told. We don't want the police to pay us another visit now, do we?"

"No, we wouldn't want that," Ari responded tersely.

They were soon speeding home in Gloria's Jaguar. The trees whipped past them in a blur of branches just sprouting with the first signs of green. Ari couldn't wait to get in the bath and slip under the water. When she was little, Irena would let her bring a snorkel in the soaking tub so she could stay under for hours. With all the noise in her head, she just might want to go looking for that snorkel. The important thing was that she came out of Silver Hill with her mind intact; she could certainly handle a few more tests and another doctor.

Five days later, Dr. Raad arrived at the Parker estate. His Honda Civic felt out of place as it crawled past the imposing gates and up the gravel drive. The housekeeper, who looked like a sixty-year-old linebacker, directed Raad to the book-lined library. Curled up in a chair by the expansive windows, Ari was deep in concentration as she read an SAT prep book.

She was the picture of youth on the cusp of full bloom. Raad was not one to remark on a woman's looks, much less a girl's, at least not since his wife died nine years ago. But even he noted that Arianna Parker was stunning. Her face reminded him of a carefully crafted sculpture. Her pale skin was like alabaster as she held herself in an unconsciously graceful pose. She had a natural pink flush to her makeup-free cheeks, and her chestnut hair hung loosely around her shoulders. What complexities did this young Aphrodite have hidden away in her mind, Raad wondered.

"Excuse me, Arianna. I'm Dr. Raad." The black Lab at her feet eyed him lazily and, after determining he wasn't a threat, went back to his nap. Raad was at first taken aback by the girl's sharp gaze that snapped in his direction at the interruption, but she quickly gave him a shy smile and stood to shake his hand.

"It's nice to meet you, Arianna. Studying for the SATs?" asked Raad.

"Yes, I'm taking them in a month," she answered softly.

"It's been a while since I've been in school, but aren't you a few years early?"

"Well, I've never been to school—in the traditional sense—so I wouldn't really know."

"Well congratulations then."

"Thank you. Would you like to sit here in the library or would you prefer to go somewhere else? My mother said that you would likely just be asking me questions today."

"Here is fine," he said as they settled into leather wing chairs facing each other. He didn't take out a pen or notepad, which surprised Ari. "I do want to ask you some questions, but I mostly want to have a conversation to get to know each other better. I thought we could start by me telling you about myself and then vice versa?" Ari gave a curt nod in agreement.

To Ari, Dr. Raad looked nonthreatening. He was slightly disheveled, with a wrinkled button-down under a wool V-neck sweater covered with animal hair. His shoes were scuffed, as if they were his favorite and only pair.

"I'm a neurologist, but I also have a degree in psychiatry," he said comfortably. "I used to have a practice in the City, but I've since given it up and I'm now living in Connecticut and working at Silver Hill. I didn't have the pleasure of meeting you in person during your stay there, but I came across your case. I'm interested in helping you explore some alternative treatments and taking another look at your diagnosis." No reaction registered on Ari's face. She truly believed no one could help her.

"I've only been at Silver Hill a few weeks, and I was expecting to encounter patients of the garden variety. But . . . you on the other hand are unique," said Raad.

"Unique? That is an interesting way to put it," said Ari as she pulled the sleeves of her cashmere sweater partially over her hands so she had something to hold on to.

"I'm renting a cottage on the Silvermine River. It has a beautiful garden and view, and it's great for reading and writing. My dog, Luna, loves it, but she keeps bringing dead squirrels home. I don't have the heart to get mad, she is so proud," Raad laughed. Ari gently brushed her foot over Beau's coat and gave her dog a smile that conveyed nothing short of adoration. At least they had something in common.

"I live alone with Luna. My wife died several years ago, but the two of us get along all right," Raad said pleasantly. But underneath the tone that conveyed a surprising positivity, he was still very much a broken man.

"I'm sorry to hear that," she sympathized. While Ari felt sad for his loss, she reminded herself to keep her guard up. She'd encountered enough doctors to know that they often tried to build a feigned connection only to get her to trust them. As far she knew, Raad could very well have a wife, children, and cats waiting for him at home.

"Why don't you tell me about yourself, Arianna?" he asked. She looked at him squarely and said nothing for a while. He could tell the gears were turning.

"Dr. Raad, I don't mean to be rude, but we can skip the pleasantries. I've always been a cooperative patient. Understanding my likes and dislikes and my feelings isn't going to make a difference," replied Ari.

"You're direct, I'll give you that," Raad said. "But we are going to be spending time together, so I at least think we should try to be friends."

"The only way to have a friend is to be one," she said pointedly.

"I see you like Ralph Waldo Emerson. I've read your report, Arianna, and know you are exceptionally smart. I promise you, I will never insult your intelligence and not respect your wishes. I will also never ask you to try a treatment that you don't want to. All I ask is that you show up for our appointments. If something makes you uncomfortable, you say the word and we'll stop."

This was the first time a doctor spoke to her like an adult. Before this, she had never been given options when it came to doctors and her condition. Yet this man was giving her a choice.

"Okay," she said hesitantly. She'd cooperate and show up for their appointments. But she still wasn't going to lay all of her cards out on the table. Several silent minutes ticked by.

"Where are you applying to college?" Raad asked.

"Yale," she responded confidently.

"And . . . ?"

"That's it. Nowhere else."

"So I guess you aren't hedging your bets then?"

"No."

"As I told you before, I won't insult your intelligence. But can I ask an obvious question?"

"Sure."

"You've never attended school and you are fifteen. Do you think you are capable of living on your own?"

She began to chew on her bottom lip and diverted her gaze out the window. He could tell he hit a nerve.

"I'll be sixteen when I go, if I get in. I don't know how it will all work out. But I have to try," she said firmly.

"Do your parents know?"

"That I'm applying? Not yet. But I've just completed my GED. Yale is one of the best schools in the country. It's my father's alma mater. Plus it's only an hour away. When I get in, they won't have a choice but to let me go," she said passionately.

Oh, they'll have a choice all right, thought Raad. He rubbed the stubble on his chin and didn't say anything. The likelihood her parents would understand or accept Ari attending college was slim to none. Plus, she was still a minor. They, or at least her mother, believed she was a danger to herself and others. They'd likely want to avoid any potential embarrassment at all costs.

"I know you probably think this is stupid, but I can do this," she said, sensing his skepticism. "I really can't live here any longer. I know what my parents think of me. My mother can't stand to be around me."

He didn't refute what was likely true. "Okay, let's say you go. How do you think you'll feel around the other students? You'll have roommates and classes with many people. And you'll have to go to the dining hall at some point."

She reached down to stroke Beau's neck. "If I concentrate enough and breathe, it's not unbearable, you know," she said defensively.

"Tell me more about that. What exactly do you do to shut out the voices you hear?" Ari flushed. "There is nothing to be embarrassed about, Arianna. You hear voices. It's a fact. I just want to figure out why and what I can do to help."

Ari looked out the window. "There are voices, but it's nothing I can understand. It sounds like gibberish or a tape recording on fast-forward. If I concentrate on the sound of my breathing, for example, or the number of taps of my foot, I can kind of tune them out. You probably already read this in my file, but it gets worse when I'm around more people."

"Do you ever feel so overwhelmed you want to hurt those people?"

"No! Never. Did my mother tell you that? Sometimes my head is completely muddled. If I don't focus and I let the sounds wash over me, I don't know where I am, who is around me, or who is touching me. If I ever hurt anyone during an episode, it is by accident. I swear.

The situation with Howard was different . . ."

"How so?"

"I don't want to talk about it."

"Okay. Do you think any of the medicine you've taken has helped?"

"No. The best medicine I've found is being alone or being underwater."

"Tell me what it's like underwater."

"Let's say I'm at a pool party. There can be thirty people around me, which would normally drive me crazy. But if I'm under the water, the noise quiets. It's still there, but on a scale of one to ten in terms of how loud it is, it's like a four instead of a ten."

"Have you ever used noise-cancelling headphones or listened to music?"

"Yes. It doesn't make a big difference, but it helps a little."

"So where do you spend most of your time?"

"In my room."

"Is it soundproof?"

"Yes. My parents had soundproof boarding installed when I was born. I was a very light sleeper, and any sound would wake me."

"Arianna, I've been thinking a lot about your case. I need to take more images of your brain, but I don't think you are schizophrenic. I think what you are hearing is real. And when I say 'real,' I don't mean real because you perceive it to be. The key neural bridge between the hemispheres in your brain is wider compared to most peoples. I found it when I saw your MRI. It may be something that's been growing slowly over time. Last night, I received your last brain scan from five years ago. I had it sent over from the specialist you saw in California. Five years ago, that neural bridge was only slightly enlarged. No one noticed, though, because it was so minute. Now, it has increased by two centimeters."

"Is it like a tumor?" she asked nervously.

"No, and I don't think it is going to affect you adversely, other than what I think it's doing to you now," he assured.

"What about my headaches?"

"They may not be cluster headaches but rather the pre- and after effects of what you are hearing. I want to pose this thought to you, Arianna—you'll have to just go with me on this. What if your enlarged neural bridge has opened up extrasensory abilities in your brain, and you are picking up on the thoughts of those around you? Kind of like a frequency the rest of us can't hear? The more people around you, the louder the frequency."

"It sounds like science fiction, but if it means I'm not crazy, I'll go with you on this for now."

"We can try to reduce the enlargement, which may abate your symptoms, or we could try some natural remedies and techniques to control the symptoms. I'm a neurologist and a proponent of pharmaceuticals, but I've seen the range you've been given and I think we need to try something different. This isn't a cancer and isn't something we can or should try to get rid of with radiation, chemotherapy, or surgery."

"Well that's good to hear. The less meds the better. And I definitely don't want surgery. So do you have some special homeopathic treatments or something?"

"Some herbs that may help, yes, and I also want to try a special type of yoga and tai chi to start," Raad said. Ari laughed. "I know it sounds ridiculous. But I think we both know that if your dream of college is going to happen, something needs to change, and soon."

She took a deep breath and held out her hand. "I agree . . . as long as you call me Ari and stick to your promises." With a firm handshake, the beginnings of a friendship were solidified.

CHAPTER 4: BINDING

52 BC, JUNE
TENTYRIS, EGYPT

Almost all of their belongings were moved. This was their last night in their beloved homeland. But it wouldn't be one of sadness; it would be one of celebration. The past ten months had been filled with preparation for everyone's relocation, and all week they had readied for this evening. The ceremony, feast, and dancing would commence at sunset. Nearly six hundred Tentyrians—entailing all twelve Covens, the Tentyrian Guard, the Zodiac Council, and the royal family—would pay tribute to Tentyris. They would honor the prosperity and leadership they had experienced for nearly 130 years and look toward their future.

The Covens had selected their new homes, spanning the globe. Although the Tentyrians would no longer be in close proximity, their geographic dispersal would work to their advantage by promoting a global blending with the humans. The Rising of Sirius was in approximately two months time, during which they would convene as a Council at the Sanctum. The new location was now ready for their arrival, and they would celebrate the New Year there.

The royal Tentyrian cooks worked for days to prepare the array of food for the night's feast that included buttery cheeses, fattened fowl, beef, fish, numerous breads, cakes, and fruits. Rich aromas of rosemary, cumin, and garlic wafted through the Royal Villa. In addition to the wine and beer that would be served aplenty, golden chalices were filled to the brim with blood. The chalices of blood were the Tentyrian signature drink—some human, some animal, the blood was obtained humanely. No one, except for the animals that were being eaten for the feast, suffered.

The night's festivities would begin with the binding ceremony in the Temple of Hathor as soon as the last rays of the sun dipped out of sight. Attendees would don their ceremonial pallas and pallium over their stolas and tunics. Colored and embroidered as designated by their respective Covens, their ceremonial garb was fastened with gold and jeweled pendants called fibulae. After the ceremony, the Tentyrians would go to the Royal Villa, where the celebration would take place. Acrobats, dancers, and musicians would entertain the party as food-laden trays and bowls made of blue faience were passed. The Tentyrians would lounge on white linen divans and join in the singing and dancing that would fill the Great Hall of the Royal Villa.

Most of the Egyptian humans at the party were fiercely loyal and were moving to the Sanctum. Some were servants who were well compensated for their duties. Others were Guardians, meaning they were charged, like their mothers and fathers before them, with the well-being of the Tentyrian children. In return for their loyalty, the human Guardians received prolonged life. They could never become like the almost immortal Tentyrians, unless they were fully changed. And that never happened. However, with the drink of Tentyrian blood they were offered every full moon, their aging slowed considerably—making it possible to triple a life span. The human servants, like the Guardians, never wanted for shelter, food, or wealth. Compared to the average Egyptian, they lived luxurious lives, which was guaranteed for as long as they kept the true nature of the Tentyrians a secret.

Any servant and even an occasional Guardian who violated that secret, and consequently the Code, would have their memories fully wiped and they'd be left on the streets outside of Tentyris. When one wanted to leave Tentyris voluntarily, it was an entirely different matter. The Guardians and servants were rewarded generously and given new homes sponsored by the Tentyrian clan.

It was eight-thirty and the sun's arc in the sky was almost complete. Hathor stood barefoot on her balcony—feeling her power heighten, despite her headache. She looked upon Tentyris and the Sacred Lake. The view was breathtaking. She could see the lights of the Tentyrian villas as their occupants were preparing for the evening ahead. Merchants were closing their shops, and the farmers were retiring from the fields. The balmy air smelled of lotus. She wrapped the crimson silk tighter around her shoulders, as if to ward off an impending chill—not that she could feel one, of course. Nevertheless, it was a protective instinct.

Hathor turned her back on the view and surveyed her bedchamber with a sigh. The raised down-filled bed with feather pillows felt like an open invitation to sleep forever in its folds. She once shared that bed, made love in it, and even held her four newborn daughters there. Now, it was just a quiet escape for one. Hathor knew it was where she would draw her last breath.

She walked over to her dressing area. Hita had organized her table with a general's precision. Picking up an ivory-handled brush from the array of instruments, Hathor ran the coarse bristles over her fingers. When her girls were little, they loved it when she brushed their long wet hair in front of the fire. Meanwhile, she would regale them with visions of the future filled with new discoveries. She hoped they would get to see them one day.

Hathor's own long black hair was piled on top of her head. The mass of curls was held in place by tight braids that formed an interlocking crown. Selene did an excellent job. Rubies were woven throughout, making her hair sparkle with sin, just like her tinted red lips. Egyptians who saw Hathor called her the most beautiful woman in the world—a goddess incarnate. Their descriptions graced papyrus pages and temple walls throughout Egypt. To the Tentyrians, she was their leader. To the Luminaries, she was their mother. Hathor was the beauty she appeared, but she was also a hardened ruler nearly three hundred years old.

"My lady, your daughters are here," Hita interrupted Hathor's thoughts.

"Wonderful, send them in. You may tell Argus and Cadmus we will be ready to depart for the temple in ten minutes."

The wooden door to Hathor's chamber opened, and her four daughters entered. Their scarlet robes rustled as the silk brushed against the stone floor.

"My darlings," Hathor said, holding out her arms to her smiling daughters. Although they were grown women, they were never too old for a mother's embrace. Hathor held tight.

"Mother, don't be sad," said Narcissa, who was first to pull away. "Tonight is going to be wonderful. And tomorrow we leave for our new home."

"Yes. Indeed. I just get sad when I realize how my little girls have grown. Before we go over to the temple together, I have something to give you four." Hathor then walked over to her bookcases. On the bottom row, she removed a cluster of books and reached behind to pull out a black leather volume that was lying flat. It was about ten inches thick, and on its cover was an engraved zodiac symbol in gold.

"This is the book that I've been writing in since we first founded Tentyris," Hathor explained. "Some of the writings are my silly musings, but they also include my visions of the future. I want you four to keep this book safe. It will prove useful."

As the eldest, Daria took the book into her hands. "Mother, if this book has your prophecies, are we supposed to act on them?" she asked.

"When we are at the Sanctum, we can discuss the implications. Not tonight. But just know that you all are now responsible for this book. Keep it safe."

"I'll shift to the Sanctum now. I have just the place for it," said Daria. The air around where she stood seemed to reverberate with motion. And in an instant, Daria shimmered away.

"In the meantime, Calypso, what is the status of Auletes?" asked Hathor. "The compromise we struck should be in motion."

Like a soldier reporting to her commander, Calypso explained that over the past month she successfully dosed Auletes' nightly wine with orpiment, a tasteless and odorless poison.

"I've heard the palace doctors say it's likely his liver is diseased. Too much wine. His death will appear natural, and by my estimates, he will be dead by tomorrow. I put an extra dose in just this evening," said Calypso with a smile.

"That better not be a flippant attitude, Calypso," said Hathor warningly. "Death is serious and permanent. All we can hope for is that the Egyptians will be in better hands now. I don't know if what we have done is right. But it is done." The women stood silent.

"Why so solemn?" interrupted Daria as she reappeared.

"Auletes will be dead tonight," replied Phoebe.

"Well, let us not dwell on it," Daria said quickly. "We must go soon. I can hear Argus and Cadmus pacing outside. Our clan and celebration await."

With the expectation that they would live forever, the women understood that emotional pitfalls would be momentary components to their lives. But if moments of joy could be equally fleeting, they needed to be celebrated to the fullest. The royal family looked at each other with the knowledge they needed to seize this joyous night and not dwell on the life of a man who had only brought them pain. Auletes was forgotten.

"Does Hita have our candles?" asked Phoebe.

"Right here, my lady," replied Hita. She had a knack for always appearing when needed. Hita handed each of the five women a long, black beeswax taper. With a snap of her fingers, Phoebe illuminated the candles.

The Luminaries and Hathor exited the chamber, escorted by Hathor's bodyguards and five members of the Tentyrian Guard. Outside the villa, the women crossed the lantern-lit courtyard to the main garden path that wove its way through the royal gardens and into the heart of Tentyris. Drumbeats calling from the temple could be heard. It was the signal for all Tentyrians to meet at the sacred Temple of Hathor.

The main path merged with dozens of others, all offshoots of the Covens' villas. To the north were Capricorn, Aquarius, and Pisces. To the east, Libra, Virgo, and Scorpio. South was home to Aries, Gemini, and Taurus. And in the west, closest to the Royal Villa, were the Leo, Cancer, and Sagittarius Covens. The royal processional was joined by hundreds of other Tentyrians as they walked together by candlelight to the ceremony.

A pair of shifty eyes watched the parade from afar. The lights flickered as they snaked through the city and entered the temple. He thought their ceremonies were pathetic—a testament to unnecessary rituals that served to pacify and give meaning to the meaningless. He knew what the Tentyrians were capable of. They certainly knew it. So why the charade? The end would begin tonight, he vowed to himself.

Two minutes until nine. All the Covens were present. The Zodiac Council stood on a raised dais, set up specifically for the ceremony, with Hathor at its center. The temple walls glowed with light, and the crowd of Tentyrians chattered as they waited for the ceremony to begin.

With a shake of Hathor's sistrum, silence followed. She addressed the crowd: "Brothers and sisters. We are gathered here tonight not to just say farewell to an era but to remember who we are. We are Tentyrian. And together, we celebrate our future!" A cheer rose from the Tentyrians, who raised their candles in salute.

Hathor continued her address. "We are here to remind each other that the blood in our veins is unique, and we must cherish that. This is a world of constant change. Governments, famines, riches. They come and go. But for us, there is a constant. The Tentyrian way. The way is written in our Code, which we have pledged to follow. We must remember that way if we are to continue. The future for us will be different. We may not have Tentyris anymore, but we will remain united as one clan. With the leadership of your Covens and the values you carry with you, this will be possible. As you go forth, I urge you to remember this. Some of you may doubt these values. You may ask yourself, would it not feel liberating to feed openly and without restraint? Yes. Would it not feel empowering to share our immortality with the world? Yes, it would. But that would be counterintuitive to our self-preservation and legacy. Your Coven leaders have explained the purpose of our relocation, which undoubtedly you have been mulling over, discussing, and acting upon within the last year. I want to sum up that purpose in one word. Longevity."

With a rallying cheer of approval, the crowd raised their candles in agreement.

"Our future will not be without its challenges. But by granting further independence to your Covens, you will be able to thrive freely in your new homelands for hopefully centuries to come. Maximos will now lead us in prayer," completed Hathor.

Maximos took Hathor's place in the center of the dais. The gold lion clasp with sapphire eyes on the shoulder of his pallium seemed to roar with silent fierceness.

"Blessed be," he began. The crowd and Council all moved their right hands to hover over their candles. They let the flames lick the underside of their palms as they continued to pray in unison.

"We are he who is clothed with the body of flesh yet in whom flames the spirit of the eternal gods. We are the Lord of Life. We are triumphant over death, and whosoever partaketh with us shall with us arise. We are the manifester in matter of those whose abode is the invisible. We are the purified. We stand upon the universe. We are its reconciler with the eternal gods. We are the perfecter of matter, and without us, the universe is not."

By the end of the prayer, the candle flames burned deep enough into their flesh that blood was now dripping from all the Tentyrians' hands. But they felt no pain, only exhilaration. Their senses were fully alive. And the pricking in their gums they felt at the beginning of the prayer was no more. With their fangs exposed, they stood with each other as they truly were.

"Let us rejoice in the blood that binds us!" exclaimed Hathor. The Tentyrians turned to each other and clasped their hands with their neighbors. The connection of Tentyrian blood caused a ripple of energy to course through their palms, like a shock of electricity that traveled up their arms and into the core of their bodies.

"Blessed be the blood that binds us," they cried out in unison as the feeling of united power hummed through their veins. With a snap of her finger, Phoebe doused the lights in the temple. It was pitch black and silent. But Tentyrian senses allowed them to see as if it were daylight. They could even hear the buzz of the nighttime insects from the distant gardens.

A soft blue glow began to grow from the center of the dais. The Council members encircled it. The glow originated from a small rotating orb of light that spun and began to increase in size. Together, the Council controlled the orb within their circle as their outstretched arms urged and willed the orb to grow bigger. It rose higher and higher, and with one intentioned push, the orb exploded into a cascade of sparking lights that rained down upon the Tentyrians, who cheered at the beautiful display.

Phoebe reignited the temple's torchlight, and Hathor addressed the crowd once more. "We would like to welcome you all now to celebrate this glorious night at the Royal Villa. Please join us!" The Tentyrians clapped their hands, which were already healed, in exuberant applause. The ceremony had been short, but it was a unifying reminder of who they were. As the crowd exited through the temple's newly erected portico, they admired the ceiling's bas-relief of the zodiac that honored Tentyris and its Covens.

As a planisphere, or map of the sky's stars and planets, the zodiac relief portrayed the symbols of the twelve Covens within a circle—from the image of Taurus' bull to Libra's scales. The four Luminaries appeared as maidens supporting the circular zodiac while Hathor's outstretched body stood alongside. Hathor commissioned its design shortly after the decision to leave Tentyris was made. It was a masterpiece that would surely be cherished long after the Tentyrian race became a distant memory.

It was time for the festivities to begin. The Royal Villa was packed with guests. A fire and acrobatic show started in the main hall as a well-muscled Egyptian tossed flaming batons effortlessly and caught them in his mouth after a series of backflips. Plates filled with chickpeas, lentils, cucumbers, and onions were passed around, as well as sweet cakes drenched in honey and nuts.

Daria hung back from the festivities. She could see Aristos laughing with his best friends and fellow Council members Maximos and Pello. Ammon was holding Darrius on his shoulders to help him get a better look at the acrobatics. It was a happy sight, but she had a pit of worry in her stomach. Daria's thoughts drifted to her mother's book. Hathor brushed off the discussion, but Daria knew the book was a viper sleeping quietly in its hiding spot at the Sanctum. And why would her mother give it to her and her sisters now? Daria wished she could read her mother's mind. There was something serious brewing.

Spying Phoebe and Narcissa talking to a group of their friends, Daria walked over. It was rude to shift into a conversation. "Ladies, a pleasure to see you," said Daria. The three Tentyrian women from the Cancer Coven bowed their heads reverently. As the oldest and First Luminary, Daria intimidated people. It was the same effect her mother had. Admittedly, she wasn't as understanding as Phoebe, as frank as Calypso, or as sensitive as Narcissa. But it wasn't her intention to come off as intimidating. Aristos said it was her eyes that created the effect. "No one likes looking into emerald eyes of judgment—except me," he would tease.

"If you can excuse us, ladies, I need to speak with my sisters," requested Daria. The women politely curtsied and left.

"You could try being a little friendlier, Dar," said Narcissa.

"Yes, well there are other more important matters on my mind. Where is Calypso, anyway?" Daria replied.

"She said she went to grab a mind-settling potion. She was feeling a bit dizzy. I offered to help with my own power, but she said she had just the right medicine. You want to talk to us about Mother, don't you?" said Phoebe.

"Yes. I'm worried about the book and why she gave it to us tonight," Daria answered.

"I think we are all feeling the same way. Mother obviously thinks she will die," Phoebe said as she chewed on a fingernail.

"Yes, but we've all taken the appropriate precautions. It would be virtually impossible for Auletes' men to hurt her," replied Narcissa in earnest.

"I do think we should speak further with her tonight. It can't wait until tomorrow. I have a terrible feeling . . . Shall we convene in the library?" asked Daria.

"Yes, I'll go find Calypso. Phoebe, you get Mother," said Narcissa.

The women agreed to meet in twenty minutes.

Narcissa scanned the party for Calypso. She did a few circuits around the room and finally found her speaking with Calix. A pang of anger stabbed at Narcissa. She knew what they were discussing was harmless, but the hatred Narcissa had for Calix ran deep. She forced a smile.

"Calypso, sorry to take you away, but we're having a quick meeting. Luminary business," Narcissa emphasized while staring pointedly at Calix.

"I'll come," said Calypso tiredly, "but let me first tell Alexander so he doesn't worry."

"Hurry up then," Narcissa replied as she turned on her heel. With an inscrutable smile on his lips, Calix watched her stride away.

Calypso found Ceres and Alexander on the dance floor. Ceres loved the drumbeats, and she tried to move her hips and arms like the belly dancers. Calypso wrapped her arms around Alexander and whispered in his ear, "She's going to be a handful when she's older, isn't she?"

"When she's older? She already is a handful," replied Alexander as he pulled Calypso into a dramatic spin in front of him. "Did you know I found her underneath a table earlier with Darrius? They were playing warrior and warrior queen."

"Well, she is a little queen, so why not?" grinned Calypso with effort. She was feeling exhausted; the medicine she took hadn't kicked in yet. She briefly wondered if she was carrying a child. She smiled up at Alexander. "I have to speak with my mother and sisters for a bit, but I'll be back as quickly as I can."

"All right, but are you feeling okay, my dear? You look paler than usual," Alexander asked with concern.

"Yes, of course I am," assured Calypso.

"Well in that case . . ." Before she could object, Alexander picked up Calypso by the waist and tossed her straight into the air ten feet. Calypso pulled in her arms tightly, like a pinwheel retracting, and twisted her body so she spiraled down effortlessly into his waiting arms. Her man could dance; she had to give him that. But he certainly didn't help her nausea. With a wink, Calypso vanished.

Daria took a sip of her drink and handed it back to Aristos as she absorbed the revelry around her. Even Maximos looked like he was having fun as he spoke with Stavros, Aglaia, and Asia. Maximos was always so serious; a bit of fun would be good for him, she thought. The liquid was invigorating, and she could feel the blood nourishing her.

"Ah, I needed that. I can't remember the last time I ate," said Daria.

"The past few months have just been so busy. It's hard to believe that tomorrow is the day we leave. It's come quickly, hasn't it?" she said, mostly talking to herself.

"Yes, it has," Aristos replied. Wanting Daria's full attention, he took her hand in his. "Thank you for being so amazing, Daria. I don't know if I tell you enough . . ."

"You do, I promise," Daria said, trying to shush him.

Aristos brushed her fingers away and kissed them instead. "I was speaking with Maximos and Pello earlier, and they say all the Covens are confident their new homes are ready and secure. It bodes well."

Daria replied with a smile and said, "Thank you, love. All in a day's work, though. I must go for a bit; I'm meeting my sisters and mother in the library. See you soon." Daria gave Aristos a kiss and disappeared.

After speaking with Hita, Phoebe found Claudius relaxing on a divan sipping from a chalice. "Phoebe sweetheart, I've been waiting for you," said Claudius as he patted the seat next to him. "Come sit and enjoy."

"I need to tend to some Luminary business for a short while," Phoebe replied. "Are the twins okay?"

"Yes, I checked on them a while ago," answered Claudius. "Sleeping like angels. Tale is watching them like a hawk, of course."

"I would expect nothing less. Save me a seat. I'll be back soon. And keep those eyes off the dancers," chided Phoebe playfully.

"You know I only have eyes for you, kardoula mou," said Claudius sincerely as he reached up to run a hand through her long blonde hair. Within seconds, Phoebe disappeared before his eyes. "Damn Luminary," laughed Claudius as he settled back with his drink.

All four Luminaries stood in the library around the circular table. The table, twelve feet in diameter, had been carefully carved with the zodiac of Tentyris in its center. The floor-to-ceiling bookshelves of the library took up almost the entire room, with the exception of the windows on the south side that overlooked Tentyris. The library functioned as their place for royal deliberation and conference.

"Where is Mother, Phoebe? Did you find Hita?" asked Daria impatiently.

"She said Mother went to lie down and that we shouldn't disturb her. We all know she hasn't been feeling well," Phoebe replied.

"I would normally agree, but I have this lingering feeling that I know won't go away unless we speak with her. Let's go to her bedchamber," said Daria. But before the Luminaries could leave to find their mother, they heard piercing screams from outside.

The sisters ran to the windows to see flames bursting from at least fifteen villas. "We must hurry and direct the firefighting efforts," exclaimed Daria. Instinctively, the sisters held hands and shifted outside. Daria took charge immediately, organizing the Tentyrian Guard to direct water from the Sacred Lake to the burning villas through their telekinetic abilities. Zoe of Aquarius, who could manipulate water, set to work handling the fires that burned the strongest. Some of the Coven villas, particularly those to the east, were too far away for their abilities to reach. Consequently, the Tentyrians had to use a long siphon to draw water away from the lake to douse some of the villas. The coordination of the siphon and pump took precious time they didn't have.

Under Calypso's and Phoebe's direction, the Coven leaders began shifting in and out of the villas looking for trapped servants, Guardians, and young Tentyrian children who were left sleeping during the ceremony and celebration. Narcissa directed the injured humans and Tentyrian healers to the Sanatorium, where they began healing burns and injuries immediately.

Fortunately, the majority of the complex's inhabitants were at the Royal Villa, which was untouched by fire. All of the Luminaries' husbands and children were safe. However, the fires in the fifteen homes raged aggressively. Fires in the villas almost never happened since they were constructed of limestone, and the kitchen layouts, fire pits, and ovens were purposefully designed to prevent such disasters. The fires were clearly not accidents, as they were coordinated and well timed.

After hours of labor, the flames were out. But the night's suffering was just beginning to unfold. Daria and her sisters turned their attention to the Sanatorium, where about a dozen humans were being treated for burns. They would be fine in a matter of days. Unfortunately, six servants, one Tentyrian child, and one Guardian had died. The child was Karis and Damian's, as their villa was the farthest to the east and the farthest from the lake. It was also likely one of the first homes that ignited.

Karis' inconsolable cries of grief for her daughter Calandra could be heard for miles, as she lay next to her daughter's burned body. Damian tried to move Karis, but she resisted anyone's touch. Even the pleading of her Virgo sisters didn't help. Damian turned his grief into anger while he exploded several of the Sanatorium stone benches into dust. Karis and Damian had shifted to their home, but they were too late: Calandra and her Guardian had died of smoke inhalation. Their daughter was found clutched in the arms of her Guardian, who had tried to cover the girl's small body with her own. The damage was too severe to be healed.

In the panic of the fires, the sisters did not see their mother, which was unusual. Hathor would normally be on the front lines of any disaster, regardless of illness. Horror washed over Daria. She shifted immediately into Hathor's bedroom and vomited at what she saw. Minutes later, her sisters realized where Daria went, and they shifted in to see the gruesome sight.

Hathor's head was severed, just like their father's had been. The once crisp white sheets of her bed were drenched in blood.

Cadmus and Argus burst through the doors, hearing the Luminaries' cries. "This is impossible!" Cadmus shouted when he saw Hathor's body. "I checked on her not more than fifteen minutes ago, and she was alive. When the fires broke out, we immediately went into her room to ensure it was secure. She was fast asleep. We bolted the balcony door and remained stationed at the front, in case we came under siege. There are guards stationed in every hallway and entrance. The balcony door has not been penetrated. Look! It is still locked. Plus no one can scale those heights!" Cadmus was frantic.

"Hathor never awoke, and we checked on her repeatedly!" said Argus desperately. "No one has entered through these doors. Cadmus and I have been watching vigilantly. And we would have heard a struggle. This situation is impossible!"

Without hesitation, Daria breached their minds with a mind tap to see if they spoke the truth. The two guards stood frozen while she combed through their thoughts. Except for her husband and sisters, Daria now trusted no one. However, what Cadmus and Argus said was true.

"What they say is accurate," said Daria solemnly.

"How can this have happened?" cried Narcissa hysterically.

"I don't know, but it will be found out," replied Calypso solemnly. "Cadmus. Get Hita. My mother's body needs to be wrapped and taken to the Sanatorium. Sisters, there is nothing we can do here. We need to discuss our plan of action and call all Tentyrians to the temple for a meeting—quickly."

"I am not leaving Mother!" said Narcissa defiantly.

"Narcissa, there is nothing we can do. Even you can't help her. She is dead. Hita will be here any minute," consoled Phoebe.

Cadmus returned running and delivered yet another blow. "I didn't need to go far. I just heard from another guard. Hita is dead. Her body was found in the gardens, and her throat was slit." Daria took a deep breath. Narcissa's cries grew louder. This was a well-crafted plan, indeed.

"Cadmus and Argus, stay with our mother's body until we return. Don't leave this room or say anything to anyone," Daria commanded.

"Mistress, it is not safe. I can't allow you to leave without guards," said Argus. Daria didn't register Argus' demand.

"Sisters, let us go now," she ordered.

With clasped hands, the Luminaries shifted to the library. Daria checked that the room was empty and bolted the door. Narcissa found a chair to curl up in and continued to cry. Phoebe kneeled by her side to try and comfort her while Calypso remained standing near the windows expressionless as she surveyed the scene below. The commotion outside had calmed. The fires were out, but the heavy scent of smoke permeated the air—even inside the villa. Meanwhile, the lights from the Sanatorium burned brightly.

Several dozen Tentyrians remained in the courtyard, trying to make sense of what had happened. At Aristos' command, the Guard was vigilantly patrolling and keeping the peace. They urged all Tentyrians home until further notice was given. The handful of Tentyrians who lost their homes was at the Sanatorium tending to their servants, or they sought refuge with their fellow Coven members. From the windows, Calypso could see the Guard brigades riding horseback by torchlight, scanning Tentyris for suspicious activity. It was going to be a long night.

Daria knew they needed to move quickly as she paced the library floor. She was upset and frightened but resolved to be strong for her people. "Our grief will have to wait, sisters," Daria said. "We need to address the situation. Tentyris' Visionary is dead, which means that we are now the Primary Rulers. We will need to conduct a full-blown investigation as to how this happened and who is responsible. If it was at the orders of Auletes—who is undoubtedly now dead—then he received help from the inside. Outsiders alone could not get past the Guard, kill our mother, and set the fires. The perpetrators received help. Whether that help is human or Tentyrian, we will find out!"

"We were planning on leaving tomorrow, Daria," said Phoebe. "Do we delay and conduct the investigation? That will take months. And we need to give Mother a proper Tentyrian service. It should be done right."

"I agree," answered Daria carefully. "It will be done right. How-ever, our people are not safe here. I think we should stay an extra month, no more. That will give us enough time to discover who or what is behind this and pay homage to our dead. After which, we will leave for the mountain and the Covens will disperse. The Council will then convene at the Rising of Sirius, which is fifty-seven days away."

"I think we need to lock down the complex," said Calypso. "We can confer with the rest of the Council, but we will need to systematically question the people. The best way to do that is to ensure no one leaves or comes into Tentyris."

"Hopefully there are some witnesses," said Phoebe. "Although, to-night is likely linked to Father's death. And there were no witnesses to that crime. The method of our parents' execution is the same. Who-ever is responsible knows how to kill Tentyrians. I think it's obvious someone from inside Tentyris is helping take us down."

"Like Stavros or Calix?" suggested Narcissa between her teary hiccups.

"Maybe. It's true they didn't want us to abandon Tentyris," rea-soned Daria. "But they have been with Mother since the beginning. They are like family to us, despite our recent differences. I saw them helping put out the fires. And I saw them in the hall throughout the night. I'll admit, the fires make me suspect Aglaia and Asia. No one is as skilled with fire as them. But I also saw them in the hall. I suppose they could have slipped out, but fifteen fires at once?"

"What would any of them have to gain from setting them?" asked Phoebe. "Our decision to leave will not be reversed. If anything, this further supports us leaving." There was a long pause as the sisters ab-sorbed the situation.

"Mother must have been killed before the fires," said Calypso. "Otherwise, she would have helped in the rescue efforts. Therefore, the fires weren't a distraction to kill her. So what was the purpose?" The sisters had no answers, only questions.

"But Cadmus and Argus were telling the truth when they said they checked on Mother not fifteen minutes before we found her," said Daria. "This means there is mind control afoot. We should ques-tion all Council members first. We will start tonight. And no one is to leave Tentyris. We are issuing a lockdown, to your point, Calypso. Our people right now need comfort and assurance that our leadership will continue effectively. We no longer have our Visionary, but the strength of the Zodiac continues. Tomorrow at sunset, we will bury the dead.

The traditional mourning rituals will be followed, and we will grieve. Then, in twenty-eight days, we leave."

For Daria, assuming the position of leadership was one she accepted readily. As the eldest sister and First Luminary, she had been groomed for this role since birth. It was agreed that Daria would make the announcement to their people.

"Let us go, then," proclaimed Daria. "We need the Guard to notify our people to meet at the temple immediately. I will tell Aristos to inform them and begin the temple call. Calypso, tell Cadmus and Argus to wrap Mother and carry her to the Sanatorium. They should ensure the same happens to Hita. We'll need Mother's sistrum. Calypso, retrieve it from her chamber. Phoebe, can you help Narcissa repair her makeup? We'll all need to be composed for this meeting. We'll shift to the temple in thirty minutes. Remember, this sadness is but a moment of time."

But deep down, the sisters weren't so sure.

CHAPTER 5:
GRADUATION

2006 AD, JUNE
NEW HAVEN, CONNECTICUT
YALE UNIVERSITY

A ri heard the bells tolling ten as she dashed across the green between Saybrook and Trumbull Colleges to join the rest of her class already lined up. She spent the morning finishing her packing and cleaning up the dorm room she shared with her two friends, Jayne and Rosemary. Last night's debauchery had taken a toll on Ari's small but charmingly Gothic dorm, as well as on her roommates. Fortunately, Ari felt wonderful. Her head was clear, and she couldn't wait to toss her cap. Maybe if she got her aim just right, she could hit Gloria in the face with it.

From her first place in the processional, Ari scanned the crowd for Raad. She couldn't wait to see him and introduce Charles. Raad's opinion meant the world to her. After the graduation ceremony, they would all have brunch at Lena's Café, including her parents. They were in the second row—her parents and Dr. Raad. Their excellent seats certainly weren't surprising, but the fact her parents invited Raad to sit with them was. They always tried to avoid discussing her condition with strangers. Surely having to explain who Dr. Raad was to the other families would be awkward. Hi, this is our daughter's (the valedictorian's) personal doctor. Yes, she has mental problems. But she is doing much better, thanks. As far as Ari's parents knew, she really did have schizophrenia. This was because Ari and Raad had made the decision to keep her gift a secret. The potential for her being exploited was too great.

Since Dr. Raad entered Ari's life, she discovered what it meant to be independent, to feel that she could control her future, and that there was a life for her outside of her parents' house. Together, they embarked on what seemed like the impossible, treating a condition that had no historical precedence. It became clear to Raad that Ari was misdiagnosed as a schizophrenic, which had been a convenient diagnosis for many. But Raad's willingness to think beyond convention led them to an effective treatment plan that enabled Ari to lead an almost normal life and embrace rather than be tormented by her power of telepathy.

Every morning, Ari began her day at 5:00 a.m. She would start with a forty-five minute jog, followed by a thirty-minute meditation session designed specifically by Raad. The calming breathing exercises helped set the stage for the rest of the day. Rather than coffee, Ari only drank tea. She regularly infused it with passionflower and Schisandra, often referred to as the "Chinese Prozac." The soothing herbs helped ready Ari to face the world and its conflicting thoughts. The herbal-infused tea was also an excellent pick-me-up around two o'clock, when her mind tended to get chaotic. Ari would conclude each day with a tai chi session that helped center her and improve her unconscious awareness. It all sounded so "New Agey" when Ari thought about it and when Jayne and Rosemary teased her about her routines and refusal to deviate. But Ari knew that without those routines, she'd likely be in a padded room.

Ari had experienced her first breakthrough about three weeks after Dr. Raad began treating her. It was hard to believe that was over four years ago. When they'd first started their meditation sessions, Ari would just sit there with her eyes closed, mimicking the sounds Raad would make. She'd quickly become bored and often would just stare at Raad, wondering what he was seeing and feeling from all those "ommms" and death breaths. She felt like a phony because she didn't feel any different. But one afternoon in the rose garden as they meditated, Ari had felt something different—silence.

It was as if all the reverberations coming from her mouth had filtered into her mind and chased away the chaos with their ripples, leaving nothing. Ari had been able to quiet her symptoms before, but this time was different because she found true calm. She remembered she had opened her eyes in astonishment at the realization and shared it immediately with Dr. Raad.

"Very good," Raad praised. "Please continue." He then gestured for her to be silent, and they continued to meditate until the sun went down. When they were finished, Raad hugged her tightly. The unexpected affection was surprising but meant all that much more to Ari.

Over the next few months, Ari learned how to build imaginary walls around her mind, at will, to create the necessary tranquility to function normally. Through careful control, Ari learned she could successfully socialize and be with large groups of people without crippling side effects later. It was a giant step forward in realizing her dream of going to college. Raad was there for her every step of the way. He took her on experimental trips into town, to restaurants, and even into New York City as her self-control became stronger. He drove her to and from the SATs and helped proof all of her essay submissions. It was Raad to whom she confided her hopes and dreams, and it was Raad who helped gain her entrance into the real world.

Ari waited anxiously for days for her Yale acceptance letter. She checked the online blogs religiously to see if other applicants had received their letters. By Tuesday, the blogs showed chatter—the letters had started to arrive. By Thursday, Ari hadn't received anything and she felt despondent. Then the doorbell rang. Irena opened the door to the dean of admissions of Yale University himself. He personally drove down to hand deliver Ari's acceptance.

Thursday afternoons were the only time when her parents lunched together. Their therapist suggested it would strengthen their romantic connection. The timing of the visit was impeccable, just as Raad had planned. The dean was actually an old friend of his; they had met at a conference many years prior. But their relationship—as well as Ari already being a legacy candidate—aside, she was a shoe-in. Ari had top-notch grades and SAT scores in the highest percentile, spoke four languages, and had extracurricular skills to boot. Not to mention she would be a boon for the university as one of their youngest applicants. Despite her age, Raad assured the dean that Ari was emotionally mature enough to handle the experience. However, her parents were going to take convincing.

Gloria and Walter were in the dining room finishing their lobster bisque when Irena announced the dean's arrival. Walter's first thought was that his alma mater was asking for money. But he'd written his annual check just three months ago, so why the house call? Curious, Gloria and Walter abandoned their lunch to meet with the dean in the living room.

When Dean Whittaker told them the news, they were taken aback. They had no idea Ari even applied to Yale. Ari was called in to explain herself immediately. In the meantime, Whittaker flattered Walter and flirted with Gloria, just as Raad had suggested. When Ari arrived, she recognized Dean Whittaker and stopped in her tracks. She couldn't believe he was actually in her home.

Fortunately, before Ari could be interrogated, Whittaker covered for her. He said that he had spoken with Ari personally and understood that she wanted her potential acceptance to be a surprise to her parents, that she expressed to him in earnest how proud she wanted to make her parents. It was a bunch of bologna; Ari hadn't told them because she knew they would forbid it. But the words coming from Whittaker's mouth, a well-respected academic and winner of the Pulitzer Prize, appealed to the Parkers' egos. The words, "You certainly raised a talented young woman, Mr. and Mrs. Parker," sealed the deal.

Whittaker said he was aware of Ari's health issues and felt assured she would do just fine at school, with Raad monitoring her progress. He was confident that she would not only succeed but that he'd be surprised if she didn't graduate at the top of her class. The dean then shook Ari's hand and welcomed her to the class of 2006. Shockingly, her parents seemed pleased.

Today's graduation speech, though, was not to please her parents. It was about honoring Raad and all that he had done for her. With his support, Ari came to Yale a shy sixteen-year-old—she remembered she felt like a baby surrounded by older kids—but now, she was leaving a woman who people respected.

The ceremony music began, and Ari led her class up the aisle as families' and friends' cameras flashed. Raad was holding up his vintage eight-millimeter camera. Although slightly embarrassed, Ari was delighted. The only thing that would have made the moment more perfect was if Charles was next to Raad. Charles' early morning meeting prevented him from attending, but he promised to be there for brunch to make the inaugural meeting of the parents.

The music concluded, and the dean of her residential college, Saybrook, delivered his welcome speech with warmth and levity. Soon enough, it was her turn. Ari willed her long legs to gracefully take her to the podium. The black fabric of her graduation robe and the cords designating her various honors brushed her shins. She was confident and fresh, like a model from a Neutrogena commercial. Everyone there wanted to hear what she was going to sell. And sell she did.

"When I first came to Yale," Ari began, "I was overwhelmed by how intelligent and intense everyone was. Everyone wanted to participate in class, everyone worked around the clock for straight As, and everyone wanted to be a success. Even flag football was serious business, which I quickly learned through a dislocated shoulder. I actually never attended a real school before coming here. So imagine my shock when I encountered thirteen hundred A-type personalities. I thought for sure I wouldn't make it more than a week. But someone in my life told me not to throw in the towel. He told me to get my ass to class and to raise my hand. And to go back to that flag football field, throw some elbows, and even break some bones if I needed to. I just want to point out that the person who gave me this advice spent two years living in an ashram." Raad shifted the video camera and gave Ari a wink.

"So I took this wise man's advice. And soon, something amazing happened. I no longer was just one girl against thirteen hundred; I was one of thirteen hundred all striving for excellence. It felt like a harsh initiation for a sixteen-year-old, having to run alongside and oftentimes try to run faster than those who seemed so much more experienced and smarter. But as I ran in this unspoken race, I noticed two things. First, people fell. But when they fell, they were helped back up by their peers. And second, people found unique trails I would have never even thought to find, much less follow.

"Everyone up here today has participated in this race with success. But what we have accomplished is more than just finishing a one-time event; we have entered into a lifelong marathon with some of the brightest and most adventurous people of our generation. It's easy enough to get caught up in yourself and feel like you have to be first. But the reality is, being number one is meaningless, unless you have reached your destination with the knowledge that you made it with the people that matter and that you know you've explored the unique paths they've shown you. To the class of 2006, thank you for letting me run with you."

Ari received a standing ovation. Rosemary and Jayne gave her thumbs-up signs. It wasn't long before Ari collected her diploma, posed in front of the camera, and tossed her cap into the air. She had done it.

Ari decided to ride with Raad in his beat-up Civic to brunch rather than in her parents' chauffeured car. She wanted a few minutes alone with him.

"You did great up there, Ari. I was so proud," said Raad as they turned off Elm Street.

"Thanks, I wanted to keep it short. I hope it didn't come off as arrogant," she said.

"Not all. You spoke the truth. Except for the fact that you never really ran alongside anyone . . . You've always led the pack."

"Well, you have to say that."

"Because why?"

"Because you are you," said Ari with an indulgent smile as she tapped away on her phone, sending Charles a text.

"So I get to meet your new beau? Charles Dumore, is it?"

"Yep, I really hope you like him."

"Me too. But he is older, Ari, which worries me. And he works on Wall Street."

"You are just being cynical. He is smart, handsome, and kind. I've never met anyone like him."

"That's what I'm afraid of, my dear."

Wanting to change the subject, Raad said her "real" Beau sent his love. Since dogs weren't allowed on campus, Beau went to live with Raad and his dog Luna while Ari was at school—to her mother's delight. Beau became Luna's constant companion. Even though she visited every weekend, Ari missed Beau terribly. But she knew Luna and Beau were a match made in heaven, and Beau was surely happier having acres to romp in rather than being confined to her dorm room.

Ari could tell Raad was worried for her. "I'll still be able to visit on the weekends, you know. It's only a sixty-five minute train ride from New York," Ari said.

"That's true. But I still can't believe you are starting your first job," he said like a wistful father.

"I feel so lucky to even have a job. I know I'm just an analyst, but I can't wait to start!"

"You'll need to be mindful of your schedule, though. And ensure you maintain a work-life balance. College was one thing. But working in a city with over eight million people is different."

"I know, I know. I'm going to stick to my regimen," she assured.

"Have you been practicing the filtering?"

"Yes . . . sort of," Ari said cautiously. "You know how quickly I can lose my hold on it. I think I'm getting better. I practiced a little on Rosemary earlier this week. Can you believe she is actually jealous of Charles and me? She is one of the most beautiful people I've ever met, and she has a cute boyfriend. But I heard what she thought. She wanted

Charles for herself. I mean, Rosemary never let on. And she would never say anything like that to me . . ." Ari's voice started to trail off. "But still, I haven't been able to look at her the same." Ari stared out the window, face expressionless.

"It's a dangerous gift you have, but you will only learn to control it better the more you practice."

"Sometimes it's just easier to shut it all out. You know, actually be normal for a change."

"True. But as I'm always telling you—you are unique. And isn't that better than being normal?"

"The jury is still out," she replied as they got out of the car and walked to meet her parents and Charles.

As they entered the cozy café, Ari saw her parents already seated at a booth with Charles. They were laughing as they shared a joke. He looked refined, as usual, in his crisp suit that fit him like a glove and pink bespoke button-down. He didn't wear a tie, but a square of a pink paisley handkerchief poked out from his pocket. Ari loved how classically handsome and preppy he was. Raad gave him a once-over and thought he looked like an idiot. Charles "Dumbmore" was more like it, he thought.

"It looks like you found each other," said Ari, surprised.

"Well when I saw your beautiful mother, I recognized the resemblance immediately," Charles answered.

Ari could tell her mother already adored him. Charles smiled and got up to take Ari's jacket. It was good he was seeking her parents' approval, but did he have to be so obvious? As she shrugged out of her Chanel tweed, she knew she was being sensitive. Just because she disliked her parents, she reminded herself, she shouldn't begrudge Charles for trying.

"I must say, Arianna, this is an interesting place you chose," sniffed Gloria in obvious displeasure. Her bottle of hand sanitizer was within hand's reach.

"It's not Le Cirque, but I promise the food is delicious," Ari reassured.

The no-nonsense waitress soon arrived to take their orders: smoked salmon for Walter, fresh fruit and a fat-free cappuccino for Gloria, the Mediterranean omelet for Raad, two scrambled eggs and bacon for Charles, and steak (very rare) and eggs for Ari along with hash browns, toast, orange juice, and tea.

"Well I hope your diet improves now that you are done with college," said Gloria, appalled by Ari's robust order. Since leaving her parents' home, Ari never held back on what she ate. Food gave her immense pleasure, and she loved cooking it. She felt it was a shame to put rules around so satisfying an activity. Plus, she had enough daily rules to follow. And everyone had a vice—hers was food. When her waist started to object, maybe she'd tone it down. But at a size four, Ari wasn't complaining.

"Excellent speech, Arianna," said her father, more to his Black-Berry than to her as he took a quick scroll through his e-mails.

"I'm sorry I missed it, but from what you read to me, I bet it was great," said Charles, putting an arm around Ari's shoulders.

"So Charles, what is it that you do? Ari indicated you were a bit older?" asked Raad stiffly. He obviously wanted to grill him.

"I'm twenty-seven, sir, and I'm an investment banker," answered Charles.

"And what are your intentions towards Ari?" asked Raad bluntly. That raised eyebrows from all around the table.

"Dr. Raad, isn't that bold? We don't want to give the poor boy a heart attack," soothed Gloria.

"Yes we do," Raad replied. "And so, what are your intentions?" In truth, Ari wasn't surprised. Raad saw her not as a patient to protect but as a daughter. She simply rolled her eyes.

"Well, we are dating for now, seriously of course, and now that Ari is moving to the City we'll be seeing a lot more of each other," Charles replied smoothly.

"And it's not like we are moving in together," interjected Ari.

"Well that's good, because it would be completely inappropriate," Raad said sternly.

Attempting to lighten the mood, Gloria inquired into Charles' family. The Dunmores were Boston based and could trace their lineage all the way back to the Mayflower. His family's businesses stretched from real estate to tire manufacturing plants that had been passed down from generation to generation. He was good stock, in Gloria's opinion. Charles clearly endeared himself to her and even Walter. But the way Charles casually draped his arm around Ari irked Raad. He didn't care how much money this kid had or if his family had sailed the May-flower to the moon. Any man meeting a woman's family for the first time should be nervous. He wanted to see Charles sweat bullets.

"So you said you are in investment banking, Charles?" asked Raad, interrupting the pleasant interlude with the Parkers. They were discussing where Charles' family vacationed in the Vineyard.

"Yes, sir, I am."

"And what do you specialize in?"

"Financial institutions."

"Have you worked on any interesting deals recently?"

"We're in the process of looking at acquiring some firms in the mortgage and loan industry. I believe there are some great opportunities in mortgage-backed securities. Historically speaking, I think it's a win for investors and for us."

"And why is that?" Raad asked.

"Home prices keep rising. And everyone wants a piece of the American dream. The opportunities are endless," Charles answered easily.

"Right, except a lot of people can't afford that dream. So then what?" asked Raad frankly, taking a sip of his coffee. There was an awkward silence. Ari was frowning at him. He knew he wasn't on his best behavior, but he just wanted to protect Ari. And where had this guy even come from?

Just three months ago, Ari was solely focused on finding a job, pounding the pavement in New York City for interviews. And then she bumps into this guy at the train station and now he has his arm around her? He was seven years her senior; Ari wasn't even old enough to drink alcohol, for God's sake. Yet everyone sat around the table acting like it was fine, while Raad played the disgruntled old man.

"So, considering you are seven years older than Ari, do you ever find that age difference difficult? What do your friends think?" Raad asked, attempting but failing to lighten his tone.

"Well, I think we all know how mature Ari is. When I first met her, I would have never guessed she was only twenty. To me, age is just a number. We have so much in common too. Ari is more than a girlfriend; she is a real friend. And as for my friends, they haven't gotten to know her yet. But they will—and I know they'll love her as much as I do."

Gloria smiled at his impassioned speech, and Ari looked at Charles lovingly. Yep, Raad was definitely being the disgruntled old man.

The plates were cleared, and Walter paid the bill. Ari inhaled her meal. Her parents' food was barely touched. Ari said her farewell to her parents—an air kiss from her mother and an awkward side hug from her father ensued. As they climbed into the waiting car, her parents said they'd come visit her apartment once she settled in. Ari, Charles, and Dr. Raad stood on the sidewalk.

"So when do the movers come?" Raad asked.

"Around three. I'm pretty much all packed up. Charles took the rest of the day off to help me."

"I can help too. I know moves aren't easy, no matter how organized you think you are," offered Raad.

"That's okay. I know you need to get back to the dogs and your work," Ari said as she put her arm around him. She knew he was worried, but he had to relax. In time, she truly believed he'd grow to like Charles. She was in love with him. Raad gave her a big bear hug.

"Be cautious, Ari. That's all I want. And remember—you have a gift. Use it," he said to her.

Ari watched the closest thing she had to a real father walk away in the same old scuffed shoes she had never seen him without. Charles took her hand and led her to his Range Rover to head back to campus. Raad wanted her to use her gift on Charles. Yet she purposely didn't. She told herself it was because she hadn't fully controlled her power and she didn't want to risk having a relapse. It was kind of like controlling a dam. Although she had built strong walls, she could also accidentally open the floodgates—and once open, it was incredibly difficult to get them closed again. However, Ari knew the real reason she hadn't read Charles' mind. It was because she was afraid of what she would find.

When they arrived back at Ari's room, it was empty, with the exception of her boxes and the three stripped beds. Rosemary and Jayne had already left, but the trio said their farewells the night prior. They were also moving to New York City, so they planned to catch up soon over drinks at the Gansevoort Hotel. Ari hoped she wouldn't have to use her fake ID—being so young definitely had its disadvantages.

"Well, babe, looks like you're all packed. What do you want to do?" asked Charles.

"I'd say we should go for a walk outside, except it looks like it's about to rain," Ari said as she touched her fingers to the cool glass of her gabled window that looked out onto the street packed with moving vans. It was bittersweet leaving, but she was ready. "We could play backgammon," she said cheerily. "I'm pretty sure the set is at the top of one of these boxes." Ari started to inspect the various boxes she had methodically labeled.

"We could do that, or we could do something else," Charles said mischievously as he pulled Ari into a deep kiss. She loved the way

Charles made her feel: sexy and desired. But she hated how she always had to play the referee. He gently guided her over to the empty bed and lay down next to her, not stopping his kisses or his caresses.

"Charles, you know how much I love this, and you. But I want to wait." He let out a groan like a man experiencing acute stomach pain.

"I know, Ari, and I respect that. You just drive me wild. And I want to love you. Really love you . . ."

"For now, what we have is enough for me. Plus, having sex on my roommate's old and well-used mattress is kinda gross," she joked.

"Fine, you win. But you won't win at backgammon," said Charles playfully.

They passed the next couple of hours playing intently. Ari annihilated Charles. At the end of the first game, he was annoyed. By game three, he was obviously frustrated. At game four, Ari purposely lost. Charles looked like he'd blow a gasket otherwise.

"Ah ha! Finally," he said triumphantly. "I've been out of practice. I haven't played in years. It's finally coming back to me."

"Wow, I didn't even see that coming," said Ari. She figured his ego needed a little stroking.

"Well the truth is—I was going easy on you," he said.

"I'd say we should play more, but the movers should be here any minute," Ari replied quickly.

They were packing the game up just as Two Men and a Truck arrived. Loading the items into the truck went by faster than expected. Ari didn't have much, as she was planning on purchasing the furniture and items she needed after she got to the apartment. Ari wanted to absorb the space first before she made any hasty purchases. A blow-up air mattress would do just fine for now.

Charles and Ari followed behind the moving truck, but it was a slow-moving drive, especially in the rain. "Thanks for helping today; I really appreciate it, Charles," said Ari.

"Yep, no problem, babe," he said dismissively. Charles turned up the music slightly, using the control on the steering wheel with his thumb. Did he want to listen to music instead of talking to her?

"So how do you think meeting my parents went?" Ari asked.

"Fine. I think they liked me, don't you?"

"Yes, I think they did, they really did. Raad will just take a little longer to warm up to you."

"Yeah, what's that guy's deal?"

"He is just being protective," Ari said defensively.

"But he was acting like I was some sort of child molester."

"No he wasn't."

Charles let out an exasperated breath. "You're right. Let's just drop it, Ari. We have a long drive."

They sat in silence for forty minutes, listening to the Rift album by Phish. Raad's advice to use her gift nagged at her. What were Charles' intentions? How did he really feel about her? He had told her he loved her over a month ago—she remembered that night like it was yesterday. Charles whisked her to New York City; they saw Hair Spray and had a romantic dinner at the Harrison. That night she told him about her childhood, but he didn't judge her. She obviously didn't tell him everything—only that she still struggled with a mental illness that she worked to control. Ari half expected him to walk out of the restaurant.

But he surprised her. Charles told her he didn't mind, that everyone had their issues. He said he never felt this way about anyone and that her intelligence and beauty continued to amaze him. He said he wanted them to date exclusively because he loved her. When she returned back to school that night, she worried she revealed too much too soon—exactly what Jayne told her not to do. But then again, Jayne was a proponent of sleeping with your man on the third date. This was Ari's seventh. She had been nervous that Charles might have gotten a hotel room and she'd have to awkwardly reject him. But he didn't. Instead, he drove her back to school like a gentleman and left her with a steamy kiss good-bye. The next morning, she awoke to two dozen roses and a note that said he loved her. Still.

So Ari's relationship with Charles continued to flourish. They constantly talked on the phone and through e-mail. At least once a week, they would make plans to see each other in person. More often than not, Charles would make the two and a half hour drive to see her. He would even sit through the Yale Repertory Theater performances she loved to go to. And now that she was going to be in the City, they would see each other all the time.

Ari wanted to validate everything she felt and knew to be true. She rationalized she could take just one peek . . . Raad wanted her to. But she needed to wait until the car was parked. Whenever she started to filter someone's thoughts, the target of the exercise seemed to momentarily freeze. She preferred not to end up as collateral damage in the Lincoln Tunnel.

They finally arrived in Tribeca outside of the glass tower that was to be her new home—32 Desbrosses Street. The doorman building had twenty-five floors, and her apartment was the penthouse suite. The three-bedroom was a graduation gift from her parents. Gloria had given

Ari the exciting news by telephone the week before. Ari was certainly surprised by the generous gift, especially as she was already planning on renting a studio that she was going to pay for on her own. But this gift was beyond amazing. She figured she would be a fool to refuse. The gesture softened her a bit to her parents, and as she thought about it, Ari felt a little ashamed of how she had felt toward them during her graduation. She'd make sure to send fresh flowers to the house tomorrow along with a thank-you note, again. However, it didn't matter how generous her parents' gifts were—she'd never forget how they had treated her.

Charles pulled into the underground parking lot and moved to get out but not before Ari put her hand on his and stared into his eyes. He felt nothing more than a quick shock, similar to static electricity. Ari let Charles' thoughts filter through her. She saw images of herself, Charles' office, football, a blonde woman in lingerie that obviously wasn't her . . . No matter—guys fantasized about women in general, right? Then she honed in on something strange. Charles was talking to the blonde woman, who up close looked like a stripper. Only this time, she didn't have any clothes on and they were in his bed. Clearly, this wasn't just a male fantasy.

"Charles, I hate that I never see you. You are always at work. Or you are with her."

"I know, babe, but I'm doing this for us and for my family."

"Ugh," said the blonde woman, who pouted her glossy pink lips and rolled onto Charles' chest. He ran his hands through what looked like cheap extensions.

"My mother thinks she has about $10 million in her trust fund and that she stands to inherit at least $40 million. We need that money. I may have a good name and decent enough salary, but it's not enough, especially since the family businesses are on the verge of bankruptcy since my father took the helm."

"What I don't understand is why her own mother is going to pay you to marry her daughter? I mean, I've seen her picture; she isn't ugly."

"I've told you before, Amber, Ari is a head case. Who would want to voluntarily marry that and have children with her? Ari is the Parkers' only child, and they need someone to carry on their bloodline. Gloria knew of my family and thought I'd make an excellent candidate for a son-in-law, fortunately for me. I must say her idea to 'bump into' Ari at Grand Central was genius."

"Yes, but you are going to marry her. And where does that leave me?" Her pout appeared on the verge of a tantrum.

"Amber, you know how I feel about you. But you aren't marriage material. Ari will be my wife, but she'll never be what you are to me. Hot, sexy, gorgeous. I'll always take care of you."

It was too much for Ari. She couldn't breathe. Ari pulled herself away from his mind and began hyperventilating. Her hands fumbled for the door handle.

"Ari, Ari, what's wrong?" Charles asked, sounding genuinely panicked. "Should I call your mother? What's wrong? You were fine just a second ago!"

Between her gasps for air, Ari managed to get out of the car and stumble toward the underground elevator. Charles came around, frantically trying to speak to her and figure out what was wrong. But Ari couldn't hear him. The harsh intake and outtake of oxygen from her lungs pounded in her eardrums, along with her frantic pulse. This can't be happening, she said to herself. But it was. It really was. Ari crouched on the pavement near the elevator, her Birkin bag clutched tightly to her chest. Breathe in and out, in and out, she told herself.

It would be years later that Ari would look back on this moment and wonder how she was able to pull herself together. Somehow she did, as the elevator button beckoned to her. Reaching her hand up, Ari pressed it. And with unsteady legs, she hoisted herself off the ground. She straightened her skirt, smoothed her hair, and reached in her purse for her keys that had arrived from the Realtor via FedEx the day before.

Stunned, Charles said, "My God, Ari, what just happened? One second you were fine, and the next you were stumbling around like you couldn't breathe." He stepped closer to her. "I think I need to take you to the hospital."

Ari reached for her composure, which for twenty years she had seen so carefully exuded by the ultimate professional—her mother. "No, Charles," she said. "I'm quite fine—just part of my mental illness. I don't wish to inconvenience you any longer." Her voice and facial expression were devoid of all feeling. "I mean really, who would want to marry me voluntarily or have children with me?"

Charles blanched. How had she known? He had just been thinking about his conversation with Amber that morning. Had he been so stupid as to say it out loud, he wondered?

"Ari . . . I don't know what you . . ." But before he could finish, Ari put her manicured index finger to his lips.

"Best not to discuss it, Charles. I never want to see or hear from you again."

The elevator dinged, and the doors slid open. With that, Ari stepped in and hit CLOSE. She promised herself she would never be manipulated by a man again. It was time to close this chapter in her life and start a new one.

CHAPTER 6:
SIRIUS RISING

52 BC, AUGUST
THE SANCTUM (MARA MOUNTAIN IN MODERN-DAY
GREENLAND)

The Sanctum was incredible. Inside, it appeared as if there was no ceiling and no end, just upward space that extended for miles, illuminated by large orbs of light that burned like small suns. The new inhabitants were greeted by grand stone buildings with marble colonnades and artfully placed sculptures of the Egyptian gods their people had come to respect during their tenure at Tentyris. Etchings in their native Greek tongue and reliefs depicting the great stories of their kind decorated the buildings as a constant tribute to their history. The largest structure of all appeared raised on a hill. It was the Great Hall of the Zodiac.

At the center of the Sanctum, the Great Hall was accessible by sixty imposing obsidian steps that surrounded it on all sides. Pello insisted on the black volcanic rock to offset the white marble of the main structure. It served as both the main temple and the Zodiac Council's meeting place. Inside the Great Hall, in the middle of the floor, was a mosaic of the same zodiac symbol that was created for the portico in the Temple of Hathor back in their homeland.

This mosaic was much more than simple tile, however. Rubies, emeralds, sapphires, and mother-of-pearl sparkled within the detailed artwork that had been carefully crafted over several years. Hathor insisted the Tentyrian artisans take as much time as they needed to perfect it.

Sadly, it was not to be for Hathor to see it complete. Her image within the mosaic could only silently watch as the Sanctum prepared for its first Council meeting without her.

The Sanctum's inhabitants had successfully made the pilgrimage one month earlier, and the Luminaries and their fellow kinsmen were settling in as quickly as possible. With the Luminaries' shifting ability, they were able to bring the Sanctum's inhabitants to their new home in a matter of days. Crops were already in full harvest with the help of Phoebe's careful preparations and Narcissa's powerful ability to coax the plants to accelerate in growth.

It was the day of the Rising of Sirius, and the Council of the Zodiac would commence their meeting at midnight. Daria and Aristos decided to take advantage of the hour respite they had. They lay entwined in the canopy bed, fangs exposed, their breathing matching each other's. Sated, Daria lay on Aristos' chest as he stroked her back, where beads of sweat were now drying. Aristos stared up at the swags of white linen that draped above them and remarked on how blissfully quiet their bedchamber was.

Outside their stone apartment nestled in the new Royal Villa, the Sanctum was alive with activity. Everyone was preparing for the imminent arrival of the Zodiac Council, their families, and their closest friends. Being invited to celebrate the heliacal rising of the Tentyrians' honored star Sirius with the Council was a great honor. They expected nearly one hundred in attendance that night, including the entire Sanctum. Meanwhile, all of the Covens in their own homelands were also preparing to celebrate.

The moon was full, making the snow and ice outside the mountain a magical place. Ammon had taken Darrius on a late-night dogsled ride, his new favorite pastime. Daria hoped Darrius had expended his energy, at least for a little bit. The late-night Zodiac feast where they would celebrate until dawn would follow the Council's annual meeting. Normally, Daria looked forward to the meetings, where she'd talk politics with the Council and afterward take part in the festivities. But so much had happened in the last year. She wasn't sure what would happen tonight.

"Agapi mou, do you think tonight's meeting will go smoothly?" Daria whispered to Aristos. She was almost afraid if she asked louder her insecurities would become a reality.

"Truthfully, I don't know. There is a lot at stake. But I know that whatever happens, you will have done your best," said Aristos as his baritone warmed the chill in her heart—even if his words didn't. They both knew what Daria planned to confront tonight could have a serious impact.

The Covens were adjusting well to the relocation. She and her sisters had seen for themselves during their routine visits just two weeks before. They kept a steady pulse on the status of their people to understand their concerns and wants and to ensure the governing Coven leaders continued to uphold the Code.

With the help of their most trusted Tentyrian Guards and Maximos, who reported daily to her and her sisters, Daria kept her eyes and ears open. And as far as she knew, the Covens were prospering. Daria and her sisters worked tirelessly to ensure that was the case. From reviewing building plans for bridges to analyzing the current diplomacy skills of the Covens with the humans they interacted with, the Luminaries governing approach put the well-being of their people first—just as Hathor taught them.

There was enough money, food, and shelter for all. Not once were the Luminaries needed to preside over disciplinary proceedings to try a Code breaker. The most difficult incident since leaving Tentyris was handling Karis' suicide. Losing her daughter was too much for her, and shortly after arriving in her new home, a land far east of Tentyris, Karis went for a walk and never returned.

Karis was found hunched over a log with a dagger plunged through her heart, her fingers still clutched around the handle. She had been there for a whole day, and by then, even the most skilled healers couldn't bring her back. The Virgo and Scorpio Covens were devastated. Rather than having an election to appoint a new Coven leader, it was agreed that Damian would maintain dual leadership of both Virgo and Scorpio. Virgo and Scorpio had blended since Karis and Damian's marriage anyway, and no one was more experienced than Damian in dealing with Karis' people.

At Aristos' suggestion, Daria offered extra Tentyrian Guards for Damian's use to help with anything he needed. But Damian politely refused. He also refused anyone's sympathy, requesting no pity for his sake. Damian's leadership of the two Covens proceeded without incident. But since Karis' death, he had changed. The anger and grief that racked him so powerfully the night of the fires was extinguished, but so was his spirit. No comforting words from the mouths of his friends or the Council seemed to move him. Daria prayed he would find happiness again. She hoped they all would.

Fortunately, the Sanctum was thriving, and since Hathor's death, even Calix and Stavros showed the utmost support for the four

Luminaries and their ascension to power as the Primary Rulers. Burying her face in Aristos' chest, Daria let out a sigh. She knew it was not enough, though. There were traitors in their midst—and it would stop tonight.

"Tell me what you are feeling, Dar . . . I wish the sun and moon that I could read your mind, but I can't. You must tell me," Aristos said to her.

Daria stared into her husband's face and the warmth in his eyes. She had never known anything more precious, with the exception of her little boy. She wanted to tell him about her mother's book with every fiber of her being, but her duty and honor bound her to a higher calling.

It was that calling that drew her mind back to the previous month. Hathor's and Hita's ashes and those of the other victims who'd died in the fires were now part of the Tentyrian earth. Their ashes blew away, as Daria and her people watched and wept. Karis was too distraught to even attend. Instead she remained at the Sanatorium, silent in her paralyzing grief. Damian, meanwhile, stood in silence, watching his child's body engulf in fire. Daria remembered the white linen shrouds and blankets of lotus blossoms that burned to the tune of Aquarius' water hymn. The sandalwood pyres lit up the night and helped cover the stench of burning flesh.

In the days of mourning that followed, Daria and her sisters continued their interviews of all Tentyrians and Egyptians in their community to find out what happened. They started with the Council, who agreed to let Daria mind tap them. Removing their mental blocks to let her in, they too seemed to want to ferret out any traitors. However, all of the Council members came up clean, as did all of the Tentyrians and the city's people. Daria started to worry she missed something. Their investigations yielded nothing. There was no guilty party, no guilty conscience. As Luminaries, they possessed some of the greatest powers. Yet it all proved useless.

On the fourth day of the investigation, Daria had gone to the Book of Hathor. When Daria had opened it, she'd been surprised to find the Sanctum's fail-safe key being used as a bookmark. In the days prior, she and her sisters had gone through all of their mother's belongings in frantic search of it. Without the key, it wasn't safe to go to the Sanctum. Designed by Hathor, her daughters, and Maximos, the key controlled access to the Sanctum. Once locked with the key, a protective energy field was activated, and no one could enter or exit the sacred place.

In order to initiate a lockdown from the inside, the key was inserted into the center of the zodiac mosaic in the Great Hall. After that, only the one with the key could exit, while all others still inside would be trapped. The Sanctum could also be locked and unlocked from the outside by inserting the key into the grooves hidden in the rock wall of the escape exit that led to the fjord. The key was one of a kind—it had been a relief when Daria had found it.

Closing her hands around the cylindrical key, Daria's fingers had stroked the four small, elevated prongs running along the sides as she'd turned her eyes to the pages it lay between. Written in her mother's elegant hand, it had read:

My Darlings,

If you are reading this, I am dead. Words cannot express how sorry I am to leave you, but my time has come. With every day that passes, I want you to know how much I love you.

I wish I could tell you that the future ahead is bright. It is not. When you were young, I would tell you of flying machines and lifesaving surgeries. However, the future is undoubtedly filled with pain, which cannot be prevented.

As the Luminaries, it is up to you to lead our clan. To ensure that the Sanctum thrives and that the Covens adhere to the Code. You already know this. However, what you don't know is whether we have traitors among us. We do. Who they are, I don't know. The web of treachery is too convoluted for me to see.

In these last months, my gift of vision has been failing me, coming and going in intermittent spurts. I am dying, and no amount of help from the healers—even you, Narcissa—will change that. The Luminaries have been destined to rule together, to ensure that responsibility does not fall upon one person's shoulders. Power can be an intoxicating thing. It is only when the four Luminaries are united that our people can remain as such.

Keep your eyes trained on the Covens and their leaders. You need to be prepared for the inevitable: the destruction of the solidarity of our people. I don't know when it will come, but it will happen. Soon.

This notebook is filled with my visions: warfare waged by some of the most horrendous weapons imaginable, evil men and women who will rule only for their own benefit, but also amazing feats to be accomplished by future generations.

I ask that you not try to change the course of human history—except in one instance. Sadly, 2,064 years from now, there will be an event so catastrophic that all of the human race will be wiped out.

Some of our people will sadly be involved. It is up to the Luminaries to prevent this. In this book you will find all I know. Use my pictures and words to stop it.

Do not tell anyone of this book, with the exception of Maximos. He is essential to our future. Keep it safe with all the power you have. Should it fall into the wrong hands, the results could be as dangerous as the event you need to stop. I have described all I know of "the Event," as I am calling it, along with what I've seen of the future generations of Luminaries, beginning on page 986. This is my last entry.

You may be asking yourselves how it is possible for you to prevent something so far into the future. All I ask is that you try. Blessed be.

With All My Love,
Mother

P.S. I am leaving you with the one and only fail-safe key to the Sanctum. You'll know when to use it.

The note had paralyzed Daria with fear. The prophetic doom seemed inevitable. Doom for her clan and for the human race. But rather than providing details on what they could do right now to bring the traitors to justice, all they had were instructions to stop an event more than two thousand years away. It was unfathomable thinking that far ahead. Daria wasn't even sure if she wanted to live that long, or if she would.

Daria showed the book to her sisters and Maximos. They were surprised by Hathor's task, but they told no one else of it, even Aristos, Alexander, and Claudius. They memorized all their mother wrote and scoured the book for any information that spoke to their present situation. There was nothing. Hathor did not write about her own death, who the killer was, or give any inclination as to who would be responsible for breaking up the Tentyrian clan. All the Luminaries could do was rule fairly and ensure they addressed the needs of their people.

"Daria, please tell me," Aristos' voice brought Daria back to the present.

"I'm sorry, there is just so much going on in my head and I can't quite articulate it," she said regretfully.

"It's all right, I understand. What can I do to help, though?" Aristos asked patiently.

"Has the escape tunnel from the nursery been completed?"

"Yes, I spoke with Pello this afternoon. It is ready. He has worked day and night to finish it, alone, just as you requested."

"Let's pray the tunnel isn't needed. It's time to ready ourselves, though. The Council will begin in an hour. I hear Selene knocking. I hope she hasn't been waiting long."

Daria jumped from the bed quickly, wrapped a loose cotton robe around her, and opened the door to the young maid. Aristos quickly dressed in his ceremonial robe, leaving Daria with a kiss so she could finish her preparations. He could tell she was already deep in thought as he left her rubbing her temples, while Selene busily dressed her hair.

Aristos wanted to do one last check on the Guard and then see Ammon and Darrius. It was going to be a challenge to get his son in the bath. As Aristos walked the corridor, talking periodically to his men, he thought more about Daria's anxiety. He had never seen her so apprehensive. Since her mother's death, she had worked herself relentlessly to make sure she lived up to expectations, along with her sisters. He rarely even saw her except when she came to bed at dawn. But he knew Daria's concern wasn't without cause—despite his attempts to ease her fear. These were dangerous times, and tonight he needed to make sure Ammon remembered.

Aristos opened the door to the nursery corridor where all of the Luminary children slept with their Guardians. It was filled with laughter. There in the playroom was Darrius acting out his dogsled ride with a makeshift sleigh of a chair and rope. On the chair sat Ceres holding two ends of the "reins" while Darrius pulled her around the room from the rope encircling his waist, which was tied to the front chair legs. "Hurry doggy, hurry doggy!" Ceres ordered while Darrius barked and crawled. Their twin cousins clapped their hands in delight on Tale's lap.

"Ah, Master Aristos, the children are having fun, no?" said Ammon, who spied Aristos in the doorway.

"Yes, it certainly appears that way. How you manage to keep up with this energy amazes me, Ammon," replied Aristos.

"I do what I can. Mistress Daria came by earlier and instructed that all the children be ready at 2:00 a.m. sharp. And to wait for her word before going down to the feast."

"Yes, I know the children will be disappointed they must wait and won't be able to play with the other children before the feast, but we are taking extra precautions. I want this door bolted. You should only unbolt it and come down when the Luminaries or I say so. And

Ammon, keep your sword with you at all times. Tale and Nenet," Aristos addressed the other Guardians, "do you understand?"

"Yes, Master Aristos," they replied as they gathered closer to hear.

"By now I'm sure you've noticed the construction that has been happening behind this wall?" Aristos asked as he strode across the playroom to the wall lined with books and a six-foot-wide closet. The children remained oblivious to the discussion. "Behind this closet is a passageway that leads down and outside of the mountain. Should you need to escape, and you'll know when, I want you to go as quickly as possible. At the end of the passageway is a door that leads outside to a channel cut into the fjord. There are three small boats waiting with supplies. You are each to take a boat with the children, leave, and not turn back. We will find you when we can. Each of you took vows to protect our children, and we will hold you to it."

"Yes, of course," said Ammon with sincerity. "Your children are like our own." The two women nodded solemnly. Aristos knew Darrius and his nieces and nephew were in good hands. He showed them how to work the secret door and reviewed the warning signs they were to look for.

Just then, the four Luminaries, Claudius, and Alexander arrived, appearing in time to catch one final howl from Darrius. Following a round of applause, the doting mothers and fathers kissed their children and told them they would see them at the feast. Departing the nursery in single file, Daria and Aristos led the procession, followed by Phoebe and Claudius, Calypso and Alexander, with Narcissa holding up the rear.

The women all wore stolas in sea green wool with intricate scrollwork in crocus yellow. Gold metal belts cinched the fine fabric tightly under their breasts. The only jewelry worn was their zodiac necklaces. Their matching palla were the same sea green, but unlike traditional palla most Tentyrian women wore, these had hoods and were lined with ermine in honor of the cold weather of their new home. The palla also had the zodiac symbol emblazoned on the back in bright yellow. The Luminaries wore fur-lined brown kidskin boots that laced to their knees, where just a few inches above lay a blade carefully holstered and strapped to each woman's left thigh. Daria insisted they carry a weapon at all times.

The men were equally striking in sea green robes, with long cloaks on top in yellow. By the shoulders, each wore fibulae in the zodiac symbol. They too wore sturdy fur-lined boots, but they openly displayed their sheathed swords. The same garments tonight were mandatory for all, designed to create an image of unity. Dressmakers and tailors had worked around the clock to create the regal clothes.

As they approached the Great Hall, Narcissa let out a sigh of relief. Maximos awaited them at the bottom of the steps, where he took Narcissa's arm. "I'm so glad you waited for me, Maximos. You know I hate walking into these things by myself," said Narcissa.

"A lady should never walk alone, Cissy," he replied, a slight smile kicking up in the corner of his firm mouth. Since Narcissa was in swaddling clothes, Maximos had given her the endearment "Cissy" and never called her anything else, at least outside of Council meetings. Maximos was like an uncle to Narcissa and her sisters. He had been friends with their mother since the beginning and was instrumental in helping her design the Council of the Zodiac.

What Hathor and Maximos faced in building their community was against all odds. Yet they managed to do it. Maximos would give anything to protect his people, but first and foremost came Hathor's daughters. He had pledged so to Hathor, and he intended to make sure they were safe with his dying breath. Without them, there was no future.

"Did I see what I think I just saw, Maximos?" teased Narcissa.

"And what would that be, my dear?"

"A slightly ironic smile?"

"Me? Well, if I did smile, don't tell anyone. I have to keep up the stoic reputation."

"Of course," Narcissa said as she patted Maximos' arm with affection.

The Luminaries and their escorts continued up the steps, flanked by the Tentyrian Guards who stood silently, trained to stare at nothing while ready to draw their swords at any moment. The zodiac table was ready. Golden chalices filled with blood and small plates of fresh fruits and spicy nuts sat at each of the sixteen place settings—two less since Hathor and Karis were dead.

The rest of the Council was already seated around the historic round table brought from Tentyris. They sat sipping from their blood chalices. The Luminaries, Aristos, and Maximos took their places while Claudius and Alexander bid their farewells. Only Council members were allowed to remain for the meeting. Claudius and Alexander would join the rest of the Sanctum and the Council's families and friends in the dining area of the Royal Villa for the reception that was to occur during the meeting's proceedings.

With all seated, Daria placed her sistrum on the table and took stock of the room. Was it tension in the air or anticipation she felt? The meetings were ruled by formality, but Daria needed to address what everyone was thinking. Following her lead, the women removed their hoods and the Council stood.

"Before we begin, I want to thank you all for coming," said Daria in a voice full of strength. Her nerves didn't betray her. "Our meeting tonight is built on tradition, but we have never had one quite like this . . . without Mother or without Karis. In their honor, I'd like to offer up a short prayer . . .

"To our beloveds. If you are in Heaven or on Earth, in the South or in the North, in the West or in the East, you are known. Pure in love, pure in sight. Not shall you die a second time. You are known. All forms are your habitation. You are known."

"You are known," the Council responded in unison to Daria's prayer of the Divine Identity. Daria nodded and the rest of the Council took their seats, with the exception of her and her sisters.

Daria continued: "In these past months, we have prevailed with the odds stacked against us. I often worried this meeting would not happen. But we are here. The Luminaries and I are extremely pleased with the Covens' progress, and it wouldn't be possible without your leadership. For that, we must say thank you."

Affirming nods ensued. The Council members took their positions seriously and were never ones to pat themselves on the back—at least openly.

"However, as the Primary Rulers now, the Luminaries and I must know that we have your full loyalty," announced Daria. "There are traitors about. We will not proceed with this meeting until we know where you stand." Daria, her sisters, and Maximos had spent countless hours debating the best way to broach the issue. They finally determined it was best to address it head on. That's why they designed the contingency plan for the children and had the Guard on high alert.

Eyes shifted questioningly to each other, each member searching for doubt in the others' eyes. Aristos and Maximos were the first to pledge their loyalty.

"The Cancer Coven is behind you. As is the Guard," said Aristos.

"And the Leo Coven," promised Maximos.

More pronouncements of support followed: Pello speaking for Sagittarius, Sophia for Libra, Sebastian for Capricorn, Zoe for Aquarius, and Evander for Pisces. Stavros, Calix, Aglaia, Asia, and Damian remained seated, while those who professed their loyalty stood. Daria breathed in deeply and unleashed her fangs. Her sisters followed suit.

"Do you have something to say, traitors?" Daria addressed those seated with a snarl. Stavros laughed in response, letting his own fangs show.

"You call us traitors, Daria. Why don't you ask Calypso what she is?" Stavros scoffed. Eyes turned to Calypso, who looked utterly confused.

"Who do you think killed your own mother?" Stavros said. "Calypso. She is the only one who can make herself invisible. No one else would have been able to get that near to Hathor without an alarm being raised. But Daria, you didn't mind tap her, did you?"

Of course Daria hadn't read Calypso's mind. There hadn't been a need to. Calypso would never betray them like that. She was her sister. Daria told herself she needed to regain control, quickly.

"No, Stavros. The lies stop now," said Daria firmly. She didn't believe Calypso killed their mother.

"Tsk, tsk. You were always such a levelheaded girl. Why don't you see for yourself?" Stavros said as he gestured to Calypso, who stood rigid and pale. The Council waited expectantly. Doubt suddenly nagged at Daria.

"Put your block down, Calypso," said Daria with a tremor in her voice.

"What? No!" said Calypso. "I haven't done anything!"

"I said put it down," Daria demanded.

"Fine! You won't see anything!"

With a deep breath Calypso relented, and Daria entered her mind, something she hadn't done since they were children when Daria would look for her in games of hide and seek. Daria was instantly bombarded by images and sounds. She sifted through them frantically to find what she was looking for. Alexander playing chess by the fire. Ceres being rocked in Nenet's arms. A knife gripped in her hands. Her mother dead. Daria pulled herself away from Calypso's mind.

"How could you?" Daria yelled. Outrage was palpable around the table. Calypso's eyes blinked several times as she emerged from the trance of Daria's mind tap. Shame crossed her face, and she sunk down into her chair.

"Calypso, why?" asked Narcissa with tears streaming down her cheeks.

"I, I don't know. I swear it. I didn't know. I don't know what I did. I know I wasn't feeling well. But I swear I just saw what you saw, Daria, for the first time. Please believe me." Calypso looked desperately at her sisters and the Council.

"There is no need for hysterics. We might as well put all of the truth out there. It's not like Calypso did it all on her own," said Calix as he examined his fingernails. Daria's heart pounded. Her fingers itched to grab her dagger. "Before I explain," Calix said lazily, "I want everyone to know—no one shifts or makes a move. If you do, your Covens die. We have them all, and with the snap of our fingers they will go up in flames. And Daria, don't even try to mind tap us. Our blocks are up. Guards, take their weapons!" Several guards entered to remove the swords from the men.

The Council now all stood around the table. Fangs were bared. But those loyal to the Luminaries didn't move to fight. They were afraid for their people.

"I did not instruct you to leave your posts," seethed Aristos to the guards, who avoided his eyes. Aristos called for other guards by name, his most trusted. None came. It was a huge blow to him. These were men who he had trained alongside. Who had pledged their loyalty to the Zodiac.

"You've probably noticed, Aristos, but your men aren't yours anymore. They are mine," said Stavros, clearly satisfied. "Those who were loyal to you and the Luminaries are dead." No one moved. Aristos prayed the children and their Guardians noticed something was awry and had escaped.

With the spotlight temporarily falling off Calix, he was determined to bring it back to himself. "Now, back to Hathor's death . . . Let's just say Calypso did what she did, with a little push," Calix said and smiled. "But Daria, bravo for trying to figure out what we were up to. When you made us remove our mind blocks the night you questioned us, we thought for sure our work would be uncovered. But you didn't find anything, did you?" he mocked.

"How is that possible? Your powers don't work on us, Calix," Phoebe whispered.

"Luckily, we had a little help," Calix explained. "Guards!" he yelled. "Bring in Selene."

Two guards appeared with Selene, who clearly wasn't being held against her will. She stood confident, resplendent in a red silk robe, the same one that had been Hathor's. The normally placid eyes of the maid were dark with satisfaction.

"Selene has been most helpful," said Calix. "You see, she has an uncanny ability for weakening Tentyrian power. With Selene able to break down Calypso's mental block, I was able to slip into her mind and make a few suggestions. Then I wiped her conscious memory of it. Calypso was the easiest target, though, so sad and angry over Hector.

Convincing the guards that checked on your mother repeatedly, only to see her sleeping peacefully, was child's play. Now, Daria, you were a different story. The best we could do with you was prevent you, just barely, from seeing what we were plotting."

Daria remembered that when she was doing the mind taps on the Council, Selene had stood by with the other servants in stunned silence—clearly feigned. How could she not have noticed what Selene was up to?

Stavros laughed and continued. "Selene worked on Hathor for months, destroying her sight little by little. But she was too strong to yield to any suggestions. In time, I hoped Hathor would see things the way I did. I hoped you all would. I never wanted it to come to this." Stavros turned to the Council with open palms in a gesture seeking understanding. "All I wanted was for us to take our rightful place! We should have fought the Egyptians and Auletes for what should be ours—a kingdom! Not this pile of rocks," spat Stavros angrily.

"So you made an agreement with Auletes and his mercenaries, didn't you? You told them where and how to kill our father," said Daria with understanding dawning on her. "You wanted us to think Auletes was plotting to destroy Tentyris."

"Ah, she finally gets it. Yes I did, but it wasn't a lie. Auletes did want to destroy us; he just needed a little coaxing. You should have seen his lust when I promised him just a fraction of our wealth. My rebel subterfuge was a distraction to lead you back to Auletes. And I knew Hathor would eventually see that Auletes truly did want to kill her," said Stavros.

"That's not what you told me, Stavros," said Damian icily. "You told me that we would soon be under siege by Auletes' men who were responsible for the fires."

"Damian, Damian, it is a pity Karis couldn't be here tonight. I told you what you needed to be told: that the Luminaries would never demonstrate the strength needed to protect our people. If I had told you that I was responsible for setting those fires, then who would you have blamed for your child and wife's deaths?"

"I will kill you, you son of a whore!" yelled Damian as he propelled a guard's sword straight at Stavros' heart. Stavros batted it away like a fly with his mind.

"No you won't! And if either of you makes a move again, I swear on all of your families' lives I will incinerate your Covens," commanded Stavros. Calix, Aglaia, and Asia moved toward Stavros' side, where Selene and the Tentyrian Guards now stood protectively. "That's right. What you don't know is that as your Covens celebrate the Rising in their own halls, my men stand outside ready to blow them to pieces. With multiple bombs prepared to explode, courtesy of our Gemini twins here, there will be no survivors. The same holds true for all of your families and those so loyal to you here at the Sanctum—while they sip their drinks, they have no idea they could die in seconds."

"Why are you doing this, Stavros? What do you want?" asked Daria coldly.

"What do I want? Well I guess I will start with all of this," he said. Stavros' eyes drew upward as he surveyed the expanse of the Sanctum. "I must say, it is impressive here. Too bad your bitch of a mother kept it a secret from us."

"She knew you weren't to be trusted," Daria said, looking upon him in disgust.

"I was with Hathor from the beginning. Yet no matter what I did or how I showed her my loyalty, she wouldn't trust me. Not like Hector. Or you, puppy dog," Stavros directed his words at Maximos. "When she decided the clan should relocate rather than fight, she changed the rules of the game, not me. I had to take action. Killing her and setting the fires was necessary. With her gone, you Luminaries were more exposed than ever. With the fires, I was able to win Damian and the Guard over and prove how incompetent you were at protecting your own people. You can build as many bridges as you want, but if you aren't able to control by force, you'll never win, ladies."

Phoebe's hands gripped the table in anger. "You will be punished for this!" she said defiantly.

"Phoebe, my dear, have you taught your young ones yet not to play with fire?" Stavros replied. Before Phoebe could respond, Daria reached out her hand and squeezed Phoebe's tightly. She knew they didn't want to provoke him. He held the upper hand.

"By seeding doubt," Stavros gloated, "I was able to win over the men and women I needed to infiltrate the Guard and take over the Sanctum, which I must say is amazing, Pello. At least it is a nice pile of rocks. Lying low all of these months, pretending to support the Luminaries, has been worth it, as this all is mine now."

Pello spat at Stavros, who rewarded him with a punch to the face. But the Sagittarius Coven leader barely registered the blow that left him with a bloody nose.

"Watch it, Pello. You may not have a spouse or children you care about, but the others do," sneered Stavros. But to Pello, his Coven was his family, and he knew all too well the danger. Stavros, Calix, Aglaia, and Asia appeared triumphant while the rest of the Council looked murderous.

"You are pathetic, Stavros," said Maximos. "Whining because you weren't loved best. Hathor never trusted you because she knew of your insatiable lust for power. And sure enough, it brought you here. We will kill you," he vowed to the traitors he once considered friends.

"There you go again. No, no one is going to kill us. Do you want see the lions and cubs of your Coven again?" Stavros taunted. Maximos' jaw clenched. "I thought so. And because of that you will all do exactly as I say. We will now go to the feast, where you all will formally abdicate your power, giving it to me, the new Primary Ruler. Calix and the Twins and I will make up the new Council. Four is a much more reasonable number than sixteen, yes? The rest of you are banished and may go back to your Covens, which I will leave untouched if you cooperate. However, I suggest you do so peacefully, for as an insurance policy, your children will now be our wards—indefinitely."

"You cannot do this!" said Zoe, panicked. "The Aquarius and Pisces Covens will never agree to it, and neither will the others."

"Yes they will," said Stavros. "They will agree to it, if you agree to support me. If you don't—the children die."

Evander put his arms around Zoe, who began to sob. Daria couldn't mind tap Stavros, Calix, Aglaia, or Asia, but that didn't mean she couldn't hear what the others were thinking, if they opened their minds to her and did it fast. As the sickening admission of treachery continued, Daria tested the other Council members' minds—those who hadn't betrayed the Zodiac. They were all willing to fight, despite the cost. It was the reassurance Daria needed.

"We will go now," said Daria, "and get this farce of an abdication over with."

"Excellent," replied Stavros, who called for the guards that soon filled the room to escort them.

The Council walked solemnly down the Great Hall's steps, now littered with dead Tentyrian Guards—murdered by their brothers who had given up loyalty for promises of power.

CHAPTER 7:
DARK COVEN

Daria felt like a lamb being led to slaughter, along with her people. Stavros' quest for power created the web of treachery her mother had been unable to understand. Now that Daria understood it, there was no way that Stavros was going to let any of them live. They were all just bugs caught in his sticky thread. Stavros was not sane; the man she once knew was gone. Now she only hoped he would burn in hell with Calix and the Gemini twins.

When they arrived at the dining hall, it was filled with song and dance. Guards lined the room. It was still early, as the feast wasn't to begin for another thirty minutes. Plenty of libations were flowing, and those in attendance celebrated unaware of what was about to happen. Daria looked around furtively for her child. He must still be in the nursery with his cousins, she thought. Or hopefully he was safely with Ammon in the boat. However, there were no other children there at all. It wasn't a good sign.

Daria's muscles were taut as she looked from her husband to her sisters and the Zodiac members who remained loyal. Their emotions were masked. Stavros paraded them to the stage at the front of the room. Daria needed to act quickly to get as much information as possible. The audience hushed, curious at their early arrival. Alexander and Claudius knew instantly something was wrong. The doors to the Great Hall slammed shut and were bolted.

"Good evening, or I should say good morning everyone!" Stavros addressed the room a bit too enthusiastically. Confusion and unease was evident as the crowd wondered why Stavros was addressing them and not Daria or her sisters. "You are likely wondering why this feast is proceeding differently. I'll get right to it. After much deliberation, many of our Council members have expressed the desire to pursue other endeavors. These past few months have been difficult for us all, and they feel it would be better to step aside and have a smaller Council preside. The Luminaries no longer want the burden that was passed down to them from Hathor. They have decided to live amongst the Covens and turn the Primary Rule over to me. Zoe, Evander, and Pello wish to pass on the Aquarius, Pisces, and Sagittarius torch to their Gemini neighbors, Aglaia and Asia. Calix of Taurus will now rule Capricorn and Libra, while Sebastian and Sophia will step aside. And I will also lead the Leo and Cancer Covens."

Angry protests emerged from the crowd. It was obvious to all this was a coup. You couldn't just tell people that after nearly a century and a half of leadership, things were changing. Stavros pulled Daria toward him with a smile and hissed in her ear, "Pacify them now, my dear, or Darrius dies."

Daria stepped forward and said, "My people, I'm here now to tell you that the Council of the Zodiac as it was is no more." She paused, letting the reality sink in. "There is a dark one now in its stead." Stavros gave her a warning glance, but before he could stop the words from coming out of her mouth, she said, "I implore you to reject this and fight for Tentyris!" Daria was willing to gamble that Darrius, Ammon, and the rest of the children made it out safely. As for the people of all the other Covens being burned alive, she knew it was done.

She found one guard, out of the dozen she quickly tried to read in the few minutes she had, who heard a rumor that all of the Covens were being "removed" tonight. If it was true, Stavros not only was eliminating his own people, but he was planning on killing everyone in the room.

Chaos erupted, and fangs came out. Stavros barked orders at the guards now under his command as they moved on the crowd with swords drawn, ready to cut them down. Tentyrians and humans alike grabbed anything they could use for a weapon: knives, plates, chair legs. The hall erupted in hand-to-hand combat. With superior strength and skills, the Tentyrians of the crowd positioned the weaker humans behind them as they fought like feral animals. The turncoat guards outnumbered them four to one. Snarls, the crunch of bone, and screams of pain replaced the joyous music that had filled the room earlier. The weapons did little. The Tentyrian punches and kicks—powerful enough to break a human body—created the real destruction.

On the stage, the Council was fighting with a different caliber of power. Pello was literally ripping stone from the walls and hurling it at the guards. Aglaia and Asia threw fireballs at the Luminaries, who shifted in and out to avoid the flames and pursuing guards. Maximos and Aristos went for Stavros, who saw them coming and shifted out of reach.

With his mind, Stavros heaved a long table in their direction. It crashed into the wall behind them as Maximos and Aristos disappeared into the air and reappeared behind Stavros. Aristos threw a dagger the guards hadn't confiscated from his boot toward Stavros' back, only to have it repel and come straight back at him. Shifting away, Aristos narrowly missed the blade. Maximos went in for the attack next. Stavros and Maximos circled around and ran at each other full force. The impact as they collided would have taken down a pyramid. Maximos managed to get the better angle and put Stavros in a hold, trying to get his hands around his neck.

"Where are the children?" Maximos demanded.

"Dead," Stavros replied as he ripped a chunk of flesh from Maximos, exposing the bone of his forearm. Maximos lost his grip, and Stavros shifted away.

A series of explosions shook the building moments later. The fight continued. Calypso slipped into her invisible form and, using her knife, stabbed Calix in the ribs. He sunk down to his knees in surprise and staggered to pull himself up in search of the assailant.

"That's for my mother, you bastard," he heard Calypso say behind him. Calypso next threw herself at Calix to get her hands in position to decapitate him. But she wasn't strong enough. He threw her onto the floor, spun, and cut off her head without a second thought. Alexander saw what was left of his wife appear on the floor as her invisibility faded away. His sudden shock left him vulnerable to the guard who delivered his own similar fate just seconds later.

Aristos came after Calix, but he managed to shift out of reach to recover himself. Aristos saw Maximos, bloody arm and all, approaching Daria and Narcissa to provide support as they fought back to back. Four guards surrounded them. The sisters shifted away and then returned, catching two of them by surprise as they ripped their heads off. Maximos took out the other two. Aristos kept his eye on Daria, but with Maximos now positioning himself near the two Luminaries,

Aristos convinced himself she would be all right. He needed to get to the children. Aristos quickly subdued one of the Tentyrian Guards he had trained with his own hands.

"Tell me where you put the children and I'll spare your life," he demanded.

"We were instructed to separate the children . . . for their own celebration. Check . . . solarium," the guard managed to choke out from Aristos' death grip. "The Luminary children . . . in nursery." With that, Aristos ended the man's life.

Leaving the fight, Aristos shifted to the solarium. It had been a domed glass structure filled with exotic plants and flowers—Narcissa's pride and joy. Now there was nothing left, just flames and shattered glass. He then went to the nursery. It was the same mind-numbing scene. Char and fire greeted him. Where the closet had once stood, the rock wall door behind it was closed and, to the unsuspecting eye, looked like a blackened wall. Just as he moved to open it and check the passage, a four-foot-thick metal beam from above fell on him, knocking him unconscious.

Back in the dining hall, Phoebe was shooting shocks of energy at the guards who were successfully backing her into a corner. When she thought she brought down a couple, only more pressed in. She could shift away, but like her comrades, she wanted to eliminate the enemy. Seeing her plight, Damian threw himself in front of her and, using his energy, pushed the onslaught of guards into the wall behind them. They were dead on impact.

"Shift away from here," Damian yelled to Phoebe. Before she registered the command, Damian's head was separated from his body by Calix, who'd emerged suddenly behind him.

Sophia, Sebastian, and Evander teamed up. Not having any telekinetic abilities to leverage like many of the others, they were at a disadvantage. Evander didn't want to leave Zoe, but she assured him she could take care of herself and do more good by putting out the fires. Aristos had shifted to them earlier to explain he was getting the children. In the meantime, the trio focused on shifting out many of the humans who didn't stand a chance. Sebastian was doing his best to protect Sophia, taking on many of the blows that were meant for her. But his wounds couldn't heal fast enough relative to the blood he was losing.

"Sophia and Evander, you must leave. We are not going to win this fight. Look around. I've done the math," said Sebastian. There were at least forty guards in the fray and only a handful of Tentyrians still fighting.

"No, we can't give up!" Sophia cried. It was then she noticed how badly hurt Sebastian was. "Evander, you must help him. Sebastian is dying."

"I can't heal him here," said Evander. "Daria showed me where the infirmary is. I say we take what injured we can there. We need to find Pello and Zoe and convince the Luminaries to get out of here too. This place is an inferno."

Meanwhile, Phoebe found Claudius through the smoke battling Selene, who was about to lose. Selene soon gave up and threw herself at Claudius' feet, begging for mercy.

"Don't give it to her. She is a conniving bitch," advised Phoebe with blood spatters on her face. But as Claudius lifted his sword, his entire body lifted off the ground. He then slammed into the rock ceiling first, followed by the floor. It was Stavros. Phoebe instinctively went after Claudius, leaving Stavros to rescue his prized weapon and disappear with her.

Maximos, Daria, and Narcissa formed a triangle to protect their backs while they fought on. Constantly shifting in and out to avoid the fireballs while trying to take the guards out, they were quickly becoming exhausted, especially Narcissa. Using any Tentyrian power—whether it was telekinesis or shifting—sapped one's energy. Not to mention they were already using every ounce of their physical strength in addition to the mental exertion.

"Cissy, you need to leave. You are going to get yourself killed," yelled Maximos.

"No, I'm fine," she panted. That's when a combined fireball from Asia and Aglaia engulfed her.

"Zoe! Water over here," Daria screamed. She could hear Narcissa's skin sizzle as Zoe directed water on her sister. Bile rose in Daria's throat at the smell of the charred flesh just inches from her. "Maximos, take her to the infirmary now," commanded Daria. Maximos scooped Narcissa up in his arms and shimmered away.

Daria surveyed the room. There was blood everywhere—even on the tapestries. Bodies were strewn about the floor like broken toys. From what she could tell, Calypso, Alexander, and Damian were dead. Claudius was down, and Narcissa was seriously injured. Aristos hadn't come back from getting the children, which he told her was his priority as soon as the fight broke out. Stavros and Calix weren't in sight.

The fire was raging out of control. Zoe burst a water pipe and was dousing the flames as best she could. But the room was now practically impossible to breathe or see in. Almost as if on cue, Zoe, Sophia, Evander, and Sebastian appeared. Sebastian was leaning heavily on Evander; he was unconscious.

"Where is Pello?" Daria asked.

"Crushed under a rock," said Evander. "I can't help him. We need to evacuate to the infirmary now."

Daria agreed to meet them there, but she needed to get Phoebe first. She found Phoebe clutching Claudius' shattered body that had hit the stone floor with so much force his brain matter was strewn about. It was too late.

"Phoebe, we must go," Daria urged. "You know we can't save him."

"Why, why! Why is this happening!" screamed Phoebe.

"We're going now." Daria pulled Phoebe from Claudius with all her strength and shifted them to the infirmary, where the rest of the injured were taken.

It was mayhem. Rows of examination tables were filled with the wounded. Approximately twenty Egyptians, Guardians, and the Sanctum's servants were in critical condition along with thirty Tentyrians who had fought bravely. Another twenty or so were unhurt but were brought to the infirmary by Sophia, Sebastian, and Evander for refuge. The infirmary was built under the central area of the Sanctum and was accessible through a series of intricate passageways that also led to the core processors of the Sanctum. By placing the infirmary under the main buildings, there was ample space to build the observation and research rooms and the necessary quarters for quarantine should an epidemic strike the Sanctum's humans.

There were still a few loyal humans and Tentyrians who remained fighting above. They would need to go back and rescue as many as possible and soon. Maximos stood by Narcissa's side holding her hand. When he saw Evander, he yelled for him immediately. Narcissa was barely breathing. Before turning his attention to the badly burned Luminary, Evander called for all Tentyrians capable of healing to stand to one side of the room. There were only three, plus Evander, who had healing skills. He organized teams with volunteer nurses and prioritized the victims.

"Daria, Phoebe, I can do my best here, but what next?" Evander asked.

"We need to get to all the Covens and warn them," said Sophia.

Daria called the remaining Council members to her. They were covered in sweat, soot, and blood. "It's too late. It's already been done," she said. "Stavros never intended to let them or any of us live. But we should still send someone to check on every Coven and report back. Phoebe, can you go?"

Phoebe managed to quell her hysteria upon arriving in the infirmary. Seeing the devastation was sobering. They would have to grieve later. "Yes, I will go," she said. And with that, Phoebe left.

"What about the children?" Zoe choked out a sob. "They weren't in the dining hall. Aristos said he'd find them, but he hasn't returned."

"I know," Daria replied. "That is why I'm going to find them. Maximos, I need you to come with me. Sophia, I need you to do a sweep to look for any more survivors—no more fighting, just a sweep. Zoe, you stay here and help Evander with whatever he needs."

"Who else knows of this place, Daria?" asked Maximos.

"Not many since we haven't technically completed it or toured it. Only the Luminaries, Aristos, you, Pello, probably a handful of Tentyrian builders, and Evander. But the builders are all celebrating the Rising of Sirius with their Covens. Or at least they were. And the Tentyrian Guards aren't allowed to come down here since it's a sanitary area and is so close to the processors."

It was sheer luck Daria had shown Evander the infirmary weeks earlier at Narcissa's insistence to ask for his input on refinements. His quick thinking gave the injured a fighting chance. Daria wiped her brow, and her hand came away with blood.

"We can't stay here long," Daria said. "Stavros will find us eventually. Zoe, make sure those who are well enough stand guard. And keep the door shut."

Daria and Maximos went to the nursery first. The entire corridor was burning. Fortunately, since it was predominately stone with few support beams needed, the structure didn't risk collapsing. Through the heavy smoke, they saw Aristos, pinned to the floor. Daria ran toward him, sidestepping the remnants of burned toys, blankets, and furniture. As she picked her way toward him, she noticed the blast pattern. A bomb had exploded. Please let them have escaped in time, Daria prayed.

Aristos was severely burned, especially the left side of his face that had been licked by the flames from the rug. Together, Daria and

Maximos lifted the beam off Aristos, their own flesh bubbling under the heat of the metal. Fortunately, they would heal fast. Maximos' arm had already started to self-repair, and the bone was no longer visible. Daria put her ear to Aristos' mouth. He was hardly breathing. Feeling his pulse, it was beating sluggishly.

"Maximos, give him air while I see if the boats are gone," Daria said as she rushed over to the wall that led to the secret tunnel. When she pushed on one of the stones that was raised ever so slightly, the door opened. Daria didn't have time to run down the hundreds of steps; instead, she shifted to the bottom.

All three boats were gone. She wasn't sure if she should feel relieved or upset. She told herself she would see her son again. But what of Zoe and Evander's child, or the children of their friends? They had come to the Sanctum expecting a celebration, not a massacre. Daria and her sisters didn't anticipate treachery on this scale. They had discussed that a play for power tonight could be made, but they thought it would be done through words. They figured it was possible their own children might be threatened . . . but certainly not the families and Covens of the rest of the Council, or their entire Tentyrian clan. The devastation was unfathomable.

Returning to the nursery, Daria saw Maximos working on Aristos, giving him oxygen from his own mouth. They shifted back to the infirmary. By then, Phoebe had arrived too. She reported that all of the Covens were gone. The halls had exploded with such force there wasn't a trace of the people inside.

Aristos started to come to. Now under the bright light of the examination table, it was obvious the left side of his face was ruined. Evander would need to work a miracle.

"Matia mou, Aristos, it's me—Daria. Can you hear me?" Daria asked. Aristos tried to move his lips, but only a gravelly moan escaped. He couldn't open his eyes. "Do you know where the children are? Ammon, Tale, and Nenet must have used the tunnel. But what about the rest of the children?" Aristos' head rolled side to side. Zoe found something for Aristos to write on and encouraged him to do so. "Do you know where they are?" Daria repeated.

With his good hand, Aristos scribbled: Solarium. All dead. It was too much for Zoe, who collapsed in grief. Her only child she shared with Evander was dead. The Tentyrians were systematically wiped out. Sophia returned with four more survivors. This was the last of their race.

"Stavros intends to keep the Sanctum as his own. Which means he is still here with Calix, Aglaia, and Asia, or they are coming back. We need to plan our next move carefully," said Daria as she paced. "Sophia, based on your assessment, about how many of the Guard are left?"

"Fifty, give or take a few," Sophia replied breathlessly.

"We're too weak to take them on," Daria rationalized. "And there aren't enough of us. Between us we are only six, and Evander said there are only ten here who can fight. We need to move everybody. Maximos, do you have any ideas?"

"I know of an island not far from Greece that is deserted," he offered. "There are a few abandoned huts, but they are rudimentary at best."

"That's fine; we can shift what supplies we need later. After we get everyone out, I can lock the Sanctum down. All of the Sanctum's energy inside will be switched off, and the outside barrier will be turned on," Daria commanded.

"Those left here will remain trapped and they'll die," finished Phoebe, her voice devoid of emotion. She felt she had lost everything.

"Maximos, take us there now so we can see where we are going," requested Daria. In order to shift, they needed to know exactly where they were going. If the destination or physical surrounding was unclear, it could have dangerous consequences. The six Zodiacs held hands and Maximos took them. Within minutes, they were on a balmy island surrounded by fruit trees. They returned to the infirmary. The Council—or what was left of it—agreed they'd do one last sweep for survivors before moving everyone.

Narcissa's prognosis didn't look good—her internal organs were severely damaged. Sebastian's situation was more positive, but not much better. And Aristos slipped back into unconsciousness. Splitting into teams, Daria and Maximos planned to shift throughout the central buildings of the Sanctum, including the Great Hall, Royal Villa, and library. Sophia said those areas were where most of the guards were stationed outside. Phoebe and Zoe would take the outer buildings, which entailed the kitchens, bathhouse, and dormitories for the Sanctum's residents. They all intended to get in and get out quickly. Evander would stay in the infirmary with the rest of the survivors until they returned.

Daria and Maximos shifted themselves behind the colonnade that encircled the Great Hall. From their post, they saw the Tentyrian Guards piling the dead in the central courtyard. Amongst the pale corpses, there was no one to save. They quickly covered the library and surrounding areas without managing to be seen. No survivors were retrieved. Daria and Maximos went to the Royal Villa next and started with the lower level.

"Maximos, I want you to know that if something happens to me, I need you to take the book and protect it with your life," Daria whispered to him. "That needs to be your priority. You'll need to lock down the Sanctum. Calypso is gone. Narcissa will die. That leaves Phoebe and me. My mother said our people can only be unified when the Luminaries rule as one. My mother told us you were essential to the future; she never said my sisters and I were by name. And there is the prophecy about the next generation of Luminaries . . . You are destined to reunite them."

"Daria, shut up. Nothing is going to happen. Let's get who we can and get out of here," said Maximos. Despite his dismissive words, Maximos knew Daria was right. Hathor had alluded that much to him . . .

Daria and Maximos went from room to room, hallway to hallway; they were all empty. After searching the upstairs, their last stop was Daria's bedchamber. Fortunately, the treacherous guards had made an effort to prevent the fire from spreading from the nursery corridor to the other areas. So far, no fire or smoke reached the quarters she shared with Aristos. That meant the book was safe.

In the corner of the room, Daria had designed a small hiding space under a marble tile. Noticing the tile was loose when the construction on the villa was first completed, Daria decided to pry it off completely rather than asking Pello and his team to fix it. She borrowed a chisel and dug a hole two feet deep, creating the perfect hiding space. At the time, Daria didn't know what she'd use the hole for, but she figured having a space of her own that no one knew about would come in handy.

Daria quickly lifted the tile and reached her hand in to get the book. It was then that Stavros emerged from the shadows.

"I was hoping you'd come back here," he said. Stavros didn't make a move toward them. "My guards caught Phoebe and Zoe picking up a few stragglers, and I knew you'd be back also. Always putting the well-being of your people first . . ."

"That would be something you know nothing about, Stavros,"

Daria replied icily as she clutched the book to her chest. He dismissed her comment with a wave of his hand.

"That's Hathor's book, isn't it? I've heard the rumors, but I never knew it actually existed. This day is looking up. I'll make you a deal. Give me the book and I'll let the people you've managed to collect go." Dread filled Daria and Maximos—Stavros knew where they were hiding the survivors. "Oh yes, I know exactly where you are keeping everyone. Unfortunately, we can't shift inside because we don't know what it looks like. But the Guard is searching for the architectural plans as we speak. They are also gathering the appropriate resources to break down the door. It looks like you lose again, Daria."

"Your word means nothing," said Maximos.

"Maybe, but are you willing to risk it?" Stavros answered. "And Daria, I suggest you weigh how much your own sister means to you. You've already lost Calypso. Do you really want to lose another? If you give me the book, I'll also throw in Phoebe. Just to sweeten the deal. Selene is keeping her company."

"And Zoe?" Daria asked.

"She's dead," Stavros said bluntly. Evander would be devastated. "I know my word means little to you, but the truth is that I didn't want to kill you or your sisters. I could do without the others, though." Stavros directed the last bit at Maximos. "You and your sisters have the strongest powers, and I thought over time we could come to an agreement. I'd allow you to see your children, and you could do the occasional favor for me. But that little rebellion you stirred up changed that. So what do you say? Phoebe and what remains of your people for the book?"

"I won't agree to anything unless I see her first," Daria said vehemently.

"Let's go, then, to the bathhouse gardens, where it smells a little less of death?" Stavros suggested. Daria looked at Maximos. He nodded in agreement. The three of them then shimmered away.

Daria saw Phoebe lying on a garden bench. She looked peaceful, as if she had been lulled to sleep by the trickling fountains. Her torn robe, disheveled hair, and blood-spattered body told a different story. Selene stood above her with eyes fiercely focused.

"You said she was unhurt," accused Daria as she stood with Maximos about ten feet away from Stavros and from where her sister lay. They wanted to ensure there was ample distance in case it was a trap.

"She is," Stavros said, "at least relatively. She took a mild blow to the head, and Selene has been keeping an eye on her since. We can't have her shifting, now can we? So what next, Daria; what is your decision?"

"Wake Phoebe up and have her walk towards us," Daria demanded.

Stavros challenged her in return, "No, give me the book."

"Not happening. You've already taken everything from us. If you kill the survivors, it won't make much of a difference," Daria lied. "Now give me my sister or I'll take this book somewhere you'll never find it. I doubt that bitch can prevent all three of us from accessing our powers."

"Selene," Stavros snapped. "Wake her up." The traitorous maid gave Phoebe a shake and altered her piercing gaze. Phoebe sat up suddenly.

"Phoebe, come towards me," Daria called. Phoebe tried to shift but couldn't; Selene kept her mentally tethered. Phoebe started to walk toward her sister and their gazes locked; she saw the book in Daria's arms and realized the magnitude of the trade. She couldn't let it happen. Phoebe wasn't strong enough to take on Stavros. But if she took out Selene, Maximos and Daria had a better shot at killing him and getting away.

Phoebe took one step toward Daria and said, "I love you." With a quick pivot, she turned and wrapped her hands around Selene's surprised neck and ripped off her head.

"No!" Stavros yelled. He lunged at Phoebe, who put up an electric wall in front of her, trying to hold him off while her power flickered like a dying lightning bug.

"Go now, Maximos," said Daria as she shoved the book at him with the key closed between its pages. "The key is inside. Get them out of the infirmary if you can. Lock the Sanctum."

"Blessed be," Maximos said as he shifted away, knowing he would never see her again.

A strange calm came over Phoebe as she channeled the last of her energy. The world became quiet, and the next few minutes occurred in slow motion: Stavros coming closer as he screamed something unintelligible, Daria handing the book to Maximos, Daria's outstretched arms enclosing her, the sun on her back—bright and hot, spreading its rays over them together, no feeling, their mother's arms wrapped tightly around them, white light.

After giving the Book of Hathor to Maximos, Daria catapulted herself toward Phoebe. If she could reach her before her energy barrier completely failed, she could get them both away. But it was not to be. Just as Daria reached her sister, she saw Aglaia and Asia. Flames swallowed them both. Daria's last prayer was for the future Luminaries to prevail.

PART II

CHAPTER 8: INTERVIEW

2010 AD, JULY
NEW YORK, NEW YORK / SUWANEE, GEORGIA

"**M**y name is Arianna Parker. I'm here for a 9:00 a.m. meeting at Leo Capital," I hear myself say to the attendant at the World Financial Center security desk. She looks up from her phone, clearly irritated I've interrupted her texting.

She slides her chair over to the computer screen and with a few impatient taps asks, "Meeting with Allison Fox?"

"Yes," I reply with a smile.

She picks up her phone, calls up to the respective floor, and drawls, "A Ms. Parker is here." I take a seat in the waiting area while I wait to be retrieved. A quick scan through my BlackBerry shows I already have over thirty e-mails awaiting my attention. It's only been fifteen minutes since I replied to the most urgent. I take out my personal phone and shoot Laura a quick text: Laur: Waiting for the interview start. Can't wait to debrief you tonight!

As much as I hate being away from the office, this is an opportunity I couldn't pass up. Leo has been recruiting me for months, along with dozens of other private equity firms. My "all-star" status as proclaimed by Town & Country's "Top 25 Under 25 Movers and Shakers" propelled me to the top of headhunters' lists. While it's an uncomfortable notoriety, it has been helpful in pursuing my next job.

My five years at Crest Rock have been great. It was daunting at first, having to pay my dues as the lowest analyst on the totem pole. But the seventy-hour weeks and chauvinist verbal abuse helped harden me into the businesswoman I am. I know Crest will pay to keep me, especially after the last opportunity I tossed in their basket, but money isn't the appeal. I need something different, a new challenge. At least, that is what I'm telling myself.

In the last year, a sense of anticipation started to creep up on me. It feels like walking around with butterflies in my stomach—all the time. I am waiting for something . . . but what? Raad chalks it up to my impending twenty-fifth birthday and tells me to keep up my tai chi. Laura thinks love is just around the corner. But I can't help but feel something greater is on the horizon. Maybe Leo is it.

"Ms. Parker?" I look up at the severe woman calling my name. "Right this way if you'll follow me. I'm Allison," she says as she extends her hand toward me. It's a weak handshake. I gather my laptop bag and purse. Sometimes a handshake can be just as helpful as doing a mind filter. You can always tell the extent of someone's grit. Allison's severe look and glasses are misleading, but then again appearances can be. I should know.

When I started working, I purposely tried to look innocuous. I only wore black suits, a striped button-down, black pumps. Hair held back with a headband. No makeup. At first, I was just the analyst asked to get coffee and order the late night dinners. But while I ordered those chicken parms and trudged on with my own work, I carefully learned the lay of the land and the intricacies of the business.

I first proved myself on the discarded acquisition of an energy plant. Crest Rock had been working on the deal for at least three months, and they were in the final stages of negotiation. Analyses were complete, showing the acquisition would be profitable if we could restructure the company and sell it as two separate entities within two years. The partners met with the plant's management teams several times, and the contracts were all but signed. That's when I stepped in.

I wasn't part of the deal team, but the investor presentation came my way for some additional formatting. It was mindless busy work with charts. That's when I decided to dig into the supporting data, which showed some flaws. They were nuanced flaws, but I realized they could have crippling effects within a month if we went forward. I didn't even need to use my telepathic powers to determine the deal was a lemon. I suppose if I had hard-core scruples, using my power in the workplace would never be a consideration. But I'd be lying if I said I didn't occasionally do it. And why not? In a world dominated by men,

I figured my ability only helped level the playing field.

Rather than cleaning up the presentation, I worked all night on my own analysis. At 7:00 the next morning, my manager expected to see the fruits of my graphic work. Instead of pretty graphs, he saw a ten-page report showing the pitfalls of the deal. He was furious and told me to take the day off. I took it with a grain of salt and went for a walk by the water. As I sat watching the ferry cross the Hudson, my cell phone rang. I was told to get back to the office immediately. Later that morning, I walked the investors through my report, and it was agreed the deal would be tossed. We found out only three weeks later the plant filed for bankruptcy. It was clear our infusion of cash and expertise wouldn't have been strong enough to save it. Crest Rock would have lost over $330 million.

I was promoted from the "bull pen," which was the open area of desks filled with data monkeys like myself, and was given my own personal glass cage with a view. I soon abandoned the headbands and black pumps and began to show my true colors—in more ways than just the sassy Louboutins and bright Hermes scarves I sported. By then, I had spent six months understanding the minds of my colleagues, their motivations, and the business. My quick learning landed me the plum deals and the right to speak up in meetings. Instead of ordering the dinners, I was taken out to them.

My meteoric rise was wonderful, and the extra money in my checking account didn't hurt, especially since I was financially independent. But aside from Raad, I didn't have anyone to truly share it with. Occasionally I saw Jayne and Rosemary, but with my work schedule, I spent any free time I had sleeping, trying out new recipes, or focusing on my health—a precarious thing to manage.

Fortunately, not long after my promotion to director, I bumped into Laura Delia on the red line. I hate taking the subway and I normally prefer to walk. But it was raining hard that morning and I couldn't justify spending $15 for a one-mile commute. So I braved the crowded subway car and found myself a nook in the corner to stand. As I was going to my happy place in an attempt to ignore the stifling air and thoughts of those around me, I felt a tap on my shoulder. It was Laura, all grown up. Miraculously she recognized me, because at first blush I wouldn't have recognized her.

Her lean, boyish frame had filled out. Her runner's body, once awkward, now stood confidently in front of me. She had cut her long blonde hair into a short bob that angled down in the front. But her friendliness and quickness to smile hadn't changed one bit. In the five minutes we could talk before my stop, I learned that Laura worked in advertising and lived uptown with three of her sorority sisters from Vanderbilt. We exchanged numbers and agreed to meet up for drinks that night.

We met at one of Laura's favorite haunts, the Roosevelt rooftop deck. It was a beautiful summer night, and for once I was genuinely glad I left the office before nine o'clock. It was true I didn't get out much, but it didn't mean I was out of touch with fashion. Shopping online, next to my obsession with the Food Network, was an addiction I readily embraced. I had chosen a Carolina Herrera ivory and black degrade silk and organza cocktail dress. The pleated skirt gave it just enough poof to keep it girly, and the thin black leather belt gave it an air of sophistication I loved. I found Laura at the bar in sky-high heels, a sequined tunic dress, and with two martinis in hand. She was talking to a hunky businessman, but as soon as she spied me, she yelled my name and pranced her way toward me. The poor fellow didn't get a glance back.

A drink was shoved in my hand immediately, and she gave me a hug. Even in her heels, Laura was still a good six inches shorter than me.

"Jesus, Ari, did you just step off the runway?" she exclaimed.

"Ha, well apparently you just did too!" I said. Laura gave me a little twirl so I could get the full effect of the Tahari dress.

"I was a little worried it was too disco. But I couldn't say no!"

"You look wonderful" I assured. Laura grabbed my hand, just like she did when we were children, and found us a lounge settee.

"I can't tell you how great it is to you see you, Ari! It's been forever!" she said.

"I know. It's been at least eight years since we've actually seen each other in person."

"And really, a brief sighting at the New Canaan Starbucks doesn't count. Did you know when we were little I came by your house, like once a week, to see if you could come over to play?"

"What? No, I had no idea!" I was genuinely surprised. The only thing I wanted more than to get out of my house as a child was to have a friend like Laura.

"Yeah, that housekeeper of yours was a real gem."

"Ah yes, Irena. I haven't seen or spoken to her in . . . well, a long time."

"Really? But she still works for your parents. At least I think she does. I still see her car every now and again when I'm home for the holidays."

"Yep, she probably still does. But I don't have a relationship with my parents anymore, so I can't really confirm or deny." Laura looked at me with a raised eyebrow. I took a big gulp of my martini. I rarely drink, but the U'Luvka vodka went down like water.

"I know, it's sad," I replied, "but you know what my parents are like."

"From what I remember, they seemed cold . . . and a little stingy on the desserts at their holiday party. Plus you were always in that house. What did they do, keep you locked in your room all the time?"

"Not quite. My parents didn't know what to do with me growing up. I had some health issues, and the best way they knew to deal with that was to keep me isolated. Although they did attempt to stick me in Silver Hill."

"No way! Seriously?"

"Yep."

"Well at least you could have hung out with Mariah Carey."

"Ha, possibly. But I didn't belong there. That incident was really the beginning of the end for us."

"I'm sorry, that really sucks," Laura said sympathetically. She waved to the waiter, who practically panted around us as she directed for another round.

"It mostly comes down to my mother. She is manipulative, and my dad supports it. I realized it wasn't something I wanted in my life anymore. So after I graduated college, I stopped speaking to them."

"Good for you! But it still must be hard."

"One of my proudest moments was about two years ago when I wrote them a check in full for the apartment they gave me."

"Wow, really? You actually own your apartment? You're in your twenties, Ari."

"I got a good jump start after college, and I've been working pretty hard. I almost refused the apartment after my parents gave it to me. But I sucked up my pride. I knew there was going to be a day when I'd write that check and consider myself paid in full."

"So now that you are 'paid in full,' how does it feel?"

"I'm still trying to figure that out. But I know right now—I feel pretty great!" I said with a tipsy giggle.

"Excuse me, ladies," interrupted a lawyer type with his tie loosened. "My friends and I were admiring you, and we wanted to know if we could buy you a drink?"

Before I could say anything, Laura smoothly replied, "Sorry, girls' night tonight." He attempted to segue into getting our phone numbers but left empty handed. Four martinis and several rebuffed men later, Laura and I were sure we were the best friends we never had. She lamented about her lack of luck in love and the string of boyfriends she'd had. We discussed work, shopping, life in general, and closed the bar down that night.

Since that evening two years ago, we've been best friends. Speaking of which, tonight is Bachelor night, and Laura will be expecting a full recap on the interview when she comes over. I should make a chocolate soufflé—the perfect complement to red wine and terrible television . . .

"We are so pleased you agreed to meet with us today," says Allison as she directs me to the elevator she waves her key card in front off. Funny, she doesn't look pleased at all, but I suspect she looks like that all the time.

"I know I took some convincing, but I think this could make for an exciting opportunity," I say genuinely. Hopefully, the rest of the group is a bit more chipper.

"As I stated in my e-mail, today, you will meet with Robert Murdock. He is one of our three managing partners," says Allison. After our ascent, the elevator doors slide open to a marble reception area. A silver graphic lion on the white Carrara marble wall above the reception desk silently greets me. So this is Leo Capital. The offices are modern and sleek, with a minimalist vibe, unlike the old-school boys club I'm used to.

The floor, overall, looks like a solid mix of both men and women working amongst the open layout of desks and LCD computer monitors. It's a good sign; too much testosterone can be difficult to work with. Around the outer edges of the main floor are the executive suites and conference rooms. Allison parks me in one overlooking Ground Zero, where the World Trade Center once stood, still a stagnant construction site. It's hard to believe that even after nine years, construction has barely moved forward. There is a knock on the glass door, and an older gentleman with slicked-back silver hair walks in.

"Arianna Parker! Or should I say number fourteen?" he greets me warmly, referring to my ranking in the Town & Country article.

"And you must be Robert," I reply. We shake hands. It's a very firm shake but not one meant to intimidate.

"Welcome to Leo. We've been trying to get you in here for months. I've heard from Allison it hasn't been an easy task." We take a seat side by side in leather swivel chairs at the head of the conference table.

"I needed some time to think about it. I hadn't yet digested a potential move from Crest," I say.

"Well, we are certainly glad you are here, as is Mr. Vasilliadis himself." That comes as a surprise to me, for the elusive founder himself to take note of my recruitment. I'm good at my job, but really? I hold my skepticism to myself. If they want to woo me, then woo away. "I'm not going to waste our time, Arianna, and have you take me through your resume and skill set," Robert says, looking at me intently. "Instead I want to spell out our proposition for you. If you join us at Leo, you will become the fourth managing partner. I think that sets some kind of record in the industry when it comes to your age. Over the last ten years, we've only had three MPs. The base salary is $500,000, and you know how bonuses go. You will also receive a ten percent stake in the company, which is practically unheard of." He pauses to gauge my reaction. I have my poker face on, but really I'm in shock.

"However, there is a catch," he continues. "In fact, the catch is two-fold. First, this offer is only good until midnight. Second, we want you to visit a company we are thinking of investing in, in Georgia. We want a verbal analysis, and we also want it tonight."

"Excuse me?" I ask, confused. "You want me to visit a company in Georgia and provide you with an analysis this evening? It's already 10:15 in the morning. I'll never be able to get a flight on such short notice. And I am due back at my office at twelve."

"I apologize for the short notice. The company jet will take you. It is already fueled and prepped on the tarmac. If you take the helicopter now, you should be able to take off by eleven and be in Suwanee by two. This is a once-in-a-lifetime opportunity, Arianna. Your meetings should not be a concern."

"With all due respect, this is not what I was expecting. I haven't even met the rest of the team. And you want me to hop on a plane. Right now." I never have been one for spontaneity; maybe it's because I live such a methodical life. The last spontaneous thing I did was splurge on Jo Malone shampoo. But I think most would agree this was taking things to a whole different level.

"I understand your concern," Robert tries to reassure me. "You will have the opportunity to meet the rest of the team when you return. We are having a party this evening to celebrate our second quarter earnings. Mr. Vasilliadis wanted me to extend an invitation to you. The entire Leo group will be there."

"So you also expect me to go to Georgia and come back in time for this party, which I'm just hearing about?" I ask, even more confused.

"Yes, the plane will take off from Mathis Airport around 6:00 p.m. I think it's fair to say you can make it back to the City by 9:30. You may miss the dinner, but we'll ensure there is something for you on the plane. The party is at the Four Seasons. Allison will give you the itinerary and ensure you are where you need to be." Robert looks at his watch impatiently. "Arianna, if this is something you are interested in doing, you are going to have to take a leap of faith. We are asking you to do this because we think you are capable. If you aren't, then that's a different story. The helicopter is ready."

I look at Robert in disbelief. This is the strangest interview process I've ever heard of, much less experienced. But my interest is piqued . . . The compensation is unheard of. And of course I'm capable! Laura is always telling me I need to live a little . . .

"Okay, I will go. Do you have any debriefing documents on the company and the management team?" I ask.

Robert smiles proudly, clearly thinking he has won some victory. "Yes, of course. Allison will provide you with everything you need." On cue, she arrives. Robert shakes my hand and says he hopes to see me this evening. Allison ushers me out of the conference room, hands me a thick manila folder, and takes me once again to the elevator. She hits H on the keypad and swipes her card in front of the screen.

"Everything you need is in that file," says Allison pointedly. "It includes a full itinerary, including travel logistics, contact numbers, as well as the bios and financials on Apex Pharmaceuticals."

"Great, at least I know what company I am going to," I say sarcastically as I shove the file folder into my laptop case. Allison gives me a reproachful look. Whatever, she can scorn me. It's not like I'm desperate for a job. I have one right now, thank you very much. As soon as I get to the airport, I'll need to tell Sarah my secretary to clear my calendar for the day. Guess this will be my first sick day, ever.

The doors open onto the roof. I clutch my purse and laptop case tightly. My hair whips around my face as I teeter slightly on my heels. The wind is blowing hard, and the helicopter propellers are still spinning. It's too loud to speak, but a man who looks like a security guard with an earpiece takes my elbow and walks me to the helicopter door and helps me inside. The door shuts, and the propeller above me begins to spin faster. We lift off.

The view of the City is undeniably breathtaking. It looks like a children's toy set with play cars, boats, and skyscrapers. It shines perfectly from so far up. No grime or cussing cabbies. But the reality is that grime and those crazy taxi drivers make New York real to me. There is no other place I would rather live. Last New Year's, I took Laura and Raad to Paris. Laura and I annoyed him with our shopping, but he put up with it. Fortunately, he brought plenty of reading material—lots of medical journals that would make my eyes bleed if I attempted to read them. We saw all of the sights, from the Eiffel Tower to the Arc de Triomphe, and dedicated an entire day to the Louvre. But the City of Lights just can't compare to my Big Apple. Wait till Raad and Laura hear about this adventure . . .

We touch down at Islip Airport a short fifteen minutes later. An escort in the form of another nameless security guard retrieves me from the helicopter and walks me to the awaiting Gulfstream GIV-SP. At least that's what I'm told the plane is by the friendly flight attendant, Diana. I settle into a beige leather seat of the twelve-passenger plane and am offered my choice of refreshments.

I take a sparkling water and bowl of fresh fruit from Diana and power up my laptop. I make a quick call to Sarah, telling her that I'm not feeling well and that my meetings need be cancelled ASAP. I also remember to leave Laura a message that we'll have to reschedule Bachelor night; something important has come up but I promise I'll give her the dish tomorrow. The pilot indicates we are right on schedule, and I realize I only have about two hours and forty-five minutes to learn everything I can about Apex Pharmaceuticals. Let the digging begin.

Just before 2:00 p.m., we begin our descent. I've crammed as much information as I can into my mind. I've begun a model on the company that I think I'll have just enough time to complete on the flight back. It's rudimentary, based on the time crunch, but I think it will give me the information I need. So far, Apex looks like an excellent investment opportunity—provided that the information I've received is accurate.

Whenever I do an analysis of a company, I always seek out as many resources as possible. Those resources can vary from store clerks to third-party suppliers of parts. Once, when I first started at Crest, I rode every MTA bus transit line in Manhattan and Brooklyn when we were looking to enter into a partnership with the city to help them close the $600 million gap in its operating budget.

I like to dig all the way to the grassroots level when I do my due diligence. But sometimes, no matter how thorough an analysis you do, it can be worthless if you don't understand the management team. A management team, alone, can determine the success or failure of a deal. It's important to understand their motivations, how they run their companies, and their dedication to the partnership. Fortunately, I happen to be an expert in that area. Town & Country attributed my success to my "killer instincts;" Raad calls it my unique gift. I'm not sure exactly what I'd label it—some days I view my telepathic skill as a pain in the ass; other days I view it as a godsend. Regardless, I know I'll need to use it today.

The passenger door opens, and Diana helps me down the stairs. There is a black SUV with a driver standing by. According to Allison's itinerary, it's a thirty-minute drive to Apex. From what I know of the company, the Suwanee, Georgia, based facility produces generic antibiotics. It is also known for being first to market on several key drugs once their patents have expired, leaving Apex approximately thirty percent market share of generics. While clearly not as big as some of the larger drug companies, this is a sizable company for a one-town pharma company that only began production about fifteen years ago. Helping Apex prepare for an acquisition by a larger company could be an interesting and profitable opportunity.

We bump along many a dirt road before finally arriving at the plant. It is huge, sprawling across approximately twenty football fields. The whole town must be employed by this place. Per the itinerary, I am to call a number and inform them of my arrival. No sooner do I do that and step outside of the car when I am greeted by a pleasant-looking admin who ushers me inside. I am brought into a conference room where the management team is already waiting. The CEO, their head of council, CFO, and COO are all in attendance.

I feel like I'm walking into a firing squad, and I don't even know why. I wonder how much they know about me. It's likely they have no idea I don't even work for Leo Capital. Well, I'm certainly not going to be the one to dispel them of that notion.

"I'm Arianna Parker. I appreciate you meeting with me this afternoon," I say as I shake the various hands and make the introductions.

"It's a pleasure to meet you," says the CEO, Morris Finley, a rotund man with flush cheeks. "Mr. Vasilliadis told us you would be instrumental in Leo's decision to invest, and we are happy to extend you every courtesy as you conduct your analysis."

"I appreciate that," I reply. "Unfortunately, my trip today must be cut short. I typically spend several days learning about the companies I visit. Since I only have a few hours, I'd love to sit with you all individually for about twenty minutes. I know you likely have a presentation to share, but if you can just provide me with a copy, we can skip that and then perhaps conclude the day with a tour?"

The chiefs of financials and operations look displeased. Obviously, I've thrown a wrench in their plans. I don't have to read their minds to see they are wondering who this Yankee biddy is that looks fresh out of the schoolroom.

"Of course, whatever you wish, Ms. Parker," says Finley.

"Excellent. If it's all right with you, can I start with you, Mr. Finley?"

"Please, call me Morris," he says with a wink. He seems like the type who wants to call you "sugar" or "honey," but not in a derogatory way. He is more like an affable grandfather. The rest of the room departs, and my interview begins.

I start by asking him how he got started at Apex. Even though I have already read his bio, I need him to talk awhile to fill up the twenty minutes before I filter through his mind. He is a sweet man and clearly passionate about the company. I jot down notes of our conversation on my notepad. Then, leaning back in my chair, I absently toy with my pen. It drops and we both lean down to get it. My hand brushes his. He freezes, and I begin the mind filter.

I see he is genuinely excited about the opportunity. He constantly motivates his employees and believes in adhering to the strictest protocols and Food and Drug Administration standards. He's familiar with the accounting. The numbers are sound. There are several other private equity firms that want to invest. Leo is his first choice.

This is a good sign. I remove my hand, and Morris gives me my pen. We finish out the interview, and he thanks me like a gentleman for my time. Next, I interview the CFO and COO in succession. They think some pretty disparaging thoughts about me. "Bitch" and "whore" are some of their choice words. That's always the worst thing about using my gift, finding out what people really think. You'd think you'd want to know, but deep down, you really don't. I learned that lesson with Charles.

In this case, it doesn't hurt my feelings because they don't even know me. And they are just being pigheaded men threatened by a woman half their age. Deep down, their anger at me is driven by fear—fear that I'll tell Leo not to invest. I see that they have all worked hard together to get Apex to where it is today. They believe it is solvent and the drugs they create are of the highest quality. From what I can tell and based on the numbers I've seen, Leo would be foolish not to invest.

Three down, one more to go. Next is the lawyer, Travis Ridgefield.

Travis explains he joined Apex in 1995 and has worked closely with the management team to navigate the difficult waters of pharma lawsuits and regulations from the FDA. Everything with Travis seems on par, until I touch his hand. He is involved in some shady dealings and has engaged in talks, unbeknownst to Morris, with a company called Trebuchet. Not to mention, Travis has also been embezzling money from Apex for the last ten years and has knowledge of an impending FDA warning letter for one of the firm's drugs called Sitorin. He obtained that knowledge through the illicit affair he is having with the director of the Center for Drug Evaluation and Research. It really couldn't get much worse.

No private equity firm would touch this deal with a ten-foot pole if they knew what I did. It is time to wrap this up, I think. I remove my hand. Travis looks like he's lost his train of thought. Before he can continue, I say, "I'm so sorry my phone interrupted you, Travis. But it looks like I need to head back to New York immediately and I'll be unable to go on that tour. I appreciate your time, however. Meeting with you all has been very helpful."

I stand to shake his hand as he is trying to remember exactly when my phone rang. "Please give my regards to the rest of the team," I say quickly as I collect my things and power walk out to the waiting car. I know I was rude. But better social graces aren't going to improve the situation, I tell myself as we speed toward the airport. I realize I'm exhausted as I kick off my heels and turn up the AC. My cream Ralph Lauren blouse with its ruffled Victorian collar has lost its starch, and I feel like a wilted flower in this southern heat. We'll likely take off at 5:00 p.m., forty-five minutes ahead of schedule. Fingers crossed I will have enough time to run home and take a quick shower. I certainly don't want to show up to a black tie event like this to explain how the Apex deal is a mess and likely can't be fixed.

Now, how do I explain the viability, or lack thereof, to Robert and presumably Mr. Vasilliadis? I have no idea what this dinner will be like and how they want my opinion presented. He said verbally, so I won't need to hand in a formal report, which is a relief. It's difficult to source information like: Apex general counsel—conflict of interest due to affair with CDER director; current embezzlement amount—$25 million; knowledge of FDA citation letter, re: adverse events associated with cholesterol-lowering drug.

My best bet is to keep it vague and explain that I suspect, based on my observations, that Travis Ridgefield is engaged in illegal activity. I will suggest to have an additional internal audit conducted and for

Leo to look into Apex's close ties with CDER. Surely they'll find the embezzlement and misconduct. Based on my review of the financials and my model, the numbers are all clean. That means the records Leo has are either inaccurate or incomplete. It also means I have no data to support my thesis. In fact, my model completely contradicts my recommendation.

It is one thing to be the harbinger of bad news when you have cold, hard facts on your side. But it is another thing entirely when you only have information that is factual to you and theoretical to others. We pull into the small private airport and drive up to the tarmac. Diana lets down the plane stairs.

"Ms. Parker, you are back earlier than we expected," she says happily.

"Yes, change of plans. Can we take off, or do we need to wait for some special runway clearance?" I ask as I make my way into the plane.

"We should be good to go. The pilot will radio up to New York to let them know of our changed arrival time. Traffic control at Islip isn't a problem for us."

I plop myself into a seat. My head aches from the extra energy I've exerted.

"You look peaked. Can I get you a cocktail?" Diana asks.

"No thanks. I save those for special occasions. Could you make me some green tea, though?"

"Of course. Would you like a snack? I know you haven't eaten lunch."

"No, thank you." I'm too tired and nervous to eat.

"And I assume you will be freshening up for later this evening?" Diana gestures toward the bathroom.

"I'm planning on going home first."

"There is no need, Ms. Parker. The plane is equipped with a full shower, and several clothing options have been provided for you," Diana says cheerily.

"What?"

"I know, it's surprising that we have a full bathroom on here, but I assure you it is fully functional and quite comfortable."

"No, I mean, why are there clothing options for me? How would you all even know my size?" I ask tartly. I'm irritated. So this is why the itinerary had me going straight from the airport to the Four Seasons. I don't like feeling like someone's chess piece, and I'm not playing dress-up for my future employer.

"I'm so sorry, Ms. Parker. I didn't mean to offend you. I was just told that you'd want to change before the quarterly dinner."

"It's quite all right. I'd simply prefer to wear something of my own," I reply crisply.

She nods. "I'll go make your tea now." Diana goes to the rear of the plane to the small galley area.

I head to the aft lavatory to splash some water on my face. I look more than a little frazzled as my pale complexion stares back at me. "Girlfriend, you need a tan or at least some blush," I say to the mirror. Unfortunately, no matter what I do, I know I can never get that golden glow, at least not without self-tanner. And the last time I tried that, I ended up looking like an Oompa Loompa for a week. No matter; I've come to accept my paleness as a fact of life. Laura says it makes me look like a Madonna. Maybe that's why I'm destined to die a virgin, I think wryly. That thought is just too embarrassing and depressing.

I quickly survey the bathroom, which is surprisingly large and elegantly appointed. But even so, the Pretty Woman moment isn't happening. Curious, I take a peek in the small closet adjacent to the powder area. There are three fabulous ball gowns inside, and they look like my size—exactly. Same with the shoes. Amazingly, everything is to my taste: conservative but subtly sexy. The black Valentino is calling my name as I shut the closet door firmly. No, I'm not a puppet; not my family's and certainly not Leo Capital's. I rack my brain for everything I know about the man behind the firm that has managed to throw me completely off guard.

From what I know of Leo's founder, he shuns public attention and as a rule never gives interviews, unless it is for a charitable cause. Rather than himself, Vasilliadis positions his managing partners as the face of the company. In fact, I could only find two publically available photos of him. He certainly was easy on the eyes. No wife or known girlfriends. I'm sure if there were any more details they could get their hands on, the media would love to proclaim him one of New York's hottest and most eligible bachelors.

Looking back on the day, everything was predicated on presumption and the arrogance of a firm used to getting its way. And what did that say about Vasilliadis? Everything. But then again, I did have to respect the man who started a firm on his own and successfully grew it from nothing to having over $20 billion in assets under management—in less than five years.

I go back to my seat and settle in with the steaming cup of tea. The sun is still bright in the summer sky as we head north. I close the shade to shut out the light. The warm liquid relaxes me, and I feel myself getting drowsy. I need to gather my energy if I'm going to tell Maximos Vasilliadis exactly what I think of Apex . . . and of him.

CHAPTER 9:
INTOXICATED

2010 AD, JULY
NEW YORK, NEW YORK
THE FOUR SEASONS

"Where is she, Robert?" I ask my trusted friend as I take a sip from the crystal champagne flute. "The plane landed over an hour ago."

"It seems Arianna had her own plan and insisted the driver take her home," replies Robert. "She said that she'd manage to get herself to the party just fine—that is what the driver said. He is still outside her apartment, as is the surveillance team."

"Very good. When she arrives, please let me know." I place my empty glass on the silver tray that sails past and decide to make the rounds. The Bulle de Sucre dessert, a purple sugar bubble filled with violet cream, blueberry sherbet, and lemon jam, is being served. It looks delicious, but I prefer to drink my calories—at least tonight. As I visit the tables, I make it a point to say a few words to as many employees as possible. While I find these affairs boring, they are important. I want my people to feel appreciated because they are. Without them, we wouldn't have any earnings to celebrate.

The criticism that the rich keep getting richer while the poor keep getting poorer isn't beyond me. I hear it loud and clear. But the reality is our earnings help fund some of the city's most important projects, including the NYC Children's Hospital, the Manhattan Institute of Medical Research, and the new ADR housing project in the Bronx solely sponsored by Leo Capital.

The ADR "American Dream Realized" housing project was an idea of mine to provide affordable but beautiful and safe housing for struggling families. Administered by an independent council, the program calls for interested families to submit applications stating their situation and plans for the future. If approved by the ADR board, the family will receive a home for three years and pay a flat rate of $300 a month. We just broke ground on fifteen new townhouses last week. Job counseling, day care, and various support services are all included, with the goal in mind that when their lease is up, the families will be more than capable of standing on their own two feet.

While the human race is fragile, it can also be incredibly strong. Sometimes it just needs a little help. As I glance around the room at the glittering jewelry and flashy watches, I recognize the decadence, but I also recognize that it is this that makes projects like the ADR possible. It is also this that funds and supports my own purpose.

Contrary to popular belief, I'm not about ripping apart companies, firing people, and making a profit. We make a profit for sure, but Leo Capital also helps salvage and improve hundreds of businesses a year. And those companies that we do take down deserve it. There will always be naysayers, but for as long as I am alive, I intend to keep Leo thriving and generating the money I need to continue what I set out to do.

The band strikes up a classic swing number, and the dance floor fills with tuxedos and ball gowns. I see Sasha coming toward me in a slinky black sequined halter gown that might as well be see-through based on the quantity of nipple I can see. Her long blonde hair is swept up into a tight chignon, drawing attention to her long, exotic neck that I have so enjoyed over the last few months. I told her I could offer little more than the pleasures in my bed and some polite dinner conversation, but that has done little to deter her. She refuses to let up on her possessiveness, despite my trying to break it off last week. I'll have to talk to Allison about allowing her into the party, and all future events for that matter.

"Maaaximos," she purrs in her Russian accent. "Vyy have you not called me?"

"Sasha, I told you I'm very busy right now . . . and I can no longer do this," I say while scanning the crowd for Allison, who may need to call security if this escalates. I can tell Sasha has already had too much to drink.

"But vvy?" she demands. The sharp, almost emaciated features of her face that have made her a world-famous model contort into an un-attractive scowl. "Vy are you not pleased with me anymore?" I really don't want a scene right now.

"Sasha, I like you, I do, but I can't give you the attention you need. You should be with someone else."

"But I vaant you," she cries. "I thought ve made a vonderful couple!" I can see the tears starting to well up. I spy Robert out in the throng, talking to the other two managing partners, Satish and Samson. They are almost certainly discussing Arianna and what she means for the future of Leo. I hired them because they are smart and trustworthy. They are all men of integrity, and they can keep a secret. But their concern is not misplaced. If Arianna is who we think she is and she accepts the job offer, a new type of visibility will undoubtedly reach us that could be dangerous. If she refuses, it means she may never accept my help and we will be unable to protect her.

With my men occupied, I'm going to have to deal with Sasha myself. And I'm going to do it once and for all. I typically despise using mind control on humans, but in the long run this will help her.

"Sasha my dear," I say, lowering my voice to draw her in. She steps closer, and her eyes widen. The sound of my voice and my dilated eyes are starting to enthrall her. I reach out and tenderly brush her cheek with my palm; she leans her face against it. "Sasha, look at me. I want you to listen. You don't like me. You do not like Maximos Vasilliadis. You are going to turn away now and leave this party. You want to go home . . . and eat something . . . with carbohydrates."

Her eyes, which fluttered shut as I spoke, are now fully open. She takes a step back in confusion and excuses herself. That will be the last I'll hear from her. While her company was enjoyable, it was becoming too complicated. I have enough on my hands. One of which is Arianna Parker.

My study of Arianna over the last few months has certainly been an interesting one. If an outsider were to look inside the contents of my desk, they'd likely think I was a stalker. My file on her has everything from her medical records to her senior thesis. My team has snapped enough photos of her to fill an art gallery. And an art gallery wouldn't be an exaggeration, because that woman is like looking at a work of art. Whether she is jogging at 4:30 in the morning, cooking in her apartment, or working intently, Arianna is one of the most focused and striking people I've come across—and that is saying something.

I normally don't read anything but financial or news publications or the security reports my men give me. But the head of HR sent me the

May issue of the magazine containing a profile on Arianna. She suggested I take a read through. My heart almost stopped in my chest when I saw the picture. The resemblance was astounding. At first I thought I was hallucinating. Maybe my blood sugar was low. But after a double take, I realized I'd recognize that sharp chin and those green eyes anywhere. I called the Brothers to let them know what I suspected. They were incredulous at first, but when I e-mailed them the article, they couldn't deny the resemblance.

I immediately set my team to finding as much information about her as possible and had a security team watch her at all times, yielding the thick file. Her extreme intelligence, obvious struggles with mental health, and physical resemblance were all key markers. If Arianna is who we think she is, then big changes are about to take place. This is what we've been waiting for. It also means others have or would soon recognize her too.

According to my records, Arianna's birthday is only three days away now, which means the window is getting smaller and smaller. Of course, it would have been much easier to simply retrieve her and lay out our theories immediately. But we need to tread carefully. Arianna is too valuable an asset to mishandle. We need her to want to work for us. Once we have her in the door, we will be far more capable of controlling the events to come.

"Excuse me, Mr. Vasilliadis," says a young waiter. "Here is the drink you requested from your private stock."

"Thank you," I say as I reach for the glass of vintage merlot infused with a special blend of O and A negative. But before I take in a pull of the aromatic scent, I catch the scent of something else. It makes my gums prick, and it's definitely not the wine. It smells like lily and honey and carries a pulse beating a few skips faster than an average human's. Not quite as fast as mine. I turn toward it. Arianna. I breathe in. She is coming down the curved staircase leading into the ballroom. I'm not the only one who has taken notice.

Several of the guests have looked up from their cocktails and conversations to admire the new arrival. Where Sasha is pure sex appeal, Arianna is pure elegance. She is wearing a long chiffon skirt. Silver. High waisted, with pleats cascading silkily around her hips. Hips any man would want in his hands. A knit top hugs her closely and dips seamlessly into her skirt. The small cap sleeves reveal slender, creamy arms; the scoop neck shows just enough breast that I take a gulp of wine to take the edge off. She's worn her hair down, its chestnut color enhanced by subtle honey highlights and a slight wave. I can hear it brush against her shoulders and neck. God, that beautiful neck. It's adorned by a diamond necklace of flowers. On her ring finger, she wears a matching flower encrusted with diamonds. Fortunately, I know it's not a wedding ring. That would add another level of complication I don't need.

"Maximos, she is here," Robert says as he comes to my side.

"I can see that," I reply, a bit gruffer than I intend.

"She arrived in a taxi . . ."

I take another swig of my drink and a deep breath, forcing my incisors to retract all the way in. Certainly don't want to embarrass myself.

"Well, are you going to bring her over here?" I ask.

"Of course." She's made her way down the stairs. Robert hurries toward her and extends a hand. Arianna gives him a gracious smile as he offers to escort her. She takes his arm. With her free hand, she clutches a small, sparkly box that must be a purse. What can a woman possibly fit in a contraption like that?

They are coming toward me; Robert is walking, Arianna is gliding. She sees me. Her eyes lock on mine. They are mesmerizing. Surprise registers on her face. But just as quickly as it's there, it's gone. Her emotions are now masked to me.

"Mr. Vasilliadis," she says smoothly, beating Robert to the punch.

"A pleasure, Ms. Parker," I respond calmly. I take her hand in mine. It would be too cliché and inappropriate to kiss it, but I'd love to. Our touch is hot . . . like fire. We quickly separate in surprise, and she takes a step back. Her scent completely overwhelms me, and I must swallow convulsively. Lily, honey, skin, blood. She is intoxicating. I swear on all that is holy, in the 2,225 years I've been alive, I haven't experienced anything like this. My demeanor appears calm, at least I hope it does, but inside, my body and mind are screaming at me. I didn't see this coming. Could this be the woman that Hathor's prophecy predicted?

In the months leading up to this moment, the Brothers joked I was becoming obsessed with Arianna—routinely checking in with the surveillance team and reading her file to find any pieces of information I had missed. I told myself it was because I wanted to protect her and keep her safe if she was one of us. She was just a child to me. But standing before me, it is clear she is no child. Praise Hathor for that.

I can see the pulse in her neck beating furiously, and her fingers are now clenched around the sparkling box. Her careful smile doesn't betray her, but I know she is as rattled as I am.

"I hope your travels went well today?" I inquire.

"Yes. So how do you wish to go about this, Mr. Vasilliadis?" she replies coolly. Clearly, she wants to skip the niceties.

"Please, call me Maximos. Robert, if you will excuse us?" Robert nods and walks over to Satish and Samson, who are eagerly awaiting an update. "Can I get you a drink?"

"Some sparkling water with lemon would be lovely." I nod to a waiter, who comes over and eagerly takes her order. I wouldn't be surprised if all the men in her life await her beck and call.

"I'd like to have this conversation in private," I say firmly. "Even though we are amongst my employees, I like to keep confidential information concerning live deals quiet. Let us go to the roof."

"Will the managing partners be joining us?" she asks, unsure.

"No, I keep them apprised of the information they need. I want to hear your analysis firsthand. I've gone to great lengths to hear your opinion, Arianna."

I can tell she is pondering the prospect of being alone with me on a rooftop. She slips a hand into the fold in her skirt and pulls out a phone to look at the time.

"Well, that's clever to have pockets. Surely you couldn't fit that in your purse," I remark—somewhat of an obvious comment. But then again, it's hard to bring your A game when you can barely focus on anything except for a woman's scent and neck.

"No, I couldn't, and I like to keep it with me at all times." She gives me a hard look. Is she warning me that she has her phone with her? Does she think I'm going to make a move and she'll have to call 911? Surely not, if I ever hope to gain her trust. I merely raise an eyebrow at her. "Yes, let's go," she agrees. "It is getting late, though; I will leave here in an hour." She states it as a fact. Arianna is obviously trying to put some parameters in place.

"Very well." I nod. The waiter comes back with Arianna's water, and we make our way to the roof. As the elevator doors close, the air grows thick between us. It's not caused by dread or fear—rather, it's pure anticipation. I can almost feel the air crackling with energy.

The elevator doors open, and we make our way through the lobby toward the empty roof deck that is closed due to our party downstairs. I open the door for her, and she steps out into the summer air, with me in tow. Watching her from behind is just as stirring as it is from the front. I find myself wondering what she looks like with her clothes off. The night is warm. Fortunately, being over fifty stories up eliminates the humidity. Not that it matters to me—but I want her to be comfortable. Before I can begin the conversation, which I've planned, Arianna starts in with a determined look.

"Mr. Vasilliadis," she says.

"Please, call me Maximos."

"I want you to know up front that I think your interview methods are presumptuous and inappropriate." So much for treading lightly. I tilt my head, indicating I'm listening. I've found the best way to respond to verbal confrontations, especially from women, is to listen. She clearly has already played this out in her head, and to interrupt her and tell her differently won't help. Plus, she has her hand on her hip. And it's sexy. I keep my thoughts to myself. I probably am as inappropriate as she thinks. Get a grip on yourself, man. I swallow again.

"I agreed to take this interview under the impression that I'd be meeting Robert, not an entire management team over eight hundred miles away. From the moment I stepped into your office, you expected me to be flattered and do whatever was on that itinerary of yours. I don't appreciate being toyed with."

"I didn't expect you to be flattered; I thought you would be interested," I say genuinely.

"That's not to say I wasn't and am not interested, but your methods are calculating, and I cannot work for someone who intends to move me about like a game piece."

"So you're saying you don't want to work for me?"

"No . . . yes. . . I'm not sure yet." She is flustered. "You haven't even heard my take on Apex, and I just accused you of being manipulating. Why would you even want me to work for you?"

"Okay, let's start with Apex," I say carefully. "What is your opinion?"

"Based on the documentation that was provided to me, which I used to build my model, the numbers look very good. And to the unsuspecting eye, Apex would appear an excellent investment opportunity. But I am advising you against it. I think there is some unscrupulous activity occurring that will have serious ramifications. I suggest you conduct an internal audit on their financials and look into Travis Ridgefield."

"The lawyer? Why? What type of unscrupulous activity do you suspect?"

She pauses. "I can't say for sure, but my opinion is that it is detrimental to the company and your investment in them."

"So you don't have any numbers or proof to back this up? This is just your opinion?" I ask caustically. She looks out at the skyline and unconsciously bites her lip. I'm pushing her intentionally; I want her to share what she really knows. Her head snaps back in my direction. I can hear the tendons crack.

"Yes, it's my opinion."

"You are going to have to do better than that, Ms. Parker."

"Unfortunately, I can't Mr. Vasilliadis. I've given you my recommendation. If you don't like it, I suppose there is nothing more for us to discuss." She turns on her heel and starts to go back inside.

"Ms. Parker."

"Yes?"

"So, what is your answer? Midnight isn't too far away."

"Excuse me? You can't honestly want me to work for you?" she asks incredulously.

"Yes, I do. Otherwise I wouldn't have extended you an offer in the first place."

"But why?"

"Because I trust your opinion."

"But you just said . . ."

"I said that you are going to have to do better. And I mean that. I expect everyone who works for me to be honest—completely. I don't know how you know what you do about Ridgefield. But clearly there is more here than meets the eye. Our team is about trust, and I can tell you don't trust me. I know we've only just met and it's true—I have moved you about today with my own considerations in mind. But I think if we learn to trust each other, our work could be mutually beneficial and very successful."

Arianna looks unsure about what has just transpired. "Are you going to invest in Apex?" she asks.

"No," I reply.

"Would you have invested, regardless of my opinion?"

"No."

"Why?"

"Because Travis Ridgefield is a crook and Apex is about to be fined millions of dollars by the FDA."

"So this was a test you already knew the answer to? And I suppose I passed?" Her voice has taken on that cool quality again. I'm not sure what to say. My bowtie is feeling a little tight.

"Yes."

"So, what you just said about trust doesn't apply to you?" She is definitely angry.

"It does—but I wanted to test your skill set. How is that any different than if I asked you to do a case study or asked you how many pencils it would take to fill a room? That's how an interview works,

Arianna. I know you are young, but don't be naïve." She doesn't respond right away, but I can see the fury in her eyes.

"Mr. Vasilliadis, I do have an answer for you. Thanks, but no thanks. Leo Capital is not the right fit for me—just like the clothes that were provided this evening," she says with a smirk. This time she really does leave, taking her honey and lily scent with her. I don't say anything to stop her. I don't know what to say. How did I lose control of the situation so quickly? She wasn't supposed to react this way.

I knew Arianna was the type of person who never did anything unless it was challenging to her. We all agreed that it would be good to give her a test, which she accepted. If I simply offered her money, she wouldn't take it. I mapped everything out flawlessly, and Allison ensured any and all complications were taken care of—just as I instructed. Most people, especially women, were appreciative of the lengths I went to. But just then, she threw it in my face.

If I learned anything about Arianna tonight, it's that she doesn't like to be controlled. I clearly miscalculated on this one. But I didn't miscalculate who she is. Meeting her in person confirmed everything I suspected—to my relief and fear. Her aura is pure Tentyrian. My body recognized it as soon as she entered the room. She must also possess a psychic skill. Otherwise, how would she know about Ridgefield? I wonder if she found anything about the Trebuchet connection . . . Regardless, in the files I gave her, I ensured there was no indication that the deal was anything but flawless. For her to find out what she did about Ridgefield would have been virtually impossible without telepathic powers. If I had to put my money on it, I would say she is a descendent of Daria. I wonder how Aristos will react.

We knew that the Luminary descendents were out there. But after the massacre, it became impossible to find them. Wherever the Guardians took the children was beyond our reach. We had also considered it possible that the escape wasn't successful and they all perished. For two years straight, we searched every day with no leads. Since then, we've continued to scour the globe and our network in search of them. With the exception of the Dark Coven (our moniker for those who betrayed us), we—Aristos, Evander, and I—could find no one else of Tentyrian descent. The Covens had been methodically eliminated. If it weren't for Evander saving Aristos when he did, I'd likely be alone.

When Daria placed the book in my hand, I knew what I had to do. But by the time I arrived to help evacuate everyone from the infirmary, it was incinerated, courtesy of Aglaia and Asia. Evander had only split seconds to shift out. When the explosion hit the infirmary, he was standing over Aristos. Narcissa died just minutes before. As Evander looked up from his ministrations and saw the flames rolling toward him, he reacted instinctually and took Aristos with him to the island.

It was there I found them. Aristos remained unconscious, while Evander prayed on his knees. Picking up the pieces from that day took years, even decades. To this day, we still carry the memories of the slaughter. I haven't had a peaceful night of sleep since.

After I discovered there was no one to save from the infirmary, I went to lock down the Sanctum. I hoped that Stavros, Calix, Aglaia, and Asia were still inside. However, the odds were once again not in our favor. We returned to the Sanctum two years later to bury the dead. Our safe haven's energy shut down the moment I turned the key, and it became impossible to enter or exit. Any survivors could have subsisted for a couple of months, but two years would have been impossible. Aristos wanted to return immediately. But we determined that if the Dark Coven was still inside, we'd let them rot. Those who were loyal to us were all dead. There was no one to rescue inside, so in the interim we focused on finding the Luminary progeny.

On the day we reopened the Sanctum, the stench of death was overwhelming. Air hadn't circulated inside in two years. We searched everywhere for Stavros, Calix, and the Twins amongst the decomposing bodies. But we couldn't find them. They had escaped. We gathered the pile of corpses from the courtyard and those scattered throughout the complex and burned them in a mass pyre on the side of the mountain. Since so many of our people had been burned alive with such intensity, what was left was just ash. To honor them, we collected all the ash and released it into the Arctic wind. It was a perverse feeling, holding what was left of our friends and families in our hands.

I remember snow was falling heavily that day. Aristos and I refused to sing or pray. Our faith was gone. Evander offered up prayers to the gods on our behalf. While Aristos' physical wounds healed, leaving only the scars on his face, his emotional wounds never got better. His easygoing attitude was replaced with vengeance for Daria, Darrius, and all of our people.

Evander, in contrast, reached a level of acceptance despite losing his beloved Zoe and son Galen. He believed he survived for a reason. While Aristos is set on revenge, Evander's faith in something higher has been his constant companion. For me, I'm driven by honor and duty. I made a pledge to Hathor and the Luminaries. I intend to keep it.

With the resources we've gathered over the last two thousand years, Evander, Aristos, and I have been able to build the Tentyrian

Brotherhood. Our purpose is threefold: kill the Dark Coven, find the Luminaries, and stop the Event. Today, we are one step closer to achieving all three of these goals, which are all interconnected.

Together, we have eliminated hundreds of the blood-hungry creatures that the Dark Coven has created to carry out their dirty work. We call them "Subordinates" because they are little more than animals that do anything and everything the Dark Coven asks. The difference between the Subordinates and Tentyrians, or even the humans we have turned and brought into the Brotherhood, is that they have virtually no control over their thirst.

The decision to create the Brotherhood was a difficult but necessary one. We are now a Brotherhood of fifty-three, with several loyal humans like Robert, Satish, and Samson who help run our businesses while we track the Dark Coven and search for the next generation of Luminaries.

To this day, we have yet to find and kill Stavros, Calix, and Aglaia. We know Asia died at some point during World War II. The Dark Coven continues to evade us, as they operate in great secrecy and hide behind complex layers of bureaucracy and Subordinates. Fortunately, we are hot on their trail. The Brotherhood is a team of soldiers and business strategists, constantly hunting the Dark Coven and their money trail. We intend to take them down one Subordinate and business deal at a time.

One of our biggest breakthroughs came about five years ago when we identified Trebuchet Global, an international arms dealer, as the brainchild of the Dark Coven. Within the last year or so, Trebuchet has also branched out into pharmaceuticals. Their relationships with political figures and governments run deep, making it all that more difficult to destroy them. But the day of reckoning is near.

What makes what we do so difficult is the amount of damage control required. The Dark Coven intentionally creates Subordinates not only to carry out their plans, but also to create mayhem. As a result, we spend an incredible amount of manpower and time hunting them and eliminating reports of vampiric activity. Protecting our existence is still of the utmost importance. Sometimes, the clusters or one-off Subordinates we find are just a ruse. But, if we get lucky, they lead us to a goldmine like Trebuchet.

Until we found Arianna, it appeared that all who carried the original Tentyrian bloodline—except for me, Aristos, Evander, and the Dark Coven, of course—had vanished. We examined Arianna's lineage, or what we could find of it, very closely. No one displayed any

Tentyrian markers, except for her. Evander theorized that somehow our genetic code had gone dormant but reawakened and manifested itself in Arianna. This means the other Luminary descendants could be alive, but their Tentyrian genes haven't yet activated. Hathor's vision of four Luminaries in the future is coming true. Unfortunately, I managed to screw it up already. Damn it.

I reach into my pocket and pull out my iPhone. I call Aristos. He answers with his characteristic rough tone. Any levity in Aristos died the day that Daria was murdered and his son disappeared. Since then, the happiest I ever saw him was in battle.

"Brother, we were right. She's one of us," I say.

"Good."

"She not only looks just like Daria, but I think she has a psychic ability." I hear Aristos suck in his breath. If Arianna is his lineage, it could be life changing for him. He will be reclaiming part of his family.

"What is she like?" he asks in a strained voice.

"She despises me and she refused the job."

"Shit, Maximos!" Aristos says in frustration. He switches into strategy mode. "It's time we change tactics. You've done everything to ease her into this—but time is running out. The choice is no longer hers. The Dark Coven is going to find her unless we extract her. And pretty soon, she's going to be completely helpless."

"You're right. I thought I could earn her trust if she joined us voluntarily. What does Evander think?"

"If I can pull him out of the lab, I'll ask."

Ever since we provided Evander with some of Arianna's DNA from a hairbrush we took, he hasn't left the sterile room filled with test tubes and equipment. Evander managed to find wonderment in the world through science. To him, the beauty and complexity of science was another testament to a higher power. As our resident doctor and expert on all things medically and genetically related, Evander successfully unlocked several hundred years ago what separates Tentyrians from humans.

Our unusually wide neural bridge promotes extensive brain activity and growth—75 percent more compared to humans. Our hearts also pump twenty times faster—making us stronger, faster, and capable of self-healing. The Tentyrian digestive system is one of our more unique qualities. After coming of age, our stomachs shrink to the size of a baby's fist. It's when our fangs also begin to show. The need for food virtually vanishes. Instead, our rapidly moving blood flow becomes powered by blood itself—a testament to our unique evolution but also our curse.

Since the massacre, there have been no young Tentyrians to analyze and observe the changes they undergo over time with modern technology. All we have are our own memories of what we encountered when we reached the ripe old age of twenty-five. Of course, Aristos and I, along with the rest of the Brotherhood, are Evander's constant guinea pigs. But our blood and DNA are old news—in more ways than one. Our cells don't age. Strengthened by the constant replenishment of blood, our cellular makeup is the equivalent of the fountain of youth. Provided that we feed regularly and avoid deathly injury, we can live forever.

Living forever is not all that it's cracked up to be, especially when you are alone. Although I have the Brotherhood, it's not the same as a family, which is what my Coven was to me. Back when Tentyris was in its golden age, I always planned on marrying and having children, but it was something I just didn't get around to. I enjoyed the company of human and Tentyrian women alike—maybe too much so. But I had so many years ahead of me. Or so I thought. Settling on one commitment just wasn't in me. Narcissa called me the "perpetual bachelor." To this day, thinking of her and all of my people makes my heart ache.

When everyone was killed, everything changed. The responsibility of ensuring that I would be there when it came time to reunite the Luminaries and prevent the Event became my top priority. I could find room in my life for a lover, but a girlfriend, much less a wife, was too much. Seeing firsthand how deeply the loss of a partner imprinted itself on the heart as it did for Aristos made me avoid love at all costs. And besides, my life would only stay the same while my mate's would progress. To hold someone back from experiencing the joys of life and changing with her would be to force my own immortality on her. And I won't do that to a woman.

I admit, after our families and friends were taken from us, Aristos and I briefly contemplated taking our own lives. But Evander persuaded us against it. The selfishness of the act outweighed the relief it would bring. We have a duty to do, and we owe it to Hathor and all of the dead Tentyrians to see it through. We long for the time when we are able to close the Book of Hathor and our task will be done. However, that day is not yet guaranteed. Getting to Arianna is the top priority, right now. She is the one ray of light in the grim future we face.

CHAPTER 10:
RUNNING

2010 AD, JULY
NEW YORK, NEW YORK / NEW CANAAN, CONNECTICUT

The nerve of that man! Just as arrogant as I thought. Who did he think he was? I inadvertently slam the door of my apartment in frustration. The jarring noise is a jolt I need. I'm overreacting. There is just something about him that has gotten under my skin. Seeing him for the first time was like being struck by lightning. I felt hot and shaky all over. It was a miracle I was even able to make my way toward him in that ballroom. I remember the feelings of anticipation I had reaching a fevered pitch when I saw him.

He was standing away from the crowd, looking relaxed and debonair in his element, undoubtedly relishing in his success while he casually sipped his wine. The black tuxedo he wore fit him perfectly, accentuating his muscular and almost-too-tall build. I've always been considered tall, but Maximos Vasilliadis' stature—he had to have been nearly seven feet tall—made me feel unusually small. His midnight black hair was meticulously combed and cropped in the traditional style favored by finance guys. But what really differentiated him from all of the men I've met, and ever known for that matter, were his eyes.

They were an electric midnight blue that practically shocked me when they connected with mine. If it wasn't enough that I felt like I was being scrutinized by a Greek god, the baritone of his voice threatened to lull me into submission. The man was devastatingly handsome. The sharp angles of his cheekbones and nose gave him a severe look, but that severity exuded such power. No wonder he was successful. I remember my blood was practically humming. Miraculously, I had managed to snap myself back to reality, reminding myself it was about business and hiring me was just another deal.

It's about business, I'm still telling myself now. So why was I so unprofessional? I acted like a petulant child and stormed out of the party. I close the white linen curtains of my living room to block out the pouting reflection of myself in the windows. If I'm going to be sullen, I'll do it alone. I slip off my skirt and let it pool around my ankles. The smooth silk sliding down my skin feels good. It makes me wonder what his hands would feel like. Jesus. I was going to take a hot bath, but maybe a cold shower would be better.

I head toward my oasis, discarding the rest of my clothing in the process. I'll put it all away before bed, but right now it feels good to be careless and leave it on the floor. Look at me, reckless Arianna. My bathroom is always an excellent antidote to a bad mood. But the floor mosaic of pearly white penny rounds and the fresh white hydrangea on my pedestal sink do nothing for me tonight. I let the water from the rain showerhead beat down against my back. I wish I could do this night over.

But if I did it over, I still don't know if I'd take the job. A challenge is one thing, but drastic change is another. Maybe that was my problem. I was afraid of giving up what I was used to—my careful routines and the life I had built for myself. In a period of twelve hours, Leo completely uprooted me and expected me to say how high when they asked me to jump. I'm not a jumper, and if I'm going to take a chance, I need to know all of the risks as well as the rewards. Jumping into things gets you hurt; I know that firsthand. Maximos Vasilliadis may as well have "RISK" stamped on his forehead.

He called me naïve. But it wasn't naïveté; it was a refusal to lose control. In the half hour I spent with Maximos tonight, I felt like I was barely able to keep it together. My reaction to him was an overreaction because for the first time in a long time, I didn't know what I wanted to do or what I should do. And why hadn't I used my gift? I intended to, but when his hand touched mine, everything I planned to say and do disappeared. Instead, I was careless with my words and subconsciously—or maybe consciously?—ruined the Leo opportunity. The good news is, it is done and I won't have to see him again. I scrub my face vigorously. Tomorrow will be a new day.

I wrap myself in a fluffy towel and put on my robe. The waffle cotton folds are comforting. Speaking of which, a comforting voice sounds good about now, and so would a cheesesteak. I opt to just call Laura and Raad instead of delivery. It's late, but both of them are night owls.

To no surprise, I get Laura's voicemail. She is probably out with her latest boy toy. I leave a message: "Hey girl, it's me. Sorry I bailed on you tonight. I know, I'm a jerk. Some interesting developments, though. I can't wait to give you the scoop. I met the founder of Leo tonight and need some advice. He's hot all right, but a real asshole. Anyway, call me. We still need to finalize plans for Monday night."

Raad on the other hand picks up on the second ring. I imagine him sitting in his leather Eames chair, his reading glasses on, Beau and Luna by his feet. It's too hot for a fire, but maybe he's opened the sliding glass doors and is enjoying the summer night.

"Ari! What a wonderful surprise," he says excitedly as soon as he picks up.

"How did you know it was me?" I ask.

"Intuition, my dear."

"You finally got caller ID, didn't you?"

"Maybe." I can hear him smiling.

"So what's going on? You rarely ever call this late. Is everything okay?"

"Yep. I just wanted to say hi. I was thinking of taking the day off tomorrow and visiting for the weekend." I didn't really know I was thinking about visiting, but it just came out. Said aloud, it sounded like a great idea.

"You never take the day off. And you told me you were going to have to work this weekend. Are you sure everything is okay?"

"I just need a long weekend and to get out of this hot city. That's all. I'll take the train out tomorrow. Can you pick me up at the station?"

"Of course—just let me know what time."

"11:15?"

"Perfect. This is great timing. I thought we were going to have to wait to celebrate your birthday until next weekend. Now we can do it Saturday night! Also, I started to clean out the attic earlier this week. You can help me finish." I groan inwardly.

"Great, I'll be sure to dress for the job. And a Saturday night birthday dinner sounds perfect. See you tomorrow."

"Sleep well, but make sure you meditate before bed," he reminds me.

"I will," I assure.

I put my phone in its charger and tidy up my mess. Or what is a perceived mess to me. My apartment is immaculate, but in keeping it that way religiously, if one thing is ever out of place it drives me insane. Like my hairbrush; I can't find it anywhere and I've turned the apartment completely upside down twice looking for it. It's a liability of living alone—making yourself crazy. At least I don't have cats. Dogs are more my speed.

It is going to be great to see Beau tomorrow. I wasn't able to go for a visit last weekend, and I'm sure he is missing me. When I moved to New York, I did a trial period with Beau in the apartment. He did fine, but he just wasn't happy without Luna. I can't deny him anything, so he went back to our old arrangement of living with Raad—who loves him as much as I do.

It's almost midnight and I want to put this day past me. I take an oversized down pillow in blue ikat from the tufted sofa and place it on the floor. Perching myself on top with legs crisscross, I start to slow my breathing and clear my mind. I rebuild the walls around me that have weakened. I lay the bricks, one by one. I fill myself with white, clean space and go to the white room in my mind. No frustration, no upset. Just white, clean space.

But I see Maximos. His chiseled face fills my white space. Instead of calm, my pulse quickens. That's enough for tonight. I put the pillow back and shut the lights off.

As I slip underneath the covers, he is still in my head. I sleep fitfully, tossing and turning. Even in my dreams I can't stop thinking about him. He really did have some nerve.

I wake up at 4:30 and go for my morning run. It feels good to sweat and make my lungs burn, with loud techno music drowning out my thoughts. The West Side Highway path is mostly empty. People are still in bed with their spouses and lovers, whereas I awoke with my BlackBerry next to me.

When I get home, I quickly shower and spend two hours responding to e-mail. I tell Sarah to clear my schedule again—I'm still not feeling well. I opt for steak and eggs for breakfast (my favorite) and make sure that the steak is extra rare. The garlic butter sauce on top melts right into the steak juice. Daniel Boulud would be proud. My mother would be appalled.

I pack my Louis Vuitton duffle and don a pair of worn-in jeans. It's been forever since I've worn them, but I like their soft feeling and even the tears. Today, I want to relax. I put on a simple white scoop-neck T, my tan leather ballet flats, and a pair of pearl earrings. I may be covered in attic dust by the end of the day, but I can't forgo all jewelry. After running through my mental checklist ensuring everything is tidy, I lock the apartment and head out. I decide to pick up dessert and stop at Magnolia Bakery.

Three chocolates, three vanillas, and an iced green tea to go later, I try to hail a cab to Grand Central. Without one in sight, I end up walking. Fortunately, I've given myself plenty of time. After a block, a weird feeling starts to creep up on me. I sense I'm being followed. Off and on for the last couple of months, I've definitely had moments that felt like someone was watching me. I'm probably becoming paranoid. But this time, it feels different . . . it's ominous.

I stop. Pretending to balance the cupcakes and reach into my purse for my sunglasses, I look behind me. I notice that the same man who was behind me in line at the bakery is now walking a short distance away. It's probably a coincidence.

When I get to the station I check the arrival board. The 9:07 is on time and on track 26. I still can't shake the feeling of being watched. So I decide to walk to track 25 and pretend to wait. If I am really being followed, I don't want him to know where I'm going. He's probably a pervert. At 9:06 I run to track 26 and get on right before the doors close. Fortunately, I manage to find a row with an empty seat in the middle, separating me from another train passenger who is busily reading his paper. I don't see the cupcake man. But again, I'm probably just being paranoid . . . I did barely sleep.

I close my eyes and put in my earbuds, turning on my classical mix. "Don't be naïve, Arianna," I hear him say. Damn it. I need to talk this out with Raad; he always gives the best advice. Maybe he has a new herbal infusion that will help clear my head. Today wasn't the new day I thought it would be. For now, I let my thoughts take me where they want—to Maximos.

I wonder how he manages to look so good. Not a wrinkle or extra ounce of fat. Rather than making his athletic build look awkward, his tux last night enhanced it. The man was born to wear formal wear. He should be in his mid-thirties but he looks much closer to my age. I try to imagine him getting Botox or eating vegetarian food. No, not him. He is a man's man through and through. He probably has a bevy of bimbos. The good-looking ones always do.

We arrive at the New Canaan platform on time. Raad is waiting for me with Beau and Luna pulling on their leashes and barking like psychotic animals. As much as Raad and I are animal lovers, we aren't disciplinarians at all. Beau and Luna are as friendly as can be, but they rule us rather than the other way around. We talked about taking them to obedience school, but of course we never followed through. Raad gives me a big bear hug, and I'm showered with sloppy kisses by the dogs. We pile into Raad's car, and with the windows rolled down, the dogs continue to bark at the passing scenery. It makes it difficult to have a conversation. But this is what I'm used to, and it's bliss to my ears.

As we drive along the winding roads out of town, I think about my parents. Coming back to my hometown, but never actually going home to the house I grew up in, is a strange notion. I used to get nervous I would somehow see them in passing, whether it was on the sidewalk on Main Street or driving to the farmer's market. But in the past five years, we haven't had a chance meeting once. Mostly it's because we stay at Raad's house or go to the park, two places my parents would never go. But they know I come back—this town is simply too small. Plus, in the last few years, I've run into several of their friends. I wonder what they think of when they think of me. Do they even miss me?

When I told Raad what happened with Charles, he was the shoulder I cried on. He suggested that I talk to someone professionally, aside from him. He worried that my relationship with my parents had become so convoluted and damaged that I would always harbor resentment toward them. And he was right; I still am angry. But I don't want to get over it. I told Raad that going to the spa was plenty enough therapy. He never brought it up again.

We arrive at the house, and I unpack in the guest room, which for all intents and purposes is my room. Raad let me decorate it, along with the whole cottage. The summer after my freshman year, I scoured country consignment and antique shops to make over what he called home. The little cottage on the Silvermine River had practically no furniture, and Raad saw nothing wrong with it. The man would live like a Spartan if I didn't intervene. He let me do it because he wanted to appease me and get me to stop shoving pictures from design magazines in his face. But I know he appreciates it. When I took a colorful throw, made by hand by his late wife Seda, and framed it in a shadow box to hang in the living room, I saw tears in his eyes.

We decide to start tackling the attic right away. He's already made significant progress, and there are less than ten boxes to sort through.

"Wow, I can't believe you actually started to clean this place up," I say in surprise.

"I know. It looks like you've finally gotten your wish. Maybe you can do something with the extra space?" answers Raad.

"You mean like a decorating project? Really? You are voluntarily asking me to decorate?" I'm now suspicious. "But you never wanted me to do anything up here before. What's changed?"

Raad looks at me sheepishly. "I was thinking of putting it on the market."

"What! You want to move? Why? You can't. This is your home!"

"It's just something I was thinking about. Maybe moving to the beach . . ."

"But where? Florida? California? Outside the US? There are a lot of beaches." My voice is panicked as I spit out my questions rapid fire.

"Ari, my dear, I was just thinking of moving over to Darien or Westport. It wouldn't be any farther for you to come visit. I don't need all this space, and I think Beau and Luna would love the ocean." I breathe a sigh of relief.

"Do you want me to have a heart attack?"

"I didn't think you were going to get so worked up." Raad looks concerned. He puts a comforting hand on my shoulder. "Are you sure you are all right? You seem apprehensive."

"You're right, I'm not being myself. I had this weird and terrible interview yesterday and I don't know . . . I'm just unsettled."

"Then let's pause on the sorting and I'll make you some tea."

"That would be great," I say appreciatively. "If you have any magic potions to stick in there—please feel free."

We head down the creaking staircase and into the kitchen. Raad makes my favorite, and we sit in the little garden that the kitchen opens on to. The sun shines on my face, relaxing me as I sip the warm beverage from my Adirondack chair. Coming out here is so much better than the Hamptons. It's quiet, peaceful, and without the pretentiousness of the Manhattan crowd. But then again, how pretentious could it be out here? It's just me, Raad, and the dogs.

"I'm going to miss this place if you sell it," I say.

"I know. I will too." Raad's voice is equally wistful. "But things can change, Ari, for the better." I look at him skeptically.

"Tell me about this interview," he asks. I lay out my story as Raad listens patiently.

"So that's what happened . . . I handled it completely wrong," I say, frustrated.

"Well to be fair, you were expressing what you felt at the time."

"I was, but that feeling was and still is utter confusion."

"Do you want my opinion, Ari?"

"Of course."

"It sounds like you are attracted to this man, and it sounds like you want the job, but . . ."

"Yes, there is always a but . . ."

"But you are scared of what will happen if you admit that attraction or take the opportunity—which represents everything you hate."

"What do I hate?"

"Taking a chance."

He nailed it. He always does, and he doesn't read minds like me. I let out a sigh.

"It's too late, though. The offer expired."

"Something tells me that if they were pursuing you that hard, they will make an exception if you change your mind."

"Maybe." I'm doubtful.

"Ari, you are responsible for getting what you want out of life. But if you fight change, you will stagnate." I know he's right.

"I don't mean to pry where I'm not wanted, but you do realize you haven't had a relationship in four years?"

"I have plenty of time, though. I'm only twenty-four. And that's not true, I go out on dates."

"Yes you do. But they are all first dates only. Right?"

"Yes. I just haven't met anyone I want to go on a second with."

"Okay. And when are all of your first dates?"

"Thursdays."

"And where do you go to dinner—every time?"

"Locanda Verde."

"And do you let him pick you up?"

"No, I meet him there."

"Do we see a pattern here, Ari?"

"Yes, I get your point. I know it's weird and freakishly routine. But I think of it like a science experiment. If I am going to test if a relationship can go somewhere, then I need to control for certain things . . . like when, where, and how the date takes place." Raad doesn't say anything. He just sips his tea and suns his face. "I've been really happy with the way things are. I like my job, I like my friends, and I like my life." He opens one eye and squints at me. "Fine. I'm going to call Leo on Monday and see if the job is still available." He smiles. Raad always manages to get me to the place where I need to be. "Do you want a cupcake? I brought them for tonight, but I could use a pick-me-up."

"Absolutely."

"Stay right there. I'll grab them."

I bring out the cupcakes on a blue and white Chinese platter. Like two naughty kids, we spoil our lunch.

"So I found something when I was cleaning out the attic," Raad says, brushing the crumbs off his wrinkled khakis. The man doesn't iron and certainly doesn't make use of the one I bought him. I should call the maid and ask her to do his ironing; he'll never remind her. Mental note, check.

"And what's that?"

"I'm not sure exactly, but it looks like a journal."

"Can't you read it?"

"No, that's the problem. The text is pretty faded and the paper is crumbling in some places. I didn't recognize the language, and I didn't want to touch it any more than I did; otherwise I'll ruin it."

"It sounds really old. Can I see it?"

"It's with a friend of mine back at Yale—you remember Professor Sorrell. He is an expert on languages, and I asked him if he could translate it."

"Well that's exciting! A Raad relic," I say thoughtfully.

"It was in a trunk that actually belonged to my father, buried at the bottom. I don't know why I didn't know of it before. Anyway, Sorrell said he would get back to me next week when he had a chance to look at it."

"Do you think there is anything more in the attic like it?"

"Probably not. I'm pretty sure everything else up there is Seda's clothes." Sadness washes over his face. I place my hand on his.

"Do you still miss her?" I ask.

"Every day. She was the love of my life. One day, I hope you will find that same happiness."

"You know I can go through those boxes myself. Do you want me to take the clothes over to the Salvation Army?"

"I can help. It's not going to make me cry, I promise," he says with a wink.

"I've never even seen you cry."

"You never watched Titanic with me, or The Blair Witch Project."

We sit in companionable silence enjoying the sun. My stomach is starting to cramp with all the sugar I just shoved into my body.

"I made dinner reservations tomorrow night at Bonne Nuit. I was thinking tonight we could grill," Raad says.

"Sounds great. In that case, I should probably take a run and work off these calories. Do you want to come?"

"Not on this stomach. But why don't you go ahead and take Beau? Luna's arthritis has been bothering her, so leave her here."

"Okay. I'll be back in a couple of hours."

I give him a quick kiss on the cheek and run inside to change. We'll clean the attic later. It really is a beautiful day, and we should enjoy it while it lasts. I'm pretty sure I saw something in the weather report about late afternoon showers. Beau and Luna start jumping up and down as they see me rifling through the leash basket by the door. "Now Luna, I can't take you but I'll give you a biscuit instead." I reward both dogs with treats and lead Luna outside to sit with Raad while I take Beau for our run.

We start with a fast-paced walk on the gravel road. I notice Beau has gotten a bit chunky, so this will be good for him. Picking up the pace, we start to jog and veer onto the running trail that goes into the woods. This is one of my favorite routes. It's hot, but the trees offer shade as we run through. After an hour, Beau gets fatigued. I also start to hear the rumblings of thunder. Good, some rain will help wipe this summer humidity away. Our jog winds back to a walk so we can cool down. Raindrops start to patter on my head as they sneak between the trees.

A bolt of lightning streaks across the sky, and heavy rain clouds come rolling in. This looks more like an oncoming downpour rather than a few showers. Beau makes a whining sound. We need to sprint home to avoid getting soaked. "Come on, boy, come on," I encourage Beau as he runs alongside. He slows and whines again. Beau normally isn't afraid of thunderstorms. Maybe Luna is making him soft.

"Come on, boy, we're almost home. You can do it." The sky is now dark gray. You wouldn't believe the sun was shining just minutes earlier. Looks like the weather is as volatile as my temper. With the house now in sight, I notice the front door is open. That's strange. It was closed when I left, and hardly anyone comes to visit down the road. Maybe a neighbor needed a cup of sugar. Did Raad even have sugar?

My sneakers are now caked with mud from the road. I kick them off and leave them outside on the front porch so I don't track mud in the house. The rain starts to come down in sheets. I pad inside and take off Beau's leash. He starts whining again and circles around me. "It's okay, boy, it's okay." I run my hand through his fur, which is standing on end. "Let's get you a treat." I'm probably the one making him fat.

"I'm home!" I yell as I make my way toward the kitchen. "I was thinking I could make an early dinner since we skipped lunch. You in the mood for burgers?" No answer. "Hello, Raad, Luna? Burger time . . ." No answer. The car was definitely still in the driveway when I came back, so they didn't go to run an errand. Were they in the back? In the rain? I look through the window and don't see them. "Come on guys," I yell again.

I dash up the stairs and check the attic, the four bedrooms, and three bathrooms. Nothing. I do a sweep of the downstairs from Raad's study to the living room and even the kitchen pantry. Still nothing. I check the basement and see only garden tools. Beau is now lying on the floor whining. I run out to the backyard in my socks. They aren't anywhere. I call their names again. Maybe they really went to the neighbors? It's about two miles down the road, though. Is there a note somewhere?

I go back inside and take my filthy socks off. I'm dripping water everywhere and working myself into a panic for no reason, I tell myself. I look on the kitchen countertops, the fridge, and the front hall table for a note but see nothing. I go back into Raad's study; also no note. But I notice his normally organized papers are a mess. The articles and health periodicals, which he keeps in meticulous stacks, are toppled over. I didn't notice it when I first looked for Raad in the office. Upon closer inspection, his papers look rifled through. I'm in full panic mode now. I grab my phone. No missed calls. Raad's home answering machine shows a red zero. I'm going to the neighbors.

"Come on, boy, we're going for a car ride." Beau whines in response. He knows something isn't right, and his strange behavior says it all. We run to the car and he gets in the passenger seat. We head over to the neighbors driving fifty miles per hour. We're there in two minutes. I run to the front door and bang on it like a crazy woman. I realize I have no umbrella and no coat, socks, or shoes on.

A kind-looking woman opens the door. "My dears, I was worried . . ." she starts to say. "Oh, I'm sorry, I thought you were those little Girl Scouts selling cookies who came by earlier. I was worried they were going to get caught in the rain." I think the woman's name is Mrs. Lansing.

"Hi, I'm so sorry to bother you, but I'm looking for my friend Dr.

Aman Raad. Have you seen him or his dog Luna?"

"Oh, Dr. Raad, of course—you're Arianna, aren't you?"

"Yes, ma'am, I am. Have you seen them?"

"No I haven't. Is Luna lost? I know she and that other dog are rather rambunctious."

"I don't think she's run away. But I can't seem to find them. You're sure you haven't seen them?"

"Yes, I'm sure," she says, confused.

"Have any cars come down the road in the last two hours?"

"I don't know. I haven't exactly been watching . . ." I can tell I'm alarming Mrs. Lansing.

"Thanks very much," I call to her as I leave her staring after me inquisitively. I dash back to the car. Maybe they're back already. Maybe they went for a walk in the woods. And here I am freaking out. Raad is just going to laugh at me and tell me to go do some tai chi to center my unbalanced self.

Within minutes we're back. I call again throughout the house, but still no answer. Still a red zero on the machine. I decide to take Beau into the woods for one last look. If we can't find them, I'll call the police. I let Beau run free as I call for Raad and whistle for Luna. The woods go straight back for about three miles until they back into someone's lawn. I won't be able to cover all the square acreage, but if they're out here I have a good chance of finding them. Could Raad have had a heart attack? He is getting older . . .

Beau starts barking, and it's not his usual, curious bark. It's strained and mixed in with whining. I run toward him, barely able to see him through the sheets of rain coming down. It's Luna, collapsed on the forest floor. I put my ear to her chest. It's not moving, and I can't hear a heartbeat. I wipe the mud from her muzzle and cradle her head. My hand comes away with blood. It is seeping from the left side of her skull. I can't believe what I'm seeing. It looks like a bullet hole.

"Oh my God. Oh my God! Raad, Raad! Are you out here?" I scream. Beau circles around Luna's body and me and licks her face in an attempt to will her back to life. What does this mean for Raad? And why would someone take him? Or kill Luna? Was his body stashed here in the woods too? Aside from his files being rummaged through, it didn't look like a robbery had taken place. I leave Luna. I can't carry her back to the house easily, and I need to call 911 immediately.

For a split second I consider the intruder may still be lurking inside. But I've been in the house twice and it was fine. Beau is on my heels and will sense if something is amiss. I should have trusted him when he was whining on our run. He sensed his friends were in trouble. But I didn't. What did that say about me?

I shove open the sliding glass door and run to the phone. But before I reach it, I slip on the wood floor that is now soaked with puddles I've left from traipsing in and out. My head bangs the floor hard as I land flat on my back. The wind is knocked out of me but my adrenaline is pumping hard. I start to get up. I'm a bit dazed and still trying to catch my breath when behind me I hear a growl. I turn quickly. That's when I see him. The next thing I know his arms are around me. Sweet–smelling fabric is shoved in front of my face. I inadvertently inhale between screams. Why? is my last thought before I pass out.

CHAPTER 11:
LIABILITY

2010 AD, JULY
NEW YORK, NEW YORK / AMBROSINE ISLAND, IONIAN SEA

My head is achy, and so is my back. I pull my duvet up closer
to me; its cool folds are soothing against my protesting
muscles. Thoughts of getting the flu briefly flicker through
my mind. I pull the covers off and fumble for the bedside lamp. I usually never feel this disoriented. I must be coming down with something. I turn the light on but can't find my BlackBerry, which I use for
my clock. Throwing off the sheets in a flurry, I check the bed, behind
it, and under it.

What the hell? Maybe I left it in my purse in the front hall? That's
when I notice what I'm wearing. Running shorts and my "No one likes
a vegetarian" T-shirt. I never would wear this to bed. I look at myself in
front of the starburst mirror above my dresser. My hair is a mess, and is
that dirt smudged on my cheek? The room around me starts spinning.
I grab the dresser for support and put my head between my legs. Deep
breaths, just take deep breaths.

Bile is rising in my throat. My forehead is beading with sweat. But
it's not my physical condition that worries me. It's the memories that
begin to come back. Cupcakes, the attic, running, Luna's blood, more
running, Maximos. I have to call the police. I throw open my bedroom
door. But before I take a step forward to get to the kitchen phone—I see
two men in my living room. They are dressed all in black with closely
cropped hair. Not to mention they are huge. With my not-so-quiet

yanking of the door, they turn toward me.

"She's awake," one of the military-grade men says.

"Clearly," responds the other.

They start to walk slowly toward me. I must look like a deer caught in the headlights. I immediately slam the door shut and lock it. With all of my strength, I manage to push the dresser in front of the door. I hear knocking. My pulse is pounding so loud it's hard to concentrate and understand the voices on the other side.

"Ms. Parker, I know this is confusing and you are probably scared, but we aren't here to hurt you." Who were they kidding?

"I've already called the police!" I yell. "They are on their way. You better get out of here now!" No response. Did they know I was bluffing? What feels like hours tick by . . . I can't tell if they are leaving or not. I swallow continuously to keep from throwing up. I silently climb on top of the dresser and put my ear to the door. I hear shuffling outside.

"Get Max up here now. He'll know how to handle this. She wasn't supposed to wake up so soon. We should have had another hour."

"At least she can't get out of there. I checked," I hear the other man say.

Maximos Vasilliadis. He was the one behind this. He was the one who took me from Raad's house. I remember after I slipped trying to get to the phone, I had turned to find him standing there. We briefly grappled, but he put something over my mouth. That bastard drugged me. No wonder my mouth tastes like bad grapefruit. But why? And why did he bring me to my own apartment? Behind that suave façade, was he insane? And most importantly, why hurt Luna and Raad? I have all questions and no answers.

I need to get out of here now. But how? This is a modern condominium building, and it's not like there is a convenient fire escape outside. I'm also twenty-five stories up. Of my wall of windows in the bedroom, only the left side slides open about half a foot wide. I'm not sure if I can even fit my body through it. I press my face to the glass and look out the window. If I position myself right, I may be able to fling myself down and over to the balcony of the resident below me. If I land successfully, I might break a few bones. If I miss, I'll die. I don't know what to do . . . I hear more knocking on the door.

"Ms. Parker, please open the door. We are trying to help you." What is it going to be, broken bones or death? Or should I wait until they break down the door and try to overtake them? I know I don't stand a chance against two well-muscled men who are over six feet. There isn't much of a choice after all. I slide open the window and suck in my breath. The night air kisses my face, and the metal window frame feels cool against my hands and bare feet. I start to inch the left side of my body through. It's a tight fit. I suck in harder as the window frame scrapes against me.

All of a sudden, vice-like hands grab my right arm and leg and pull me inside with one swift yank. I hit the floor hard. Fortunately, the carpet and the person who pulled me cushion my fall. Unfortunately, it's Maximos. And I'm lying on his chest. I fight against him and scream. His hand clamps down on my mouth.

"None of that," he commands. "Otherwise we are going to have to do some explaining to the neighbors, and we don't have time." I bite down and can feel his flesh break. "Damn it, Arianna!" yells Maximos. He pulls his hand away but flips me over onto my back. His blood touches my tongue. But it doesn't taste metallic, like the times I've bitten the side of my mouth or had a nosebleed. It's different. Spicy, warm, arousing . . . delicious. My head swims with the heady flavor of his blood.

"Arianna, listen to me." Maximos brings his face close to mine. He is holding my wrists down. I can see where my fingernails have raked the side of his face. He is going to have some serious welts. Good. "We need to leave here. I know you are confused, but I promise I won't hurt you. Hale and Philip are finishing the sweep. Before we got here, someone else had already gone through your apartment—just like they did at Raad's house." I give him a vicious look.

"I did not hurt or take your friend. I promise. I'm here to help," he says. I close my eyes and focus on my breathing. I need to calm myself; otherwise it won't work. "Arianna?" Maximos asks, unsure if I'm falling unconscious. I calm my mind and push my energy out. His hands are on mine, which should make it easy. But rather than feeling myself drifting into him, it's like hitting a wall. I push again. No luck. There is only one other person who is able to do that. Raad. I open my eyes to find Maximos staring down at me with a slight smile. Bastard.

"I knew it," he says smugly. "I can feel you. Your power is still raw, but I know a mind tap when I feel one, matia mou."

"I don't know what you are talking about! Get off of me, now! The police are coming!" I scream, coming back to my senses.

"No they aren't. I'm only going to explain this to you once more. You are in danger. I'm here to protect you. I didn't hurt your friend. If I can save him, I will. This is what is going to happen . . ." Maximos' deep blue eyes stare into mine, and I see the dark orbs of his pupils dilate. "I'm going to get off you and you are going to pack a bag—calmly . . ." I can feel his own energy push against mine. It's cold and tingly. He is trying to get inside my head. I push back with all my strength. He laughs. "Well, it was worth a try. This is your choice. You pack your bag or I drug you again."

I'm unsure of what to do. But I know a threat when I hear one. It's unlikely my neighbors or the doorman will come to the rescue. The walls and floor are all soundproof. I have three men in my apartment. And Maximos clearly has a psychic ability. Not to mention he is probably unstable. My escape plan will need to be shelved.

"Fine, I'll do it. Get off of me!" I say vehemently.

Maximos gingerly removes his hands from my wrists and stands up. He eyes me suspiciously as I sit up from the floor, rubbing the circulation back into my hands. There is a throbbing ache. I will likely have bruises. Maximos looks contrite as he sees he's hurt my wrists.

"I'm sorry I grabbed you so hard, but you could have gotten yourself killed! What were you thinking?" He has the audacity to scold me?

"I'm not going to explain myself to you or your henchmen!" I assume the henchmen are "Hale and Philip" he referenced earlier. They must still be on the other side of the door. The still blocked door. How is that possible? "Wait, how did you get in here? The door is still locked!" I stand up quickly. My heart is beating a mile a minute, and I still have the taste of his blood in my mouth.

"I'll show you, if you pack," he says with an arched brow. "Five minutes, Arianna." Maximos strides over to the dresser and pushes it aside effortlessly. He opens the door to a grim-looking Hale and Philip. One of them looks incredibly familiar, but I can't place why.

"We're leaving in five," Maximos addresses them. They nod in unison.

"We found this, Max," says the henchman who I think I've seen before, as he hands over a black plastic disc no more than a quarter big.

"Thanks, Hale. Not a surprise. You deactivated it?" asks Maximos.

"Of course," responds Hale.

"Good. We'll have Aristos look at it back at the lab." Maximos turns toward me sternly. "Four minutes, Arianna. Philip, go with her to make sure she packs. I'm going to make a call." What was that disc?

"Miss, I'm very sorry we frightened you earlier," says Philip in an impeccably polite English tone. "Can I help you with your luggage?" Is this guy a bellhop?

I don't know what the hell is going on, but I manage to say the words, "Top shelf, closet." My mind is racing, but before I can organize my thoughts into a cohesive story, Philip arrives with my rolling suit-case. The next few minutes go by in slow motion. I open my dresser drawers and methodically fold T-shirts, underwear, and jeans into the suitcase. I don't even know where I'm going or for how long. But I don't want to ask. I figure the longer I draw this out the more time I'll have to gather my energy and think. It's not long before Maximos is back.

"You still aren't ready? Philip, what have you been doing?" Maximos asks impatiently.

"I didn't want to upset her," the Englishman responds defensively.

"That's the least of our worries." Maximos begins to open dresser drawers, reaching for handfuls of clothes and throwing them carelessly into the suitcase. He paces over to my closet, scoops up some shoes, and grabs a few things off the hangers. "Do you have toiletries you need?" he asks. He might as well be speaking another language. I still don't understand why this happening. And he is asking me if I need toiletries?

"Okay, well whatever, you won't need it. We are out of time," says Maximos. Philip zips up the suitcase, efficiently tucking in the loose pieces of fabric poking out of the bulging bag. Am I going on a one-way trip? Will I ever see anyone again? Laura, Raad, Beau? That thought helps snap me out of this surreal daydream.

"Where is my dog? He was at the house when you took me," I ask, as the power of speech begins to dawn on me.

"He is safe; in fact, he is where I'm taking you."

"And where is that?"

"You'll see, matia mou."

Kidnapping 101—your chance of survival plummets if you get moved to another location.

"I need to use the bathroom before we go," I say with feigned calm.

"Fine, hurry up. Philip, go with her," Maximos orders. A faint blush colors Philip's pale cheeks.

"I don't need an escort; plus there is nowhere for me to go," I respond defiantly.

Maximos' pocket vibrates. He answers in what sounds like Greek, the same language of the absurd pet name he's given me—matia mou. Distracted with answering his phone, he dismisses me with a wave of his hand. He probably treats everyone in his life like that, dismissing them when it's convenient for him. I've never met someone so arro-gant! As I walk out of the bedroom, I eye the front door that looks unguarded. This is my chance. I sprint to the right. But just as my hand reaches for the handle, the door opens to Hale. Foiled again.

"Hello, ma'am, pleased to meet you again." He grins cheekily and extends his hand. This time I look closer at him, absorbing his features. He is of medium height with a muscular build. His face is on the rounder side, and his hair is a fiery red. I saw that red hair yesterday poking up from a newspaper. He is the man who sat next to me on the train! I want to stamp my feet and scream. I can feel tears of frustration at the corners of my eyes.

"Enough is enough," I hear Maximos say. "You're becoming a liability." He grabs my hand and pulls me toward him. Maximos wraps his arms around me. My own arms are locked by my sides. My face is buried in his chest, undoubtedly making it wet with my tears that I know are coming down. I hope I ruin his shirt. I don't try to move because it's pointless.

"Philip, Hale. We're ready," Maximos says brusquely. He leans his head down and whispers in my ear, "I'm sorry, Arianna. Please don't cry. I only want to keep you safe." He kisses the top of my head. I sense that Philip and Hale have moved closer to us. They reach out to hold onto Maximos' shoulders. All of a sudden, the air grows cold, like the inside of a freezer, and I feel as if I'm spinning like in a teacup saucer ride at Disney. Yet another childhood dream never realized.

I'm so dizzy. So confused. I decide to give up—just for a bit. There is nothing I can do right now. The control my mind has been struggling to hold onto slips away like sand through fingertips. I let my legs buckle, and the ground beneath me disappears. I don't fall, though. I'm still held tight by warm arms. This must just be a dream.

A dream is what it feels like when I open my eyes to sunlight filtering through gauzy curtains that surround a canopy bed. It's warm, but I can feel a sea breeze, as if I'm outside by the ocean. I can even hear ocean waves crashing. What? I sit up. A white silk satin sheet slips down my skin. My naked skin. Oh no. This is definitely not my bed. Where are my clothes? I take quick stock of myself; no cuts or aches. Even my wrists are fine. And I'm clean, very clean. My skin tingles as if I've been thoroughly scrubbed.

I smell like—something flowery and spicy I can't quite put my finger on. My skin is soft and moisturized too. Normally when I wake up, my hair resembles a bird's nest. But touching my fingers to my head, I feel silky intricate braids. It's a disturbing thought to have no recollection of having been bathed or dressed. Or in this case, undressed. I also have no memory of how I got here. The last thing I recall was standing in my front hall. Maximos had his arms around me, the room started spinning . . .

I start to panic but try to remember that I'm unhurt. In fact, by most people's standards, I've likely been pampered. Even my nails have been buffed. I wrap the sheet about me like a toga and, pushing the canopy's curtains aside, I see that I am practically outside.

The bed is centered atop a travertine floor that is open on three sides. The fourth, which is behind the bed, has thick wooden doors that must lead elsewhere. Is this a house or a hotel? I can see the full-length shutter walls that roll on tracks have been pushed aside to give me this panoramic view. If I hadn't just been kidnapped and awoken naked, I'd think the view was breathtaking.

I can see that I'm on a cliff. About fifty yards in front of me, where the grass lawn and palm trees stop, there is a sharp drop about a mile down toward jagged rocks being swallowed by crashing waves. Beyond the cliff drop is sparkling ocean. Where is this place, and how did I get here?

Before I can even ponder my next move, the doors open behind me. I barely keep my gasp of surprise in check while I clutch my makeshift toga. A woman enters carrying a heavily laden tray with silver-domed tops.

"Good morning, Ms. Parker," she says sweetly with a Middle Eastern accent that reminds me of Raad's occasional lilt. She is wearing a turquoise sari that displays a tanned and firm stomach. Yet looking at her face, I figure she must be around sixty.

"Good morning," I say tentatively, looking into her warm brown eyes.

"I've brought you a wonderful breakfast. The master hopes you enjoy it," the woman says. She sets the tray down on the ottoman at the foot of the bed.

"And who is the master?" I ask cautiously.

"Mr. Vasilliadis, of course. Would you like your breakfast in bed?"

"No, thank you. Where is this place?"

"Well, how about at the table then?" The woman moves the tray to a small table accompanied by two bamboo chairs. She's obviously avoiding my question.

"Excuse me, ma'am, where am I?" The woman smiles at me

warmly.

"I'm Shashandra. And no need to call me ma'am. It makes me feel old." She extends her hand toward me with a wink. I won't shake it. She is one of them, and I already can tell she won't help me. "Don't be angry, Ms. Parker. The master will explain everything to you. Let me fetch you a robe," she says in an attempt to pacify me. Shashandra walks over to the wooden armoire and pulls out a white seersucker robe. Without even asking, she tries to pull the sheet from around me, which I've knotted tightly.

"Excuse me, I can do it myself!" I say. My voice comes out practically a screech.

"I'm sorry, madam; I was only trying to help." I can tell I've hurt the woman's feelings. Well, she shouldn't be so presumptuous.

"I didn't mean to be rude," I say, mollified, "but can't you understand my predicament? I just woke up naked in someone else's bed."

"Ms. Parker, I assure you, this is just your bed. No one else has slept here, except for you," she says with a smile. "And if you are concerned for your modesty, I promise I was the only one who saw you as you are. Last night I gave you a bath and put you to bed. I just wanted you to be comfortable." Thank goodness.

"Ah, thank you," I say with obvious relief. Now that I think about it, I actually feel refreshed. It's surprising considering all the turmoil of the last twenty-four hours—or at least what I think has been twenty-four hours . . . "Shashandra, what time is it?"

"10:00 a.m., mistress. Now, why don't you eat? I understand you didn't have any dinner."

I eye her warily. She seems kind, but I remember that she is part of this strange kidnapping conspiracy. Proudly, she lifts the tops of the dishes and explains the delicacies revealed: hickory-smoked bacon with peppercorns, a Gruyère and spinach omelet, sliced mango, a papaya smoothie, and tea. It looks delicious, and my growling stomach agrees.

"I'll leave you to break your fast," says Shashandra, who gives me a small curtsey and leaves. I don't hear a click of a lock. Then again, I suppose I could easily exit with the majority of the room exposed to the open air. But a man as meticulous as Maximos isn't going to let me escape easily. From what I've seen, he probably has a private military stationed throughout this place. My stomach rumbles. I'm not in imminent danger, so I might as well eat. I admit it, I'm a glutton.

The food is delicious—cooked to perfection, with lots of surprising flavor. The cayenne in the omelet gives it just enough spice, and the cinnamon mixed with papaya in the shake adds the right dimension. It's not long before I've eaten everything. Nice control, Ari. Although I've had my fill, there is a lingering hollowness in my stomach. Even after all of that, I could still eat an entire steak. But isn't that how I always feel? One of these days I'm bound to blow up. I decide to sit on the coral steps that lead down from the bedroom into the grass and finish off my tea. With cup in hand, I breathe in the salt air and look out at the rolling waves.

This is a paradise. Only I have no idea where it is or why I'm here. Deep down, I realize Maximos isn't going to hurt me. And I believe that he didn't take Raad. But the whole situation is so bizarre it's hard to wrap my mind around. Maximos' words, "If I can save him, I will," echo in my head. Aman Raad is the kindest person I know. Why would anyone hurt him? Why would anyone want to hurt me?

"Arianna?" I hear a man's voice ask.

I stand up and walk back nervously into the bedroom. I tell myself to be confident and strong. I'm going to find a way out of this mess, and I will find Raad, with or without Maximos. And I'm not going to be anyone's prisoner in the process.

I see it is Maximos, and he looks as handsome as ever. He is wearing white linen drawstring pants, a navy T-shirt that fits him like a second skin, and brown leather flip-flops. I shouldn't stare; it's inappropriate. But the man is gorgeous. His black hair is still wet, as if he came straight from the shower. Its natural wave is like an open invitation for a woman to run her hands through it. He smells like mint, and the dark stubble that graced his chin yesterday—or what I think was yesterday—is gone. My pulse quickens.

"Hello, Mr. Vasilliadis," I say hesitantly.

"Please, I thought we agreed you'd call me Maximos."

"I agreed to nothing." Despite the warm weather, there is an obvious chill in my voice. I place the white ceramic teacup with painted pink flowers on the table and cinch the belt around my waist tighter.

"Did you enjoy your breakfast?" he asks pleasantly. He's clearly immune to the look of anger I'm directing at him.

"Why do you care?"

I need to keep my guard up. He looks so confident, and the way he is looking at me, I feel like he is looking within me. Most people, when you talk to them, don't look right into your eyes. They focus on your face as a whole, your lips, or more often than not, your breasts. Not Maximos, though. He goes right for the eyes. It's unnerving.

"I was hoping you at least sensed by now that I genuinely care about your well-being. I'm sure you have plenty of questions," he says seriously.

"Yes, I do."

"We can talk now, or if you'd like a few minutes to get dressed we can wait . . ."

"Where is my dog?"

"Last I checked, he was eating his breakfast. But I can get him now if you'd like."

"Yes, I'd like," I say firmly with my arms crossed. We'll play by my rules, thank you.

"The boudoir and bathroom is just down the hall to the left if you'd like to get dressed while I get Beau." I don't reply but instead just stare back.

"Okay, I guess that's my cue to go." Maximos smiles, turns, and strides casually from the room. A man shouldn't be that graceful.

I count slowly to twenty before I make a dash down the hall. After tentatively opening the door, I find that the dressing room and bathroom are twice the size of mine at home and twice as luxurious. The floors and double sinks of compressed coral speak to the natural elements of the seaside paradise. The mirrors above them are outlined in mother-of-pearl. There is even a chandelier comprised of cubes that look like they are made from crushed seashells. It's magnificent.

What's most surprising is the rectangular bath that is already filled and steaming. It's about eight feet long and four feet deep. The water doesn't look like it's stagnant, though. Instead, it's constantly flowing. I take a closer look and dip my hand in. It's hot. There are no jets, but the water flows in from a horizontal slit inside the front of the tub and is sucked out through another at the back. The water smells faintly of sulfur. This must be a natural sulfur spring tub. If it wasn't, it certainly was a waste of water. Speaking of which, I need to stop wasting time. The last thing I want is for Maximos to barge in while I'm using the toilet. I wouldn't put it past him.

I quickly lock the door and make use of the facilities. It's a relief to have a moment to myself. Toothpaste is definitely in order. I scan through the various apothecary jars on a silver baker's rack filled with cotton balls, Q-tips, gauze, and bath products from mini shampoos to lotions. I find there is a whole jar dedicated to dental care products. I select a pink plastic toothbrush and a mini-sized toothpaste tube and bottle of Scope. This bathroom is a traveler's paradise. I wonder who he brings here.

As I brush furiously, I examine myself in the mirror. I look . . .

surprisingly good. Shashandra's braid work—at least I assume it's hers—is intricate. And while unusual, it gives me a graceful Grecian appearance. I don't have the heart or the time to undo it. I also notice my skin has a glow about it. It's not pasty; it's porcelain. I'll have to ask what type of lotion or oil Shashandra uses. Should I do that before or after I ask why I've been kidnapped? I ask myself wryly.

I take a white washcloth from a sea grass basket and run it under cold water. Blotting my face and neck, the coldness feels invigorating, especially in the heat. I go to the dressing area next, where all of the clothes that were haphazardly tossed into my suitcase are hanging up or neatly put away on the built-in shelves.

I select a simple black maxi dress that miraculously made it into the suitcase. If I had known we were heading to an island, I would have packed more things like it. But that's the thing when you are being threatened and have visions of being chained to a wall in a basement—it's difficult to think of bathing suits and flip-flops. I don't see any shoes that will work. There are only four-inch heels. Screw it, I'll go without. When your whole life is turned upside down, the small things certainly don't matter as much.

When I return to the bedroom, I see Maximos sitting at the table reading the paper with Beau loyally at his feet. The ocean breeze lightly ruffles the New York Times in his hands, and I notice his dark locks are getting curlier in the humidity. Oddly, the image seems like it fits. The man is just as at home here reading the paper with a dog as he is in a tux working the socialite circuit. I run my tongue over my lips, which have suddenly gone dry. When he sees me, Maximos stands suddenly, and Beau trots over. Beau jumps up to lick me, as if to apologize for his newfound allegiance.

"You little traitor, I was worried about you," I say to Beau. I feel such a sense of relief to see him again as my fingers massage his thick coat.

"He's been fine. Bothering Cook, of course, but I think your dog loves the beach," says Maximos pleasantly. A stab of heartache hits me. Raad had thought the same thing . . .

"Let's talk," I respond quickly. This is no time to get caught up in emotion. I need information now.

"Do you want to take a seat?" asks Maximos, gesturing to the chair. I determine it's best to act like a composed adult, even though I don't feel like one. I sit down awkwardly; my tension is palpable as Maximos sits and puts his paper aside.

"Where should I start?" Maximos asks with a strained smile.

"How about at the beginning?"

"The beginning is a very long time ago, so I may need to abbreviate it for you . . ."

What the hell does that mean?

"I'm sure you've noticed that you aren't like other people."

"I don't know what that is supposed to mean," I respond automatically.

"Let's cut the crap; you can read minds," Maximos says as he leans back in his chair and looks me squarely in the eye. It's amazing how quickly he went from nonchalant to accusatory. And Laura says I have mood swings.

"How do you know that?" I ask with my arms crossed.

"Because I can sense it. People like us can sense it."

"So you can read minds too then?"

"No, not like you. I have my own talents. Telepathy is a gift that belongs to only a select few. I've known only one master of it in my lifetime."

"I don't see what that has to do with why I'm here."

"Because your talent is one of a kind, and people would kill for it."

"So people are trying to kill me because they know what I can do?"

"Yes."

"But why now? And no one except Raad knows the truth. And, well, I guess except you. But Raad would never tell anyone . . ."

"He probably didn't. But regardless, they've figured out who you are," Maximos says ominously.

"Who is 'they'?" I ask.

"A very dangerous group of people. Think of them as terrorists. And they want to either kill you or use you against my people and me. I believe they were looking for you when they took your friend." Hold on there, crazy town.

"'Terrorists'? 'Your people'? I don't know who the hell you are, but as far as I'm concerned everything was perfectly fine until I met you. Which means that you are either behind this or somehow you've helped paint a target on my back . . . and put the people I love in danger."

Rather than replying immediately, Maximos looks out silently at the ocean with a furrowed brow. "Yes, you are likely right. My association with you probably piqued their interest. I believe you were watched leaving the Leo party, and they broke into your apartment the next day and planted a listening device. We removed one from your apartment. They tracked you to Raad's house. You were never in any danger; my men have been watching you. Unfortunately, we didn't know they would take Raad in your absence. Somehow, they have figured out who you really are. It was inevitable."

"You've had people watching me! And what do you mean, who I really am?"

"Arianna, you aren't human." He pauses to let the words sink in. I'm not sure I've heard him correctly. I'm still coming to terms with the fact I've been the subject of a surveillance team.

"Not human? What are you talking about?"

"You actually have a different DNA sequence that has been changing as you get older."

"I'm human. I've seen the pictures—surprisingly—of my mother holding me at the hospital. I was born to two humans, I can assure you."

"Yes, you were. But your genetic code is in the throes of changing. Your twenty-fifth birthday is tomorrow. That means there are some big changes in store for you. When you experience 'the Turn,' you'll know what I'm talking about."

I begin to rub my temples. I feel a headache starting to set in. The cause? Talking to an insane person. Up until this moment, I started to believe him. Maybe people were really after me. It would explain why I felt someone following me to Grand Central and why someone had potentially taken Raad, if they were looking to kidnap me and use me for my mind-reading abilities. But now, I know Maximos is just crazy and I've been stupid enough to think otherwise.

"Look, you obviously need help. I'm not an alien. I'm completely human. And I need to get home and find Raad. It's time to call the police. You are wasting my time, and this sick game needs to stop. So let's get back on your jet, or however you brought me here, and go home."

"I knew you wouldn't believe me," he says with a sad shake of his head. I can hear the obvious frustration in his voice. "When you bit my hand, Arianna, what did it taste like?"

Delicious. The memory of that heady flavor is almost as intoxicating as the blood was itself. But I'm not going to admit it. My reaction was likely the side effect of the drugs he'd given me, which must have altered my taste buds.

"Blood, obviously. It was disgusting!"

"You are a terrible liar," Maximos chuckles. "We'll have to work on that . . . Arianna, you are a descendent of a race of people called Tentyrians. We are not aliens but rather evolved humans."

It's now my turn to laugh. "Oh great, and that makes you Professor

Xavier?"

"Ah, I know that reference—you are likening me to a comic book character?"

"Fitting, considering you are talking about fiction," I say, my laughter disappearing. "Can you please stop this? Please take me home!" I now sound desperate, something I vowed to never sound again.

"Damn it, you aren't hearing me!" Maximos says angrily as he pushes his chair away from the table and stands up. The delicate teacup rattles on its plate and falls to the floor, shattering into dozens of pieces. The noise is a harsh interruption to the soft ebb and flow of the ocean waves. It marks the obvious change in Maximos' mood. His good-humored patience has now turned into anger. We both hurriedly reach down to pick up the pieces.

"Arianna, leave it alone. You'll cut yourself!" he yells.

"It's not a big deal!" I yell at him with equal fervor.

Our hands reach for the same shard, and our fingertips inadvertently brush. The same jolt of electricity I felt at the Leo party shocks me again. Hot, delicious. I shiver and pause, looking into his eyes. I can feel his fierce energy pushing against me. I hold my mental block firm as I teeter on the balls of my feet, refusing to drop my gaze. I notice the blue azure of his eyes has become more vibrant, the muscles in his body more tense—they seem to ripple under his clothing. That's when his lips curl to reveal sharp incisors, like fangs.

I quickly stand from my crouched position, but I'm not scared enough to scream. This must be part of some elaborate ruse. A really sick one.

"Arianna, another name for Tentyrian is vampire," says Maximos as he rises and places the china shards on the table. He walks toward me. "That is what I am, and that is what you will become."

"This is getting really messed up," I say, a slight tremor betraying me. "If you take me back home, I'll make sure we get you the help you need . . ." I should calm him. He obviously believes he is a vampire. He is wearing fake fangs, for God's sake. How did I not notice them earlier? I've heard stories of people who believe shit like this, but experiencing it is something entirely different. For all I know, I'm at some secret cult location with "his people" that all believe in this craziness too. Shashandra did call him master. What have I gotten myself into?

"I don't need help. You need mine," he says as he comes closer. "But I need you to understand the truth. This is also about life and death. I made a pledge to protect you a long time ago . . ."

His hands reach for me. I've backed myself into the ottoman at the foot of the bed. There is only one thing I can think to do . . . run.

CHAPTER 12:
TRANQUILIZED

W hy didn't he stop me? I think as my feet pound against the closely cut grass. There is a dim pain in my left foot I'm determined to ignore. Is he giving up? Jumping off the cliff isn't an option, so instead I run as fast as I can around the perimeter of the building, what appears to be a massive white stucco home. Bougainvillea has threaded its way into the plaster; their red blooms offer an air of lazy romance to the Spanish villa. I can hear the trickling of a fountain flowing in relaxed contradiction to my panic and hurried pulse.

If circumstances were different, I'd stop to admire the Moorish architecture of the curved window arches and terracotta roof. However, I don't have time and most importantly, I don't know where the hell I am. I don't see any other buildings or even roads. The house that looks like a postcard from Seville is literally perched on a cliff edged by brushwood and palm trees. The front of the home doesn't even have a driveway; instead, it butts up against what looks like miles of unending orchard.

How was this place even built? I search for a path that leads away but can't find one. There is no choice. I make a beeline for the orchards. My dress is bunched tightly in my hand to avoid tripping as I run. I need to get to the cover of trees as fast as I can before they catch up. Are they watching me now? When I ran from Maximos, he didn't follow, but I can only assume he'll send his men after me. I'm too scared to look back as my legs pump hard, and the rocky soil cuts into my feet, exacerbating the burn I already feel in my foot. The scent of olive trees fills my nose.

The unrelenting heat of the sun bogs me down. But I don't stop. After what feels like an eternity, I worry I've gone too far. I may not be able to find a path leading out, and all the rows of trees look exactly the same. I see a tree with thick roots that have risen out of the ground to form small nooks around its base. Perfect for a resting place. I limp over to one and lean into the natural crevice. I roll onto my back to feel little patches of light warm my already hot face. I just need to catch my breath.

I open my eyes to the beauty and sheer size of the trees all around me. But instead of feeling enthralled, I feel small and helpless. Which is what I am. Don't cry. My heart is still pounding, and I begin to shake. I lift my leg and pull my foot toward me to survey the damage: blood is oozing and dirt is caked into a three-inch gash. It will need stitches. I must have cut it on a stray china shard when I ran. So stupid, Ari. I realize I'm going into shock, and I need to stop it before it's too late.

My dress is now soaked through, and I'm dripping with sweat. I may as well be in a sauna. I pull myself into a sitting position and focus all my energy on meditating. My first task is to lower my heartbeat, which is out of control. If I don't slow it, my shock could easily spiral out and I'll lose my mental block. That means the chaos of the world will come crashing down. Any minute.

I rub my twitching palms on my thighs, back and forth. The friction of the cotton and the steady motion is soothing. Back and forth. The air passing between my lips transforms into a low hum. I focus on the vibration and the feel of the fabric. Back and forth. But just as I'm making progress, I hear the crunch of rock. My eyes open immediately, and I see them.

It's Philip and Hale along with another man, approaching. Dressed in black cargo pants, lace-up boots, and black tees, the muscular men are an intimidating force. Their grim expressions certainly aren't reassuring. I notice they don't carry weapons, which is a good sign. They must not intend to kill, only capture me.

"I can smell her, this way," says the one I don't recognize. He also has a buzzed haircut and looks like a GI Joe on steroids, just like Philip and Hale. How can he smell me? It's only a matter of seconds before they find me. I'm afraid and panicked, but I'm also angry. Angry that I'm cowering. Angry for what has been done to Raad.

Time and time again my freewill has been taken from me, and it's all because of Maximos. Enough. My once calming heartbeat is beating rapid fire again; so much for stopping the shock. I stand up, leaning my weight on my good foot, and yell, "If you want me so badly, come and get me. But I will fight you!"

Their attention snaps in my direction, where I stand less than ten yards away.

"Target found," says the one I haven't seen before, his voice cold and devoid of all emotion.

"Screw you!" I yell at him.

"Ms. Parker, we don't want a fight," proclaims Philip cordially as ever, as if he's discussing the weather.

"Your actions speak otherwise." I position myself into a fighting stance.

When Raad learned I was good at fencing, he thought it would be an excellent opportunity to build on my skill set. Especially after he learned the truth about Howard. Raad taught me techniques that combine karate, jujitsu, and some good old-fashioned street moves he learned as a kid. Now was as good a time as ever to put them into action.

"You've cut yourself, ma'am. Why don't you just come back to the villa and Shashandra can bandage that up for you?" Hale says calmly, with a faint southern twang I didn't notice before. "Otherwise it's going to get infected. And there is no one around here for miles . . ."

"No, I'm not going anywhere with you psychos! I'm not joining your messed-up cult!" I scream hysterically. The men look at each other quizzically.

"For God's sake, we have better things to do then chase this one," murmurs the unnamed GI Joe.

"You heard what Max said, Ryan. We are to retrieve her and quickly," says Philip, looking at his watch.

"Fine, let's get it over with," answers the guy who I guess is Ryan. He starts toward me. I'm ready.

I brush the strands of hair that have come loose from my braids off my sweaty forehead and prepare to engage. That's when Ryan laughs. "Come on, little one, let's not fight," he says between chuckles. He isn't menacing, just mocking. It only makes me madder.

"Go ahead and laugh. You won't be when I put you on your ass," I say between clenched teeth.

"You have a sassy mouth," he says as he lunges for me. I duck quickly and deliver a sidekick to his shin that causes him to stumble and catch himself on his hands. His buddies are the ones laughing now.

"Looks like she almost got you on your ass after all," says Hale enthusiastically.

Ryan stands up with determination and comes for me again. Philip and Hale watch in amusement. I bend my right hand at the knuckles, forming a flat edge, and jab at his throat. I make contact, but it doesn't hinder him. Instead, he grabs my wrist so fast I barely even register any movement. In a blur, my arm is now pinned behind my back. Damn.

"You had a lucky hit, but now the game is over. Let's go, little one," says Ryan as he throws me over his shoulder, knocking the breath out of me as his muscular shoulder digs into my diaphragm. I instantly make my body go limp. Let him think I've given up.

"Let's go, boys, the show is over," he says, and the group starts to make its way silently and quickly back to the house, like an army task force on a stealth operation.

My arms are dangling like a rag doll, and my breathing is labored. Red spots start to fill my vision; it's time to act. I dig my fingernails into his back with all my strength.

"Ahhhh! Jesus Christ!" Ryan exclaims, and his grip on me loosens. I manage to flip myself over and land on my feet, crouched like a crazed cat but without the grace. It feels like a knife has been shoved into my foot. I cry out but manage to stagger into a standing position and hobble away feebly. My vision isn't very clear, probably from all the blood that's rushed to my head. The red spots start to dissipate, and over my shoulder I can see the men standing and talking amongst themselves. What are they waiting for?

"Damn it, get the gun from your boot," I hear one of them say.

Tears flood my clouded sight. But I don't have any more energy in me to do more than continue with my pathetic hobble. If those cowards are going to shoot me, then so be it. I hear a click, but it's surely not loud enough to be a gun. A sharp prick in my back gets my attention, and warmth begins to spread like a bad rash. It feels hot and itchy. I reach behind me to touch what it is. I stumble. With a pain that is almost nothing compared to what I feel in my foot, I rip it from my back and stare at its feathered tail. What the hell? It's a dart.

But now, I notice that my foot doesn't hurt as much anymore. Actually, nothing hurts. The dart slips from my fingers. And I can feel myself slipping away from reality. My muscles are soft and pliant, like Irena's kneaded dough for her black bread. My legs collapse, with only the dirt to cushion my fall. It feels like I'm moving in slow motion as I roll over and gaze up at the orchard trees above. So beautiful and peaceful.

I can't lift my arms or move my neck, but I'm vaguely aware of arms lifting me. It's Ryan. I struggle to lift my heavy eyelids.

"Quiet, little one," he orders.

His chin is above, as are shafts of light filtering through the leaves. Like the air particles dancing in the sun, I'm floating along with them. If this is what dying feels like, it isn't that bad. Then all I see is darkness. Again.

"How much ketamine did you give her, Ryan?"

"Enough."

"It smells like enough to take down a pride of lions, damn it!"

"Well last time she woke up before she was supposed to, didn't she?"

"If she has an adverse reaction, I'm holding you responsible, Brother."

"Don't worry, Max; Evander said her system will burn it off in a couple more hours. Underneath that sedative, can't you smell her adrenaline? I've never smelled anything like it. It's amazing . . ."

"Get out, Ryan. And get Evander in here now!"

A door slams. Through my eyelids, I see white light, but I can't manage to lift them. I vaguely hear voices and, if I'm not mistaken, I just heard I've been drugged with ketamine, enough for a pride of lions. Beneath me, it feels like I'm lying on a bed, and I can smell antiseptic. I must be in a hospital. Hands are now moving over my arm, and there is a faint pinch in my wrist . . . Are they drugging me again? I have to get out of here.

"She needs more fluids to flush the drug out of her system," I hear someone say.

"She's been asleep for almost an entire day, Evander. Is this normal?" I recognize that voice: it's Maximos.

"Yes, it can be expected. But I want to show you her EKG results . . ."

"These are just lines on a paper to me, Evander. Translation, please?" I hear Maximos ask.

"Look how erratic the lines are . . . especially this one. The Turn is starting."

"How much time does she have?"

"I don't know for sure, but I would expect it to begin in a couple of hours. And after that, you know what will happen . . ." What will happen? What is wrong with me?

"I'll keep her with me and I'll take care of her," says Maximos.

"She should stay in the lab where I can monitor her, Max. The data . . ."

"No, you've seen what a fighter she is. She is scared. Keeping her strapped to machines and IVs isn't going to help our cause."

"As you wish. But you're the one who has to tell Shashandra. She fixed up Arianna's foot earlier, and I heard her tone. You're in trouble . . ."

"Ha, I always am with her. After the state I brought Arianna home in last night, I got a well-deserved tongue-lashing. You should have seen her, Evander . . ."

"Shashandra?"

"No, Arianna. She was prepared to jump from a twenty-fifth floor window before I brought her here."

"Sounds like she's a Luminary all right."

"By the gods, she's going to be the death of me, Brother."

I don't understand what they are talking about, but I do understand that I need to get out of here. But my body won't obey my commands. I've heard nightmare stories of people who went in for surgeries and were given anesthesia. But instead of putting them to sleep, it only paralyzed them and they could feel everything. I'm not in pain, but I'm aware of my own unresponsive body. I'm trapped inside myself.

Beep beep beep.

"Evander, why is her heart monitor going off like that? And her adrenaline, it's increasing," Maximos says.

"She is waking up. And panicking. This isn't good for her. She needs to be kept calm. If she isn't kept calm, it will bring the Turn on faster, which will make it more painful. I can't give her more drugs, though, and my healing energies won't work on her in this stage. Her body needs to be toxin-free when the Turn takes place; otherwise there could be damage to her organs. Max, can you try to talk to her?"

"Last time I did, she didn't respond well. She ran off! She thinks this is a cult and I'm the evil mastermind."

"She will come around. She can't deny what she is forever." What am I?

Beep beep beep.

"Have you tried reaching her in her mind?"

"Yeah, but she has a wall like a fortress. And since she isn't human, I couldn't even apply any basic suggestions."

"Try it now. She has enough of the drug in her still so she is in a slight dream state. Her subconscious will be more open."

A warm hand smoothes my brow. I hear a whisper, "Matia mou, let me in." The warm hand is replaced by a cool energy on my forehead that grows stronger and starts to tingle. His energy, it's crackling, it's pushing at me. I'm weak, but rather than fighting against it, I accept it. Maybe because I'm too tired? But maybe it's because too much of what I've heard and seen indicates I've misunderstood something . . .

Within a flash, I'm no longer aware of what's happening outside my body. Instead, I'm acutely aware of what's happening within. I'm standing inside the pristine white walls of my mind, the safe place I go to in meditation. I appear as I always do in my safe place, in a white simple tank dress with my hair loose. But this time, I'm not alone. I see Maximos. I know that I am not imagining him . . . He is actually standing there as if it's real life. No one has ever breached my mind or my dreams before. But there he is, standing with his hands clasped behind his back like the devil himself. Or a vampire. His jaw is locked tight, and his eyes are glowing like sapphires.

"I didn't think you were going to let me in," he says, letting genuine surprise show on that chiseled face.

"I'm tired. And I let you in because I need answers. I can hear what you are saying about me, out there." I gesture beyond the white room we are standing in. "Something is going to happen to me. What is it?"

"Your body is embracing your genetic code and undergoing the final process for you to reach Tentyrian adulthood." He says it matter-of-factly, like this is all supposed to make sense to me.

"You told me you . . . were a vampire. That . . . I'm going to be a vampire." My words come out an awkward stutter.

Maximos comes closer and takes my hand in his. This time I don't run. There isn't a rational explanation to the events of the last couple days, and there isn't a rational explanation as to why Maximos is in my head. For the first time, the reality of what Maximos has been saying sinks in. I feel . . . lost.

"I'm going to help you through this. You have nothing to be scared of," he says.

"Now you are the one that is lying," I reply. The hard lines of his mouth soften in sympathy.

"When you undergo the Turn, you will experience the Tentyrian thirst for the first time. It's difficult to control. The first twenty-four hours are the hardest, but after that, it will get easier . . . I promise."

"You mean for blood? You are saying I'm going to want to drink from and kill people?"

"Yes. But you won't kill anyone. I'll make sure you have the nourishment you need. You aren't in control of your powers yet, which means you won't be ready to feed on humans."

"Oh my God, oh my God, feed on humans?" I start to pace the white expanse of the room. My bewilderment is now full-fledged panic. This is not a reality I want to live in.

Beep beep beep

"You need to calm down."

"How am I supposed to calm down!"

"You must try. Can I show you something?"

I stare at him in disbelief. What can he show me that is going to make what he's telling me palatable, or even calm me? But that innocent question, combined with the melody of his voice, is enough for me to pause.

That's when I feel something cold and wet on my feet. I look down to see that it's water. A small stream is now flowing between us. How did water get in my white room?

"Are you doing this?" I ask in disbelief.

"Yes."

"How? This is my space. I control it. No one has ever even come in here . . ."

"My skill is in dream walking. I can create things—experiences in dreams that we have when we sleep. You aren't in REM sleep right now, but it's still possible for me to enter your dream because the lingering drug is keeping you in a transitional state. With humans, it's much easier."

Maximos waves his hand at the water, and it becomes wider and deeper. I step back quickly to keep my bare feet from touching the icy water. But when I step back, it's onto soft green grass. I see now that we're in a meadow dotted with white hydrangea. My favorite—how did he know? I even spy a family of rabbits. The white walls around me are now gone. Instead, there is only beautiful blue sky and downy white clouds. The stream between us bubbles, and I can hear a faint hum of cicadas.

"This is amazing," I remark.

"Watch, what do you think of this?" Maximos coaxes his finger at the ground, and a young sapling starts to inch its way upward. At first it's just a small thin trunk, but with more urging, it grows into a fully aged tree. The limbs and vines then groan, bend, and twine to form two swings.

"Shall we?" Maximos asks as he smiles playfully and hops over the river to my side. He then sits on one of the swings. I'm not sure what to say, so I mimic his actions and sit on the swing next to him. My hands hold onto the green vines that serve as rope, and I give myself a light push with my feet. The tips of the grass tickle my toes. My dress billows with the motion. I could never dream up such a tranquil place on my own.

"Feel better?"

"Yes." I breathe deeply. Rather than reflecting on how only moments before I was about to have an aneurysm, I find I'm captivated by the air. It's lightly perfumed with that same flowery but exotic scent I smelled on my skin earlier.

"What is that scent?"

"Lotus and myrrh. It's an ancient Tentyrian perfume. It reminds me of home."

"Tell me about your home?" I ask. Maximos looks at me with an arched brow. I'm surprised at myself for even asking.

"I will, but are you ready to hear it?"

I keep swinging and ponder the thought. The wood seat underneath me is firm. The vines I'm holding are strong. I'm not about to fall, but I can't shake the feeling that I'm Alice, fallen down the rabbit hole. Since I first met Maximos, I had been followed, my mentor kidnapped, my apartment invaded, and I had tried to escape Maximos not once but three times. Not to mention I had been shot with a tranquilizer dart. Or I think all of this happened. Is it possible that I've gone crazy?

"I don't know. I don't know what's real anymore—like these beautiful flowers and this stream. Maybe I've lost my mind? Maybe I've been a schizophrenic this whole time and my hallucinations have finally caught up to me. You may not even be real . . ."

Before I can finish my thought, in a blur of motion, Maximos plucks me from the swing and places me on the soft grass in his lap. My arms instinctually reach for his shoulders.

"What was that for?" I ask.

"Does me holding you right now feel real?"

"Yes . . . but it's not."

"But it is, though. A mind, Tentyrian or not, is a powerful thing. What you can experience in a dream, for example, can feel just as real as 'real life.' Just because it isn't happening out there doesn't mean it's any less significant." I look at him doubtfully, but his strong arms don't falter. I push myself away into a sitting position across from him. I already miss the comfort of his arms around me. But the sensation and confusing emotions I'm feeling are overwhelming. For me to accept everything that's happening requires faith, which I'm not sure I have.

"It's difficult for young Tentyrians to come of age," says Maximos. "And it's been especially hard for you, I imagine, because you haven't understood what's happening."

"I still don't." I roll a dandelion in my palm, scattering the fluff into the breeze.

"You will, with time. You were fortunate to have someone like Aman Raad who recognized your unusual situation. I've read your file, and it's a miracle he found you and developed the treatment regimen he did."

"He did what no one else could figure out," I say softly.

"He did what we call 'Guardians' do," replies Maximos.

"You've lost me." I know I'm staring helplessly at him, but what else can I do?

Maximos patiently leans back on his hands and smiles like he is about to begin a teaching moment. He hands me a dandelion.

"When every Tentyrian child is born, a Guardian is appointed to him or her. They are sworn to protect and help the child grow into his or her legacy. Guardian families run in parallel to Tentyrian ones, and their ancestors carry on with the duty to protect the Tentyrian children."

"But why? What's in it for them?"

"Honor, love, protection, wealth. They aren't like employees or even your modern-day notion of slaves, Arianna. They are part of our own families too, and they are treated as such."

"You said Guardians help them grow into their legacies. What does that mean?"

"Every Tentyrian has a unique ability that starts to show in child-hood, but it isn't until they reach the age of twenty-five that they have full control over it. Until then, they must grapple for years trying to hone their skill. Guardians help with this learning process, and when the Turn happens, they are the ones who help their charges get through the thirst and embrace their power."

"So are there others like me?" I ask.

Deep sorrow shadows Maximos' face. "No, unfortunately not. You are now the only one with your unique skill."

"You said 'now,' though. What happened to the others?"

"They were massacred."

"Oh." I'm not sure what else I should say.

"It was 52 BC when it happened . . ."

"Wow. That was a long time ago. And you're really old . . ." I can't stop myself before the words tumble out. Maximos laughs.

"So what happened?" I ask, trying to calm the growing bloom in my cheeks at my comment.

"We were betrayed by those who were power hungry."

"Who?"

"The Dark Coven. They are the same people who are after you."

"You've lost me again."

"I'm sorry; I know this is a lot to take in. And we don't have to talk about everything now if you don't want. I'm just glad you aren't trying to run away from me again."

"Sorry about that . . ."

"Don't apologize. I put you in an impossible circumstance. And you wouldn't be who you are if you didn't try to fight." Is that a look of respect he's giving me?

"Why didn't you come after me, though? When I ran from you." I can see his nostrils flare.

"Because I was afraid I would hurt you."

Now I'm really confused. "Why? You said yourself you are trying to protect me."

"I am, but when you cut your foot on that china—something overtook me. I was afraid if I went after you right away, I could have hurt you."

"So it was because of my blood?"

"It's more than that. You'll soon come to see, blood is an intoxicating thing. Especially the way yours is for me. Combined with a chase or hunt, it's easy to lose control."

"Will all blood taste the way yours tastes to me?" I ask tentatively.

"Oh, you mean the blood that was so disgusting to you?"

"Yes . . . well no," I say awkwardly.

"Hmm?" says Maximos slyly. He knows . . .

"Fine, it tasted amazing," I admit.

"And that was just now. After the Turn, blood will take on a whole new meaning for you. But all blood tastes different. No two people are alike, and neither are the way they taste."

"Am I going to be bloodthirsty and evil? Like in the movies?"

"Not unless you decide to be," he says seriously, "and don't believe what you see in the movies."

"So it's a conscious choice?"

"Yes. Although at first it may not feel so black and white. I'll be there to guide you, though. You aren't alone in this."

"What if I don't want to drink blood?"

"You'll die."

"Is that how you die, then—starvation?"

"No, but it can be. Think of Tentyrians as super humans. We are stronger, faster, and healthier. Our bodies are also able to regenerate and self-heal. If an injury is bad enough, we'll die just like any other human. However, it takes a great deal of trauma for that to happen."

"Will I live forever then?"

"It's possible."

"It sounds lonely."

"It can be. But there are others like us. And you'll get to meet them when you wake up."

"Are you referring to your Navy SEAL team?" Maximos laughs again. His rich voice gives me butterflies.

"I'll have to tell the Brothers you said that."

"Are they your real brothers?"

"Not in the biological sense. But we've been together a long time, and I think of them as such."

A question is nagging at me and I want to ask, but I'm . . . what? Scared. It feels like rubber bands have somehow gotten around my heart. My chest feels tight. I want to ask . . . but I don't . . . Oh hell, just ask.

"Do you have a family, like a wife . . . and children?"

"No." Snap, the rubber bands are gone.

"Did you ever?"

"Not in the way that you think of a family. But I did have my own people who were like that to me. We were called the Leo Coven, and I was their leader."

"Leo, like the horoscope sign?"

"Yep. Who do you think invented it?"

"You? You've got to be kidding," I say, incredulous.

"No, I'm not kidding." Maximos looks slightly affronted.

"It's just, I thought horoscopes were fake?"

"They are—but Leo as an astrological sign is very much a real thing. It's just that time erases the memory of creation."

"What about the other signs? Were those made by other Tentyrians too?"

"Yes. There were twelve Covens in all: Cancer, Leo, Sagittarius, Libra, Virgo, Aquarius, Aries, Gemini, Taurus, Scorpio, Pisces, and Capricorn. The signs which are now affiliated with astrological horoscopes were our Covens' symbols," Maximos says. He then pauses, seeming to search for the next piece of information to reveal in this dizzying explanation of what I am and where I come from.

"Have you ever been to the Louvre museum?" he asks.

"I was there last New Year's, actually."

"Do you remember seeing the Zodiac of Dendera?"

I quickly run through the catalogue of images and memories from our Paris trip and find the one of the stunning Egyptian bas-relief I had seen at the museum. I remember the tour guide told us it had been removed from the ceiling of an ancient Egyptian temple. The sandstone carving portrayed a large circle and within it were hieroglyphs representing twelve constellations. In each of the four corners of the circle was an Egyptian maiden.

"Yes! I do. It shows the twelve main constellations. Those are your Coven's symbols!" I say excitedly as the pieces of information start to click.

"Precisely. Dendera, also referred to as Denderah, is a town situated on the west bank of the Nile in Egypt. Tentyra is the Greek name for Dendera, and from which my . . . or I should say our people obtained their name. Our city was called Tentyris, and it was there the Dendera Zodiac, which is how people now refer to it, was found in the Temple of Hathor. Our queen commissioned its design to commemorate the twelve Covens and the royal family. The four Egyptian maidens that you may remember seeing in the corners of the zodiac represent Hathor's daughters . . ."

"What exactly is a Coven, though?" I ask hurriedly. This is just another in the unending amount of questions I have.

"Each Coven consisted of around fifty Tentyrians. The Covens' leaders, like me, were elected to council seats, where we formed the Council of the Zodiac. The Council formed the government for Tentyris. We were a small but prosperous city . . . long ago," he says. I can hear the sadness in his voice.

"And you said in Egypt? But you seem Greek. I've even heard you speak it. With the last name Vasilliadis, I guess that's what I assumed you were."

"While our homeland was in Egypt, our heritage is fundamentally Greek blended with Macedonian bloodlines. We're an evolved people who emigrated from Greece."

"So you were a government official?"

"Something like that. I was also a trusted advisor to our queen— Queen Hathor."

"And what happened to her?"

"She died. As did her daughters and the majority of the Council members who were my friends. There are only six of us left now, of the first generation."

"How does the Dark Coven fit in?"

"They are three of the six of us who are alive—Stavros, Calix, and Aglaia. They are responsible for killing our people." Maximos' hands, which seemed so calm moments before, are now clenched.

"And you intend to do what with them?"

"Kill them, among other things," Maximos says seriously.

If you asked me a day ago what I thought of someone who openly admitted to wanting to murder people, I would have said they belong in a psychiatric ward or jail. But in this new world that seems to have swallowed me up, the legal system appears irrelevant, along with the basics of biology.

"It's been thousands of years; I guess that is not something you could forgive?" I ask.

"Could you forgive it if you saw everyone you loved slaughtered in front of you?"

"No, I suppose not."

"They are Tentyrian. Not simple humans you can put behind bars."

"You know, I was perfectly happy being a simple human."

"Maybe. But you aren't one." We both remain silent for several minutes.

"So if my birthday is tomorrow and it's July—does that mean I'm a member of the Cancer Coven? Do they even exist anymore?"

"It doesn't work like that. And your lineage never belonged to a Coven."

"What did my ancestors belong to?"

"The royal family."

"Does that make me royalty or something?"

"We use the term 'Luminary.'"

"To be a luminary, don't you need to be inspiring?"

"Yes, that is the essence behind the word. And like the Luminaries before you, you are inspiring, Arianna."

"How?"

"Well for one, no one has a power like yours. There has only been one Tentyrian ever who was able to read minds the way I suspect you will be able to. Her name was Daria."

"Who was she?"

"She was the First Luminary, the eldest of Hathor's four

daughters—the maidens portrayed in the Dendera Zodiac carving. And now that you are here, I believe you were meant to ascend to the First Luminary position, Arianna. It's a position of great power and responsibility."

I can feel my anxiety coming back. "What does that even mean, Maximos? Now I'm supposed to be a vampire . . . luminary?"

Beep beep beep.

"Arianna, take a deep breath and calm down."

"Stop telling me to calm down!"

"It's for your own good. Now breathe." But it really feels like I can't.

"I, I can't . . . it hurts." It's like an elephant is on my chest.

"Am I having a heart attack?" I sputter. "I'm not feeling well, Maximos."

"You said your heart hurts?"

"Yes." My mouth and lips are now dry. The pain is growing.

"We need to leave this dream, Arianna, and you need to wake up. The Turn is coming, and your anxiety is bringing it on now."

"But there is so much I don't understand, Maximos. You have to tell me!"

"I will, I promise. It's time to go back, though. When you wake up, I'm going to be right next to you. Do you believe me?"

My voice comes out a whisper: "Yes."

The beautiful field is now gone, as is Maximos. I'm standing alone in my white room and I'm hurting, physically and emotionally. I don't want to wake up to face what sounds like a nightmare. I am to become a vampire.

CHAPTER 13:
THE TURN

Arianna has proven time and time again she won't play by the rules. But this time she'll have to, because when the Turn happens she'll want to break every single one. Entering her mind was risky. I could have pushed her too far. And at one point I thought I had. I told her it was difficult for Tentyrians to come of age, but I didn't tell her how fragile a Tentyrian mind could be, especially one with strong power like hers. The Dark Coven is a prime example of what happens when the mind isn't kept in check . . . But Arianna is strong. And she finally seems to have accepted the truth.

Her temperature is now at 115 degrees Fahrenheit, and her heart rate has increased twofold. Evander says that the Turn is on the cusp. She is only minutes away from the intense pain that is about to take over her body. Hathor help her.

"The drug is fully out of her system, Max," says Evander. "She should be with us any moment. I had the Brothers put restraints in your room. You remember when Narcissa came of age—it was one of the most powerful I've ever seen. I wouldn't be surprised if Arianna's is the same."

"That's what I'm afraid of. The Luminaries have been gifted with the most power, which makes this experience even harder. Should we move her now?" But my question is pointless; her eyelids are lifting and her eyes are glowing. Her pupils have dilated and are rimmed in vibrant green. Like emeralds on fire. She is awake.

"Arianna, can you hear me?" I ask.

"Yes. Please . . . make this stop!" she cries. Her voice is riddled with pain.

Her body is shaking, and her fingers are twitching—reaching for something she can't quite grasp. Release from the pain. I know what she is going through is excruciating. It feels like all of your insides are moving and trying to find a new place to root themselves. Your skin begins to feel too tight, and your throat becomes a parched desert. Now mottled, her skin is slick with sweat. Before I can respond, offer her words of assurance, she bolts upright and violently rips the IV from her arm. A bead of blood forms at the insertion point. My mouth waters.

"Get away from me!" she snarls. Her hands frantically pull at the sticky plastic pads over her heart.

"The aggression is a natural side effect," Evander warns as he tries to blot some gauze on her wrist. But she writhes away.

"Don't talk about me like I'm a sideshow!"

"He's here to help, Arianna. Evander is a doctor."

She now doubles over, knocking down the heart monitor and a tray of medical instruments with a caustic crash.

"I'm taking her to my suite, Evander. No one comes unless I call. If there is a complication with tonight's mission, let me know." Evander gives me a warning look. I scoop her into my arms; she's as light as a feather. As much as I want to be out with the teams tonight, ensuring that Arianna is safe is equally important.

"No doctors, Maximos, please no doctors. Can you get Raad?" she pleads as violent spasms rack her body.

"I can't find him right now, kardoula mou. I promise I'm looking. I think a bath will make you feel better, though." I shift her to my wing of the house, where the Brothers know it's off limits. Her fingers are clutched tightly to my shirt. They might as well be clutched around my heart.

"Arianna, you are burning up. I'm going to put you in the water to equalize your temperature."

She doesn't acknowledge my words. Fortunately, the sulfur baths in the home are always running. I just need to adjust the temperature down. To imagine Arianna having to go through this alone—or worse, at a hospital, where they would likely turn her into a government experiment—puts ice in my veins. The seclusion and comforts of Ambrosine are what she needs.

After the massacre, Aristos, Evander, and I lived in temporary shelters on the island before going back to the Sanctum. When we came to terms with the fact there was nothing for us at the Sanctum anymore, we—or rather I—decided to build Ambrosine. By then, Aristos needed to work out his anger and left us for several decades. Evander threw himself into study and science. And I needed an outlet, which became the genesis for this house. Over the years, I've razed and rebuilt it at least twenty times. Although the Brotherhood has homes all over the world, I've always felt an attachment to this location. Its view, remoteness, and natural sulfur springs are unparalleled. It was also our refuge when everything went to hell. And because of that, this place has been my solace. I hope it can be the same for Arianna.

I place her on the edge of the tub, where she just about falls over onto the marble floor before I catch her. "Arianna, stay with me . . ."

"No . . . I'm dying," she cries.

With no time to lose, I place her directly into the water that I've adjusted down to almost freezing. The writhing of her body stops as she registers the stark change in temperature. The green of her eyes is electric.

"Better?" I ask.

"Numbing . . ."

"Give it a few minutes. You are going to start to cool down. Pretty soon your body temperature will swing in the opposite direction, and we'll need to get you warm." I reach over for a jar of crystallized eucalyptus and dump a scoopful in.

"What is that?" she asks breathlessly.

"One of Shashandra's concoctions. It will help relax your muscles, and it smells good."

"Hmmm. Everything about you smells good," she murmurs. It's the fever talking. "Like mint mixed with man. It's so . . . heady. Is that the right word? I don't really know. You are heady, I suppose, and so . . . big. I've never met anyone who takes up so much space. How do you do that?" Her head is lolling side to side against the stone lip of the tub. It's a strange question, but if talking distracts her from the tumult of the cell processes happening within her, fine.

"Years of practice?"

"I bet you've had lots of practice at things . . . I bet you know everything . . ."

"I have had all the time in the world, I suppose. Which has given me ample opportunity to learn," I say cautiously. I feel her forehead—still too hot.

"Would you take advantage of me?"

"I would hope not. I'm sworn to protect you." I swallow. Hard.

"Protection is nice and all, but women don't like that all the time. I like . . . I'm not sure what I like. You are awfully serious . . . Why am I still in my dress? Why is that bandage on my foot? Why did you put me in here like this?" Her attention flits restlessly from one point to another.

"Because I didn't have time to take it off . . ." Without hesitation, Arianna shreds the dress in two and rips it off her body. The sopping fabric hits the floor with a wet smack.

"Wow, I'm strong!" she says with childlike amazement. She doesn't have a hint of self-consciousness. Me, on the other hand, I'm acutely aware of how little my linen drawstring pants offer my own concealment. Beneath the greenish tinge of the water is a body women would die for and men would worship. Breathtaking. Long, lean legs, honed firm from running, gently curved hips, and a flat expanse of stomach the palm of my hand is itching to explore. Not to mention the bountiful but not excessive breasts they want to grasp. My own skin is tightening.

Arianna is different from the women I'm normally attracted to. She is so . . . challenging. It's true I've always enjoyed the pleasures of the female sex, the lush comforts of their bodies and their sweet demeanors—so giving and pliant. But what makes Arianna different from the hundreds of women I've been with is that she continues to surprise me. I wouldn't exactly call her sweet, and she is anything but pliant. Her spirit is hard, and I pray it is never broken, but can she learn to bend? Maybe for me?

I'm goddamn presumptuous, I chide myself. No matter how tantalizing she is—I can see her skin just below the surface of the bath water—she can never be mine. But when our eyes connect, I feel that electric shock again. It's hard to keep my thoughts straight. The tip of her pink tongue licks her lips.

"So thirsty," her voice rasps. Good, a task. I need one, other than staring at her.

"I'll get some water," I say immediately. Fortunately, the wet bar in my room is within sight distance to the bathroom. Within seconds, I fill a glass with ice and Perrier and return to place it in her trembling hands.

"Where did that come from?" she asks in surprise. "You never left
. . ."

"I did. It was just very fast."

"Vampire thing?"

"A Tentyrian thing, yes."

"Will I be able to do it?"

"Eventually. Drink the water, Arianna."

"Don't order me around!" The glow of her eyes intensifies, and I
notice she is trembling again. But she downs the water. Her temperature is lower. Good.

"Let's make the bath warmer, okay?" I turn up the temperature.

"I need more water." I fill it, five more times. By the sixth glass, she
throws it. Tiny pieces ricochet off the floor. Here it comes.

"I hate this!" she yells.

"Is it the water you hate?" I keep my voice level. Trying to argue
with a Tentyrian in the full swing of a Turn is impossible. So many hormones and emotions are in flux, maintaining a rational train of thought
is very difficult. It's similar to dealing with a volatile teenager.

"Yes, and you! You've done this to me!" A sob bursts from her, and
she rubs her face. "My skin is too tight . . . I feel like I'm going to break
through it."

"It will feel better soon." Her lips are now turning bluish. I put my
hand in the water—far away from her creamy thigh. It's cold. Her body
is now cooling the water off. I turn the temperature all the way to hot.

"Would you like your hair washed?" I offer.

"You are offering to wash my hair?" she asks absently, clearly
confused.

"Well, you aren't in the condition to do it yourself, and since your
adventure in the orchards, I think you'd probably like to get some of
the dirt and tangles out . . ."

"Okay," she acquiesces, staring ahead. It seems like she is drifting
elsewhere and the pain has abated. For now.

I set to work by quickly undoing the intricate braids done in the
Tentyrian style. Did Shashandra do it for Arianna's benefit or mine, I
wonder? It's amazing how well it suits her. She looks like a Tentyrian
through and through. My deft fingers remove the pins and smooth
out the auburn locks shot through with strands of gold. Following my
guiding hands, Arianna dips her head under the flowing water. Eyes
closed, her face is serene and relaxed, like a Michelangelo carving
of Aphrodite's face. I gently massage the rosemary shampoo into her
scalp, hoping to ease some of her pain. I rinse the lather away while

cradling her neck and head. To hold vulnerability in one's hands—hands capable of so much destruction—is a humbling thing.

Her eyes blink open, and her attention is once again focused. "It's my birthday, you know; I have to tell Laura I'm going to miss my birthday dinner. I have to tell her . . ."

"Don't worry, it's been taken care of. I sent her an e-mail," I assure her.

"From where?" She snaps her head up from my cupped hands.

"Do we need to talk about this now?" I ask calmly.

"You went into my phone. You took it!"

"I'm sorry. I didn't want her to worry. I said you would reschedule."

Her teeth are chattering now. Her legs are now pulled to her chest, and she is rocking back and forth in the water. The temperature is as hot as it can go.

"I'm cold. And thirsty," she whispers.

"Just a few more minutes in the water, it will warm you. I think it's time to get you some blood to drink." I can see a spark in her eye at the mention of it—it must sound appealing. That is a good sign. Instead of Perrier this time, I pour the O negative I had Shashandra store in the mini-fridge into a glass.

"It looks like V8," she says solemnly.

"Trust me, this will taste better." She tentatively takes the glass. This time I have to help hold it to her now-pale lips to keep the blood from sloshing over the rim.

"I still hate you." The vehemence in her voice isn't there, though.

"I know."

"It tastes okay. Better than water. I don't think I can drink water ever again."

"You won't have to."

"It doesn't taste like you, though. It's dull . . . Ahh! My stomach!" She wrenches away from the glass and clutches her stomach.

"Your body is having its first real taste of its new life source. It will get better," I try to assure her.

"You keep saying it will get better and it's not! It hurts!"

I can see the taut muscles of her stomach rippling in response. I touch her forehead. Her temperature is now too low but better than it spiking. Without asking, I lift her from the tub in one swift motion. The water streams down her cool-to-the-touch body. Her natural honey scent that's been haunting me since I first met her comes off her in waves. It's the pheromones her body is releasing in rapid supply—a sign of arousal, another side effect of the Turn. Normally it is the

Guardians who take care of their charges in this process. For me to be doing it, especially as I'm clearly attracted to her, is risky. But I couldn't leave her in the lab . . .

I place her on the white cotton bath mat and reach for an oversized towel. I wrap it around her and rub her down vigorously to increase the blood circulation and warm her. I'm careful to control my pressure so as not to leave bruises. This happens in what appears as seconds to her. For me, it's like slow motion. Every inch of her is caressed by my gaze, burned into my memory.

I ignore the pricking of my gums as I wipe the droplets of water off her neck and the stray ones between her shoulder blades. Hathor help me. I quickly towel-dry her hair, and before her legs buckle again, I carry her to my sleigh bed that's been turned down. The sun has set, and the blinds of the arched windows have been shuttered. The room is pitch black, but I can see her as if it is daylight. I suspect it's the same for her too, as the glow of her eyes indicates her night vision has been activated.

I tuck the white duvet around her as her dazed eyes look up at me. Her teeth are clenched in response to the intense pangs of pain that are spiraling in her stomach. I reach behind her to prop her up with pillows when Arianna clutches my arm.

"I'm so cold," she whispers.

"I'll get more blankets."

"No, warm me now. I need body heat, Maximos." Her face looks so pained, and she is shivering with cold. I can't deny her. You can't deny yourself is more like it.

I strip off my soaking-wet shirt I paid no heed to when I pulled her from the bath and slip underneath the covers. Her eyes are locked on mine as I pull her body toward me. I try to mentally detach myself as my hands reach for her body. Our flesh connects, and she flinches away in surprise.

"You're so hot," she murmurs.

"You're so cold. We need to get your temperature up. Once it normalizes, your natural temperature will be around 105 degrees. Tentyrians run on the warm side." She leans into me, her face buried in my chest. I run my hands over her skin and try to rub it with indifference.

"Why?" Arianna asks. She is trembling like a leaf.

"It's because of our increased blood flow. Our hearts beat twice as fast compared to a human's."

"I can already feel it."

"It sounds beautiful . . . like a hummingbird," I say.

"You can hear my heart?"

"Yes, and you will be able to as well once you get through this. Your senses will soon come alive. What you will be able to see, taste, and hear will be magnified. It's like an awakening."

"Ah!" she cries out, and her body gives a violent wrench, like a helpless puppet yanked from its strings.

"Please, distract me! This hurts too much," she pleads. I struggle to find the right words to say and find I'm at a loss. The only thing I can think of to talk about is the island. So I begin to prattle . . .

"I named this island, and subsequently the house, Ambrosine. It means immortality, and I chose it because this is a place I felt would live on forever with me. I'll have to show you where we are on a map—Ambrosine is part of a collection of islands in the Ionian Sea. It's about an hour's flight from Athens. There aren't any natural resources of note here, and because it's so small, no one tried to settle it. Many of the surrounding islands were settled, however, around 1200 BC. That was before my time, though . . ." I realize I probably sound like an old professor to her. What am I thinking?

"Tell me more?" she asks gently when I pause, burying her face deeper into my chest. My hands continue to stroke her back, which is already much warmer.

"Since we found Ambrosine, our slice of paradise has been protected by the Brotherhood. I'll have to give you a full tour of the house when you are better. And even show you the Control Room. That's Aristos' favorite place. I'm sure he is eager to meet you . . ."

Her trembling has subsided, and it seems like the gut-wrenching pain has too. Somehow her legs have become entwined in mine. Our layered legs are sweet torture, just like the press of her naked body against me. With every chill she feels, I can feel her skin change against me. Sweet torture, indeed. I clear my throat.

"I have so many favorite places here; I'd love to show them to you," I continue. "One of the best things to do is picnic at the beach. We'll pack cold chardonnay infused with blood and strawberries. I don't know if that sounds appetizing to you yet, but I promise it tastes delicious. And we'll snack on stuffed figs with spicy lentils and sweet baklava dripping in honey. One of the things I appreciate the most about being Tentyrian is how much flavor I can taste." I inadvertently nuzzle her neck and take a deep breath, letting her honey scent envelop me.

Arianna lifts her head and looks up at me; the green of her eyes is hypnotizing. Her mind has naturally gone to where mine was leading me—to a dangerous place. She is unconsciously sucking on her lower lip. And it's downright sexy.

"It doesn't hurt anymore, Maximos. The pain is better . . . and I'm not cold or too hot. But I'm starting to feel . . . thirsty again. I want something hot . . . and alive," she says. Arianna has now pulled herself up and is straddling me. If she didn't notice I was turned on before, she'd have to be practically blind not to see it or feel it now. The cascade of damp hair around her shoulders frames her face that I once thought angelic. But now, there is something fiercely beautiful and knowing—not so innocent.

With lightening speed, I remove myself from her tantalizing grip to stand by the bed. I need to put distance between us.

"I'll get you more blood . . ." I quickly pour another glass and hand it to her. It's an effort to keep my own hand from trembling.

"No! I don't want that! I want . . . you. I feel restless . . . and my throat is on fire." She is now kneeling on the bed in all of her natural glory to come face-to-face with me.

"Arianna, you feel like this because of what is happening in your body. Everyone reacts differently to the Turn. Some become violent, some become . . ." But it's difficult for me to finish my sentence. "If you don't keep yourself in check, you will start to get out of control."

"I want to be out of control!" Arianna exclaims.

"Just drink this, please." She haltingly takes a sip and makes a face.

"I don't want it." Her voice is defiant. Arianna places the cup on the mirrored glass night table.

"I want this . . ." Her hands grab my shoulders, and she pulls me into her body, now thoroughly warm. My hands instinctively move to the small curve of her back.

"We can't do this," I manage to say. My response sounds weak. I try to push her away as my hands move to her hips. But her grasp holds tight; her strength is growing. It must be midnight by now. You are being weak, Maximos. Arianna's mouth kicks up in a mischievous smile. The paleness of her lips is gone. Instead, they are pink and soft. Sweet Hathor, help me. She places her luscious mouth on mine, and I know I'm lost.

When our lips touch, it's impossible to block out the sweet honey of her that has been my constant companion. It fills my nose and mouth and ignites the animal in me I've tried so hard to keep in its cage. My fangs release automatically. A roar like that of a waterfall fills my head.

"You don't know what you are doing here, Arianna. This is wrong," I growl. She removes the press of her lips and looks at me intently, her eyes searching for answers. This time, she doesn't pull away at the sight of my fangs.

"Why? Because you think I don't know what I am doing?"

"Because I don't know what I'm doing. We shouldn't be together. I am supposed to protect you."

"You've said it before, and I don't want to hear it," she interrupts. "Your idea of chivalry is antiquated. I don't need a protector. I need . . . you . . . right now, just as you are. I'm flesh and blood, not a china doll."

I know she is no doll. She is temptation incarnate. From the night she walked into that ballroom, I knew I had been wrong. I was a fool to think I could take on the role of a protective uncle, like I had with Hathor's daughters. I thought she would follow my direction—my centuries-old wisdom. Laughable. There is nothing wise about me now. The truth is—I've wanted her for myself the moment I began to track her and obsess over her like a miser does his gold.

"I want you, Maximos." Her soft plea followed by the lick of her tongue on my mouth is as much as I can take. Like an addict who has his first pull of a drug after trying so hard to stay clean, I let go of my hesitation with only a flicker of shame. The roar is so loud now; I give up trying to listen to my conscience. I tip her onto her back in one swift motion, and my mouth begins to devour hers. Her mouth opens slightly as she lets out a soft moan. The sound is so beautiful and arousing, like the call of a lioness to her lion. The animal I am, I take advantage of her open mouth and taste her deeply. I am not patient. I'm demanding and hungry. She responds just as eagerly—holding to me tight as her tongue dances with mine. Delicious.

I can hear her blood literally humming; it's singing to me. I stroke my thumb over the pulse of her carotid and replace it with my lips. Just feeling the heat pulse beneath my mouth drives me further to the edge. But I won't take her blood. And I cannot let her take mine. I travel from her neck down to her breasts that want to be loved.

"You are so beautiful, Arianna. I could just stare at you."

"Well I want you to do more than just stare. Make love to me," she murmurs.

"You don't know what you are asking, matia mou."

"Don't I?" I can see pricks of white now. Her fangs have manifested. It's almost too much for me to handle.

"If we do this, you have to resist the urge to bite me, Arianna."

"Why?"

"Because it is going to take us to a place that's difficult to return from." She nods in vague agreement as I caress her. I have to stop.

"Do you understand what I am saying, Arianna? It's important."

"Fine, just don't stop. I need more," she pants.

"My demanding princess, be careful what you wish for," I growl. Her impatient hands struggle with the ties of my pants, and in her frustration, she tears them off in shreds. The sound of the tearing fabric helps pull me from the erotic haze that is swallowing me.

"Matia mou, maybe we should take a breath."

"No!" Before I can blink, she has me flipped me over on my back.

"Did you see what I just did?" she says in amazement. Her strength likely equals mine.

"Yes. You are amazing."

Her hands lock on my wrists, and she is in the position of control as she holds me down. Her body is locked around mine, now just as naked as hers. I can feel myself against her thigh. I'm rock hard. Feeling this close to her almost drives me to the brink. It would be so easy to let go of that last bit of control I'm struggling to hold onto. To lose myself.

Her fingers dig into my wrists, and I can feel the crescent moons of her nails leaving their mark. It's her turn now to explore me as she kisses my neck and chest. Her trailing mouth leaves gooseflesh in its wake. Her mouth is magic. She lazily strokes my nipple and gives it a nibble. The small pulse of pain makes me groan. There is so much I want to do to her body, but I can feel the clock tick. I want her the way I've never wanted another woman. And it's making me impatient.

"Arianna, if you continue to tease me, I'm going to lose myself, and then it will be over quicker than this started." She gives a throaty laugh and stops the play with her mouth. This time, she slowly rubs her body along mine. Her breath slows but deepens; the softness of her touches my hardness. She is biting her lower lip, and while she looks excited and aroused, I sense uncertainty that wasn't there before.

"Matia mou, what is wrong? Something is troubling you." I reach my hand up to brush a lock of hair, which has now dried in sexy waves, from her face.

"I don't have doubts about us and what I want. It's just I'm not sure exactly what to do. I know you have a lot of experience. I can only imagine how many women . . ."

"Only you matter, Arianna," I interrupt. "And as far as I can see, taste, and feel—you are doing everything right."

"No, you don't understand." She shakes her head. "I know what to do up until now . . . but not what comes next . . ."

What she is alluding to finally hits me. She is a virgin. My inner reaction is a mixture of surprise, worry, and pleasure. This bold vixen of a woman is an innocent. In my time, it was expected one waited until marriage to have sex. In fact, there was great dishonor in not waiting, for the woman at least. But cultural norms change, and to expect that of today's modern female is unrealistic and ignorant. I've always believed women have the right to embrace their sexuality, and making love is to experience life. To be chaste for one man until their marriage bed was certainly an honor for him, but for her it meant forever being tied to one man. Who would want that?

It is the idea of that invisible tie that has always made me avoid virgins like the plague. And marriage, I suppose. I have enough duties keeping me on a tight leash. But as I look at Arianna and the alluring glow of her eyes, my attraction is heightened, rather than tempered, at the prospect of making love to her. The idea that she has been untouched by any other man strokes my ego. She would only be mine. And for that I feel like a hypocrite. I also recognize the gravity of the situation. She deserves for her first experience to be just as sweet and pure as herself. And what I would do to her now would not be that. She is in the midst of the Turn, and it's wreaking havoc on her hormones. If I were to take her innocence tonight, she would regret it and so would I.

"Ah, I see. How about we stop for a while and talk?" I say calmly. I don't want to upset her.

"I knew you'd do this. I shouldn't have even told you!" she says, frustrated as she shoves me hard into the pillows behind me. "I'm ready. I don't see what difference it makes."

"It matters to me. If I were to take your virginity tonight, you'd wake up tomorrow fully aware of yourself and regret it."

"I won't, I know I won't. I can't explain it . . . but this feels right," she whispers in my ear with the full press of her body against me. It does feel right, and my body is failing to agree with the reservations of my mind.

"How about this. I will show you something amazing tonight . . . and we can talk more about this tomorrow." She looks at me in surprise and triumph; she thinks she's won. And she partly has. Tonight I will not be the beast I want to. But it doesn't mean it won't be satisfying. I sit up, pulling her onto my lap. Her flesh is exposed and beautiful. I kiss her deeply as she pulls herself tighter to me. Ignoring the urge to bury myself in her, I lay her down on her back while not stopping the assault on her mouth.

My fingers find the delicate rosebud of her, and I begin to stroke it softly. Her moans intensify. But before she becomes too frenzied, I pull away, to her immediate frustration.

"Maximos!" she cries.

"Be patient." I abandon her mouth and start my descent downward, trailing kisses along her stomach. There I find her again and tease her with my tongue. She practically lurches off the bed in surprise and pleasure. I have to hold her thighs in place with my hands. This is what the gates of paradise look like. And they are beckoning to me.

"Please, Maximos, I can't last much longer."

"You have to matia . . ." I urge her. When she reaches her release, I want to look into those amazing eyes and see the gratification on her face. So I leave her on the brink again with my mouth—her nail marks on my shoulders proof of her frustration. I pull her under me, her body trembling with desire. I kiss her deeply again, the taste of honey lingering on my tongue. She is pulsating with heat, making it easy for my fingers to reach her core and apply the pressure she is seeking. She is sleek and narrow, and by the goddesses, so tight. Her muscles clench and pulse around my fingers. I'll give her just enough to take her to the edge of the place she wants to reach so badly.

"Look at me, Arianna, and say my name." The intensity of her gaze is arresting, and I feel as if she can see through me.

"Maximos, please . . . now." I want her so badly, and my ability to say no is practically nonexistent.

"Not yet. I'm giving . . . you what you need," I struggle to say. The fangs in my mouth ache. I can tell she is almost there, her moans peaking. Her right hand clutches my neck, and in one swift motion, she pulls my neck to her before I can resist. Her bite is swift and painless. It's also excruciatingly pleasurable. With the first pull of my blood, her body gives a violent shudder and she cries out with her release, a wild and beautiful sound.

But just one pull of my blood isn't enough. For her or for me. She takes more from my vein hungrily, and the natural aphrodisiac of her venom seeps into my neck. I'm at my own brink of release, and if she doesn't stop soon, my own hunger will overcome me. And I'll take everything from her.

"Stop, Arianna, you have to stop . . ."

PART III

CHAPTER 14:
TREBUCHET

2010 AD, JULY
NEW YORK, NEW YORK / HAMILTON, NEW JERSEY
TREBUCHET GLOBAL

The melody of Beethoven's Für Elise does little to quell my anger. How typical of a Subordinate to screw up a simple order. Fortunately, he won't have the opportunity to fail again since he's dead. That's the problem with leaders of today, corporate and government alike: they're too lenient. You'll never have the respect required for success if your employees think they'll be forgiven. I press the buzzer on the intercom to connect with my secretary.

"Bridget, can you please have someone come in here to clean up this mess?"

"Yes, sir, right away," she replies. The carpet is ruined. Fortunately, I was never a fan of the green Turkish weave.

"And Bridget, can you please order a new rug? Let's try something red this time."

"Yes, Mr. Papadakis."

The auburn-colored scotch is almost drained. A gift from the Japanese pharmaceutical plant we just acquired. While I prefer my private label with its infusion of B+, this does the job. After all, I've had my fill of blood for the day. Ignoring Marcellus' body on the floor, I turn up the music and rotate my leather swivel chair to see the view of Central Park. I prop my feet up on the windowpane and lean back, admiring my black velvet driving shoes embroidered with a cheeky red devil dancing on the tongue. A gift from Calix; he thought them ironic and irreverent. I suppose they are. Lucifer and I are both misunderstood light bearers.

How far my feet have come from their Tentyrian leather sandals. I like how today's fashions are more comfortable and practical, yet I find I gravitate toward the refinement of the Victorian style. Nothing beats the sophistication of a waistcoat, or "vests" people call them these days. Because I'm rarely seen in public and I keep my meetings small and intimate, which is essential for anonymity, I typically wear whatever I want. No one gives a shit, because I'm in charge.

This morning I've chosen a light charcoal cotton and silk single-breasted lapel jacket with matching bespoke pants that run on the slim side. My frame has always been long and lean, not as muscular as most Tentyrian men. Like Maximos—that bastard. My shirt is a cream linen button-down fastened at its French cuffs with ruby cuff links. The wool vest I wear is a darker shade of gray and is lined on the inside with scarlet silk. I'm a firm believer in always looking your best. After all, if you don't have personal convictions, then what do you have?

Speaking of convictions, from my penthouse view I can see the humans everywhere; running, walking their animals, pushing baby strollers. It's disgusting. They are like an infestation, breeding in mass and leaving destruction wherever they go. They consume resources and destroy the planet and each other. I'm not an avid environmentalist by any means, but what I've seen happen to this Earth in the thousands of years I've walked it is sickening.

Blood doesn't even taste the same. Now, it's tainted from pollution and the hormones in livestock. If humans are allowed to continue as they do, this Earth will die and so will I. Tentyrians may be able to live forever, but we still need oxygen and blood for survival, two things that may not exist in the future—if the humans aren't stopped. But that will happen soon enough. A few more kinks just need to be worked out.

One of which is Arianna Parker. I gave Marcellus a simple task: retrieve her. But he missed his opportunity before she got on the train. Mistake number one. I should have pulled him from the job right then and there. But he assured me he'd have her back in the City by nightfall. Instead, he botched it again and only brought me back the worthless doctor, who by then he'd practically drained and tortured so much he was useless. Mistake number two, which was his last.

Subordinates are notorious for getting distracted with their need for blood. And that is exactly what happened with Marcellus. Arianna somehow slipped out of the doctor's house while he followed two delectable Girl Scouts selling cookies. Fucking Samoas. By the time he came back to the house, she was gone, and all he managed to do was slaughter a dog and take the word of an old man who'd likely take the truth with him to the grave.

The doctor told Marcellus that Arianna had gone back to the City, and the fool believed him. If he had any brains at all, he'd have seen that her bag was still there. If only he had waited . . . Now, she has disappeared. No doubt the Brotherhood is responsible. Even the listening device he planted is now deactivated. Useless. I throw the crystal tumbler at the wall and watch it shatter into hundreds of glittering pieces. My tension feels a fraction better, but only a fraction.

I've been following the Brotherhood's movements and their businesses for quite some time. And likewise, they've been doing the same with mine. For centuries, we've tried to dismantle each other, and there have been ample successes on both sides. Out of all the destroyed homes, compounds, and facilities, I still miss my castle in Romania the most. Fortunately, the Brotherhood hasn't been able to kill me or the rest of the "Dark Coven," as they so aptly call us. The layer of Subordinates we have between ourselves and them is thick. I'm untouchable.

The difference between my own methods and those of the Brotherhood is that I don't get my hands dirty. The Brotherhood may have its soldiers, but I have Subordinates willing to obey my every whim, as long as they don't let their bloodlust get out of hand. Subordinates can be unfocused at times but they are loyal; they don't have a choice. Additionally, they pose no threat to power. When they get out of control, they are eliminated.

Calix has been whining for centuries for us to create our own army. The Tentyrian Guards we used to help carry out the coup had long ago been eliminated; most of them died locked in the Sanctum. Thank the goddesses that the four of us got of the Sanctum when we did. But I keep telling Calix, it's about the bigger picture. Why would you want to be a god among equals? That's why we removed what was of our race to begin with.

It feels like I've waited my entire life for this moment. The years of hiding, planning, and amassing the business contacts, resources, and wealth I've needed to get to this point have been slow and methodical. But when you have forever, you have plenty of time. We've had to evolve our strategies over the years. And with every evolution, it seems the plan has become grander in design. Making it all that more beautiful to execute.

At first, it was just about having the freedom to do what we wanted without rules. We turned as many humans as we wanted into mind slaves and we fed as often as we wanted, without restraint. Since it was just the four of us initially, and we moved around so often, the Brotherhood didn't stand a chance of finding us back then. But after more than a thousand years of our nomadic and gluttonous lifestyle, we began to put down some roots, and our real plans started to take shape.

Even as we settled down, the world was still a much simpler place. We could rule as kings and queens, without question, and we did. The feudal system was wonderful, and we made quite a name for ourselves in Europe. But as time went on, the humans became more numerous, practically swallowing up any unpopulated lands. They also became smarter, more organized, weaponized, and dangerous. I'll admit it; I never saw the progression of humanity come as far as Hathor predicted. The days of our unchecked freedom were numbered.

It was about the time of the Industrial Revolution when I determined change needed to occur and that the Dark Coven would pave the way to a new Eden. We started to selectively push dominos over among the humans, causing ripple effects of destruction and death. We dabbled in both the world wars, plague outbreaks, famines, and even assassinations of political leaders. We made events happen in our favor and profited from the results—whether it was from the purchase of our weapons to the chaos itself the events created. The beauty of it was that the net outcome was always the same—humans killing each other without us having to actually do it. Meanwhile, we reaped all the rewards.

I had thought by now that, even without our help, the humans would have made more progress in obliterating each other. We should have had a nuclear war, at least. They came close several times, especially during the Cuban missile crisis, which we played a not-so-subtle role in. But somehow, they've been able to prevail. If Tentyrian evolution is a miracle, so is humanity's ability to live this long. With seven billion strong, it's time to wipe the slate partially clean and recalibrate the Earth's balance. And that's exactly what will happen—soon. Funny, it seems like just yesterday the Council was talking about resetting the balance.

I'm not sure exactly how Arianna Parker fits into this, but the Brotherhood's interest in her is significant. They've been recruiting her aggressively to join Leo, and they even sent her to look at Apex, which is one of my holdings they are investigating. If it weren't for her shocking resemblance to Daria, I wouldn't give her a second thought. But after seeing the footage of her the night of Leo's party, I know she's more than just a prospective employee.

I need to get my hands on her and figure out who or what she is. My stomach is curling into knots just thinking about the possibility she is a Tentyrian descendent . . . or worse, a Luminary. I still don't know how it's possible. We took great measures to ensure that everyone was dead . . . If she has power like Daria's, or worse, Hathor's, there will surely be more complications ahead.

My hunch that she was once a patient of Dr. Raad seems accurate, but her medical records have vanished. We searched his home and office and the hospital where she may have been treated. There was no paper file on her, and unfortunately the hospital hadn't digitized her records. No one questioned at Silver Hill, even with Aglaia's persuasive methods, recalled her name. Likely the Brotherhood at work. Additionally, her parents are out of the country, and only their useless cleaning staff—who don't even know Arianna—is home.

It all seems too convenient. Fortunately, it's only a matter of time before we find the information we're looking for. Aglaia will uncover if Arianna has anything to hide, once she locates the girl's friends and acquaintances. And the good doctor is bound to crack eventually, which reminds me I should call Calix to check on his progress. Better yet, I should see for myself.

I press the buzzer again. "Bridget, I'm leaving. Clear my afternoon."

"Yes, sir."

She's a good girl, obedient. That's what I like. She lost her spark when I turned her into a Human Subordinate, but that's what happens. Sometimes I miss that spark, especially of Tentyrian women in general. Hathor used to give me a run for my money. Too bad she turned into a heartless bitch. I thought Selene would be a good mate. But she didn't make it to the end. Pity, considering her power was so useful. I figured I would mourn her loss for a while, but surprisingly I didn't. It must not have been love after all.

It's a beautiful day out. The summer heat has lifted, and the City doesn't stink as bad. Compared to how it smelled in 1900, it's like a spring garden out there. I wouldn't mind riding in the Bentley, watching the vermin try to see who's behind the tinted glass. But using human transportation makes one a target, and the Brotherhood has been closing in lately. Better to be safe than sorry.

I lean back in the chair and close my eyes, envisioning the sterile lab in New Jersey where so many of our Human Subordinates are hard at work engineering DTPA12. DTPA12 is our unique formula of diethylenetriaminepentaacetic acid, designed to bind to metals and particles of radioactive elements in plutonium, americium, and curium. Soon enough, I'll be the sole distributor of the only drug capable of treating the unique radiation sickness when it sweeps the globe.

I imagine the interrogation room where Calix is keeping the doctor and direct my energy toward it, embracing the familiar cool that comes with shifting as it brushes over my skin.

"Stavros, I wasn't expecting you," says Calix nonchalantly as he looks up from the syringe he's filling. Arrogant, per usual. The sleeves of his purple gingham button-down are rolled up, and he's tossed his blazer aside. I notice a few spots of blood on his leather Gucci loafers. How unusual for him, as he always looks pristine.

The combination of Calix's slick demeanor and his boyish good looks, akin to a California surfer without the tan, make him irresistible to women. While I may not have his golden curls or cherubic face, I make up for it with my power and intelligence. It's been amusing to watch Calix and his female dalliances all these years, but it's almost impossible to be jealous of him. At the end of the day, Calix will never have the foresight to be a rival.

The doctor is a mess, but white cotton bandages cover his damaged neck and the lacerations on his body. The smell of his blood is tainted by the smell of antiseptic, making him not even remotely tempting. He appears unconscious in the examination chair he's strapped to, as his head hangs limply. The harsh fluorescent lighting really isn't doing anything for his bruised and bloodied complexion.

"Any progress?" I ask.

"Marcellus did a number on him, but he'll heal," answers Calix. "I've given him antibiotics, steroids, and painkillers to help. Torture is not the way to get to him. But I'm not sure if I can get into his mind just yet. I haven't encountered a mental block in a human like this since we killed those Shaolin monks. Remember that raid?"

"Ah yes, 1351, the Red Turban Rebellion. Those monks put up a good fight."

"They did but not good enough," Calix says with a smirk. He flicks the syringe, and clear droplets squirt out as he applies pressure to the plunger.

"What's that?" I ask.

"A psychoactive medication."

"Truth serum? Will it work?"

"In conjunction with my power, I should be able to get something out of him."

"Be careful; don't scare him to death with a heart attack."

"That's what the defibrillator is for," says Calix as he points to the set of paddles bolted to the wall. This should be interesting. Calix injects the doctor, and we wait a few minutes in silence. Calix checks his pulse. He then slaps the doctor with a loud thwack. A white mark appears on the doctor's golden cheek and quickly turns to red. His eyes flutter, and he lets out a groan.

"What . . . do . . . you want?" he asks, his tongue thick in his mouth. Calix looks to me, giving me the honors.

"How do you know Arianna Parker?" I ask slowly, allowing him time to register my question.

"She is jusssstt a friend," he says with a slight slur. The doctor's almond eyes are glazed as he looks straight ahead, at nothing.

"He's lying, Calix."

"I know. He's been trained in counterinterrogation techniques. We'll just need to give it some time. Don't worry, I'll work my magic."

"Now Aman, we know that's not true. Arianna is in great danger right now, and we need to find her. We can't do that unless you help us," coos Calix.

"Where is sheee?" he asks calmly.

"She's been kidnapped."

"Funny, I thought that was whaaat happened to me," he says wryly. His split lip is still bloodied, and the saliva in his mouth is pink.

"Is it? Is that what happened to you?" Calix asks innocently. He places his hands on the doctor's head. I can feel the energy in the air that he is directing at the doctor, trying to instill a false memory in him—likely something that will scare the shit out of him. Raad's head vibrates slightly in Calix's grasp, and his eyes roll into the back of his head.

"Fuck! He's still too strong. He won't let me in," responds Calix as he pulls away with obvious frustration.

"You won't get anything out of me," whispers Raad as he blinks repeatedly, trying to clear the haze of Calix's attempted mind manipulation. Calix ushers me outside of the room to stand in front of the pressure-locked door to the general lab area.

"I just need more time, Stavros."

"That's a luxury we don't have, Calix. I need to know why the

Brotherhood wants her! Hopefully Aglaia has found something helpful. Call me when you break him."

"I'm not your Subordinate, Stavros. Remember that," Calix warns.

"No you aren't, Calix, but you don't want me as an enemy." I keep my voice calm.

"Old friend, of course not," he says, trying to diffuse the tension, placing a hand on my shoulder. "But you forget yourself with me sometimes. In the interests of our partnership, I'm only trying to remind you." Like hell you are. I smile.

"Forgive me. It's been a stressful couple of months. Are the shipments ready?" I ask. I'll put him in his place later.

"Yes, the DTPA12 is prepped to ship to São Paulo, Mumbai, Hong Kong, Tokyo, Washington, DC, Los Angeles, London, Paris, and Berlin."

"Excellent. Full speed ahead then. Have you heard from Aglaia, by the way?" Calix smiles in response with an arched brow.

"Right, still aren't speaking yet, are you? Give it a hundred years or so. She'll come around." I leave him with a pat on the back and shift to my brownstone.

In my townhouse, it's most convenient to find Aglaia in the parlor. She's lounging on the Queen Anne settee, her leather skirt showing plenty of thigh. Upon my arrival, she doesn't look up from the screen of her iPad, but she knows I'm there.

"Really, Stavros, I don't know why you insist on keeping the most uncomfortable furniture around," she says in her typical, bored voice.

"I see you're being useful again. Online shopping, are we?" I make my way over to the bar cart and pour myself a generous scotch.

"Well, it's unlikely Saks Fifth Avenue is going to be thriving after most of the human race dies, isn't it, Stavros?" Her finger doesn't stop its swipe as she peruses the digital pages of designer clothing.

"Well we all must make sacrifices. Try buying some real clothes this time, Aglaia; you look no better than a hooker." That gets her attention.

"And I should be taking fashion advice from you? You look like you just walked out of a Sherlock Holmes novel. Do you have a pocket watch too?"

"All I'm saying is that erring on the conservative side, my dear, isn't a bad thing. Leaving something to the imagination, hmm?"

"Your idea of attractive is a corset and legs swallowed in petticoats. No thanks, Stavros. Been there, done that. I like my freedom."

"Well that's evident. What was his name last night?"

"None of your business. But he was a sweet boy," she says, tilting her head with a lazy smile on her heavily lipsticked red lips.

Aglaia is gorgeous, the spitting of image of her now-deceased sister. Between their long chestnut curls, heart-shaped faces, and curvaceous bodies, I used to have a difficult time telling them apart. But since her twin's death in 1941, Aglaia had cropped her hair short and insisted on an overtly sexual look. So different from how she used to be. Asia's death was hard on Aglaia; it was like losing her other half. In part I guess that's why they were both so flippant about men. At the end of the day, the two of them preferred each other's company. But World War II changed that.

Initially, we played both sides, supplying weapons to both the Allies and the Nazis. Essentially we did what we always do—supply the toys and let the children hurt each other. On a routine trip to Berlin, however, Asia didn't come back. Somehow she had been careless in her feeding, and our Nazi partners received a tip she was a vampire. She was followed, ambushed, and before she could shift away, a grenade rendered her powerless and on the brink of death. But death would have been a better fate than what she received.

The Nazis took her dying body and experimented on her. By the time we recovered her, it was too late. Her powers were useless, and her mind was completely gone. We tried everything to heal her. Aglaia patiently nursed and cared for her for years. But there was nothing that could be done—she was a vegetable. One day, Asia jumped out the window of their London apartment and fell to her death four stories below. Some part of her must have recognized that she no longer had a life worth living.

Aglaia was devastated, constantly ranting about the evilness and fickleness of humans. I never pointed out the hypocrisy of her beliefs; I'm too much of a gentleman and strategist. But who is she kidding? She murders people every day. It wasn't until something precious of hers was taken that her hatred of humans was solidified. I suppose that is always the genesis of motivation, though. It has to become personal for it to become real. Fortunately for me, it is just that type of conviction I need for our cause.

"Aside from your own personal exploits, did you manage to accomplish what I asked?" I finish the drink in one swift swallow.

"As a matter of fact, yes," Aglaia taunts me playfully as she un-crosses her long legs. She abandons her new iPad and slinks over in her patent leather heels to the armchair I'm lounging in. She perches herself seductively on my lap. Aglaia loves to tease, but her overtures are innocuous, and right now she's just angry at Calix. Their on again, off again relationship is enough to drive me crazy. She's smart enough to know I won't take the bait.

"I left you a present upstairs in your bedroom," she says.

"A present? What's the occasion?" I ask, surprised.

"There isn't one. But hopefully you'll stop acting like such a bore. Her name is Laura. She's Arianna Parker's friend."

"Very good, I'm impressed. And may I ask what condition she is in?"

"Don't fret. I didn't touch her—not even a taste. She looks like your type. Thin and blonde. . ."

"What does she know?"

"You can see for yourself. But it's clear she doesn't know where Arianna is. She can tell you, though, about our mini Daria's relation-ship with the doctor. You were right. She was his patient."

"Did anyone see you take her?"

"Yes, as you requested. The Brothers were watching her. Really, they are such simpletons."

"Excellent. It's time we step up the game. Aside from her friend, did you find anyone else who knew anything?"

"Her parents are still off the grid. I found an old boyfriend who seems like a sleazebag. Not particularly helpful. But he did say that their relationship ended abruptly when she figured out he was cheating."

"Aglaia, how is that even remotely insightful?"

"He was genuinely surprised that she figured it out. He used the words, 'It was like she read my mind.'"

"Shit."

"Exactly. On that note, I'm going to head out." Aglaia gets up from my lap slowly, allowing me a generous view of her behind. She isn't wearing underwear.

"Where to?" I ask.

"To the office. Trebuchet Global isn't run solely by you, Stavros."

"I never said it was."

"You didn't have to. Enjoy my treat," she says over her shoulder before she disappears.

CHAPTER 15: AWAKENING

"**O**h Laur, you shouldn't have done this!" I exclaim.

"Are you kidding me, Ari?"

"Yes I am. But really, these are too beautiful and expensive."

"Girl, it's your twenty-fifth birthday, and since you wouldn't let me throw you a party, this is the only alternative."

"I love them, I love them, I love them!"

"I know you eyed them last time we were shopping. They are faaaaabulous!"

I give Laura a heartfelt hug and kiss on the cheek as I tear the tissue paper off the Ferragamo hot pink Blejan heels.

"Now where do you want to wear them tonight? This is part one of your present; part two is getting ridiculously drunk and dancing inappropriately all night. Maybe even some tabletop action, give or take a few kamikazes," says Laura.

"Your pick. You know everyone and the best places to go. I'm just the tagalong, Laur." I give her a twirl in my heels, and I get the nod of approval.

"More champagne?" I ask, reaching for the Veuve chilling in the crystal ice bucket on my coffee table.

"Yes, please. Of course you put the onus on me. That's fine, I'll let it slide. You are the birthday girl, after all." I fill Laura's glass to the brim, and she quickly drinks the bubbly foam before it flows over. After a healthy sip, she leans back into the sofa, where we've been lounging for the past hour attempting to recover from the birthday dinner food coma. I think we've only done more damage with the champagne.

"That reminds me," continues Laura. "I have one more gift for you. It's not wrapped, so you'll have to close your eyes." I shut them immediately and hear Laura rustle around in her bottomless Marc Jacobs. Several lipsticks and tampons later, she finds what she is looking for and places it on my hair. I open my eyes and touch it. It's a plastic tiara. "Now, I expect you to wear this out tonight. We're bound to get free drinks!" Laura enthuses.

"Laur, this really is the best birthday. Dinner was amazing, the cake was amazing, and the shoes are amazing! And the tiara, you remembered . . . I'm so lucky to have a friend like you."

"You say that every year, Ari. I think it's because you had a childhood devoid of birthdays."

"That's not true," I say defensively. Laura gives me a knowing look.

"You're right. But this time I really mean it; this is the best birthday!"

"Yeah, yeah, yeah. You'll say that next year! Now hurry up and change your dress. You should wear the pink Kate Spade one that makes your breasts look fantastic."

"Are you sure it's not too revealing?"

"Again Ari, are you kidding me? It's Kate Spade. I don't think her clothes exactly scream 'slut.' Now hurry up, it's almost midnight!"

I rush to my closet to change, but when I open the door, the rows of shoes, shelves, and clothing are gone. In fact, my whole closet is gone. Instead it's a party. What the hell? I step inside and make my way through the crowd. What happened to my closet?

"Laur, can you come here?" No answer. I turn around, but there is no door anymore. It's just a posh room with a sea of people. "Laura! Laura! Where are you?" People are staring. I elbow my way past the elegantly dressed men and women and blank-faced waiters. They are holding cocktails—all red cocktails. "Laura?"

"Looking for someone?" I know that voice. I turn around. It's Charles.

"Why are you here?" I ask.

"I came to see you, Ari. Happy birthday, baby. I have a surprise for you." His hand grips my wrist, and he starts to pull me through the crowd. His fingers are cold and clammy and too tight. I try to resist, but my new shoes slide on the floor. The conversation around me grows louder; the murmurs are overpowering my thoughts. The control I've worked so hard to nurture and strengthen is slipping.

"I'm not your baby! Let go of me! Help! Stop him!" I scream. No one hears a word I say as Charles keeps pulling me. Why won't these people help me? They are just standing there, glassy eyed. We reach a side door he yanks open and pushes me through. The door locks behind me and refuses to open despite my efforts. I whirl around to see I'm now standing in a richly decorated office with burgundy tones and dark walnut paneling. A fire is blazing in the fireplace. I thought it was summer? The carpet is a deep rich red, but there is something not right about it. It's making a squishy sound underfoot. I look down, and there is red liquid seeping through my pink shoes. It's blood.

"Beautiful, isn't it?" I hear a man say. But it's not Charles. When I look up to face the voice, there is a man in a black velvet smoking jacket leaning against a desk. He's tall, with pale white skin and thick dark hair that stops just above his shoulders. He has a narrow face and high cheekbones; his nose is slightly hooked. While not handsome by traditional standards, there is something alluring and catlike about him.

His eyes are blue, but where Maximos' eyes are brilliant sapphires, this man's are the color of dull, dark ink. He stands up and walks toward me. That is when I see Laura in the desk chair. Her head is cocked to the side, and blood is pouring from two punctures in her neck. Her eyes and mouth are open. She is dead. The man's tapered fingers point to her. "Isn't it beautiful, Arianna?" he says.

That's when I wake up with a start.

"Arianna, are you okay?" Maximos says, tossing the book down he's been reading in the chair pulled up next to the bed. He stands by my side immediately and checks my temperature with his hand.

"I think so, just a bad dream," I say, sitting up, slightly out of breath from the terror of the nightmare that felt so vivid. But wait, my voice sounds different—it doesn't sound panicked; it's soft and calm, with a singsong quality. It's alluring. Like the way Maximos always sounds to me. "My voice, it's different," I whisper to Maximos as I touch my throat with my fingers. To my relief, there are no puncture wounds.

"It's the Turn. It's complete. You are going to feel slightly different," Maximos says as his eyes seem to survey every inch of me. Self-consciously I survey myself too. That's when I notice I'm wearing an oversized pinstripe nightshirt and pajama bottoms. Judging by the size, they must be Maximos'. At least I'm not naked.

Maximos looks beautiful per usual, albeit slightly rumpled with a bit of black stubble showing. Effortlessly sexy is more like it. He's changed into navy blue linen drawstring pants and a simple white V-neck T showing plenty of muscle and sinew. Muscle I just want to run my hands on and explore . . .

"Your temperature is normal," he says, interrupting my mini reverie. My temperature may be normal, but I certainly don't feel normal. It's daylight outside, and the balcony doors of his bedroom are open. The white linen curtains flutter gently in the breeze. Although I recognize the room from last night, I now see it in sharp detail. But it's more than just seeing detail. I can smell it, hear it, and sense every facet of it. It's like I was an out-of-focus camera lens that has suddenly been set to the right aperture.

I can see deep between the seams of the painted white floorboards, I can taste tiny salt crystals on my tongue, and I can feel the individual threads of the finely woven Egyptian cotton sheets on my skin. I can even hear what sounds like Shashandra and someone else discussing a lunch menu. It must be the afternoon. For the first time, I feel alive. Maximos was right. I have awakened.

"Geez, how many times am I going to wake up in a strange bed?" I say, trying to fill the awkward silence that now pervades the room. Maximos clears his throat and looks embarrassed. Whether it's for him or me, I'm not sure. Probably for me, considering how I acted last night. Flashes of our skin touching and his mouth on mine crowd my memory. Kate Spade would definitely call me a slut now. I scan his face, trying to read his expression. One thing is clear—it's filled with regret.

Before I know what I'm saying, I start blabbering. "Maximos, I just want to say how sorry I am about last night . . . I was out of line." The words tumble out awkwardly. His brow furrows, and his mouth draws into an unreadable expression. Why isn't he saying anything? "I know I practically threw myself at you. I swear, I don't normally do that." Then, like an avalanche, all of the memories come raining down on me. I remember fully now, beyond just the sensual moments we shared . . .

"I drank from you and I almost didn't stop!" I get out of bed in a flurry of sheets, pulling them with me to inspect his neck. I touch my hand to the muscular column and feel his skin beneath mine. But there is no broken flesh or even a mark. Did I imagine biting him? Did I imagine that spicy hot liquid filling my mouth, driving me to the edge? "Did I hurt you?" My voice comes out a tremble.

"No, of course not. I'm fine, I promise. You stopped when you needed to," he says dismissively as he takes a subtle step back from me. But I see the movement and what it communicates. The distance forces my hand to drop from his corded neck. He clears his throat again and shoves his hands in his pockets. "We're fast healers, you and I. All Tentyrians are. I see you remember last night; I was thinking you might not," he says, rocking back on his heels. Thinking or hoping?

"Yes, I remember," I say. My blush is likely visible, at least where I'm not covered by the oversized pajamas.

"You have nothing to be ashamed of. Sexual arousal is a natural part of the Turn, and it's not like I was a saint. If anything, I'd understand if you were angry at me," he replies. The man definitely was not a saint. The way his hands, his mouth, oh my God his mouth, touched me . . . But I have no anger, only desire. Even now. But does he feel desire for me or just regret? In the daylight, he seems like a different person. Where last night he was passionate, almost carnal, now his body language and tone are restrained. I was sure of his desire and tenderness last night, conveyed by his touch and the Greek endearments that made my heart ache with every word. Now, I am anything but sure.

Maximos told me I would regret what we almost did in the morning. But the more I think about it—and believe me, I'm thinking about it, because it's nearly impossible to forget—I don't think I would be sorry. My first instinct was to apologize out of that innate female defense mechanism that we have to protect our respect. No woman wants a man to think she is easy. And that look he just gave me, it certainly wasn't one of desire. What else was I supposed to say?

The truth is—I wanted Maximos, and I still do. In all the craziness that has become my life, this may be one of the craziest aspects: being attracted to the man who turned it all upside down to begin with. "No, I'm not angry . . ." I begin to say. But before I can explain how I feel, to recant my dumb apology, Maximos interrupts.

"Arianna, I'm the one who must apologize. How intimate we were . . . it should never have happened, and I promise it won't happen again. It was a mistake, caused by the Turn. I'm ashamed of myself." Well I guess I have my answer about how he feels. A mistake. Ashamed. The words leave their stinging slap. I cross my arms in front of me and look at him squarely.

"So now what? I guess I'm a vampire now? Can I be released back into the wild, or are you going to keep me here to observe my absurd behavior? You'll need to keep a respectable distance, of course. I don't want to shame you, after all." I keep my voice level, but I know he can hear the dripping sarcasm. His expression is one of surprise and confusion. I can tell he is reaching for the right words. But there are no right words; he said what he felt. Maximos turns to face the view off the balcony, giving his back to me. Silence ensues.

"The Turn is over. So yes, you are a full Tentyrian. Not a vampire. It was something you always were, Arianna. You will stay here, though. It will be some time before you can go back to your old life, if at all," he says solemnly, turning to face my questioning gaze. In the seconds waiting for him to respond, some part of me held out hope he'd say that what happened between us really wasn't a mistake. That he wasn't ashamed. But instead, the only words out of his mouth were a command, highlighting that my freedom was gone.

"What is that supposed to mean, 'if at all'? I will be going back to my old life, whether you like it or not! And I'm not about to go on a bloody rampage, Maximos. You said I would have an uncontrollable blood thirst. But I feel fine. Maybe you don't know as much as you think you do." I am seething. The room starts to waver slightly, so I take a seat on the edge of the bed. Too angry to even look at him, I reach down to rip the bandage from my foot. To my surprise, the cut is completely healed. Not even a twinge of pain.

"You feel fine because you've recently had my blood. Your thirst will come back with a vengeance. But it's not that it's you, Arianna— you have plenty of self-control, and I think over time that would never be put into question. It's simply not safe. The Dark Coven wants you." Well at least someone does.

"I can't live my life in hiding, Maximos. And I need to find Raad," I say vehemently.

"That's what we're working on right now. What you need to do is rest and hone your power."

"When you say 'we,' who are you referring to?"

"The Tentyrian Brotherhood. That's what we call ourselves."

"Right, your 'brothers.' Then why . . ."

Maximos holds up a hand to stop my inquisition. "Before we get into this, let me help you get dressed first. You may feel a little shaky and unsteady." My first instinct is to protest immediately. But I hold my tongue. Now that he's called attention to it, I am feeling really dizzy. "Vertigo is natural when all of your Tentyrian senses are first awakened. But it will disappear in a day or so."

"Okay, sure. Lead the way. I don't think I have much of a choice, anyway."

"I can call Shashandra if you feel it's improper."

"I think it's fair to say we already crossed the boundaries of propriety last night," I say dryly. Since he feels so ashamed, I might as well rub it in.

"As you wish." And with that, Maximos sweeps me up into his arms. This time I do protest.

"I'm not an invalid!"

"Trust me, it will be quicker." I feel a cool tingling on my skin. It's what I felt right before I woke up on the island . . .

In the blink of an eye, we're in the dressing area with my clothes. There's no party in here, which reminds me, I need to call Laura. Maximos sits me on a cushioned bench in front of the floor-length mirror while he rummages through the contents of the shelves. I'm speechless.

"Is this okay?" He holds up a pair of blue jean shorts and a white tank top.

"Umm, can we talk about what just happened? We were just in one room and now we're here."

"It's called shifting. We'll have to see if you are able to do it. Only Tentyrian Council members were able to, to my knowledge. But maybe I don't know as much as I think?" he chides. I can't think of an intelligent quip. Must be the vertigo.

Maximos hands me the clothes along with a basic white cotton bra and thong.

"We don't know what you are fully capable of yet. It's possible you'll be able to shift as well," he says.

"That's how you got me to this island, isn't it? And here I was thinking we hopped on your private jet." I fold and refold the clothes in my lap to keep my hands busy while I ponder the possibility of being able to go wherever and whenever I want. Maybe I can get myself off this island . . .

"It's the fastest and safest way to travel," he explains. "You just need to have a clear visual picture of the place."

Eager to experiment, I close my eyes and visualize my apartment, directing all of my concentration there. No luck.

"You need to give it time. And I would prefer it if you only try it with me or when one of the Brothers is with you. If you do succeed in shifting to where you want to go, that means I'll have to find you again. Not that I won't, but I want you where I know you are safe. Understood?" He's definitely back to his controlling self.

"I must say, I prefer your bedside manner . . . Before I forget or you shift me someplace else against my will, I need to call Laura. She is probably frantic."

"I wouldn't worry about it. I told you last night I took care of it."

"Yes, I recall you did, but that does little to reassure me."

"See for yourself," says Maximos as he fishes out his iPhone from his pocket and brings up my Gmail account.

"You hacked into my Gmail?" I ask in disbelief

"It was necessary," he says as if it should be obvious. "Text messages and phone calls can be traced. An e-mail sent from an undisclosed IP address can't." I give him a dirty look and grab the phone from him to scroll through the last e-mail exchange:

From: laura.ash.delia@gmail.com
To: arianna.e.parker@gmail.com
Bitch, where are you? You aren't picking up my calls or answering my texts. What gives? Sorry I missed your call last night. Jake was over J So many deets to share! Not sure if you'll be ashamed or proud? I'm going to assume the latter for now. I have fabulous plans for your bday dinner. Can't wait to celebrate the big 25!!!! If you don't get back to me by 5pm I'm coming over there and breaking down your door. It won't be pretty.
XO L

From: arianna.e.parker@gmail.com
To: laura.ash.delia@gmail.com
Laura, can't make dinner. Have to go on another business trip. Will be out of the country so phone won't work. So sorry to mess up your plans. Please forgive me. I promise I'll make it up to you!
XO A

From: laura.delia@gmail.com
To: arianna.e.parker@gmail.com
Are you insane? It's your birthday! Who agrees to go on a business trip on their birthday? Is this about that job at Leo Capital? Is he really that hot? You said he was but I'm questioning your taste if you are ditching me for him. And you don't even call me! Hos before bros girl.
XO Your former best friend
P.S. you never address me as "Laura" what gives?

From: arianna.e.parker@gmail.com
To: laura.delia@gmail.com
Not insane—but unfortunately this was unavoidable. I'll let you know what's going on as soon as I'm back . . .
XO A

From: laura.delia@gmail.com

To: arianna.e.parker@gmail.com

You didn't answer the most important question. Is this about him? And when in the hell are you coming back?

XO Your dying-to-know former best friend "Laura"

Since Laura's last e-mail there has been no reply. I'm positively mortified that Maximos has been in my e-mail and had the gall to pretend to be me. Who knows what other types of exchanges he's read between me and Laura? The snarky material is endless. As if my embarrassment couldn't get worse.

"So are you going to monitor my e-mail now? I assume you have my phones too?" I ask snidely.

"They had to be destroyed to prevent tracking. By the way, who has two BlackBerry smartphones? I only put your e-mail on here for convenience sake."

"A lot of people use two phones. One is for work and one is personal. But I guess you have no respect for anything that is personal. You better replace them."

"I can ask Aristos to provide you with a secure device, as long as you agree to keep our location and the obvious details of what has been happening out of any communications. Your friend wouldn't understand. And the more she knows, the more danger it will put her in."

"Is she in danger?" The terror of my dream flashes in my mind.

"I don't think so. She knows nothing about what you are. Only Raad would have had any knowledge to help the Dark Coven. The Brothers have her under surveillance, though, just in case. If anyone tries to hurt her, they'll be there."

"They better be. If anything happens to her, I'll never forgive myself. Raad and Laura are like my family, Maximos." His face is sympathetic with understanding. Of course it would be; he has already lost what was his family.

"Come on, let's get you dressed, Arianna." Maximos pulls me to a standing position like a parent dealing with a stubborn child. He is more than a foot taller than me, and I have to lift my chin to connect with his eyes. The sapphire blue of them is still just as beautiful as they were last night.

"But what about my work? The office is going to be freaking out. I haven't responded to an e-mail in forty-eight hours, not to mention I haven't shown up."

"You have resigned, Ari."

"Are you fucking kidding me? You did not!" I push him, and he stumbles back, to my utter satisfaction. I'm strong.

"I had to! You are in no condition to start work again anytime soon."

"How dare you!" I throw the clothes at him.

"I'm sorry, I truly am. But this is the way it has to be."

"I want you to know that when this is all over, I am walking away from this and you. I am going back to my life."

"Let's just see what happens, Arianna . . . And I am sorry. I promise, your career and reputation won't be marred by this. I'll make sure it isn't."

I take a deep breath and try to calm myself. I need to go with the current rather than fight it.

"If you are going to insist on ruining my life, then I'm going to insist you call me Ari," I challenge. Maximos seems so set on establishing the rules I must follow. But rather than making me want to follow them—I want to throw them in his face. So I begin to unbutton my shirt slowly, trailing my fingers provocatively along the exposed skin.

"Okay," he replies calmly, his eyes not wavering from mine. But I see his convulsive swallow and clench of his jaw. Not so in control after all.

Before I can make it past the fourth button, Maximos takes over. Within seconds, I'm dressed. But this time as Maximos moves with his superhuman speed, I can actually see him. I see the way his fingers linger as they travel up my legs. Thank goodness I'd had them waxed recently. I feel the gentle way he folds the bra over my breasts and clasps it behind my back. His movements are graceful and smooth, and his touch leaves my skin tingling. The synapses in my brain must be firing on all cylinders. I have to reach for his arm to steady myself.

"Easy there. Do you want use the bathroom?" Maximos asks. As soon as I say the words, he shifts me there.

"Can you wait outside? I'm not going to pass out," I say to him with more than a hint of sass. He looks skeptical. "You are going to drive me crazy. If you don't leave right now, I will flip out. And you saw how volatile I can be. Like last night." That should get him to leave.

"Okay, fine, but I'm right outside the door."

He is infuriating. As soon as I inch my way toward a little control, he tries to take it. After Maximos disappears, I survey myself in the mirror and am shocked at what I see. It's still me, just a more enhanced version. My hair, even my eyelashes, are thicker, shinier. I graze my fingers along my cheek. My skin feels smoother and softer—like a child's. The color of my lips seems pinker. I've always been fit, but even the muscle definition of my arms is more refined than it was yesterday. Between my amazing senses, strength, and appearance—maybe being Tentyrian isn't so bad? I wonder if people would believe it if I told them that I owe my newfound "rejuvenation" to the spa?

I quickly brush my teeth while holding firmly onto the sink so I don't topple over. The room may be spinning, but at this rate, I'll never be able to do anything on my own if I don't assert myself. I take the wooden comb and try to detangle the natural waves that are springing up in the humidity. I manage to get the knots out, but doing anything manageable with it is impossible without a hair tie. Whatever; like the lack of lack shoes, I just let it go. I take a deep breath and try to remind myself that the quickest way out of this mess is to work with Maximos, not against him. When I open the door, he is standing right there. What a surprise.

"Here, put these on. It's bright outside, and your eyes are going to be very sensitive," Maximos says as he hands me a pair of Ray-Bans.

"So the myth that vampires can't go out in the daylight isn't true after all."

"Like I said, you aren't a vampire. You are Tentyrian. But I suppose there is some truth to the myth in that we prefer the nighttime. Vampire legends tend to take their attribution from our kind. With our heightened senses, you'll see you'll appreciate the quiet and darkness that falls with the sunset. It's also when our powers can be wielded with the most strength. You've probably heard the term the 'witching hour'? Midnight for us is when we feel the strongest, the most powerful."

"Then why aren't we asleep now?"

"Because in today's society, it's difficult to only function at night. The world doesn't work that way, so we mostly keep human hours. Shall we eat?"

"Yes, I'm starving," I say enthusiastically.

"I bet."

This time, Maximos has the decency to leave me standing as he wraps his arms around my waist and we shift to an outdoor pavilion with a fountain and amazing view of the sea. He's right, it's blindingly bright. But the beautiful sounds, smells, and scenery quickly eclipse the annoyance of the light. Now that we're outside, my senses are buzzing with the ocean air and crash of the waves. I can smell the rich greenery of the orchards and even the ripening pomegranates. A table is set for us with bamboo chargers, sea-green glasses bespeckled with air bubbles from their artistic blowing, and simple silver flatware. Like the gentleman he is, Maximos pulls the chair out for me under a white umbrella.

"What would you like to eat?" he asks.

"Whatever is on the menu. It sounds like there already is one."

"Ah, you heard that?"

"I feel like I can hear everything."

"A whispered conversation now will sound normal to you. It's a matter of tuning out what you don't want to hear, which in your case is more than just sound."

"It's funny, I almost feel like my ability to block thoughts now is stronger. I obviously didn't run or meditate this morning, which I used to feel compelled to do to quiet my mind every day. My senses feel alive, but my mind is surprisingly quiet."

"Now that the Turn is complete, your physical state has been fortified. For years you've been building your own mental block through routine exercise, both physical and mental, which is essential for all young Tentyrians. It teaches discipline, and it also makes the difficult symptoms in our youth easier to manage. But now, your body is in tune with your mind. From here on out, the headaches and overwhelming thoughts of those around you should be much easier to control. That's how it was for Daria, who shared your gift. You should always remember to keep your guard up, however. You can lose your grip on reality if you aren't careful . . ."

The sound of a sliding glass door and Beau's toenails clicking on the Spanish tile can be heard. Following close behind on Shashandra's heels, Beau jogs over and obediently sits next to me, eager for some attention.

"Look at you sitting so patiently. Who taught you that trick?" I purr to Beau, giving him a loving back scratch. Maximos smiles smugly.

"If you were firmer with him, he'd obey you more," he says.

"I'm an indulgent mother, so bite me."

"I see you have a sense of humor this morning," he says, the corners of his mouth lifting. Maybe it is possible for us to communicate like civil people.

"Master Vasilliadis, Mistress Parker, are you ready to eat?" interrupts Shashandra. "Cook has prepared a delicious lunch."

"Yes, thank you. Please bring out the food," says Maximos.

Maximos plucks a plump grape from the cluster sitting in a white ceramic bowl at the center of the table. He examines it carefully before popping it into his mouth.

"Did you know we grow these here on the island?"

"You have nice orchards. I've seen them. But I don't want to talk about fruit. What were you saying about being careful?"

"Are you always this demanding?" Maximos shakes his head with a smile. "There are other Tentyrians who have powers, Ari. You saw that I can enter people's dreams. That's child's play compared to what others can do. For example, Calix of the Dark Coven can make you think and remember things that never happened. If you don't keep your mind carefully shielded, they can hurt you from the inside out. You also need to be careful not to let your Tentyrian power and strength go to your head. I told you before, blood is an intoxicating thing. Coupled with your superior strength and ability to manipulate humans, it's easy to think you belong in a position of superiority. That's why the Dark Coven began and ultimately destroyed our people."

"We can manipulate humans?"

"To some extent. When we want to, we can offer up commands if we direct our energy at them. I tried it on you, but you resisted and it didn't take. It was another confirmation that you were different."

"That's crazy. We can actually command people to do things?"

"We are natural-born hunters, Ari, and that ability helps us. Even the sound of our voice works in our favor to draw our prey in. However, as civilized people, we've made it a conscious choice not to give in to our baser instincts. And to prevent humans from finding out what we are . . ."

"How?" I ask.

"Well, when we can't fight the urge for human blood and there is no one to give it willingly, we take great care to obtain it humanely. After we feed on humans, our venom makes them more susceptible to control. So we wipe their memory of having been bitten. Back when Tentyris was in its golden age, we had plenty of willing hosts—either the Guardians or our human servants. We didn't need to manipulate humans within our community. They knew our secrets and were sworn to protect them. But in instances where we needed blood and a willing host couldn't be found, we took what we needed, in a nonviolent manner . . ."

"So you wouldn't kill humans—or 'hosts,' as you call them?"

"No. It was against the law, and it still is within the Tentyrian Brotherhood. We respect all life."

"So you don't think you are superior to humans?"

"Absolutely not. Their blood gives us life. And we have unique powers that enable us to protect them. In theory, we should live in symbiosis. That is the foundation for the Tentyrian Code, which for us is law. The Code was drafted by the Tentyrian Council and forbids the killing of humans unless warranted by self-defense or war. In fact, it was punishable by death. While the Dark Coven no longer follows the Code, we the Tentyrian Brotherhood do."

"How many Brothers are there?"

"Around fifty."

"But you said there were only six survivors?"

"Some of the Brothers were changed from their human states and made to become like us. The Brothers are stationed all over the world. Right now, most are in the United States . . ."

The sliding glass door opens again, and Shashandra appears with lunch. A heart of palm and fig salad with pine nuts and a dressing I don't recognize, along with a tall glass of blood, is served. I can feel my gums pricking like they did last night. I subconsciously run my tongue along my teeth and can feel the sharp incisors. In last night's frenzy, I barely even noticed . . .

"It's okay, your fangs will come out when you get hungry. See, I have them too." Maximos bares his pearly white fangs to me in a boyish grin.

"Well I guess we're both freak shows now." I poke at the salad with my fork.

"Aren't you going to eat?" asks Maximos.

"I've never been a salad girl . . ."

"You'll see, you'll like it. It has wonderful flavor. Plus that's not really your lunch. The blood is. That is what your body wants."

After a minute of contemplation, I take the glass and chug it down greedily. It's definitely not as good as what I experienced last night—that was like the nectar of the gods.

"It's human blood we get from a blood bank," Maximos explains. "Since you are newly turned, you especially won't like animal blood. The fresher the blood for you right now, the better. It will help you reach your full potential. In a few days, once you get stronger, I'll take you to the mainland and you can practice drinking from a human."

"What if I don't want to?"

"It's your choice, but your body is eventually going to want hot blood from an open vein. And you'll want to hunt."

"It sounds barbaric."

"You weren't complaining last night."

"Touché."

"So what's with the salad then if all I need is blood to survive?"

"Eating human food is enjoyable, provided that it has lots of flavor.

Our palettes are very sensitive and delight in rich foods in small quantities."

"I guess that is going to take some getting used—small quantities."

"Before the Turn, your body's energy consumption was much higher than a human's. Your diet likely tried to compensate for that."

"And I always wanted rare meat . . ."

"Because it was high in blood content. See, it's all interconnected. And you thought I was a cult leader." Maximos lets out laugh. I ignore him.

I tentatively take a bite of the salad, and instantly my mouth is flooded with intense flavor. The dressing is a mixture of sweet pomegranate, a buttery olive oil, spicy pepper, and tangy blood. The palm is crisp and the fig is tender.

"Wow, this is amazing. It's like fireworks in my mouth."

"Just like blood, food also takes on a whole new meaning."

After three bites, though, my stomach feels stretched full. My fangs have retracted.

"You said you made some of the Tentyrian Brothers. How do you do that?"

"It's complicated. But they are given a combination of our venom and blood."

"So you can turn humans into vampires?"

"Tentyrians, Ari, not vampires. It's like calling all Asian people Chinese."

"So you take it as an insult?"

"Yes."

"Interesting, I didn't take you to be the sensitive type." He gives me deadpan look.

"Fine. So you can turn humans into Tentyrians?"

"Yes, but they are different from us. They don't have the unique powers that come to every naturally born Tentyrian. They have our strength and self-healing capabilities, and they feed on blood. But beyond that, their powers of persuasion over humans are limited, and they'd never be able to read minds like you or enter dreams like me. They are also incredibly bloodthirsty if they are not trained very carefully. It can take years to train a human you've changed to control himself."

"If your whole race was eliminated, why don't you just create as many Tentyrians as you want? And maybe add some women while you are at it. Aside from Shashandra, I haven't seen a woman around here."

"Because I wouldn't impose this life on a human, man or woman, unless there was no other choice."

"Wow, that's a solid vote of confidence for our kind."

"I'm sorry to say it, but it's true. I wouldn't choose this life if given the choice." Neither would I, I think. "All of the Brothers were chosen because they were on the brink of death and they wanted this life. They proved themselves capable of the burden and responsibility that comes with being a Tentyrian Brother. As for why no women, there hasn't been a need . . . It would only be a distraction. It would also be a significant time investment. Unlike the Dark Coven, we change a Brother only after much deliberation. It also requires one of us to give him a significant amount of our blood to become his maker. We then have to work with him intensely for long periods of time to help assimilate him back into the human world. Because they are created by our venom, as opposed to natural cell process, their urge to feed is very powerful."

"So the Dark Coven has changed people too?"

"Yes, but those they have turned are called Subordinates. There are two types—Human Subordinates and Tentyrian Subordinates. The first are humans who have been practically drained of all their blood and given just enough Tentyrian venom to turn them into mind slaves. They will do anything that is asked. The second are humans who are also drained of their blood, but they are given large doses of our venom combined with natural Tentyrian blood. This is what was done to the Brothers. The difference, though, is that the Dark Coven intentionally never trains their creations. They let them run wild, as long as they basically follow orders. Unfortunately, the Brotherhood spends a significant amount of time hunting them and cleaning up after them."

"So that's what the Brotherhood does? Kills Subordinates?"

"We are always looking for the Dark Coven and their disgusting creatures. Not to mention their destructive enterprises. We intend to eliminate them all. It's for vengeance, yes, but it's also to protect the humans. That is what we were tasked to do."

"By whom?"

"Hathor, our Visionary Queen, goddesses rest her soul . . ." The whoosh of the opening door interrupts, again to my frustration. I consider ripping it off its tracks. With my strength, I probably could do it. But instead of Shashandra emerging, it's Ryan, Hale, and Philip. They are still in their black fatigues. You would think they'd be hot in the tropical-like weather, but they appear perfectly cool. Maybe it's their stern expressions that give the effect? But now that I think about it, I should be hot too. The shadow cast by the umbrella doesn't offer much protection from the Mediterranean sun. I register that it's warm, but instead of sweating or even my skin getting burned, I feel perfectly comfortable. It must be part of my new powers. Now all I have to do is "hone them." Easy task, right? As soon as the GI Joes leave, I'll ask just how I'm supposed to do that . . .

"Max, we need to speak with you in the Control Room," says Ryan, who I eye suspiciously.

"Hello, little one." He smiles. I bare my fangs at him and am surprised, if not a little proud, by my own viciousness. Even though Ryan may have been trying to help me, he mocked me and dragged me back to the compound like a sack of potatoes.

"You can say it in front of Ari. It's better that she become accustomed to what is going on," says Maximos. Ryan eyes Hale and Philip with doubt. "Spit it out, Ryan," Maximos demands.

"It's her friend, Laura Delia. The Dark Coven has her."

CHAPTER 16: PROPHECY

2010 AD, JULY
AMBROSINE ISLAND, IONIAN SEA

“How did this happen!” I demand. “Laura Delia was to be watched 24/7. We assigned her a designated surveillance team to prevent this, damn it!”

If they were careless, they will be answering directly to me. Ari’s hand is gripped tightly in mine, and her face is stricken with worry. Since Ryan delivered the news, she has gone completely silent. She didn’t say a word when I shifted us into the villa’s Control Room. The Control Room is the heart of our operations, filled with cutting-edge computers, plasma screens, and state-of-the-art weapons. Ari looks fragile and out of her element—so different from last night when she was in the throes of passion. Or even this morning when she looked ready to rip my hair out. I’ll take her anger any day, compared to her fear.

“It was Aglaia,” Ryan explains. “The Brothers say she went right into Laura’s office after she arrived for an early morning meeting and shifted her out. There was no way we could have anticipated this, Maximos.” That may be, but I promised to keep Ari safe, and that also means the people she loves.

“The Dark Coven rarely show themselves in person. For Aglaia to do this, it’s significant. Was there any indication of where she took her?” I ask the obvious question.

“No,” responds Ryan, “according to Dimitri.”

"I'm working on getting him and Estaban online now," answers Aristos, who is furiously typing away at his triple-monitor workstation. The technology that keeps our operations thriving is his pride and joy. "They should be arriving at the NYC safe house and will be logging onto the secure telecom system in a matter of minutes."

I guide Ari over to the massive black granite conference table that can seat the entire Brotherhood. She sits down slowly into a chair, as if her body is still trying to catch up to what she has heard. I crouch down to come face-to-face with her.

"We are going to get her back," I say. But her piercing green eyes are filled with doubt.

"Yes, but in what condition, Maximos? Dead or alive?" she whispers. "If you haven't found Raad yet, how will you find her?" I don't have an answer.

"The link is up. Conferencing them in now," says Aristos curtly as the plasma monitors come to life with Dimitri and Estaban's faces. Although they only became Brothers ten years ago, they are two of our most trusted. I stand up immediately and am joined by Aristos, Evander, Philip, Hale, and Ryan around the table that faces the main teleconference screen. We're all too anxious to sit. Ari remains in the chair to my right with her head in her hands.

"What went down?" I ask firmly, keeping the anger out of my voice until the Brothers explain themselves.

"Max, she was sitting in her office when Aglaia literally swept in and took her out," Dimitri says in his heavy Italian accent. "I was less than ten yards away, watching her from my temp cube. There was no indication that the Dark Coven had even been watching her. Estaban had periphery surveillance and didn't see anything."

"I swear I did not," chimes in Estaban, Dimitri's routine surveillance partner and biological twin brother. They have never slipped up—until now.

"Shit," I hear Aristos say under his breath. His gaze flits nervously over to Arianna.

"Did people see?" Evander asks.

"Yes, a few. We took care of it, though." Dimitri runs his fingers through his brown locks; his olive complexion is marred with stress. It's clear he is taking this failure personally.

"Aristos, where do we stand with the remaining facilities?" I ask.

"Same as it was eight hours ago. We have it narrowed down to five." Aristos touches his fingers to the conference table keypad, and the projected image on the screen splits to show a map with the locations the team has worked tirelessly to find.

When we started going after the Dark Coven's latest crop of businesses and facilities about five years ago, we had over a thousand possible targets. After dismantling them one by one, we are down to just a handful as of now. The problem is that every time we take one down, another pops up. There is also no indication that Raad or Laura are at any of them. With their shifting abilities, the Dark Coven could stash them anywhere. What Ari doesn't understand yet is that there is more at stake than just Raad and Laura's lives . . .

"The Dark Coven is either getting sloppy or they are inviting us to engage in all-out warfare," says Evander in his blue lab scrubs.

"Maybe the crackdown we started is changing the game. Maybe they are getting desperate?" suggests Ryan.

"I think we are putting a serious dent in their Subordinate head count," Hale says with a smirk.

"We may have been successful," I announce to my men, "but it's not enough. Something has changed, and I don't feel it's us who are prevailing. Stavros is too smart. The Book of Hathor says the Event is two years away, but maybe if they've figured out what Ari is . . . they've accelerated their plans? We forget sometimes that Hathor's visions were not always guaranteed. We could already be out of time."

Aristos moves his hand over the touchpad, and the screen splits again to reveal six locations the Brothers raided during the night. After Ari slipped into sleep, following what I can only describe as the most intense and mind-altering experience I've ever had with a woman, I went to the Control Room to monitor the mission. Missions, my businesses, and my men—these are all things I understand. The same can't be said for how I feel about Ari. I'm more confused than ever before. But now isn't the time to ponder my emotions; there are too many lives at stake.

"In the last twenty-four hours, we've deployed our teams to these six facilities," Aristos explains. "We looked for weapons, drugs, illegal activity, Subordinates, and Raad. It took us three months to plan this mission, and we leveraged almost the entire Brotherhood in this coordinated effort. These were the most high-risk facilities." Aristos points one by one. "But when we arrived, they were abandoned. We came up empty. We usually find something, which means the Dark Coven could have consolidated or already moved their assets. They may be gearing up for an attack. Now that they've taken Laura openly, I'd say they are ready for a fight."

"So there are five more facilities we have left to check," I say.

"We labeled them as low risk, but at this point we have no other options. We should consider raiding them. And we don't negotiate with the Dark Coven. I know you've been monitoring them throughout the morning—any new movements in personnel?"

Aristos points to the red dots on the map in New Jersey, New York, Virginia, Georgia, and Texas. "These locations have significant numbers of human personnel. If they are being used as weapons caches, for example, it would be highly unusual to have this many people present. The Dark Coven is notorious for keeping a streamlined staff while utilizing select Subordinates to protect the locations. The Brothers on the ground, who are standing by, report no suspicious activity. We aren't even completely sure these are Trebuchet's . . ."

Ari's head snaps in my direction. "You said Trebuchet? When I went to Georgia to look at Apex, Travis Ridgefield was working with a company called Trebuchet. I don't know about what exactly, but he was doing business with them," she says.

"Which is what we suspected and why this facility in Georgia is Apex," Aristos explains as he points to the corresponding red dot.

"Trebuchet is a front for the Dark Coven, Ari. They sell weapons, and from what we can tell, they are now dabbling in pharmaceuticals. A dangerous combination," I say to her confused expression.

"What are we waiting for? If we suspect in the slightest this is the final wave of Trebuchet's holdings or they are affiliated with the Dark Coven, then let's get in there and bust up the party," enthuses Hale. While I appreciate his spirit, the cowboy in him needs to be reigned in every now and again.

"Because it may be premature," I reply. "There is a process to everything, and with every raid we do, there is always the inevitable fallout."

"Damage control isn't a problem. We'll secure the area like we always do and give the humans mind wipes," Hale replies breezily.

"It's not as simple as that and you know it," Aristos growls. "To raid the six we just did, it took us months to plan—everything from securing the floor plans to understanding the surrounding areas. Now we want to go into five with less than one day's planning and put dozens of humans at risk? You all know how I feel about the Dark Coven, but I'm not one for being careless."

"Not to mention none of the Brothers are rested," warns Evander.

"I'm ready to bust up those Dark Coven Subordinates any day," says Ryan as he cracks his knuckles. "Sleep or no sleep."

"Maximos, it's your call," responds Aristos as the room turns their eyes to me.

I nod in agreement but propose we wait until we hear back from Evander's contact at the Food and Drug Administration and Aristos' at the Department of Defense. Both of them have been quiet, and we need an update before we engage.

"I should be hearing back from Perry in the next hour," says Evander. "He is checking the FDA internal system to see if Trebuchet is doing anything unusual. Last we heard, they were the holding company for smaller subsidiary plants, producing a few harmless generic drugs that have been on the market for decades."

"Aristos, any word from David?"

"I just received an e-mail from him. There is minimal chatter right now at the Department of Defense. No weapons purchases have been made from Trebuchet in the last year by the US or any other country for that matter. The status is unchanged from what it was last week. Still quiet. Maybe too quiet . . ."

"Then we wait until we hear from Perry," I say. "In the meantime, Aristos, are the teams in place?"

"Yes. I can get them online by telecon if you'd like."

"No, not necessary. We will join them in person when it comes time to strike. Our shifting abilities may be needed. I will take the New Jersey facility, Evander will take Virginia, and Aristos will take Georgia. Dimitri and Estaban, I want you at the New York one, since you are close by and can get there by car. Head there now. Hale, you get Texas since it's your home state, and I want Philip with you. Ryan, you will stay here with Ari."

"Why do I have to stay?" protests a disgruntled Ryan. All of the Brothers' heads whip in his direction.

"Because I said so. Do you have a problem with that?" I respond with an obvious edge in my voice. The Brothers know not to question my orders, as their leader.

"No, Maximos," he replies, mollified.

"Good, we also need you to man the Control Room while we are gone," orders Aristos. "You will be playing an integral role in this mission, Ryan. We need you on board." As much as Aristos appears gruff—in fact, we all do—we value each Brother and his respective skills.

"I understand," Ryan says solemnly.

"Evander, once you hear from Perry, we need you to take Hale and Philip to the Texas location since they can't shift. Everyone is to keep their earpieces and mics turned on and follow mission protocol,"

I command. The room nods in unison, except for Ari. "We will meet back here in an hour, after which we will debrief with our teams in person. Aristos and Evander, stay. The rest of you are dismissed."

The Brothers leave swiftly, and Dimitri and Estaban log off. Ari sits frozen in her seat, barely acknowledging the hand I place gently on her back. "Ari, I want to introduce you to Evander and Aristos," I say. She gives me a questioning look and stands up.

Evander is first to extend his hand and address her warmly. "The Turn suits you, Ari. Maximos told me you made it through without incident." Even now that she is full Tentyrian, I can see she hasn't lost her ability to blush. It looks beautiful on her. Who am I kidding? Everything looks beautiful on her. Humans will be unable to resist her—from the sound of her voice now richer with its lulling melody, to the creamy skin now absolutely perfect. She has been subtly refined through the Turn. I suppose it's a consequence of evolution, a predatory advantage. But I'm not sure who was whose prey last night. She could have easily become mine. I came so close to biting her and completing the sacred Tentyrian blood ritual. A ritual sacred to the marriage bed and that would link us forever.

There was so much I wanted to say to her this morning and so little time. So I told her that last night was a mistake. I played on her insecurity. The pain that registered on her face wasn't lost on me. But it's what she needed to hear. I couldn't explain to her that last night was incredible or that I've never felt this way about anyone. And that her willingness to give herself to me so completely is something that I don't deserve but something I covet all the same. If she is the First Luminary, and there is no doubt in mind that she is, then I am supposed to protect her as a brother—not a lover. As the human colloquialism goes, the truth sucks.

"We met briefly yesterday, but you were quite ill," says Evander to Ari.

"Yes, I remember," she says softly, "nice to meet you." She manages a hesitant smile.

"I'd love to run some tests on you tomorrow if you are up to it," says Evander. Ari's smile immediately sinks into one of panic. Damn it, Evander. He is like a dog with a bone sometimes.

"Not now, Evander. We'll discuss this some other time," I interrupt through gritted teeth. "Maybe you should go see if you've heard anything from Perry?"

"An excellent idea. I'm sorry if I alarmed you, Ari," Evander says apologetically. "The tests can wait." He nods cordially and shakes her hand good-bye before retreating back to his lab.

Aristos, who has been hanging back, keeping his fingers busy on his keyboard, steps forward. I haven't seen him this nervous since . . . well, I can't even remember. Throughout our meeting with the Brothers, I couldn't help but notice how he looked at Ari. It was with a combination of recognition and nervousness. Seeing a picture is one thing, but seeing Ari in person is another. She is the spitting image of Daria, even in her modern-day cut-off shorts and tank top.

"This is Aristos, my longest friend," I introduce him.

"Pleased to meet you," Aristos says formally as he gives her a small bow, opting for the Tentyrian form of respect, instead of a handshake.

"And you," she says, her voice not as timid as it was with Evander. Her eyes look at him intently, and she tilts her head. What she says next completely takes me off guard.

"I can see some of you in me. Are we related?"

I had purposely not called out her lineage, as I thought it was a conversation the two of them should have. But their resemblance is hard to miss with their same chestnut hair and the shape of their eyes. An obvious difference is in Aristos' scarred face, riddled with raised white lines—a token from the Sanctum fire that even Evander couldn't completely heal. But Aristos wasn't the vain type. He told me that every time he looks in the mirror, the scars remind him of what is important: killing the Dark Coven.

"Yes," Aristos says, shifting uncomfortably. "Daria was the name of my wife," he continues with his voice tight, looking down. When he looks up, I see tears in his eyes. "You look just like her. If we had a daughter, I always imagined she would look like you." Ari's face is equally filled with emotion. There is a slight tremor in Aristos' hands, which he clenches by his sides when he sees me assessing them. Ari steps forward and wraps her arms around Aristos without hesitation, which isn't an easy task based on his size. He looks at me in surprise, and his own arms, awkwardly but slowly, enclose around her.

To see my friend actually held in the arms of another is a strange sight. Since the massacre, I've never seen Aristos share an emotional connection with anyone. Not even Evander or me. Post-battle celebrations don't count. "Evander has looked at both of our DNA; you are of my blood," he chokes out.

"So how many 'greats' come before grandfather?" she asks as she steps back and smiles up at him.

"Very many." He smiles. He actually smiles.

"We are still piecing together your family tree, Ari. There are some significant gaps, so we don't know exactly how many generations separate you, but we estimate it to be around sixty-eight," I offer. "Unfortunately, the bulk of those gaps start with Aristos' and Daria's son, Darrius. We don't know what happened to him after the massacre and how your family's line continued. For a while, we thought Darrius must have perished along with the rest of the children. But your existence proves that didn't happen. Which means it's also possible that there are more direct Luminary descendants out there . . ."

"How many do you think there could be?" Ari asks.

"We have no way of knowing. But we suspect four, including you. What's interesting, and Evander could go on about this for hours, is that you are the only one in your family line that has the markers of a Tentyrian descendent. Somehow, when you were born you carried the Tentyrian gene and for the first time it was activated. If any of the other children of the first generation survived and they managed to procreate, there could be more like you . . ."

"You told me no one else survived except for you all and the Dark Coven," Ari says in confusion.

"That's what we thought, until you came along," Aristos replies. He looks like he is still pulling himself together.

I interject for him. "There were four Luminary children, including Aristos' son, that we managed to secret out through an escape tunnel. We sent them along with their Guardians. We intended to find them afterward, but they disappeared. Eventually, we had to come to terms with the possibility they had died. However, the Book of Hathor told us that there would come a time when four would be born to unite and bring glory to our kind. So we held out hope . . ."

"You mentioned that book earlier. What are you talking about?" she asks.

"It's called the Book of Hathor. Aristos, can you work your magic and show Ari?" Aristos looks relieved to have a task to snap him out of his uncharacteristic emotional state. He walks over to his desk and picks up an iPad. He brings it over to the conference table and puts it in front of Ari. With a few taps, scanned pages of a book appear on the screen.

"The pages are too fragile for us to work with, so we've had them scanned," Aristos explains. "The original book is kept safe in a special vault. If you look here in the notes sections, the translation can be found in English. It was originally written in our native Greek, the language of Tentyris." Aristos quickly flips through the pages to show Ari the prophecy of her birth. She reads it aloud:

"Beginning in the year 1985 after the death of Christ, four stars will be born. They will fall to this Earth unrecognized at first, waiting to illuminate their brilliance. The first star, surrounded by her brothers, will lead the way. Without her, her sister stars will be lost. Her sight and ultimate sacrifice will mean salvation. The second star's light will flicker. The loss of her half, a painful lesson. Yet her energy must endure to bring light to us all. The third star will burn with fury, both an asset and a danger. Through temperance and patience, destruction can be overcome. The fourth star, unknown at first but still beloved, brings with her the possibility of peace. Yet olive branches can break and so can hearts. Together, these four stars will form a new constellation, guiding humanity and our people home. To guide is a blessing and a curse, the paradox of the Zodiac's beginning."

After a pause, Ari asks, "And you think the first star is me?"

"Yes," replies Aristos confidently, as if seeing her now solidifies our theory into conviction.

"I explained to you before that Hathor was our queen. She was also our Visionary, meaning she had the gift of foresight," I explain, trying to provide more clarity. "Hathor wrote down all of her premonitions in this book. It was only shortly before her death that I learned of the book's existence. She kept it secret for fear that it would fall into the wrong hands. Only her daughters and I knew of it. She left us with the instruction that we not try to change the course of the future, with the exception of preventing one event, which will ultimately bring about mass destruction for all mankind if it takes place. Since her death, we've tried to uphold that promise as a Brotherhood and locate the four she speaks of."

Aristos swipes to the last page in the book for Ari to see:

In the year 2012, after the death of Christ, the world will end. Sickness will sweep the globe and war will be waged. The siege engine will not stop until decimation covers the Earth. But even the engine will not anticipate the outcome. There will be no survivors. No medicine can stop the spread, unless the four stars and their brothers intervene. Poison must burn; gatekeepers must drown. And when it becomes dark, we must be the ones to restore the light. Tentyris can rise again in glory.

"We believe the siege engine is Trebuchet Global and the poison will come either from their weapons or pharmaceuticals. That's why it's imperative we finish off those facilities," I explain. "We have also worked hard to cripple their financials, which we hope is limiting their funding to terrorists—a favorite pastime of theirs. We know the Dark Coven's 'legal' supplying of weapons is quiet. But that doesn't mean they aren't using alternate, illegal methods. The root of the problem is that they have support from inside the US government, the gatekeepers if you will."

Just then, Evander appears from the lab. He looks paler than usual, which isn't a good sign.

"I've heard back from Perry," he proclaims.

"And?" Aristos' asks.

"There is a new drug that's just been fast-tracked for approval this month. It's called DTPA12. Perry hadn't even heard about it or its clinical trials until today. Its testing was partially funded by the government, and they mandated it be kept under wraps for security purposes. It's used to treat radiation sickness. And, no surprise, Trebuchet is the main underwriter. We have a serious problem."

It's my call now. "The mission is on," I say with a deep breath. "We don't have much of a choice. It's 6:00 a.m. on the East Coast. And while I prefer to do our raids at night, I don't think we have time to wait. We risk them moving. Plus, if these are Trebuchet's holdings, they won't be expecting us in the daytime."

"But Maximos, the collateral damage on this could be huge," Evander warns.

"I agree, but our options are limited. We leave in thirty. Let's get our men in position," I say. Aristos and Evander agree. "Proceed with the preparations; I need to speak with Ari in private."

Aristos gives her a kiss on her hand and tells her to keep the iPad until we return. It has all of his favorite books in the e-library, if she's interested. He assures her we'll be back in a couple of hours and that he's looking forward to learning more about her. She thanks him and gives him a kiss on the cheek. I don't think I'm about to be extended the same favor.

I shift us down to the beach in the hopes it will calm her anxiety that I know has been brewing.

"I want to come, Maximos," she says.

"Absolutely not," I reply. The afternoon sun is moving further to the west; we don't have much time. I need to get back and suit up for the mission and review the plan of attack with my men already on the ground.

"But I can be helpful. I can read the Subordinates' minds, or whosever you need me to. Maybe I'll find out something useful!"

"No, too dangerous. You aren't in control of your power yet. And what are you going to do, Ari, hold the Subordinates' hands before you get into their heads? Subordinates are fast, strong, and vicious. They'll rip your throat out before you get within ten feet of them."

"You just expect me to sit here and wait for you!"

"Yes, that is exactly what I expect."

"If I'm supposed to be the First Luminary, then I'm supposed to lead and you are supposed to follow. That's what the prophecy says, you arrogant jerk!" she yells at me over the crash of waves. The sunlight makes the blonder strands of her hair glow. No one should look this pretty when they're angry. Sasha certainly didn't.

"When that prophecy was written, I don't think Hathor expected you to face a pack of violent Subordinates, or humans for that matter, within twenty-four hours of your undergoing the Turn. You could get hurt or even hurt someone."

"You act like your Brotherhood is the answer to everything. If that's the case, then why are we in this position to begin with? Why is the Dark Coven even alive? Why were they able to take Raad and Laura? Seems to me you don't do your job very well," she says defiantly. It's a blow to where it hurts most: my pride. She may be right, but it doesn't mean I'll take her with me.

"Say what you want, Ari. You aren't coming. If you want to be useful, work on your powers. But before you continue your tirade against me, I wanted to give you this . . ." I thrust toward her the gold pendant on a chain I pull quickly from my pocket. I had it made for her not long after I suspected she might be the star in our prophecy. I don't know exactly what compelled me to do it, but it seemed appropriate for her to have a token of our shared past—even if it is a replica.

"It's the zodiac symbol with all of the original Tentyrian Covens. The Luminaries are portrayed here along the sides—just like the one you've seen. If you look closely you can see the four," I point out. "All of the Luminaries and Hathor wore ones just like it. I thought it would make a good birthday present."

"It's beautiful," she says in surprise as she takes the delicate chain necklace from my oversized hand into her smaller one. I'm hoping her anger is forgotten, at least momentarily.

"Will you put it on me?" She turns her back to me. I undo the clasp and put it around her neck. She lifts her hair from the back of her neck, releasing more of the honey scent and exposing that beautiful flesh that has been calling to me. Somehow, I manage to close the small gold enclosure. She gives a slight shiver as my fingers brush her skin. I breathe in the salty tang of the Ionian Sea to help bring my senses back to where they need to be. I must go.

"Thank you for the necklace, Maximos," she says genuinely as she turns around. "But I still think you should take me with you."

"You just won't let up." Okay, I decide, if she wants to come along, then she'll have to prove she's ready. "If you want to go on this mission, then meet me back up at the villa. You'll have to shift if you are going to make it in time. You seem confident in your power, after all."

"That's not fair, Maximos!"

"It's not? Well if you can't make it, take the path," I say as I point to the coral steps that lead back up the side of the cliff. It's at least a thirty-minute walk, even with her increased speed. She'll never make it in time. We'll be gone in ten minutes. When I get back to the villa, I'll tell Ryan to get her so she doesn't have to walk up the steep steps by herself.

"Be safe, matia mou. I'll see you soon." I shift away before she can say another word.

CHAPTER 17: MISSION DEPLOYMENT

2010 AD, JULY
AMBROSINE ISLAND, IONIAN SEA

I sit down on the sunbaked sand in frustration. Damn him. He knows I won't make it back to the villa in time if I have to take the path. I close my eyes and try to focus on the terracotta-laid pavilion to move myself to the villa. But all I succeed in doing is giving myself a headache. How am I supposed to learn if no one teaches me? If only Raad were here. I offer up a quick prayer for his and Laura's safe return—I don't even know who I'm praying to, but I'll do anything if it helps.

My senses still haven't adapted to the Tentyrian sensory overload. The sun's light is blinding. Unfortunately, I forgot the sunglasses in the Control Room. It was easy to get distracted in there: that place looked like a cross between the Starship Enterprise and an armory museum. In addition to the plasma screens and computers that filled the room, guns, knives, and armor lined the windowless walls. There must have been weapons from every century there—no doubt acquired by Maximos and his Brothers firsthand.

I make my way over to some rocks shaded by the cliff's mammoth height to get out of the sun. Although I don't have my sunglasses, I still have the iPad Aristos left me. I wonder if it can connect to the Internet out here and access my e-mail . . .

Within minutes, I find my attempt is fruitless. But I'm not about to sit here placidly and read Anna Karenina, an unusual favorite for a man as intimidating as Aristos. It's amazing to think that he is actually my family . . . Oh my God, my family.

The realization dawns on me. Through this whole ordeal, I've barely given any thought to my parents. Our relationship may be strained, but I should have asked about their well-being immediately. What if the Dark Coven has them too? If they took Raad and Laura, why wouldn't they take them? What kind of daughter am I?

As soon as Maximos gets back, I'll find out. I can only hope he provided them with a security detail. Meanwhile, I am to sit here on this island, helpless. I grab a rock from the sand and chuck it out at the ocean in anger. Rather than landing only a few yards out as expected, the rock travels about a mile through the air, disappearing into the foamy crests of the ocean. I can feel the tendons, sinew, and muscles of my body work together in their kinetic splendor.

The strength of my own body is astounding, although right now, it won't do me any good. I should try to be productive rather than pout like a child left home. Perhaps reading more about the Book of Hathor will help? I navigate back to the document Aristos showed me and start at the beginning.

What I find is amazing. Their queen predicted the Crusades, the French Revolution, the creation of penicillin, the rise of Abraham Lincoln and his inevitable assassination, the same for JFK, the Wright Brothers, World Wars I and II, computers, cell phones, the Afghan war, 9/11, and so much more. The predictions go on and on, stopping with Hathor's last entry dated 52 BC, where she predicts my birth and the Earth's destruction.

Hathor was a real Nostradamus. And her predictions aren't just vague visions. Some give specific names, locations, and dates. But why tell the Brothers not to act on the predictions? If that is what she wanted, then why even write them in a book? The Brothers could have saved millions of lives. Instead, they stood by and watched it all happen? I shut the device off in disgust. There are no clues in here that will help my cause. I should head back to the compound. I give shifting another try, with no result. I'll have to get to the villa the good old-fashioned way—by walking.

I begin to make my way up the winding path nestled into the side of the cliff, careful to mind the sharp edges and rough brushwood with my bare feet. I hear a crunch of rock under a boot and look up to find

Ryan standing in front of me.

"Hello, little one," he says with a grin. He extends a hand toward me. I reluctantly take it. With the way the sun is shining in my eyes and the steep incline of the path, it's a relief to have a steady hand in mine.

"You were taking too long. You had me worried," he says.

"You could have fooled me. Aren't you supposed to be in the Control Room?" I ask.

"They aren't raiding for another hour. They are still securing the areas. Maximos told me to retrieve you. I figured I'd give you some time on your own. When you didn't show up, I started to worry you tried to swim out to the next island." I raise an eyebrow at him. "Don't get any ideas. It's more than twenty miles away and you'd drown. Knowing you, you are dumb enough to try it. Hence I'm here."

"Wow, my knight in shining armor. Thanks so much."

"Just doing my job."

After we complete our ascent, we find ourselves at the top of the cliff with at least three acres of orchard stretched ahead of us before we will reach the villa. We begin to walk, and I match my pace and stride to his.

"So you're full Tentyrian now?" he asks.

"I suppose."

"We've waited for you a long time, you know," he says almost accusatorily.

"I guess I couldn't really help that, now could I?"

"No, but you could try to express some gratitude."

"Excuse me?" I feel my gums pricking in anger.

"Maybe gratitude is not the right word, but some respect wouldn't hurt," Ryan says bluntly.

"I give respect when it's due," I snap. "I read what Hathor predicted, and you all did nothing. You could have saved lives. Instead, you all were probably too busy fighting with the Dark Coven."

"You don't understand, Arianna. Maximos and the rest of us have dedicated our lives to protecting humanity. But changing the future isn't as easy as you think."

"But you are trying to do it now. So why not before?"

"When you meddle with fate, it causes a ripple effect," he explains as we continue to make our way down the alley of olive trees. "You might succeed in making a change, but it's entirely possible what you do will have a worse impact than what you were trying to prevent. Or the outcome will inevitably be the same. Did Maximos tell you why he created me?"

"No. Just that all the Brothers had proven themselves and they made the choice to be changed."

"That's right. But every Brother has their own unique story about their creation. For me, mine began in Eritrea."

"That's in the Horn of Africa, right?"

"Yes. In my human life, I was stationed there as a Peace Corps volunteer. I was young, freshly graduated from Cornell, and looking to change the world. In Maximos' time, the Ptolemaic kings of Egypt used Eritrea as a source of war elephants. The country is now run by the People's Front for Democracy and Justice. No other political groups are allowed to organize, elections don't exist, and the human rights violations rival those of North Korea.

"It was 1992, and I was an English teacher there. Eritrea had just seceded from Ethiopia, and the unrest was significant. With the help of the UN, elections were soon to be held for a president. There was hope . . . Maximos and the Brothers were in the same village as my school, investigating the trafficking of weapons that they believed to be supplied by the Dark Coven. What I didn't know at the time was that the Brothers knew that a war with Ethiopia was about break out within the country and thousands of people would be killed. Hathor predicted the war would last for two years. One afternoon, I was teaching class when gunfire erupted in the streets. Believe it or not, it wasn't unusual, so we closed the shutters, locked the doors, and hid under the desks like we always did.

"But this time, guerilla soldiers broke down the door. Despite my protests, they separated the boys from the girls and loaded them into trucks to be taken to training camps to 'bring pride to their country.' What that really meant was they were to be sent into battle, to be used mostly as human shields. When I tried to protest, they shot me. As they drove away, I was able to pull myself up from the bloodied schoolroom floor. I then ran door to door asking for help. Help to get the children back. The doors closed in my faces. Some of those doors were even those of the children's homes. People were too scared.

"That's when Maximos and the Brothers drove up. They put me into their truck and asked me if I knew where the children were taken. I told them it was to Adi Quala near the Ethiopian border. It was known as a hotspot for rebel soldiers. The Brothers had never been there before, so they couldn't shift. We drove for hours, looking for the soldiers and their encampment. I knew I was going to die. I was beyond medical help, and I had lost too much blood. But I wouldn't let the Brothers leave me behind. I needed to find my kids. And when we found them,

Maximos made sure those bastards regretted what they had done. The Brothers killed the guerilla soldiers, at least seventy of them, and they brought the children home safe.

"It turned out the soldiers were endorsing one politician who, if he came to power according to Hathor's premonition, would be responsible for the next war with Ethiopia. So the Brotherhood did what they had pledged to avoid. They moved to change the future and killed the politician who was destined to become a despot, or so they thought. The Brothers helped put in place an opposing candidate. That someone is still in power today since he was elected in '93. And that war, it still ended up happening, just a few years later than predicted. And it lasted for exactly two years. Who is to say if more lives were saved than lost?"

"So you are saying their intervention did nothing?" I ask with a pit in my throat.

"We saved the children. But close to one hundred thousand people died in the war we failed to prevent. You can't always stop fate."

"So we're all going to die then?" I ask. Ryan stops and stares at me intently.

"No, Hathor saw it was possible to stop the Event, as long as we have you and the others. I was wrong to be so harsh. I just wanted you to realize that what we do as a Brotherhood is to save humans. It's why we get up and fight every day and night. This is a difficult task. I think I just expected you to embrace your destiny rather than fight it." We keep walking, and I ponder Ryan's words. Had I judged the Brotherhood too harshly?

"Did you know what you were getting yourself into when you were turned?" I ask.

"Not exactly. But I knew Maximos was a good man . . . and the life he offered me was better than none at all. By joining him, I've been able to continue my good works, just in a different fashion."

"I'll say. Using a gun is a far cry from wielding a piece of chalk in a classroom," I point out as I eye the intimidating weapon holstered on his side.

"This isn't just any gun," Ryan says ominously as he traces the weapon's outline with his hand. "The bullets are laced with cyanide. It helps slow the Subordinates down. But whereas one bullet will kill a human, it can take up to ten just to bring a Subordinate to his knees. I'll take you to the shooting range to practice sometime. You should know how to defend yourself . . . although I know you have some tricks up your sleeve."

I give him a hesitant smile, thinking back to our first meeting in the orchard. We may have gotten off to a bad start. He actually seems like a good guy and fiercely loyal once you get past the chill of his attitude.

"I bet I can beat you back to the villa," I venture.

"I'd like to see you try, little one."

"Why do you call me that?"

"Because when I first saw you, you looked so small and helpless."

"Hmm, really?"

With that, my legs take off. The energy inside of me explodes, like the burst of a starting bell at a horse race. The orchard trees blur like a Monet landscape, and the earthy air fills my lungs, urging me to go faster. I can feel my feet on the soil, but it feels like I'm flying, only touching the ground every dozen yards or so. This is what it feels like to be free. When I run now, it's completely different from working out as a human. The dogged burn I used to feel in my lungs and body is gone. Running now is as easy breathing. This is the natural state my body wants to be in. But I can feel myself yearning for a hunt. To chase. To sink my fangs into flesh. To taste the reward of hot blood.

I land on the pavilion floor in a crouch, minutes before Ryan arrives. As I stand up from my catlike position, I notice my fangs are out. I run my tongue along the sharp surface and take a deep breath in, willing them to retract. It's a struggle to get them to obey. I want to hunt and kill. Ryan stops up short of the fountain seconds later, looking composed as ever. Meanwhile, I feel like a caged animal that's just been let out.

"What's wrong, Arianna?" he asks, concerned. I look at him wild eyed. My throat is on fire.

"I'm thirsty."

"That was probably your first run, I take it?" I nod in shamed acknowledgment. "Let's get you a drink, come on." Ryan tugs me along inside, past the sliding doors. Rather than calling for Shashandra or taking me to the kitchen, he leads me toward the living room bookcase and pushes his shoulder against the far right shelving unit.

"You're lucky, you know," says Ryan as he grunts with effort. "The Turn is much harder for us who are not naturally born Tentyrians. You have a self-control that can take years for us to master. I wasn't allowed to leave this compound for twenty-two months, most of which I spent locked in a padded room monitored by Maximos. Even though Maximos was my maker and could control me, I was so thirsty I'd have drank his blood if he'd let me."

Considering I drank Maximos' blood last night, I don't think I'm necessarily a model of self-control. But I keep that to myself. With one final push, the wall shifts inward with a scraping noise that grates on my sensitive ears. A passageway and spiral staircase leading downward is revealed. Fluorescent lights illuminate the long dark passageway, but I don't need the aid of artificial light with my newfound vision.

"This is the way to the Control Room and lab," say Ryan, "for those of us who can't shift." Ryan punches a code into a keypad that prohibits entrance. The keypad beeps in acknowledgment, and the door slides open with a sucking whoosh. "Follow me," he orders as we cross in to what I recognize as Evander's lab.

I haven't been in here since I woke up on the table with an IV in my arm and feeling like I was about to have a heart attack. The room is filled with test tubes, microscopes, centrifuges, and refrigerators. The Brotherhood certainly has a well-equipped operation. I can only assume businesses like Leo Capital help fund this. Ryan quickly opens up one of five stainless-steel fridges and pulls out a plastic bag of blood from a drawer. He tosses it to me like a beanbag. I catch it and stare at the red liquid inside. It's been labeled "B–" in black Sharpie.

"Drink up, little one. It will help." I stare at him self-consciously, and I look around for a cup.

"How should I drink this?"

"Bite in and suck. Don't be embarrassed. This is like sipping tea compared to a real hunt. Come on, I have to get back," he urges.

We head back into the Control Room and sit down next to each other in front of the main computer monitor where Aristos was working earlier. Ryan presses his finger into his ear and speaks into the tiny voice-activated microphone clipped to his black T-shirt. "All teams, report your positions." He listens intently and nods. I bite into the plastic bag, my fangs slicing through effortlessly. I purse my lips to the puncture and suck out the liquid like a juice box. It tastes dull and cold, but I drink the blood eagerly. The bonfire that began to rage in my throat during our race is now tempered to a lingering smoke. The wildness that was threatening to claw its way out of me feels calmer.

"Are they okay?" I ask while draining the last remnants of the bag.

"Yes, they are moving into position. Look here," he states as he points to the screen, where I see a series of blue dots within six different video frames. Each frame has its own label: Alpha, Beta, Delta, Omega, and Phi. "The blue dots are the Brothers. Their body armor contains tracking devices. We're still in a holding pattern."

"Can you tell if any of the Dark Coven or their Subordinates are near?"

"It looks like there are mostly humans within the buildings, but some of the Brothers have sightings of Subordinates." Ryan's fingers tap rapidly on the keyboard, and he brings up a picture on an adjacent monitor. "I want to show you what the Dark Coven looks like, so you can be prepared." The grainy photo is black and white, and the resolution is low. But one person in the image makes my breath catch. It's the man from my dream . . .

"Who is that?" I ask, pointing to the man sitting at the center of the elegant dining table in the photo. My voice is quivering.

"Stavros—the mastermind himself. This was taken about ten years ago through a fluke surveillance operation at a restaurant where we suspected a weapons' transaction was about to take place between a Saudi prince and a US government official on the sly. We had no idea it was connected to the Dark Coven. Low and behold, we find these three." I can hear Ryan grinding his teeth together.

Ryan points to Stavros and his two companions sitting to his left and right. The woman to his left is stunning. "That is Aglaia," he explains. Her short bob has an effortless sexy bed head look with its tousled layers. Her rounded chin and cheeks have a sweet quality, only to be offset by her darkened lips and ample bosom accentuated by a sleeveless cocktail dress. "Don't be deceived. She is lethal. When her sister was alive, those two decimated many a village, leaving behind drained corpses scorched by fire. They were called the Fire Twins."

"I take it they could somehow use fire?"

"Yes, and Aglaia still can. She'll burn you alive with the snap of her fingers, given the chance."

"What happened to the sister?" I ask.

"Asia died in World War II at the hands of the Führer's sick doctors in their search for Aryan perfection and God knows what else. As far as we know, Asia was experimented on and tortured. They documented what they did to her, contributing to the limited knowledge humans have of our kind. I wasn't with the Brothers then, but Maximos and Aristos managed to track down the files the Nazis kept and destroyed them. We will never work with the Dark Coven, but it is imperative we all keep our existence hidden."

"And what about him?" I point to the golden-haired man in mid laugh, offering a toast to the Middle Eastern gentleman across the table.

"That's Calix. He may look like a playboy, but don't let his tailored suits and baby blues fool you. He is just as dangerous."

"Maximos told me he has some type of mind control power?"

"That's right. He'll burrow his way through your mind and make you think you've experienced some of the most awful things you can imagine." Ryan's voice drops an octave. "There was one Brother who was ambushed many years back. Backup didn't come in time, and a group of Subordinates managed to kidnap him. About a month later, he was dumped on the steps of our old safe house in Chicago. He had been convinced that Maximos skinned alive his human family, raped his mother and sister, and mercilessly fed off them. The Dark Coven tortured him into revealing the safe house location, and he was brainwashed to murder us. Rehabilitating him didn't work, and he had to be eliminated."

"You killed one of your own?" I ask in disbelief.

"He wasn't one of us anymore, Arianna," Ryan says roughly. "He tried to kill us at every turn. Keeping him locked in a cage for life wouldn't have been fair."

"I suppose you're right . . . When this picture was taken, why couldn't you have killed the Dark Coven?"

"We tried. The Brothers were prepared to blow up the entire restaurant and accept the human casualties. But they shifted out before we could detonate the bomb. The ability to shift can make you practically untouchable. It's easy enough to kill one of their bloodsucking puppets. But getting to the Dark Coven is an entirely different matter." I can hear the anger in his voice, which turns a fraction hopeful. "You should be able to shift, though. It will undoubtedly help our efforts. I understand you have the power to read minds, too. Can you do anything else?"

"No," I say automatically. "And I don't think I can shift. I've tried." If I dreamt of Stavros, does that mean I'm capable of premonitions like Hathor? I'm torn if I should tell Ryan that I think I recognize Stavros. Then again, the photo isn't very clear. Maybe I only think he looks familiar and that I've seen that hooked nose and lanky frame before . . .

"Teams, ten minutes until deployment," Ryan commands as he presses the control on his earpiece again. Please find Laura and Raad, I pray silently

"Ryan, are there any Brothers looking out for my parents? I meant to ask Maximos earlier, but I didn't get the opportunity. Do you know if they are safe?" Ryan shifts his gaze swiftly from the computer screen to me.

"Yes they are. They are out of the country and actually on safari. The Dark Coven won't find them. It was one of the first precautions we took."

"What? How did you manage to do that?" I ask in surprise. "My father hates to travel unless it's to Bermuda or Pebble Beach."

"Never underestimate the persuasive ways of the Brotherhood," he says with a smile. I feel a weight of relief lift from my heart.

"All right, Brothers, on my count. Three, two, one, zero," says Ryan. We watch the blue dots advance on the facilities in unison. I can tell he is listening intently to the instructions and movements the teams are voicing back and forth. The minutes tick by. I realize that I'm holding my breath, only releasing it until my lungs feel like they'll burst. All of a sudden, the blue dots and three of the buildings simultaneously flicker, and Ryan rips his earpiece out.

"Ahhh, damn it!" he shouts as he presses his finger to his eardrum in pain. Some of the blue dots reappear and some do not.

"Ryan, what just happened?" I ask, panicked.

"There must have been an explosion," he says distractedly, and he quickly places the earpiece back in. "Teams, come in," he shouts. The seconds that go by next feel like hours. "I can hear you Alpha and Omega. Beta, Delta, Phi, come in. Beta, Delta, Phi, come in," repeats Ryan. "Communications have been lost with Beta, Delta, and Phi. Team Alpha, abandon your mission. Aristos, shift your team to Beta, then proceed to Delta and Phi to report on conditions. Omega, continue as planned and upon completion go to Alpha's mission in Georgia to do a sweep."

The blue dots begin to disappear on the Alpha screen while Delta's keep moving. I look hopefully on as a few of the dots move slowly on the Beta, Delta, and Phi screens. There must be survivors. Maybe only their communications were wiped out . . .

"Ryan, what team is Maximos on?" I whisper to him. But he doesn't hear me; he is engrossed with what's happening on the ground. I hear the shouts and orders of men faintly through Ryan's earpiece. But even with my extra sensory hearing, I can't fully interpret the words with so much static. I ask again, louder, and the response I hear is not what I want.

"Maximos is on Phi."

CHAPTER 18: ZODIAC PENDANT

2010 AD, JULY
AMBROSINE ISLAND, IONIAN SEA

He's going to be fine, I keep telling myself. There was only so much information I could get out of Ryan while he was helping manage the mission that seemed to fall apart right before my eyes. When he started swearing at the monitor and slammed his fist so hard against the metal desk that it left a dent, I knew I should give him space. There was no help that I could offer or that he'd take between the commands he was barking to the Brothers who were thousands of miles away. And we haven't heard from Maximos . . .

I left the Control Room. Somehow, my feet managed to take me upstairs to Maximos' bedroom, which is where I am now, watching the sunset from the balcony. Whether it was the comfort of the room itself with its white and beige colors that drew me to its solace, or the fact that this was the place I spent with Maximos in a night that was both frightening and beautiful at the same time, I don't know why I'm here or what to do next.

It's been hours since Maximos handed me the necklace now dangling from my neck. I toy with it nervously as the engraved disk flips between my fingers. The sun sparkles off the pendant, mesmerizing me with its glimmer and intricate etchings. I continue to flip it between my fingers, slower now, making the symbol all the more profound. I take a deep breath in and rock back on my heels, not stopping the movement of my fingers. I know what I'm doing, I think vaguely. I imagine the figures and symbols on the zodiac moving, as if they are dancing. But there is no music, only the sound of the waves down below.

The sound of the waves crashing is quieter now. Less frequent. My fingers are moving slower, and it's as if I can see the disk moving in slow motion over my knuckles. Time is slowing. Then, without warning, an explosion of light fills my vision. Its white light blocks out the sunset, the beach, my hands, and the necklace. I stumble back, almost blinded. I reach for the rail in front of me to steady myself. I can feel the wrought iron under my hand, and just in time, as a series of images come barreling into view.

A drawer. My hand. An iPhone. An e-mail from Laura. Help. She needs help. Smoke. Fire. Maximos lying on a floor in a pool of blood. Then, like a photograph coming into view after a dip in developer, reality fades into the picture. The white light and lighting-fast visions are gone, only to be replaced by the crimson and tangerine of the sun reflecting off the ocean that has now absorbed almost all of the rays.

What was that? My hands are trembling and my walk is shaky as I stumble back inside to sit down on the bed that has been neatly made, waiting for its master to return. Although, based on what I just saw, Maximos won't be returning. I fight back my tears. Maximos can't be dead. He just can't be. I think back to how I was playing with the necklace and how I was so captivated by the reflecting light. It was almost as if the necklace was egging me on, telling me to watch it. Using objects to focus and create a hypnotic state has been used for centuries; in fact, Raad and I had experimented with it successfully several times.

My subconscious must have led me into some type of hypnosis by using the necklace. Or was it conscious? I distinctly remember feeling aware of what I was doing . . . Nevertheless, the visions that I experienced completely took me by surprise. Was it just my imagination playing off my fears? Or was what I saw a premonition? Could I really be like Hathor? Please don't be a premonition . . . Then it hits me: the drawers. I should check all the drawers.

I spy the night table and reach for it quickly to yank open the drawer. In my eagerness and overwhelming strength I'm not yet used to, the drawer rips out onto the floor. I jump back quickly, as if a snake will jump out. But there is no snake, just one lone iPhone and a black leather Tory Burch wallet. The phone belongs to Maximos and the wallet belongs to me. He must have put them here before he left. After all, why would he need them when he is off killing Subordinates and breaking into suspected weapons facilities?

I put the wallet in the back pocket of my jean shorts, but before reaching down to snatch up the phone, I look around tentatively. Like there is anyone to stop me. "Enter Password" displays on the screen as I press the keypad with my thumb. I'm tempted to put the phone back in the drawer and close it shut along with whatever ominous portents may be inside. However, I put my fears aside.

I knew that phone was there. I saw my hand reaching for it. Something tells me that if I knew it was there, I should be able to guess the password correctly . . . And why shouldn't I at least try? Especially if Maximos is bleeding on a floor somewhere. Maybe this is my opportunity to save Raad, Laura, and him. I can only wonder if I've had this vision for a reason. I have ten tries with the password before the phone will fully lock.

I start with the basics: Maximos, Brotherhood, Tentyrian, Ambrosine. I then try adding capitalization and basic numbers after the words. Two tries left, I better make it good. I type luminary1 and press the enter key. To my shock, it works. I'm in! Luminary1 is essentially me. I am his password. I could probably torture myself for hours thinking of that implication, but I don't have time. So far my vision has been correct, which means I'm about to find an e-mail from Laura. I click on the envelope icon with the word "Arianna" below it. I sort by last name and there it is:

Delia, Laura

RE: help

I open the e-mail, with my heart thundering in my chest. Its message is numbing:

I have Laura Delia along with Dr. Aman Raad. If you want to see them alive again come to 840 12th Avenue between West 58th and 59th Street (NYC). Come alone or they die. If the Brothers are reading this and you attempt to come with Arianna, they die. Nonnegotiable.

That's it. No indication of who it's truly from or what he or she intends to do with me if I do in fact come. But I know the answer. It doesn't take a genius. It's from the Dark Coven, and if I go, they'll probably kill me. What are the odds they believed I would find this e-mail and that I would find it alone? It was sent over three hours ago. Timed for when the Brothers were gone on their mission? Which means the Dark Coven either knew the Brotherhood was coming to raid the facilities or they believed that the Brotherhood hadn't yet found me. It was a risky move, but it worked. I've read it and I want more than ever to save my friends . . .

What the Dark Coven doesn't know, though, is how far away I am from New York. I have no way of getting there, even if I was crazy enough to go without any means to protect myself. Maximos was right—what am I going to do, hold their hands while politely asking for Laura and Raad? Damn it. I shove the phone in my other back pocket. I need to talk to Ryan. Maybe he's already gotten in touch with the teams who he lost communications with—including Maximos. But if I tell Ryan, it's not like he or any other Brother is going to let me go alone into what I can only imagine is a trap set by the Dark Coven. That means my friends will die. It's not negotiable, like the e-mail said. But I can't exactly commandeer a private jet.

My only hope to save Laura and Raad and protect myself is if I can shift. Ryan said it himself: shifting makes you practically invincible. I reach for the necklace on instinct. It helped me have a vision, so why not help me shift? The sunlight is long gone for me to use its rays to capture the light like I did before. But maybe candlelight will work. There is bound to be a candle in one of the villa's overstocked bathrooms. I pad over to Maximos' en suite and find what I'm looking for on the sink countertop—a Diptyque Menthe Verte candle. Mint must be his very favorite scent, I think indulgently as I remember his heady smell. Please come home safe.

I find a matchbook under the sink. Before I proceed, I need to think about how I want to go about this. I should experiment first. I'm most definitely not going to shift right into the location cited in the e-mail. From what I know of the area, it's mostly warehouses down by the West Side Highway. If I don't get killed first by the Dark Coven, there is always the potential for getting mugged. For starters, let's see if I can even get myself beyond this bathroom.

Shutting the door, I turn off all the lights. Sitting myself comfortably on the center of the marble floor with legs crossed, I strike the match and light the candle positioned in front of me. The sharp smell of sulfur dioxide burns my sensitive nose for just a moment as the candle comes to life. The light begins to dance, reflecting off the silver bathroom fixtures and mirrored surfaces. I unfasten the necklace from my neck and dangle the zodiac in front of me.

This time, rather than flipping the symbolic disk in my hand, I twirl the gold chain to maximize the flicker of light. The zodiac spins. I give myself several minutes to just watch the golden sparkle and let myself be drawn into it, to relax. I regulate my breathing like the seasoned meditator I am. I can do this. I imagine the bedroom in detail on the other side of the door, as if I'm checking off a design list. I visualize all of the furnishings, from the tufted sleigh bed to the beautiful chest sitting at the end of it with a zodiac symbol on top. I imagine the French doors leading to the balcony just beyond the two club chairs dressed in cream linen. I want to go to that door between those chairs. I silently chant it over and over again while maintaining the picture in my head of the doors in front of me.

I'm rewarded with a cool tingling sensation on my skin. It's almost like having aloe vera spread on in it. I close my eyes, as I know what's coming. When I open them, the doors are in front of me. Not so helpless after all. I can feel my adrenaline pumping and my pride swell, but there is little time to congratulate myself. My friends and Maximos could be dying. Unfortunately, I don't have enough detail indicating where I saw Maximos. The vision is already fading like a dream. Shifting to Maximos won't be possible. I must go to Laura and Raad.

Although it's easy enough to conjure up my apartment in mind, the Dark Coven could have Subordinates waiting for me there. I want to give myself time to check out the address and plan an escape route if my once-tried shifting fails, which wouldn't be a surprise. I should shift to a place I can easily remember the detail of and to where I won't be recognized.

Then it dawns on me. What better place than Grand Central Station? I've been there hundreds of times, and I know the architecture and layout of the landmark like the back of my hand. Not to mention I can easily catch a cab downtown. It's easy to be anonymous amongst a crowd. Ironically, I used to have a fear of going there when I was younger, as it was difficult for me to keep my mental block up. With Raad's help, I learned to overcome that fear and embrace the City, tourists and all. But now there is a much bigger task ahead of me I must embrace . . .

If I'm going to shift, I'll need to change. Cut-off shorts and bare feet aren't going to fly on the streets of New York. I can feel fatigue nipping, along with my unsteadiness, at the edges of my consciousness. Not wanting to waste my energy trying to shift again, I swiftly jog to my closet. I take the lit candle and necklace with me. With my superhuman speed, I doubt Shashandra would have even seen me pass her in the hallway.

It's slim pickings in terms of what to wear, and I'm faced with the same problem again of only having high heels and no practical shoes. I eyed Shashandra's feet earlier but they couldn't be more than a size 5. I'm a 9.5, a gift my mother and I both share. It was a shame she never let me play in her shoe collection; it's vast enough to make any fashionista swoon. Well, heels it is then. But maybe this isn't a bad idea . . . If I play the confident part, I can maybe use it to my advantage. It works in business, so why not when dealing with murderous vampires who intend to destroy the world? If I need to run, I can always throw off the shoes. I select a black Stella McCartney lace dress and gold brocade platform pumps notorious for compliments but also blisters.

I have my wallet and Maximos' phone but not a purse to put them in. So I'll travel light. I take out my driver's license, $200, and the mini Swiss Army knife I keep in my change purse. I shove the contents in my bra; a trick Laura taught me. I don't have a place to put the phone, but there is no point in bringing it. I have no one's phone number, and the people I would call have all been taken. I find the spare hair tie I also keep in my wallet and manage to put my hair back into a low ponytail that I hope is somewhat elegant. I can't believe I'm going to attempt to do this. I kneel on the floor, where I've placed the candle, and hold up the zodiac pendant once again. It's showtime.

CHAPTER 19:
PRESERVATION

2010 AD, JULY
HAMILTON, NEW JERSEY
TREBUCHET GLOBAL

"Calix, I'm tired of listening to the doctor's screams; it's unsettling and bad for employee morale. The humans aren't completely stupid. They are going to realize that there is more going on in here than 'regulated human testing.'"

Even in her white lab coat, Aglaia manages to look seductive. I can only imagine what she has on underneath. Today, she is wearing her tortoise-rimmed glasses. It's not like she needs them to see with her more than perfect vision, but I guess it's a fashion statement these days. Her hair is pulled back, creating a severe effect. Since our last spat, she won't give me the time of day. Not that I mind. We probably do make better friends and occasional adversaries than lovers. But she is one of the only remaining ties I have to Tentyris and the closest thing I'll probably ever have to a partner.

I'll be the first to admit I'm vain. I have no illusions that I am a good person. But it amazes me how deeply people want to believe this about themselves. After being around for as long as I have, you realize that most people live a lie, and when push comes to shove, they will be selfish. Self-preservation always wins. When I look back on Tentyris and when we ruled as part of the Council, I do feel a twinge of regret. Mostly because it's lonely having only two peers, and Aglaia's and Stavros' company does get old after a while . . .

My biggest regret, though, is Narcissa. Our romance was brief but sweet, just like her life. But the monogamy, loyalty, and virtue she demanded were exhausting. It was impossible to live up to what she wanted—essentially Maximos—and that's just not me. The number of times I had to hear her scold me like a schoolmarm for not being more like him was sickening. No thanks.

So our relationship turned sour and ended. But I never wanted her to die. Things should have, and could have, turned out differently, but the coup went terribly wrong. If the rest of the Council, including the Luminaries, had handed over their power without a fight, they could have been spared. But I guess they too wanted to believe they were good.

"Calix, are you listening to me?" an impatient Aglaia interrupts my thoughts.

"Just following orders, Aglaia. Stavros wanted me to break Raad—but I didn't think when I did he'd go on like this for so long. You are right, it is annoying."

"Then make him shut up," Aglaia snaps as she checks something off on what looks like an endless list pinned to a clipboard. A stickler for organization, Aglaia loves her lists. Our businesses really would fail to run without her. I take a syringe from the tray of instruments and inject the doctor with a heavy dose of morphine. He'll be quiet now. It will also make his blood taste foul, but I'm quite full anyway. This will be my act of goodwill for the day, lessening the man's pain. Fortunately or unfortunately, it will all be over for him soon enough. He was stronger than I anticipated. But he finally succumbed to the visions I put into his mind of the torture of his wife and Arianna.

For most humans, when you put their own life on the line, their instinct for self-preservation kicks in immediately. They'll do what you want. Not Aman Raad, though. It was only when I instilled a vision of his wife and Arianna being staked, to die a slow and torturous death favored by my old friend Vlad III, Prince of Wallachia, did the doctor answer my questions. Vlad, who made a name for himself as "Vlad the Impaler," or "Dracula" as humans like to call him today, had a knack for torture that was even beyond me.

My how long ago that was . . . Vlad's mistake was in thinking that we would turn him. But we make Subordinates, not equals. Vlad was one of few who we let know what we truly are. Humans can be useful sometimes, especially when it comes to money and politics. But like everyone else, he coveted our power and had to be eliminated. His assassination in 1476 was a piece of cake. But amazingly enough, his legend lives on in grossly inaccurate vampire novels and movies. It's quite funny how legends start, especially when you know you are the root cause of them.

"We're still moving the product, and this room has gotten more than just a few suspicious looks from the staff," continues an irritated Aglaia. "I'm responsible for this lab, and I run a tight ship."

"Yes I know, as you so like to remind us. But it won't matter anymore. Once everything has been moved out through the tunnels today, Stavros wants this place detonated—with everyone inside. Well, not us of course," I say.

Aglaia looks surprised as she pauses her writing and gives her glasses a slight push up the bridge of her nose. "I know we agreed to destroy the facility after we moved the DTPA12, but I was under the impression we would close it down and send the humans home?" she replies.

"Change of plans. You aren't getting soft, are you? The Brotherhood now knows about DTPA12. Stavros had Travis leak the information directly to the Brotherhood's informant at the FDA this morning."

"Why?" she demands. Stavros is going to get chewed out for this. And believe me, Aglaia is a master at it.

"Because it was only a matter of time before they found out. The drug is being approved in a matter of days, and it will reach the press soon enough. Not to mention, the Brotherhood always has a way of finding out where our operations are—as you well know, based on the number of times you've had to rebuild and restructure branches of Trebuchet. This time, Stavros wants to draw them in, especially now that he knows the girl is likely a Luminary descendent."

"It sounds sloppy."

"You would say that because you weren't privy to the plan. But don't take offense, Aglaia, neither was I. You know how Stavros is sometimes—always trying to keep the upper hand over us. After I called him to explain what I learned from the doctor, he told me the Brotherhood would likely be here in a matter of hours."

"A matter of hours!"

"Yes, so how much more of this do you need to do?" I ask, gesturing to the bustling lab technicians.

"I could kill Stavros, along with you," she seethes. "You have no respect for me or any woman for that matter. Fortunately for you all, I'm almost done."

"Let's not make this about women's rights again. I get it. I really do. Now let's move on." Aglaia looks ready to rip my eyes out.

"The fail-safe system is prepped," I explain to her. "I have a Subordinate monitoring the security cameras and several more Subordinates actively patrolling. When the Brotherhood shows up, they've been instructed to notify me at once."

"And then what?" she asks.

I take out my phone to show her. "There's an app for that. I press this button and the Brothers die."

"Along with our staff?"

"Yep. That's what's great about it. The Brotherhood won't be expecting it, and they'll never think this place is rigged to blow. We've never sacrificed our own employees before—at least, not intentionally."

"So we blow this place up," Aglaia replies. "Do you really think that is going to put a dent in the Brotherhood's force? Their numbers are considerably greater than ours, lest you forget. We mostly have a bunch of moronic animals working for us."

"It will make a difference if they are going to plan a simultaneous attack on our other facilities, just like they did last night. The remaining buildings will be ready and waiting to blow. Aglaia, we've upped the ante on them. We have the doctor and Arianna's friend, and we've clued the Brotherhood in on what we're doing. They are bound to panic and focus their efforts on the only thing they can do right now—attack what they know is ours."

"Look," she says. "I'm all for killing the Brothers, Calix. Maximos' and Aristos' righteousness is enough to make me gag. But in the long run, it doesn't matter. We've designed the release of the DTPA12 and the attacks perfectly. The Brotherhood won't be able to stop us."

"Yes, but you are missing the one potential flaw. The Parker girl. She could have Hathor's power . . ."

Aglaia puts the clipboard down and puts her hand on her hip in a sign of exasperation. "You and Stavros are alarmed for nothing. You told me yourself, the doctor only knows of her having one power—telepathy. Big deal. It's not enough to foil our plans."

"Maybe. But Arianna is likely full Tentyrian now . . ."

"And how long did it take us to master our powers after we turned twenty-five?"

"Years. I get your point. But there is no harm done in trying to kill the Brothers by blowing up some of our warehouses and labs."

"Only several million dollars, but it's not like you ever paid attention to the bottom line. Whatever, it's your prerogative. I won't be mourning any deaths."

"No, I'm sure you won't, Aglaia."

PART IV

CHAPTER 20:
A PROPOSITION

2010 AD, JULY
NEW YORK, NEW YORK
STAVROS' HOME

"**Y**ou look quite fetching in that dress and hat. Turn around for me one more time so I can admire you," I say. Laura Delia turns slowly for me, a slight smile on her lips, allowing me a long look at her slim figure. The tea-length, peach-colored strapless dress compliments her blonde hair and blue eyes. It's not as conservative as I'd prefer, but it's what Bridget picked out on short notice.

When I first came upon Laura in my room, she wasn't what I expected. She was beautiful to be sure, as Aglaia implied, but there were no tears or even cries for help. She was calm and composed. So unlike the victims that usually find their ways to me. Tied to the bed as she was, it would have been easy enough to ravish and drink from her. But I found her reasonableness to confront me calmly about why she had been taken, well . . . refreshing.

Laura said she would tell me about Arianna as long as she was untied and given the respect she was due. So I had tea brought up and, in a surreal encounter, we calmly conversed while drinking a silk oolong. I even refrained from my usual scotch, I was so fascinated. Simpering females can be entertaining for a while, but they end up being the same—just another meal. This female is quietly strong, intelligent, and undoubtedly delicious. I determined to take my time before ripping into that beautiful neck of hers.

We talked about Arianna and how she has a knack for understanding people and their motivations. Laura described it as intuition, but I know what it really is—Tentyrian power. Laura said Arianna is very private and, although they are friends, by most people's standards they're more like acquaintances. Arianna's primary focus is work. Laura described her as withdrawn and "barely having a relationship with her family." Aside from knowing that, Laura rarely delves into personal details with her. The Parker woman sounds like a real ball of fun. No wonder Laura considers them mostly acquaintances. I sensed no guile in what the delectable woman was saying.

When I asked about Aman Raad, she said she knew that Arianna had a therapist of sorts. But then again, she countered, doesn't everyone have a therapist in New York these days? Reasonable enough. But what Calix later revealed to me, after breaking the doctor down, tells a much deeper story. Aman Raad knew that Arianna Parker could read minds, and over the years he helped her control that power. Calix relayed Raad's knowledge of her enlarged corpus callosum—a gift all Tentyrians share . . .

The facts are irrefutable. Arianna Parker is a Tentyrian descendent. And I suspect with her ability to read minds, she is one of the Luminaries' ancestors. I just pray she doesn't have Hathor's power. It shouldn't be possible, but somehow it happened. Which means the Luminaries' children didn't die like they were supposed to and their line somehow escaped our detection all this time.

When we escaped the Sanctum before it was locked down, we were sure of our success. Calix was fortunate enough to learn about the failsafe key from Phoebe, a fact he managed to obtain and help her forget while Selene weakened Phoebe's power after we kidnapped her. We thought the Covens were fully eliminated and there were no survivors, aside from the Tentyrian Guards we kept alive—for a while.

With our abilities and thirst, hiding what we are is difficult. So over the years we kept our ears to the ground—listening for whispers about people like us or humans who possessed knowledge of our Tentyrian existence. Aside from the Brothers, we managed to kill them all, or so we thought.

The revelation of what Arianna is doesn't change our plans. However, it does mean we need to act quickly. And bring her to us if possible. Having Laura will do just that. That's why I hatched the plan to tip off the Brotherhood about DTPA12, plant the bombs at our remaining facilities once the drugs were secreted out through the underground tunnels, and contact Arianna Parker. E-mailing her from Laura's address was a shot in the dark. Her phone number went straight to voicemail, and it appeared she had literally disappeared off the face of the Earth. According to Laura, she was on a business trip. Likely a business trip sponsored by Maximos.

I ensured the e-mail was sent when the Brothers would be distracted by the wild goose chase they likely thought would be a successful mission. Little did they know about the explosive greeting awaiting them. Laura obliged me when I took her phone and sent Arianna an e-mail. When I explained to her my rationale, she responded with an arched brow and soft reply.

"I understand you want her to come to you," she said, "because you want this power you believe she has. But what makes you think she'll even come? I explained to you that we are friends, yes. But surely not so great of friends that she would risk her life for me."

"Perhaps. But if she is anything like her ancestors, she'll protect humanity at all costs," I said. To my surprise, the alluring woman next to me simply sipped her tea in quiet contemplation. "Ms. Delia, you seem remarkably calm about this situation. Why is that?" I asked. With a cool self-awareness I've rarely seen exuded, she looked me squarely in the eye and gave me an astounding answer.

"Because there is little I can do to change the situation. You are clearly a man of great power and likely possess some type of ability I have no experience understanding. There is no way for me to escape from here, and I suspect that you aren't human. I went to work this morning and was taken out of my office and brought here in a matter of seconds. It's impossible for me to rationalize how; however, you've explained to me the why. I will not say that I condone what you are doing, as your accomplice indicated you intend to kill me. I assume you are planning on doing that after you use me as bait?" she said.

"Truthfully, I haven't yet decided," I replied.

"Very well. Then I want to offer you a proposition."

I was surprised next at my own response—"I'm all ears."

"I'm not going to beg for my life. I don't believe in playing the victim. I graduated with honors from Columbia University, and I'm a successful executive in advertising. I'm told I'm smart and make for an excellent business partner. I never want for male companionship, or friends, for that matter. To be frank, I find you attractive. If circumstances were indeed different or perhaps this was another life, I could even imagine us on a date. I'm not attempting to flatter you or even offer myself to you . . . sexually. However, I can offer you my companionship and discretion, for however long you may wish."

"So you have no qualms about your friend dying?"

"As I told you, she is more of an acquaintance. I would prefer for Arianna to live, but if given the choice between my life and hers, I would choose my own. Surely you cannot blame me for saying that I don't want to die?"

"No, I suppose I cannot. But why would you agree to be with me?"

"Aside from being a potential alternative to death? Well, I find you intriguing and powerful. Maybe with time we can learn to understand each other. Everyone has motivations for their behaviors. I have simply yet to understand yours."

For several minutes, I had nothing to say as I absorbed her fascinating proposition. This woman wasn't greedy—she was realistic. Clearly she was impressed by my power and me, but rather than offering flattery that would inevitably ring false in my ears, she gave me an unvarnished opinion. In this brave new world that I'm crafting, I could benefit from someone like her. Not that she'll ever be my equal. But as I said, play toys grow tiresome. And maybe I wouldn't grow tired of her, at least not immediately . . .

Therefore, I decided to let her live—for now. I also conveniently needed a date to the polo match being hosted at Senator Cromwell's upstate home that afternoon. I rarely make any public appearances, but this meeting warranted in-person attendance . . .

I agreed to Laura Delia's deal but made it clear that if she displeased me or proved to be a liar, I'd drink her dry without a moment's hesitation. Her eyes grew wide, and for the first time her fear was palpable. However, with one final sip of her tea and a deep breath, she offered me a curt nod and acquiescing handshake.

She clearly has breeding and is well educated. Having an intelligent woman by one's side can make all the difference between a successful and failed deal. And today's deal with the senator is crucial. I'd normally bring Aglaia, but she is angry with me. I'm going to be destroying her precious labs in a matter of hours. That is, as soon as the Brothers are dumb enough to show their faces.

They now know or have an inkling of what's at stake. Soon we'll have the only drug on the market to treat a rare radiation sickness. And when the "terrorist attacks" occur around the globe—followed by war—Trebuchet will be there to supply both the weapons and the only cure for when the humans become sick. Simply masterful.

"I do love the hat and dress, Stavros. Thank you," Laura says graciously.

"I must say, the hat reminds me of a more civilized time," I reply.

"Maybe you will tell me more about that time, along with who we will be talking to at the polo match?" she asks. I keep my face passive, but my suspicions are sparked. "If I have some basic information on who you want to engage or impress, perhaps I can be of the best use to you."

Her blue eyes are so clear and calm, could there be a woman who is conniving under there? Perhaps I've been around Aglaia for too long . . . and Hathor's memory has poisoned me. But even so, I'm not reckless enough to fully trust Laura. She is still a woman.

CHAPTER 21:
ACTING 101

Thank goodness my parents let me explore acting and psychology in college, because I'm using every skill I can remember. My assessment: Stavros Papadakis is a narcissistic sociopath. I haven't yet determined what he really thinks of me, but he's letting me live, which is a miracle. There was no time to even absorb what was happening when that woman barged into my office. The next thing I knew, I was tied to a bed in a room that looked like something out of Victorian England with its brocade canopy and thick coverings.

She said her name was Aglaia, and I learned she is just as psychotic as Stavros. I could have clawed her face off, and I tried, but what she showed me and said next made me rethink my approach. Immediately, she tied a gag around my mouth, and in a blur of motion, she had me restrained. As she was tightening the binding ropes to my wrists and ankles, making me lay spread eagle on the bed and subsequently humiliating me in my skirt, she showed me her fangs. These were no plastic fangs from Party City. As she brought her face next to mine, I literally saw them protract from her gums. Their tips were as sharp as razor blades. It was enough to make anyone faint. But I was so scared—I couldn't take my eyes off her or her mouth. A real-life vampire was standing over me.

"I might as well tell you now so you can come to terms with it, Laura Delia. Stavros, the man I brought you here to meet, is going to kill you. We're interested in what you know about your friend Arianna Parker. If you want this to be less painful, I suggest you tell the truth. If you lie, we'll find out, and when we do, I promise it will hurt," she said. I was trembling like an autumn leaf, and I would have screamed if I didn't have a handkerchief stuffed in my mouth.

The vampire then traced her finger along my face and cupped it in a gesture that was almost motherly. "I'm going to give you some advice, Laura Delia," she said. Her voice was enchanting, just like her appearance. Even in my immense fear, I could appreciate her beauty as she continued to talk. "I'm offering this advice because you remind me of myself. I like your ambition and your no-nonsense attitude toward business and men. No one likes a prude. So here it is: Stavros uses and abuses women. He can be a sadistic son of a bitch if he doesn't respect you. And he doesn't respect women, especially when they are hysterical and insipid. I know him better than he knows himself. He is attracted to strong women, as much as he would never admit that. Especially after he was scorned by the world's most powerful. I'm telling you this not because it will save your life but because it might make your death less miserable. Stavros is arrogant, proud, and he is used to getting what he wants. Be careful which line you decide to walk. Either way, it won't matter. Arianna Parker will die and so will you."

The vampire then kissed my forehead gently—her lips surprisingly warm—and left me to ponder my next move. My conclusion was that I'll be damned if I accept the fate she pronounced for my best friend or me. I will go down fighting. My only hope was to use the information Aglaia gave me and tread carefully.

When Stavros stalked his way into the room like a self-satisfied panther, what felt like hours later, I recognized the look of a lecher. I've seen it dozens of times. It's impossible not to when you date in New York City. It took all my power to remain collected, as he appraised me up and down like newfound property, and even more so as I attempted to bargain with him . . .

I intentionally downplayed my friendship with Ari, while still providing information that was accurate. I've known for years that Ari has some type of telepathic skill, not that I'm about to reveal that to the crazies who obviously intend to exploit her. Ari and I have actually never spoken about it openly because I know how uncomfortable it makes her and the struggles she's gone through because of it. I also know that one day she'll tell me about it, when she is ready. Her gift is undeniable—but so is our friendship.

Stavros is a vampire, or "Tentyrian" as he's since explained to me. However, at the end of the day, he is also a man. And if there is anything I know about men, it's how to manipulate them. This is a man who likes to be in control. It's over ninety degrees outside, and he made me use a cream-colored shawl to cover my exposed arms. That was after he had me dress up like a Stepford wife to attend a polo match. I naturally agreed to go and wear the ridiculous shawl, feigning my own Connecticut-bred modesty. I then proceeded to engage him in a politically charged conversation about Senator Cromwell's Republican position on contraception. It went over beautifully.

Conversing with Stavros in the chauffeured Bentley on our way to Bedford was easy. The trick was to ask the questions and let him respond with his lengthy diatribes. I never contradicted him, but I shaped the conversation to always appear engaged. I'm one to appreciate the art of conversation, but throughout the hour and half drive, it was downright terrifying knowing that one slip-up could cost me my life. When he received a call on his cell he clearly wasn't happy with, I thought for sure he would kill me. But after yelling about the incompetence of someone he referred to as a "subordinate" and he asked the person on the other end of the phone to "eliminate him" because he had failed in some task involving wiring, he appeared much calmer.

My mother always told me, "You don't have to be the most beautiful or even the smartest girl in the room. You only have to be the most interesting." This advice couldn't be better employed than now. I have to stay interesting. Whenever Stavros' hand would inappropriately inch up my leg, I would play the coy maiden, shifting myself away from him. Because if Aglaia was right—and she has been so far—Stavros gets what he wants. And if I give in to his advances, I'll no longer be the most interesting girl in the room.

When we arrived at the lush colonial estate that I was told was over thirty-two acres, I knew Stavros was still interested. As the valet helped me out of the car, Stavros aggressively pushed him out of the way and maintained his hand on the small of my back, just as he did throughout the afternoon. During the glasses of champagne, canapés, and watching the horses charge around the field, I kept my senses trained on Stavros' mood and on gleaning any information I could to discover the larger plan that was clearly in progress . . . and involved Ari.

Stavros alluded to this plan in the car by regaling me with the extent of his businesses. He highlighted, in particular, how Trebuchet has been supplying governments for years with state-of-the-art weapons.

He stated that his centuries of hard work were about to pay off. When I asked him what he wanted to discuss with the senator and if he would wish for privacy at that opportunity, he told me that he'd handle the conversation alone and that it was just to "ensure an arrangement" the two had made.

So when our host, along with two not so inconspicuous body-guards, made their way over to us near the polo field, I knew Stavros would eventually excuse himself with the senator or he'd cue me to leave. But first, I needed to leave an impression. So I went with what I know best—advertising. After introductions that Stavros led, calling me a "dear friend" and wrapping his arm around me protectively, I asked the senator if he had yet engaged his advertising strategist for the 2012 campaign. He said he had. I told him how fortunate that was, as his tact with the minority populations could be improved, specifically the targeted TV placements he ran in 2006. They verged on pandering.

I saw Stavros' lip curl in response; his ice blue eyes were practi-cally shooting daggers. I felt his hand dig into my waist, and I wanted to flinch under his strong grip, but I maintained my composure. The senator's reaction was my saving grace. It was priceless, in fact. He burst out laughing and almost spilled his gin and tonic.

"I couldn't agree more, Laura! That's why I fired my old strategist to begin with! He was an idiot. Now I've got some slick agency using words like 'Facebook' and 'Twitter,' not that I understand the faintest thing about technology. I'm so old-fashioned I still dictate to my secre-tary to type up my e-mails!" he said.

"Well, it sounds like you are well on your way to a successful re-election, Senator. And there is nothing wrong with old-fashioned. It's those values we need in our government. You have my vote," I replied. I wanted to vomit in my mouth, but I felt Stavros' grip gentle, and I gave him and the senator my most charming smile. "Gentlemen, if you'll excuse me, I want to say hello to some ladies I recognize from my Junior League days."

As I excused myself and walked toward a group of women I'd never met before in my life, I heard my victory spoken by the senator. "That girl is special, Stavros. Don't let that one go."

"I don't think I will Senator," I heard Stavros reply. Shivers went up my spine.

I introduced myself to the women, who looked more like vicious peacocks in their colorful ensembles and suspicious stares than social-ites. Stavros instructed me not to discuss our relationship or even bring up his name, not that they bothered to ask. While the women didn't bite, they coolly viewed me as an interloper on their inner circle and tried to ignore me as much as possible. Like I care, I thought.

As I stand here now, I'm only halfheartedly listening to the farce of a conversation about the "best" private schools. I am never having children if this is what it turns you into. These women are moronic. I keep my eyes trained on Stavros and Cromwell. They begin to walk toward the house, leaving the polo field. I want to follow, but I'm going to need a cover. I grab the arm of the unmarried woman next to me, Margaret, who looks unlikely to squawk at my rude behavior. Feigning a terrible sense of direction, I ask her to help me find the powder room. I also tell her that I saw a handsome gentleman eyeing her from the bar who I just have to tell her about. That does the trick, and she comes with me willingly.

Linked arm in arm, I prattle some nonsense about a guy in a navy blazer with dark hair, which could fit the description of half the men here. Margaret is instantly engaged. From one of the server's trays, I lift a glass of champagne and replace her empty. As we walk slowly, she starts to hypothesize on who the "mystery man" is and begins to lay out her current dating situation. With my distracted and bubbling companion, I lead us in pursuit of the men but am careful to keep a distance. Once we reach the house, I'm almost positive I see them go down the right-hand corridor. So that's where we head.

"Laura, I'm sure the bathroom is the other way," says Margaret, interrupting our stealthy pursuit.

"Yes, but those are the ones everyone else is using and I heard there is no staff monitoring them. They are verging on unsanitary. I heard someone say that there is an additional guest bathroom this way. You said that Thomas has a yacht, by the way? How marvelous!"

Between her exclamations about her heart's desire's immense wealth, I notice that Cromwell's guards are now stationed outside of two closed doors. It must be the senator's office. Who am I kidding; I have no way of listening outside the door with the security detail there. So I lead Margaret down an alternate corridor, and eventually I do find a guest bathroom. Shutting the door behind me and leaving Margaret to continue her self-absorbed chatter on the other side, I formulate an alternate game plan.

Stavros and the senator won't stay behind closed doors long—it's the senator's party, after all. I just need to kill time and keep Margaret with me as a safety, and maybe I can see if there are any relevant files or documents in the office. It did sound like Cromwell wasn't the savviest with technology, so maybe he keeps paper files? I notice there is very little toilet paper roll left. I quickly unravel it all and flush it.

"Okay, Margaret, your turn. So do you think that he'll take you to his parent's house in Antigua this winter?" I say while ushering her into the bathroom. I shut the door and let her do her thing. It's amazing she doesn't stop talking until she realizes her predicament.

"Oh no, Laura, there is no more toilet paper!"

"Are you sure, Margaret? I thought I saw an extra roll?"

"No. Not here. And there isn't any under the sink."

"Okay, no worries. Let me grab you some. I'll be back in a flash. I think there is even another guest room right next to this one . . ."

As fast as my heels will take me, I trot out of the room and back down the hall toward the office. The security detail is gone, and fortunately there is no one else in the hall. With a quick look both ways, I open the door and slip inside. I need to hustle. Stavros is probably looking for me, and I've left Margaret sitting on a toilet. The thick desk with its leather blotter is littered with papers. I have no idea what I'm looking for. But surely anything important wouldn't just be sitting out. There is no computer, which means I may be in luck. I walk over to the credenza and open the filing drawers in search of "T" for Trebuchet, the name of Stavros' business.

As my fingers crawl over the alphabet, I'm shocked they aren't trembling. If I get caught, it's over. I find the Trebuchet folder, and inside I see what looks like pages and pages of blueprints and invoices for weapons. But everything looks the same, and I can't exactly take the whole file and shove it in my dress. However, one paper catches my eye. There is no letterhead; it's just a list of ten different addresses in different countries. I fold the paper into a small square and shove it in my underwear. Shoes and even bras can come off easily but not the underwear . . .

I close the credenza and exit the study. But just as I'm opening the door, I collide with someone on the other side. I hear a clatter, followed by breaking glass. To my relief, it's just a waiter.

"Oh my gosh. I'm so sorry," I apologize. "I was just looking for the bathroom . . ."

"It's okay, ma'am. No harm done." The young man blushes as he squats down to pick up the glass shards.

"Let me help you," I say as I reach down to help. But he assures me he has it. His cheeks turn an even darker red. Not wanting to embarrass him any further, for something that is already my fault, I apologize once again and turn to go.

"Can I have some of these?" I ask, pausing to pick up several cocktail napkins.

"Sure," the waiter says, looking confused.

I hurry back to Margaret, who has likely already decided to drip dry in my absence.

"Margaret, are you still in there?" I ask breathlessly upon reaching the door.

"Yes. Where else would I be, Laura?" she says irritated.

"Here you go." I slip the cocktail napkins under the door. "There was no toilet paper like anywhere. I can't believe it! The senator really needs to get a new staff. I feel like I ran around this entire house." Margaret answers with a flush of the toilet and comes out, clearly peeved.

"Oh, don't be mad at me, Margaret. I'm so sorry." I give her a desperate smile.

"It's not you, Laura. It's Thomas. He just sent me the rudest text." She pouts as she shoves her phone at me. She probably didn't even notice I was gone while she was busy texting. Margaret is a classic case of a "clinger" with men, fortunately for me. I take one of the extra cocktail napkins and give my armpits a pat. And I thought preparing for a pitch was stressful.

"Pray tell? You'll have to give me all the details. And we need to get another drink immediately. Maybe we can find your mystery man once and for all," I say, guiding us back outside.

I'm just about to order us two lemonades when Stavros appears at my side. Literally appears.

"Oh, hello. You startled me." I keep my face as innocent looking as possible.

"I've been looking for you. Where have you been, Laura?" His voice is relatively pleasant, but I can hear the menace underneath.

"Margaret and I went to the ladies room," I say easily. "You know how complicated these things can be . . ."

"Oh you wouldn't believe it. No toilet paper!" says Margaret. "Laura is my lifesaver, though." It seems I've won the girl over with a few cocktail napkins and some boy talk. Thank God she didn't mention me abandoning her for close to fifteen minutes.

"Yes, she has that way about her," says Stavros as he reaches out to tuck a stray hair behind my ear. "I fear we must go now, Laura. The driver is bringing the car around now."

"So soon?" asks Margaret. "We must see each other again!"

"Absolutely. Why don't I give you my phone number?" I offer. Margaret, acting like we're now best friends, couldn't be better. After exchanging numbers, Stavros takes my elbow and escorts me back to the front of the house.

"Are you all right in your high heels?" he asks. "I know it's a far walk. If you'd prefer, I can get one of the golf carts over here to drive us up." If this man weren't a vampire who intended to murder my best friend and likely me, I might think the offer sweet.

"How thoughtful, Stavros. I'm fine. I have your sturdy arm." I actually manage to make myself blush as I look at him sweetly. All I had to do was visualize the waiter's reaction. Thank you, method acting. As Stavros helps me into the car, I feel the chafing reminder of what I've gotten myself into—stealing addresses and cavorting with a killer. How long am I going to be able to keep this up?

CHAPTER 22:
DESPERATE TIMES, DESPERATE MEASURES

2010 AD, JULY
HAMILTON, NEW JERSEY, TREBUCHET GLOBAL / AMBROSINE
ISLAND, IONIAN SEA

The blast took us by surprise. After hours of scoping the facilities and planning our approach, it took only ten minutes for everything to go up in smoke. The detonator was triggered not long after I discovered Raad, tied to a chair and slumped over in a bloody mess. He was barely alive, his pulse thready and inconsistent. Practically unrecognizable with his face beaten to a pulp, it was obvious he had been tortured, and knowing the Dark Coven, it likely wasn't just physical abuse Raad endured.

I directed Phi to split into pairs. Being able to shift, I went alone to cover as many of the lab's rooms as I could. Fortunately, I smelled a human through an air-locked door. It led to where Raad was held, which was more like a torture chamber than a room. Barbaric instruments, looking like a plastic surgeon's tools, were freshly stained with blood and lay neatly on a tray. Bloodied gauze bandages littered the floor.

When we burst into the lab, after cutting off the electricity and communications systems, it was absolute pandemonium. Subordinates sprang into action. Humans screamed, hid under desks, and reached for their cell phones. We had the cell phone jammer to minimize the damage control we'd ultimately have to do, but little did we know just how vast the damage would be. The Brothers went to work immediately subduing the chaos and Subordinates while simultaneously sweeping the area. As I was crouched down, undoing the leather straps that dug into the doctor's flesh around his ankles, the walls crashed down around me.

The sound of the explosion was deafening, and the force of it immediately knocked me on my stomach. Shrapnel from the surrounding walls went flying and dug its way into my skin, past the specialized lightweight Kevlar barrier of my fatigues. There was no time to react or even shift. But at least by being closer to the ground, I was able to avoid taking the full force of the blast from all sides. Raad wasn't so lucky.

I don't know how long I was knocked out for. But after opening my eyes, I lay still for several minutes, taking stock of what had happened as well as my injuries. I was bleeding profusely, but I would live. My communications equipment was destroyed, and I had no way of connecting with the other Brothers. We clearly walked into a trap crafted by the Dark Coven, who willingly destroyed their own building and everything within. Including their employees—Subordinates and humans alike. This lab was state of the art, with millions of dollars worth of equipment. The Dark Coven must not have had anything to lose.

Something heavy—either rock or metal—lay on my back and pinned me to the ground. With all the strength I could muster, I pushed myself off the floor and heaved the rubble from my back. The pain was excruciating, as I could feel the muscles in my back tear. I was losing blood quickly. I needed to drink. Struggling to stand, I surveyed what was once a room. Now it was an open array of rock, sparking electrical wires, and fire. Raad, who had been strapped to a chair, was knocked to the ground in the blast. A chunk of twisted metal covered almost his entire body. His flesh was badly burned and oozing; he also had a massive head wound.

I kneeled by his side and put my fingers on his neck to check for a pulse I believed I wouldn't find. To my surprise, I felt one. But it had only minutes left to beat.

"Aman. Aman Raad, can you hear me?" I asked. "I've come to save you and bring you home . . ." I could see his eyelids quivering, struggling to open. "You don't have to open your eyes or say anything. I'm going to get you out of here."

I was about to start prying the metal off of him when I heard a gravelly, "No." The dying man was struggling to speak through his burned lips. He tried to say more, but I knew blood was filling his lungs, making it impossible to talk. I reached inside myself for my faltering energy and managed to grasp onto some lingering tendrils. Raad was on the threshold of death, which meant I could communicate with him another way. I placed my hand on his forehead and pushed my energy out and pulled myself into his mind.

After the vertigo of entering Raad's mind settled, I saw him sitting cross-legged in a white tunic on a rattan mat. He was in the same white room I experienced in Ari's dream state—not surprising considering he taught her to build her safe space. I sat down across from him, mirroring his position. His brown eyes were warm and smiling; any surprise at my presence was absent.

"You are the one that is trying to save me?" he asked calmly.

"Yes, my name is Maximos."

"You are a soldier?

"Something like that. I am here to protect Ari. And you."

"My greatest fear has been realized. They want to use Ari for her power. I held out for as long as I could, but I fear they made me speak what I swore I would not." His face became sad, shaking his head side to side. His intake of breath in his dream state was labored.

"I can only imagine what you went through. Can you tell me what you told them?" I asked.

"They know what she can do. They know she is special—physiologically and psychically. It's my fault."

"They would have found out anyway. Ari is like me and my people. I will keep her safe." I tried to assure the man, in as few words as possible. There was so much I wanted to tell him, but I could feel his body dying. There was no time.

"How?" he asked, his eyes searching mine.

"Because I'm part of an ancient order that has sworn to protect humanity and what Ari is."

"I pray that you can. They are monsters . . . She is the second love of my life, aside from my wife who I will see soon . . ." Tears began to fall from Raad's eyes.

"I can save you if you'll let me. But it will require me to turn you into a being that will live forever."

"A vampire?" he asked. "I saw what those men were who took me . . ."

"Yes. But you wouldn't be like that. You would be like me and Ari. We're not like them . . ."

"You mean Ari is . . ."

"Yes," I interrupted urgently. "That is why she has always been different. We don't have much time. Your body is shutting down and your lungs will no longer be able to take in oxygen. You must decide if you want to see Ari again."

"I cannot. It was not meant for me to live forever. I know I was meant to guide Ari into adulthood. I've felt it since the day I met her. But my time is over. I feel it in my soul. It's time for me to join Seda."

"Very well." I bowed my head in acknowledgment and respect for the man who turned down immortality because he knew it was not his destiny. Not many would refuse the gift I offered.

"You will promise to take care of her? And help her find the love she needs?" His words were heart wrenching. Like a father pleading for his daughter.

"Always," I promised. I then saw him close his eyes and bow his own head in peace. I released the energy tethering us together and was brought back to the scene of destruction, which is where I am now.

His pulse under my fingertips is gone. I need to reach the other Brothers, but I can't leave Raad's body to burn in this forsaken place. He will burn according to Tentyrian custom. I wrench the metal off the doctor's broken body and sling him over my shoulder. My body screams in protest with the searing pain. I make my way through the broken rock and debris, avoiding the flames while calling to my men. There is no reply, just eerie silence and the crackling of flames. In the distance, I can hear the faint blaring of sirens. I have to evacuate my men before the human authorities arrive at the site. Judging by the sirens in the distance, it will be in a matter of minutes.

I see five figures in a V formation coming toward me with guns pointed. I am unarmed, as my own weapon was destroyed in the blast. I can't make out if it is friend or foe through the heavy smoke. If I have to battle, I know it is possible it could be my last. I could shift away, but I believe in facing my enemies and inflicting as much damage as possible before retreating. So I lay Raad's body on the ground and prepare to engage.

But it proves unnecessary. As the five figures reach me through the hellish fire and choking air straight out of Dante's Inferno, I see they are my Brothers.

"Praise Hathor, you're here, Maximos!" says a relieved Aristos. "We've turned this site upside down looking for you. Julian said you went off to shift through a separate wing of the facility. I was afraid we weren't going to find you—alive. Who is that poor soul you have there?" Aristos gestures toward Raad's broken body.

"Ari's mentor, Dr. Aman Raad . . . How many Brothers did we lose?" I ask. The fear and anger I feel for my endangered men is raging. Proceeding with this mission was my call and ultimately my failure.

"Two. Connor and Gabriel from Delta. New York and Texas were rigged to blow and they did along with this one. Fortunately, overall injuries are minimal thanks to the new armor that Evander commissioned. Based on the blast pattern here, though, you were one of the closest to it, Maximos. You're lucky to be alive," says Aristos.

"We have two dead Brothers. The Brotherhood has taken a grievous hit. There is no luck today," I reply solemnly.

"Guys, we need to go," interrupts Julian, one of the Brothers on my Phi team. He has a few scratches on his face but otherwise appears fine. "The humans have arrived."

"Are there any other survivors?" I ask.

"None of the humans or Subordinates lived. The rest of the Brothers have been accounted for and are back on Ambrosine," he replies.

"Let's go," I agree as I pick up Raad's body and shift with the Brothers to our island. I will now have to break the news to Ari . . .

We go straight to the lab area to treat our wounds. Only ten of us are seriously injured. The rest have superficial wounds that will heal in a matter of hours. In all, we utilized forty brothers for the mission and lost two. We now have three to mourn—Connor, Gabriel, and Raad. I was hoping to talk to Ari right away, to break the news gently, but she isn't in the lab area and I can't readily remove myself from Shashandra's ministrations and Evander's needle.

The gashes are deep in my back and require both staples and stitches. I drink six pints of blood to replace those that I have lost, eagerly sucking on the refrigerated pouches while Evander mercilessly sterilizes, removes shrapnel, and pieces my skin together. With Evander's natural healing energies, the pain lessens considerably, but it still hurts like a son of a bitch. Fortunately, I can feel the replenishing blood taking effect. I will be myself after a long healing sleep.

With bandages in place, I meet the rest of the Brothers in the conference room for an emergency meeting. I look around the table, absorbing the hardened looks of my men. But where is Ryan? His presence and perspective are essential; he was the lead on ground control.

I take the position at the head of the table. "All right let's get started, guys," I say, calling the attention of my men. "Ryan I'm sure will grace us with his presence soon. From what I know, three of the facilities blew up. Two of the others didn't. Teams Alpha and Omega, what did you find?"

"Mostly scared humans and dumb Subordinates. The facilities were used to produce DTPA12 all right. But none of it was there when we arrived. We found underground tunnels, which we think were used to transfer out the drug," says Evander, who led Omega's missions on Virginia and later Georgia.

"The Dark Coven knew we were coming," interrupts Estaban as he holds an icepack to his temple.

"After we heard teams Beta, Delta, and Phi were compromised by an explosion, we turned the facilities upside down looking for bombs," continues Evander. "With the aid of the E3500 Chemilux device, we located the explosives in Virginia and Georgia. Fortunately, they were faulty. They didn't explode because the C-4 in them wasn't connected properly to the wires. A common mistake among amateurs . . ."

"Well the Dark Coven got the rigging right in New York, New Jersey, and Texas. And unfortunately Connor and Gabriel paid for it," says Dimitri with a clenched fist.

"Every one of those facilities had at least fifty employees. The Dark Coven has never compromised their own resources like that before," comments Aristos through gritted teeth. "They no longer care about the details. Fortunately, they missed a few by not blowing up all the buildings as planned. We were able to retrieve hard drives from Virginia and Georgia that I am going to start scanning immediately."

"We're also going to conduct our own campaign against the Dark Coven by using the humans," I command. "I want the picture we have of Stavros, Aglaia, and Calix leaked to the media. We are going to target law enforcement and talk to 'witnesses' near the facilities. They are going to finger those three for the explosions. If we have to use mind control—so be it. I want the world to know that the Dark Coven is a group of terrorists, and I want their pictures plastered on the news. We aren't tiptoeing around each other anymore."

"You want us to 'persuade' the humans with mind control?" asks Hale, clearly surprised.

"Yes," I say, certain. "The stakes are too high. This is for the good of humanity. We are going to hold the Dark Coven accountable. They intended to destroy the facilities to not only kill us but stop the drug production and maintain a tight grip on the available supply."

"And sell it to the highest bidder or country," Philip chimes in.

"Exactly," I say. "And while the humans won't find Stavros, Calix, and Aglaia, the message to the Dark Coven will be loud and clear. The world is turning against them. We are also going to start a smear campaign against DTPA12. I want people at the FDA and the general public to believe it's unsafe. Whether it is or it isn't, it doesn't matter. If we take away the demand, the supply they are coveting will be rendered useless." While I avoid using mind control on humans at all costs—an example I expect my men to follow—desperate times call for desperate measures.

"But Maximos, what about the why behind DTPA12? Let's address the elephant in the room that implies the Dark Coven is going to be launching some type of radiological attack that involves nuclear weapons or dirty bombs," says Estaban. He is right, but there is nothing else to do.

"I understand your point, Estaban, but we can't address it if we don't know where they are or how to get to the Dark Coven. Right now these are your orders. And let's pray we find something on those hard drives." At that moment, Ryan enters the conference area and strides to my side. His jaw is clenched.

"Arianna isn't here, Maximos," he says.

"What do you mean she isn't here? This is an island. There is nowhere for her to go."

"I searched everywhere while you were in the infirmary. I found your phone opened up to this e-mail." Ryan then tosses me the phone, and I see the message that makes my stomach drop.

"She could only go if she could shift . . . and she doesn't know how to do that. It takes years to develop that skill," I say.

"Maybe she figured it out. Unless she decided to jump in the ocean, she is not in the house or on the island . . ." replies Ryan.

I drag my fingers through my hair. Holy shit. Arianna is walking or has already walked right into Stavros' hands. The address in the e-mail is likely a false one. They'll lure her there and soon move her.

Fortunately, we have one advantage—the necklace. It is now our only hope.

CHAPTER 23: DELIVERANCE

The terminal clock reads 2:00 p.m. in New York. As expected, no one gave me a second glance when I shifted into Grand Central's cavernous concourse under the astronomical turquoise ceiling. Raad had once explained to me that the sky is actually painted backwards, hypothesized to be based off of an old medieval manuscript. Some say it was an intentional decision and reflected "God's view." While the constellations may be backwards, I find they've taken on a new meaning for me, as I briefly glance up at their beauty in my rush to the taxi line. The stars are linked to Tentyrian history—hence they are linked to me. The Leo constellation is up there somewhere. And that gives me comfort to know some indirect part of Maximos is looking down on me.

There is a pit of worry in my stomach as I direct the taxi driver to 840 Twelfth Avenue. The zodiac necklace is nestled safely under my dress. I still can't believe that with its help I was able to shift across continents and oceans. I wonder if the necklace itself has magical properties or if it only served as an instrument to channel my power?

I concentrate on my game plan and avoid thinking, or rather fantasizing, about how delicious the cab driver's blood would taste. He isn't particularly clean or attractive. But the sound of his pulse, in such close proximity, is making my mouth water. I am disgusted at my reaction and instead I remind myself of what's at stake. The reminder serves to dampen the fire in my throat temporarily. I tip the cabbie $20 extra in an attempt to assuage my guilt.

Stepping onto the sidewalk, I feel exposed in the too-bright sun. I should have thought to bring a disguise. But the reality is, if the Dark Coven is as powerful as I suspect it is, a disguise is going to do very little. Number 840 is a tall brick building, with remnants of vintage advertising for auto parts painted on its side.

I carefully do a lap around it, scoping the surrounding area while trying to look natural and human. If that's even possible. It looks like an abandoned warehouse, with no indication that anyone is inside. Panes of glass are missing in several places, and in many instances thin pieces of plywood board up the empty windows. There are no cars parked nearby, and there certainly are no passersby, except for me. It doesn't feel like I'm in New York City anymore. It's more like I'm at a stretch of defunct warehouses in Detroit.

My heart is beating furiously. This is it. Carefully smoothing the tendrils of hair that have escaped my hair tie, I give a knock on the metal front door edged in rivulets, the numbers "840" weathered and rusty. There is no answer. I try again and impatiently wait as the minutes tick by. I glance to my left and my right. There is no one. Finally, I decide to push on the handle, and to my surprise, the door opens slowly. I step inside.

The air is cool and the room is dark. It smells like mold and filth. Moving out of the summer light, my eyes take a moment to adjust. But with my night vision, I can soon easily see the details of the room. Graffiti is everywhere. The concrete floor is littered with garbage, likely left over from vagrants looking for shelter. Rusted auto equipment is piled in a corner of the vast room, and the mold smell is coming from a stagnant puddle of water taking up another corner. But this place is otherwise empty. Did they give up and think I wouldn't come?

"Hello?" I call out. My voice bounces off the walls eerily, and it sounds like I'm inside a tin can. I walk forward, the clicks of my heels reverberating throughout the room. The hairs on my neck prickle. I feel a cool breeze behind me. As I turn to address it, there is a sharp jab in my left arm. I whirl behind me to see the man in the picture Ryan showed me. Not Stavros, but Calix. And he is holding an empty syringe.

"We were wondering when you were going to show up. Bravo, Ms. Parker." His voice is filled with mocking and contempt.

"What did you just inject in me?" I demand, panicked.

"A special serum that will prevent you from shifting. You arrived in a cab, so I can't be sure you have the ability yet. But better to be safe than sorry."

"Shifting? What are you talking about?" I rub my arm in the painful spot where the needle jabbed. I turn my facial expression into one of utter confusion and panic. The panic isn't difficult to fake, as it is very much real. "I have no idea who you are or why you have my friends, but I took your threat seriously. I came alone," I say desperately.

"Interesting, she feigns no knowledge . . ." he says aloud to himself placidly.

"Are they alive? Laura and Raad?" I ask.

"You'll have to see for yourself."

"I'm not going anywhere until you explain why you have kidnapped my friends."

"Right, like you have no idea."

"Listen, asshole, I don't!" I scream at him. "I came back from a jog to find my friend gone and his house ransacked. I immediately went to the police, and they have been actively investigating his disappearance. Now, as I just get back from a business trip, I learn that Laura has been taken too."

"There is no need to use derogatory language. My name is Calix, as I suspect you already know. And you say you have been on a business trip?" he asks condescendingly.

"Yes," I say defensively.

"I'm surprised the police let you travel and that you yourself aren't a suspect."

"I'm not a suspect! And the police know how to reach me. Just ask Officer Lefkowitz of the New Canaan Police Department. Phone number 203-922-4689. Please, do us the favor of contacting him," I taunt him.

"Excellent memory by the way. Photographic? Funny, no one in your office knows where you have been. They certainly weren't aware of any business trip. And no one in your apartment building has seen you in days. Seems like you just disappeared, Ms. Parker . . ."

"I disappeared for good reason. I've been interviewing at competitors on the West Coast. I've been using my sick days."

"Would one of those competitors be Leo Capital?"

"It was one I was considering. However, the interview process didn't work out. They told me I wasn't what they were looking for." Calix looks at my skeptically.

"Say what you want. I only said I'd deliver you to Stavros. You can tell him all about it . . ."

Calix then grabs my hand and clutches me to him in what I suspect is a vain attempt at a tease. I could have easily pulled out of his reach, but to do so would reveal my equal speed and strength. And right now, I'm playing at being human.

The next thing I know, I'm surrounded by the cool wind of his energy. Within seconds, we're standing in a library. It's the same one from my dream, with the blood-red carpet. I must have Hathor's gift . . . . Fortunately, the carpet appears dry.

Once the dizziness in my head recedes, I remember the cards I need to play. I only hope my mediocre acting is somewhat believable.

"How did you just do that?" I exclaim, feebly pushing myself away from Calix to hide my strength. I appear distraught. And I am, because I have no idea what my next move is.

"Alright, princess, stay here," he says. He leaves and slams the door behind him. The sound of a click follows, indicating the heavy wooden door is locked. I run over to the desk and open all the drawers, looking for any valuable information. They are empty. In fact, there isn't a piece of paper or a pen in sight. I pick up the phone on the desk—no dial tone. Perfect. There is nothing for me to do but stress and wait.

I seat myself in one of the plush, forest-green visitor chairs overlooking Central Park and try not to hyperventilate. I attempt to shift myself across the room with no luck. Whether it's the serum or my own lack of ability preventing me from shifting, I don't know. But I do know that the power I was relying on, to protect myself and get Laura and Raad out of here, is gone. All I have left is my Swiss Army knife tucked into my bra. I refrain from taking it out; I'm not completely desperate . . . yet.

I strain my ears to listen to any sound or conversation happening beyond the office. There is nothing but silence. I begin to nibble on my fingernails, a habit I haven't indulged in since childhood. Mother dearest forbade it. My cuticles are certainly in shabby condition and they are now raw and bleeding. Which reminds me, I'm incredibly thirsty . . . Trying to distract myself, I think of the last time I got a manicure with Laura. It was over a week ago. Poor Laura, she must be so confused . . . Staring blankly ahead, contemplating my inevitable failure and how I'll never see Maximos again, I notice the air in front of me wavering ever so slightly like the air above a hot road or sidewalk. The next thing I know, Stavros and Laura are standing in front of me hand in hand.

"Laur! Thank God you are all right!" I impulsively stand up to embrace her. Her free hand loosely hugs me in somewhat of an awkward gesture. Not what I expected. Has Stavros done something to her? I step back and pull her toward me, breaking the connection between their two clasped hands. Her face looks serious but not upset. Stavros merely looks amused. "Who are you and why have you taken my friend?" I snap, trying to keep my voice level.

"Calix said you were claiming you have no idea why you are here. Amusing," he says. If snakes could smile, they'd look like Stavros.

"I don't know what you are talking about. If you want money, I have lots of it. I'll give you what you want as long as you let me and my friend go unharmed. Laur, are you hurt?" I survey her up and down critically, looking for bruises or bite marks. She appears fine, almost expressionless. Something is definitely going on with her. She is also wearing a prim dress she would never be caught dead in . . .

"Laura is quite alright, as you can see. But let's cut to the chase. You are a Luminary." He steps closer to me, and I step back.

"You are insane. I don't know what you are talking about," I counter.

"You think so?" he challenges me. Stavros then lunges for Laura, pulling her back to him like a rag doll. His fangs are now poised over her neck. He is within seconds of killing her, just like in my dream. I react instinctually, and my own fangs come out. The next thing I know, I'm trying to snatch Laura from his arms. But Stavros is too quick, and he shifts out of reach, all the while laughing.

"Excellent. Now we can all be honest," he says, quieting his chuckle. Foolishly, I've betrayed myself with my own power. My card has been trumped. Why didn't I tell Ryan where I was going or at least leave a note? Laura is now by Stavros' side again, looking shaken but surprisingly amenable to her position. Could she have been turned into a Subordinate? Stavros and I keep our fangs out, our bodies both ready to pounce. "Arianna, I know what you are, and I want us to work to-gether—not against each other. We can do great things . . ." he coos in his suave voice.

My pride gets the better of me, and I taunt him. "Save your breath. I will never join you. You murdered your own people and you intend to eliminate humanity. Thanks but no thanks."

"Do you really think you are in a position to refuse me?" he challenges.

"Yes. The Brotherhood is on to you. In fact, they will be here in a matter of minutes."

"You are a terrible liar. I can hear your erratic pulse. And no they won't. First of all, the Brothers would never have let you come here alone. Your very presence indicates they have no clue where you are. And second of all, my plan is so beyond their knowledge base, it's impossible to stop."

He's called my bluff. All I have left is to bargain for Laura and Raad's lives.

"If I join you, would you let Laura and Raad go?"

"Well I hate to tell you . . . actually no, on second thought, I don't mind telling you at all. Raad didn't make it."

"You killed him?" I ask incredulously. He can't be dead.

Stavros' response is to simply raise his eyebrows at me as if to articulate, "What do you think?" I see red. Without hesitation, I go after Stavros. But he places himself out of reach once again. Laura steps aside, closer to the windows, to avoid the battle. However, there is not much of a battle, because Stavros is untouchable. I need to escape with Laura. Now. I grab her and make a move for the door but it's no use—Stavros blocks our exit.

"I can see you need some time, Arianna, to calm yourself and think about the options available to you. I'll have Calix take you to the room we have prepared for you." I can only imagine what type of "room" they have prepared. Stavros moves to take out his phone when Laura places a hand on his arm.

"Stavros, can I speak to Arianna alone for a moment?" she asks. Laura never calls me by full name. It sounds strange hearing it from her mouth. "I think if Arianna understands things from your perspective—and even mine—we could come to an arrangement that benefits us all. She doesn't know you like I do . . ." Laura's voice is pure sweetness, and I can see the adoration already in Stavros' eyes. Good God, she is good. But I know Laura, and I've seen her play this game. She is never one to be heartless or cruel, but she knows how to play a part when she wants. I'm always telling her she should pursue a career in acting. Right now, she deserves an Academy Award.

Stavros looks uncertain. "Haven't I proven my loyalty to you?" Laura asks searchingly. He looks at her thoughtfully and, in a shocking gesture, kisses her forehead endearingly.

"Fine. But there will be guards right outside the door. I'll give you fifteen minutes," says Stavros. As soon as he disappears in his shimmering energy, Laura runs into my arms.

"Laur . . ." I begin to say, but she quickly pulls away and puts her finger to her lips and points to the door.

"Arianna, I don't know what the Brotherhood has told you . . . or that man Maximos," she says loudly, her eyes darting from me to the door. "Stavros is not what they've described to you. He is a visionary of something great, and the world he is planning will be prosperous, simpler, and healthier. We can rule as queens together . . ." As Laura is talking, she reaches under her dress and pulls out a piece of paper that she unfolds quickly to point to a series of addresses. "Stavros is very powerful, Arianna, but he can also be very sweet . . ." Taking her cue, I continue the charade.

"It sounds as if you like him," I say, keeping my voice defensive.

"I do. I can't quite explain it . . . I might even love him." Laura points to the addresses and shrugs her shoulders, indicating she doesn't know what they are. But judging how she refolds the paper and reaches down the front of my dress to stick it in my bra, it's something she wants me to have. She sees the Swiss Army knife and gives me a nod.

"Arianna, we can't fight this. Change is coming, and we can either be a part of it or die." Laura steps back from me and continues, "I know we aren't that great of friends, but take my word for it. We are better off with them then without."

Before I can reply, Stavros appears. But rather than approaching me as I anticipate, he grabs Laura by the neck and shoves her up against a wall with a loud crack as her head connects with the paneled wall.

"You lying bitch. I trust you for a half minute and you betray me. You're just as perfidious as every other woman. Serves me right for having a moment of weakness." His grip on her windpipe is so tight she can only choke out a few gasps for air.

"Let her go!" I scream. "I'll do whatever you want." Stavros pays me no heed.

"You thought you had me fooled with that little game. But I'm not stupid, you little slut. I have video cameras and I saw you give her a piece of paper. You say you love me! What a joke."

I lurch toward Stavros with my superhuman speed, but before I can stop him, he moves out of reach and hurls Laura across the room. Her body flies over the desk, slams into the opposite wall, and crumples into an unconscious heap. Stavros looks over at her with a pitying look and appears momentarily distracted with some nostalgic thought. I only need that one moment. I whip out my pocketknife I've been coveting and sprint full speed at him with the intention to slit his throat. Stavros manages to deflect me by turning just in time. Instead of cutting his throat, I manage to leave a serious gash across his chest. The fine velvet of his jacket splits, and blood shows through the sliced fabric.

"You're a little bitch too. And now you'll die." Stavros shifts behind me and puts me in a chokehold with one arm. Will all my strength, I claw and kick. But his power is unmatched. With his free hand, Stavros fishes out the paper and also finds my necklace. He rips them both out of my dress.

"A familiar relic, I see. No doubt a gift from the Brotherhood. Hathor and her daughters wore these too. But didn't anyone ever tell you? Talismans won't save you from death—as they found out all too well." He throws the necklace and paper in the fireplace and drags me over to a switch on the wall, which he flicks. Between the red dots now clouding my vision from the lack of oxygen, I see the flames ignite. I can feel the heat on my skin as Stavros pulls me closer to the open flame. He is going to burn me alive. Through my hazy vision that is becoming darker by the millisecond, I see a figure out of the corner of my eye.

Shots of a gun fire, and Stavros reacts with a flinch, dropping me. My head connects with the brick hearth of the fireplace. Stars explode in my consciousness, and it feels like my head is a raw egg cracking. I manage to roll over onto my back, away from the blazing fire, as I hear what sounds like a series of military commands from men who have swarmed the room. Please be the Brotherhood. I open my eyes, expecting to see Stavros standing over me, but he is gone. As I begin to blink and let the chaos come into focus, I hear Maximos' voice calling my name.

"Ari, Ari, are you all right!" Maximos rushes over to me and scoops me into his arms as he kneels on the floor. Despite the abominable pain in my temples, my heart is soaring. Maximos is alive. "You scared me to death!" he says. "Praise Hathor you are alive! Tell me, are you hurt?" His beautiful blue eyes are scanning my body, looking for any sign of hurt. His face is etched with concern.

"My head aches a little," I manage to croak out. So much emotion is welling up inside of me, it makes it difficult to speak. "I thought you were dead," I say. "I saw a vision of you dead . . . on a floor. I wanted to go to you, but I didn't know where. How did you find me?" My voice is choked, and I feel hot tears begin to slide down my cheeks.

"Shh, matia mou, don't cry. I'm perfectly fine. But you will be the death of me if you do something like that again. Fortunately, I put a tracking device in that necklace of yours."

"I'm sorry, Maximos, but I had no choice—I had to try and save Laura and Raad. But they are both dead . . . Stavros said he killed Raad, and I watched him kill Laura." I am now sobbing, and Maximos is rocking me gently as he holds me close. We probably are a strange sight to the Brothers in the room, who I'm only vaguely aware of. Based on the activity around us, it sounds like they are ripping the room apart.

"Max, I can save the woman," I hear someone say. A hand reaches for Maximos' shoulder. It's Aristos. Maximos turns with me in his arms and stands to face him.

"You can save Laura?" I interrupt before Maximos can react. "Maximos, put me down. I can stand," I say as my tears are temporarily forgotten. Maximos lets me down slowly but keeps his hand on my arm to steady me.

"We only turn those who become Brothers," Maximos says quickly. He gives a look of disapproval to Aristos. "Laura is an unfortunate casualty. But we cannot turn every human who gets in the Dark Coven's way. Ari, would you wish this life on your friend?" Maximos asks me.

I'm torn with indecision. "She risked her life for me and for the Brotherhood. She was killed because she tried to give me information!" I say passionately, running a hand over my tear-stained cheeks in an attempt to wipe away the embarrassing moisture. I point to the fireplace. "She found a list of addresses that she tried to give me. Stavros burned the paper." I pull myself from Maximos' sure hold and flick off the switch to the fireplace. I try to see if even a bit of the paper survived, but it's long gone. I manage to fish out my necklace that is now blackened with soot.

The zodiac pendant is hot in my palm, and my skin puckers and bubbles in response. But within seconds, I can already feel my skin begin to heal. "Please, Maximos, we need to save her," I urge. "She is too young to die."

Maximos looks conflicted. "Aristos, are you offering to take responsibility for her?" he asks gruffly.

"Yes, I will," Aristos promises.

"Then it is done," Maximos pronounces.

"We don't have time to take her back to Ambrosine," Aristos says as he lays Laura's body on the center of the carpet. I don't see Laura's chest rising and falling, but I can hear a few sluggish beats of her heart. Cradling her body, Aristos unleashes his fangs and sinks them into her neck, which I suspect is already broken.

Several minutes go by as we stand and watch him drain her. Laura's pallor is as white as a sheet, and the sluggish heartbeats are no more. I want to cry out and tell him to stop, but surely he must know what he's doing? After all, he helped create the Brothers. That's when Maximos commands something in Greek. Aristos lifts his head and pauses in response. He looks slightly disoriented as he wipes his bloodied mouth on his sleeve. He then bites his wrist and pulls open Laura's mouth, placing his open wound above it.

At first, only a small amount of blood drips into her mouth as he gently massages the column of her throat. He then bunches his hand into a fist, increasing the blood flow. The room is silent as we stand by, watching in anticipation. Then I see the muscle of her throat swallow for the first time. Her mouth weakly purses to the punctures in his wrist, and she begins to suck. The whiteness of her skin begins to color. I breathe a sigh of relief.

"Take her to the island," Maximos commands, still shaking his head in disapproval. Aristos nods, and within seconds, they disappear into thin air.

"Thank you," I whisper to Maximos.

"Don't thank me yet. I hope your judgment was sound, Ari," he warns. "Laura will not be herself for quite some time. She won't be gifted with the control you have . . . She is not Tentyrian. She has a difficult road ahead of her."

"Then I'll help her," I promise.

"We'll see. She is in good hands for now. However, I need you to try to remember what was on that piece of paper. As you can probably see, the Dark Coven got away."

"But not before we pumped Stavros full of cyanide bullets," interrupts Ryan. "He's going to be hurting for a while."

"He really is a monster. Do you have something for me to write on?" I ask. Ryan reaches into a pocket of his black cargo pants and pulls out an iPhone.

"Can you type it?" Ryan asks. "That way we can relay it to the Control Room immediately."

"I'll try," I say as I try to conjure up the text I saw. I've always had a photographic memory, but I saw the paper only for mere seconds. Maximos questions if Laura indicated what the addresses were. I respond absently that she didn't as I begin to press the keypad to type in the words and numbers I pray are accurate.

"What if they are the locations of where the weapons will be unleashed?" suggests Ryan.

"I am hoping the same. But it will be a miracle if they are," Maximos says solemnly.

Meanwhile, I can feel his, Ryan's, and the other Brothers' eyes trained on me, patiently waiting for deliverance.

CHAPTER 24:
A FRIENDLY
GAME

2010 AD, SEPTEMBER
AMBROSINE ISLAND, IONIAN SEA

The tracking device I had Aristos embed in the zodiac pendant showed that Ari was in New York. I'm still amazed she was able to shift—it wasn't a skill I expected her to develop for years to come. However, as I suspected, she had been moved to another location. After intense deliberation with Evander and Aristos, we determined that Evander would lead the public smear campaign against the Dark Coven while Aristos and I went after Ari with the appropriate backup. It was a gamble. The Dark Coven surely knew that all the facilities hadn't detonated as planned. We were coming after them. But they had no way of knowing we knew where Ari really was...

When we arrived at the Dark Coven's penthouse office, we were prepared for an all-out battle. But Stavros shifted away like the coward he is. The Brothers found a handful of Subordinates on the premises, but Calix and Aglaia were nowhere to be found. When I pulled the trigger on my gun, I could have unleashed the entire magazine into Stavros as I saw him holding Ari's face to the fire. My rage burned just like the flames in the hearth. But Stavros' presence was short-lived. Miraculously, Ari was all right. As I held her in my arms, it was a moment that seemed to unfold in slow motion. The mayhem behind us fell away, and for a few seconds it was just the two of us. I never wanted to let her go. But unfortunately I had to—we needed to face the reality around us.

I had serious qualms about turning Laura. We've never turned a woman before. But Ari was right, Laura died trying to help us. And it wasn't that long ago I offered immortality to Raad. However, I was shocked when Aristos almost drained her completely. I've never seen him lose control like that. I had to command him to stop, before it was too late. Fortunately, the turning process was initiated successfully, and Aristos took Laura back to Ambrosine to recover.

The Dark Coven was gone, and there wasn't any documentation or computers kept at their office. Our last hope was in the address list. And Ari delivered it to us successfully. Her photographic memory captured the ten locations perfectly. We then deployed the Brothers to raid them, and within three hours they found and disarmed every single dirty bomb, all of which were rigged to detonate. We prevented disaster—barely. It was a close call.

It's been two months since we foiled the Dark Coven's attack. Our public campaign against them has been successful. DTPA12 never reached the market, and Stavros, Calix, and Aglaia are being hunted by the FBI and Interpol. We haven't yet been able to crack the hard drives that were retrieved from the facilities. It is something that Aristos has been working on diligently—when he is not taking care of Laura. As long as the Dark Coven is still out there, the nightmare Hathor predicted is still possible. Our efforts to subvert them and find the other Luminaries will never stop.

When we returned to Ambrosine, we burned our dead, and Ari had the chance to say good-bye to Raad. During the funeral pyre cere-mony, she watched stoically. I was surprised she didn't cry, and when I asked her why, she said that Raad wouldn't want her to mourn. He would want her celebrate—he had moved on to another life, and Ari was moving forward with hers.

The weeks that followed were quiet compared to what transpired when Ari first entered the picture. We spent afternoons walking on the beach, meditating, and practicing with her powers. Now Ari no longer needs the necklace, which I replaced for her, to help channel her energy to shift. She can also read minds now without physical contact. One thing she hasn't yet managed to control is her premonitions. Since the ones she experienced of Laura's death and of me dead, she has been unable to tap into that energy again. I keep telling her to give it time, but she is so eager to learn and be a perfectionist, she has little patience.

When I took her on her first hunt in Athens—which she handled flawlessly, as her prey survived the encounter without incident and memory—she was despondent with her performance. And when Ryan took her to the shooting range, she refused to leave until she shot an entire group into the red bull's-eye. She is constantly pushing herself, saying that she needs to be better and stronger for the Brotherhood. She insists on attending every meeting and training just as hard as the rest of us. It's amazing, considering it wasn't long ago when Ari was doing everything in her power to get away from us. Now she has embraced the Brotherhood and her role as one of our leaders. And every single Brother adores her, especially Ryan and Aristos. I'm certainly no exception.

Laura isn't yet ready for visitors, but we're hopeful she will come through this difficult period soon . . . once her thirst is under control. But Laura is safe with Aristos, who as her maker is able to help manage her mood swings and violent behavior. Fortunately, Laura was able to tell Aristos about Stavros' connection to Senator Cromwell, which we are currently handling. She also told Aristos to retrieve Ari's birthday present from her apartment. She insisted it must be given to Ari since Laura couldn't celebrate with her.

It was during a birthday celebration we threw for her on the island, as she was sifting through the tissue paper to reveal a pair of pink heels, that Ari confessed she knew already what was in the box. She then detailed her visions and explained that she suspected she was like Hathor. We were thrilled; however, she's been uneasy ever since, as it is a power she has yet to harness. The good news is that we have time. And that time has been a precious gift.

These past couple months have been wonderful—and that's not a word I toss around lightly. I now know Ari as a person, from her competitive spirit to her underlying sensitivity to those around her. In turn, my own controlling attitude has been softened. I no longer feel the urge to manage her. Instead, I just want to be with her . . . and as more than just friends. While we've eased into a genuine friendship, the sexual chemistry is still there. In fact, it only becomes exacerbated with every passing day. A brush of a hand here, a lingering gaze there. But I've tried my hardest to prevent it by treating her just as a friend. The words may be unspoken, but I still want her. And that is the crux of the problem.

Duty is our obligation now. I had told Ari that what we did on that magical night was a mistake. Surely she understands now what I meant by that? But I don't have the heart to bring it up and rehash what's likely to get us nowhere. What would I say? What would I do? So my answer is: nothing. I want to ask Aristos and Evander for advice, but how can I explain to them that I'm willing to put love and a woman before our duty? Not to mention Aristos is her grandfather a hundred times removed.

But the temptation is torturous. Just last night while we were playing backgammon and enjoying a crisp pinot grigio that tasted faintly of peaches, she won every single game in a row. In short, she smoked me between jokes and a pleasant banter laced with wit. I almost threw the game to the floor and pulled her to me in a passionate embrace, I was so turned on. The fantasy I envisioned of her lips and body against me while the game pieces fell to the floor—all because she dominated me with a board game—was too much. I excused myself and went to bed early, where I tossed and turned all night.

Fortunately, today is a new day—although it's unlikely I'll get any closer to coming to terms with my feelings for her. We'll be spending the entire day together, and when we're together, my ability to articulate a rational thought about my feelings seems to disappear. I promised Ari that I'd take her to visit a friend of Raad's who is currently in possession of an old book of his.

Since everything happened, Ari has agreed to put her apartment on the market as well as Raad's house, which he left to her with all of his assets. The police found some of his bloodstained clothes at the New Jersey lab facility, and Raad was declared dead. Picking up the book is one of those final loose ends that Ari wants to tie up. I don't blame her. Since we'll be in the area, we are also going to attend the award dinner for the American Dream Realized housing project tonight at the St. Regis in New York City.

At first, I automatically told Robert, Satish, and Samson to attend in my stead as the managing partners of Leo. But after Ari started to drop hints about getting off the island for a breath of fresh air and a break from the endless strategy sessions and training, I realized she was right. We need a break. It would be a good change of pace and would also generate some positive PR for the firm. Tonight, I plan to introduce Ari to the prominent donors and, most importantly, the new families receiving the homes that were just completed over the summer. If there is anyone I want to share this night with, it's her.

CHAPTER 25: AMMON'S JOURNAL

2010 AD, SEPTEMBER
NEW YORK CITY, NEW YORK / NEW HAVEN, CONNECTICUT

When we were checking into the hotel, I was practically holding my breath, waiting to see if Maximos had booked us one room or two. I knew deep down it would be two of course, but some part of me hoped it wasn't. The past couple of months have gone by in a whirlwind since the drama with the Dark Coven subsided. And while I've been focused on my new role and duties with so much to learn—Maximos is always on my mind. He's on my mind when we run together in the mornings, when we hunt, and even when I'm by myself sleepless in bed. Nights are the worst.

I've been waiting for him to say something—to tell me how he feels. Instead, he says nothing while we continue to be caught in an awkward limbo of sexual tension. The next logical conclusion would be for me to tell him how I feel . . . but how can I? Last time I was ready to give myself to him and throw caution to the wind, he said he regretted what had occurred between us. I have no desire to go through that again. And if he wanted to be with me, he would say something, right? Maybe he just wants to be friends? I wish Laura was well enough for me to talk to her. I really need some advice.

If Maximos has been anything, it's kind and patient. He's helped me work on my powers and is constantly ensuring I have everything I could ever want. He even offered to build me a separate wing at the villa, which of course I declined. For now, I'm comfortable staying in my guest room. What was truly special, though, was when he threw me a birthday party on Ambrosine with all of the Brothers attending. It was a beautiful night; we ate roasted pig and drank red wine under the stars. The Brothers sang "Happy Birthday" to me in Greek, and Maximos gave me a new zodiac necklace. For once, it felt like I had a family beyond Raad and Laura. Maximos is so thoughtful . . . I can't believe I used to think he was arrogant. Unfortunately, his thoughtfulness never translates into anything more.

But I could swear last night, while we were playing backgammon, he wanted to kiss me. The air was practically crackling with our energy. Then he abruptly got up and left. We had an amazing time and rather than growing angry at losing like Charles used to, he seemed genuinely entertained. That's why I was so surprised when he practically ran away.

We make a great pair, constantly challenging and supporting each other, and I don't think the Brothers would resent our relationship . . . if we had one. As I've gotten to know the Brotherhood, they are all great guys. And they have the utmost respect for Maximos and even me. I can only conclude that right now, it's Maximos who doesn't want to be with me.

There is a knock on the door of my hotel room. It's him. I can smell the minty scent that is distinctly him through the walls separating us. I give myself a quick glance in the mirror to make sure I'm not a mess. I apply another coat of lip gloss and smooth my hair behind my ears. It's now fall in the City, my favorite season. I'm wearing skinny jeans, brown leather riding boots, and a cranberry-colored velvet blazer over a simple white V-neck shirt. My hair is down and free. After a hunt once, Maximos remarked how pretty it was when I wore it down. I had been complaining how it was getting in my way. Ever since, I've worn it loose as much as possible. If only he would run his hands through it and tell me that he wants me.

I suggested we get off the island for a bit—for that reason. Maybe without the pressures of the Brotherhood around us he would feel . . . less bound to duty? And if there is any chance he wants to be with me he might say it? Ugh—I sound pathetic, and I hate that. I don't know what I hope to accomplish today; but since I need to pick up Raad's book, I figured I might as well ask Maximos to join me. When he suggested we attend the ADR benefit, I jumped at the opportunity. For the event, I even made a quick stop at the Carolina Herrera boutique, made all that much easier with my shifting ability.

I open the door, and there he is. I still haven't gotten used to the sight of him. Every time is like the first, and my stomach does a little flip. Today he is wearing jeans, brown leather driving shoes, and a camel-colored cashmere sweater. His jaw is clean shaven, and his black hair is slightly tousled. Now that we've spent more time together out amongst the human population, it's been impossible to miss the women who practically swoon at his feet. Granted he isn't wearing a ring, but when I'm with him you'd think most women might assume I was his girlfriend and keep their flirtation in check. Not at all. My presence does little to stop their all-too-friendly hands and cloying attention. If I didn't respect the Code and human life as much as I do, I'd rip their throats out.

"Are you ready, Ari?" he asks. I've noticed that since he rescued me from the Dark Coven, he's dropped the Greek endearments. Instead he only calls me by my name.

"Yep. Since I know exactly where to go, I'll shift us there," I say with a smile.

"As you command. Ready when you are," he responds with his hands outstretched.

I clasp his hands in mine, and I can feel my blood pump harder in response. Our chemistry is undeniable. I close my eyes and focus my energy on picturing the Beinecke Rare Book and Manuscript Library at Yale University. Within minutes of the cool air prickling over our skin, I shift us into the stacks where I spent much of my time as an undergrad. It's a great location—notorious for being deserted, and it's near Professor Sorrell's office.

As we walk down the library corridor, Maximos asks me what I expect to find in the book. I'm not exactly sure, but when I remembered it a few days earlier I couldn't believe I had forgotten about it. Ever since, I've felt the need to retrieve it. Maybe it's because I don't like the idea of having an heirloom of Raad's floating out in the universe, God rest his soul. It just feels wrong. Or maybe it's something more? When I called Professor Sorrell to tell him about Raad's death, he said that he'd seen it on the news. After sharing his condolences, he confirmed he still had the book, which he told me was more like a journal. I eagerly asked him to elaborate on the phone, but he had another meeting to get to. We agreed that when I came in person he'd tell me more. The anticipation has been nagging at me since.

When we reach Sorrell's door, I give it a light knock and hear a raspy "come in" in response. When I open it, I'm immediately struck by how much older Sorrell looks than when I last saw him. His beard is now completely snow white, and he is more hunched over than ever. The decades he's spent reading have taken their toll. I still don't think I've come to terms with the fact that I won't ever look a day older than twenty-five. Spending time with beautiful men who all appear to be in their mid-twenties is somewhat of a surreal experience, which is only highlighted when seeing someone like the professor who is in his seventies.

"Arianna, so good to see you," he says as he stands up from the desk and nimbly makes his way through the stacks of books that are clustered in various groupings on the floor. Undoubtedly they are organized in a system that makes sense to Sorrell. To everyone else, it looks like he is a disorganized hoarder of books. Sorrell gives me a hug and kiss on the cheek. His woolen gray cardigan smells faintly of mothballs.

"I'm so sorry about Raad; he was a good man. I would have come to the funeral, but I know you said he specifically requested not to have one," Sorrell says warmly.

"Yes, he was the best of men. But you know Raad. He thought funerals were too depressing," I reply.

"Well I can't say I disagree. And who is this gentlemen you've brought?" asks the professor as he pushes his thick horn-rimmed glasses further up the bridge of his nose and gives Maximos an assessing stare.

"This is my friend Maximos." Maximos extends a friendly hand to the professor, whom he practically dwarfs in size.

"You're a big fella, aren't you?" the old man remarks. "Please, both of you take a seat while I retrieve that book of yours."

The professor walks over to a stack of books and gently pulls one out as we make ourselves comfortable in two leather club chairs. Its bindings are in leather, and it's closed with a leather strap. The professor then takes a seat back at the desk, facing Maximos and me.

"Now, I mentioned to you on the phone, Arianna, that this book was more of a journal. It appears to have been written by Raad's ancestor in 1822—I assume his great, great, great grandfather. Unfortunately, we don't have Raad or his family tree to confirm."

"What language is it written in?" I ask.

"Greek—ancient Greek, in fact." Goosebumps start to rise on my skin.

"Raad is from Iran, so why Greek?" The tension in my stomach is becoming stronger.

"I'm not exactly sure. But the contents are certainly remarkable," says Sorrell.

"What does it say?" I ask eagerly. I can barely contain myself.

"May I?" interrupts Maximos, who reaches for the book quickly. The professor hands it over and begins to explain.

"The majority of the book has typical journal entries of everyday life. But it's when you get toward the end where it starts to get interesting. It's the last entry of the book, where the author named Ammon recounts his lineage. He indicates he is part of a line of people called 'Guardians' sworn to protect a people called 'Tentyrians' . . ." Maximos and I look at each other in shock. "It was the author's father who insisted he learn Greek," continues the professor, "as it was the original language of their people. The entry indicates that in fact Raad's lineage can draw its roots to Egypt! Now where it starts to get strange . . ."

But before the professor can finish, Maximos stands up and hands the book to me.

"Where are you going?" asks Sorrell, confused at the interruption.

"Nowhere," replies Maximos calmly as he walks closer to Sorrell.

"Ari, you know what I have to do," Maximos says to me while not taking his eyes off the professor. I can see the old man's eyes dilate in response.

"What do you have to do?" asks the professor, confused. Then with a blur of motion, Maximos bites into his neck, and the professor lets out a gasp. The venom that is released will now make Sorrell susceptible to a very strong mind wipe. The professor has gone quiet, and he is staring blankly ahead, waiting for Maximos to make the next move.

"Before you say anything, Ari, I had to do it. This is to protect him. If the Dark Coven knows he has this journal, who knows what they'll do to him."

"I know," I say softly. "I just didn't expect it."

"He won't remember a thing. Just put that book in your purse before I release him."

I put the journal in my Birkin while Maximos wipes his memory of ever receiving it. Maximos then nicks his own palm with his fang in order to draw blood. With his fingertip, he rubs a dab of his blood on the puncture wounds of the professor's neck, which promptly heal. Maximos then releases Sorrell from the trance.

"Now where was I?" asks the professor.

"We were talking about how Raad hated funerals," I remind him.

"Ah yes. Can't say I blame him," the professor agrees absently. But he still looks confused, as if he's trying to piece something together.

"Well we must be on our way, Professor Sorrell. I'm so glad we could stop by while we were in town. It was a pleasure seeing you," I say.

We stand up to say good-bye to the professor and quickly make our exit. The professor bids us a bewildered farewell. Rather than shifting back to the hotel, Maximos and I decide to sit outside on the central quadrangle of the campus. There, undergrads are playing Ultimate Frisbee and enjoying the innocent days of college life. It's amazing they have no idea they almost died two months ago. We find a bench under a beautiful oak tree now embracing its shades of burnt oranges and yellows.

"Something tells me you'll have no problem reading this," I say as I pull out the journal from my purse and hand it to Maximos. Maximos flips to the last few pages and pauses for several minutes while he absorbs the words. I try reading over his massive shoulder, but the words just look like meaningless symbols to me.

"Praise Hathor, this is amazing," he says.

"What! What is amazing?" I plead for him to tell me.

"This tells the story of how the Luminary children escaped. They made it through the escape tunnel and to the awaiting boats after all. This author indicates that the story was passed down to him by word of mouth through the men in his family. One of his ancestors before him was the Ammon who was the Guardian to Darrius—Daria's and Aristos' son. I actually knew the first Ammon!"

"Raad's first name is said the exact same way. I guess over time the spellings just changed from Ammon to Aman," I point out.

"I don't know why the pieces didn't click before, but it all makes sense now. Ari, Aman Raad was your real Guardian. Even though neither of you knew it."

"Coincidence or fate?" I ask.

"Fate, surely," Maximos says reverently.

"Look here at this passage," Maximos points. "It says that Ammon and Darrius managed to escape to Britannia. There, Ammon raised Darrius and they kept his Tentyrian nature a secret, afraid they would be targeted by those seeking to destroy what Darrius was. Darrius ultimately became a great warrior fighting the Romans. However, he was later beheaded in his sleep by an unknown assailant. Before he died, Darrius turned a Catuvellauni woman, who later became pregnant with his child. It looks like Ammon took care of her and the daughter she had. Many generations later, Darrius' line and Ammon's line separated from each other. It is unknown what happened to Darrius' ancestors of the Tentyrian 'blood drinkers,' as the author calls us . . ."

"I can't believe we've found this book!" I remark in awe. "Does it say anything about what happened to the other Luminary children?"

"Unfortunately, no. The three boats went off in different directions," says Maximos.

"Three boats? But I thought there would be four? There are supposed to be four Luminaries, right?"

"Yes, but Narcissa never had a child. Phoebe had two children, though, who were twins. They were newborn at the time, and they both should have escaped together with their Guardian, Tale, in one boat."

"What were the twins' names?"

"They didn't have any. Tentyrians don't name their children until around age two, when their personalities start to show. For example, all of the Luminary names—Daria, Phoebe, Calypso, and Narcissa—coincided with their powers or personalities. Daria means "upholder of the good," Phoebe means "bright," Calypso means "hidden," and Narcissa was named after the narcissus plant known for its healing sedative. Can you see how those names connect to how I've described the Luminaries and their abilities?"

"Yes . . . so what does Maximos mean?"

"Greatest."

"Fitting," I say honestly.

"Do you know what your name means?" he asks, clearly trying to change the subject.

"It's Italian for 'very holy.' My mother said that when I was born I looked like an angel. Imagine her dismay when I got older."

"I think you are an angel—most of the time," Maximos says with a smile but then finishes quickly by saying we should head back and dress for dinner. This time he shifts us back, leaving me to reflect on another missed opportunity for us to tell each other how we feel.

CHAPTER 26: EMBRACING DESTINY

2010 AD, SEPTEMBER
NEW YORK CITY, NEW YORK
ST. REGIS HOTEL

Tonight I want to wear something special. Not only to look beautiful for Maximos but also for myself. These days I feel like all I've been wearing are spandex and sneakers—items Shashandra took the liberty of stocking in my closet, contrary to my protests. At least I finally have some practical shoes. The Brothers could care less if I was wearing yoga pants or Dior. But tonight I care. So when I saw the rose-colored silk tulle ball gown with the sweetheart neckline and ribbon detail that tied around the waist, I couldn't resist. I also couldn't resist the matching heels. The price tags were outrageous, but then so was having to save the world. I'm allowed to indulge.

I decide to wear my hair back in a low knot with hair wrapped around at its base. It's simple, but tonight it's all about the dress . . . and Maximos. I'm so excited to show him; I realize it's now my first instinct to share everything with him. I've never really cared about anyone else's opinion, except for Raad's and Laura's. And in their absence, Maximos has become my sounding board. Speaking of which, I can hear Maximos on the other side of his door as I walk down the hall toward it. It sounds like he is pacing. But before I can knock, the door swings open.

"You're here," he says, surprised. "I was going to come get you." I swallow instinctively. Maximos is wearing a black tux that makes the ebony of his hair look even richer and brings a Great Gatsby elegance to his warrior's frame. Looking at him now, you'd never suspect he was more comfortable in his soldier's fatigues. He is stunning, and the way his brilliant blue eyes are looking at me, I find I'm having a difficult time forming a coherent thought, much less a sentence.

"I hope that's okay. I figured you'd be ready, and since I was ready, I thought I'd come get you. Maybe we can go get a drink?" I say awkwardly.

"Excellent idea. We should be relaxing, right? I almost feel like we've left the kids at home," Maximos replies.

"It does feel that way, doesn't it?" I agree. I come into the room, and there is a pause as I see Maximos studying me.

"Before we go downstairs, I have to tell you—you look beautiful. I think 'ethereal' is the right word." I can feel my blush creeping up my exposed neck.

"Well you clean up quite well yourself. No doubt I'm going to have to fend off the women more than usual tonight."

"Trust me, no one is going to be looking at me," he says. Maximos then clears his throat. "I know you told me not to give you gifts, except for birthdays and Christmas, and that you prefer to buy things yourself—as evidenced by the fact you cut up the credit card I gave you. But I wanted tonight to be special. So I got you something. If you don't like it, I can take them back . . ." He reaches into his travel suitcase and pulls out a blue velvet box, which he then hands to me. I'm not sure what to say, so instead I just open it. There are pearl drop earrings inside that dangle from what must be six carats of diamonds. The creamy color of the pearl is breathtaking, and the diamonds are flawless, literally.

"Oh my," I say breathlessly.

"Do you like them?" he asks nervously.

"Maximos, how could I not? They are amazing . . . You really shouldn't have."

"Think of it as a welcome gift to the Brotherhood."

"I love them. Thank you!" I say as I put them in my ears and give him a spin to give the full effect. Normally, I would never accept something like this. But it was given with such good will—how could I not? Not to mention they are absolutely gorgeous.

Maximos holds out his arm for me to take. "Shall we?"

"Yes."

In the elevators, I give him a kiss on the cheek. My lips remain longer than they should—savoring the heat of his skin. The doors open, and we make our way to the ballroom. As we head inside the room that looks like something out of Versailles, awash in a pink glow from the uplighting, my heart practically stops.

"Maximos, I've been here before," I say as I halt our procession to the head table. This is a piece of the puzzle that's made me anxious for weeks. I told the Brothers about my premonitions, but we, or at least they, assumed they were fulfilled. Maximos survived the explosion, and we were able to save Laura. But if I'm at the same party that was in my dream—then Stavros and the Dark Coven could be here.

"I dreamed this, Maximos. I think the Dark Coven is here." He places a reassuring hand on my waist.

"The Brotherhood is watching. We'll be ready. But I want you to stay close to me in case we need to shift out," says Maximos.

"I will," I agree as I eye some of the Brothers who have blended into the crowd in their formalwear. To the undiscerning, they look like guests, but I could point them out in a heartbeat. Maximos hands me a glass of champagne. I'm relieved it isn't the color of blood. Normally, just thinking of the delicious liquid makes my gums prick; in this instance, I feel nauseous imagining the blood-filled drinks of my vision.

Maximos and I find our seats along with the other guests, several of which Maximos introduces me to. I love the way he finds a way to put his hand on my waist protectively with every introduction. It's a shame this night, which is all about good works, could potentially be overshadowed by evil.

The orchestra has kicked up the music, and the first course is served. Maximos and I drank our fill several hours earlier, but we both pick lightly at the foie gras "au torchon" with pickled vegetables and brioche. Eating is the furthest thing from my mind.

The sound of a fork on crystal chimes, and the murmurs in the room grow quiet. One of the managing partners of Leo Capital, Robert Murdock, makes his way to the podium to introduce Maximos. Since unofficially becoming part of the Brotherhood, I obviously didn't end up taking the job with Leo. Instead, I've spent my time training and helping track down the Dark Coven and other possible Luminaries. But finding them is like a needle in a haystack—there are only so many news databases and contacts we have.

"Ladies and gentlemen, welcome to our Fourth Annual American Dream Realized Housing Award ceremony. Tonight we will be awarding fifteen homes to some very special families who have joined us. This evening wouldn't be possible without you all who, in one way or another, have directly contributed to this project's success. It's now with much pleasure I'd like to introduce Maximos Vasilliadis, the creator of this admirable endeavor," says Robert in a booming voice.

Maximos gives my hand a quick squeeze, and he excuses himself from the table to take the stage. The spotlight follows him to the podium as the room erupts in applause. I've attended plenty of company functions to know when there is lackluster appreciation for a leader. This is not the case. They adore him.

Maximos gives a humble thanks to the crowd. He is about to start introducing the families when the waiter clearing away the first course places a folded piece of paper at my place setting. I look up immediately with my senses exploding in fear. It's Charles.

"Hello, Ari," he says coldly. I look around nervously and catch Ryan's eye, who is sitting only a table away. I give him a nod, and he stealthily gets up to approach the table.

"What are you doing here?" I whisper as Maximos continues with his speech.

"Just delivering a message," he smiles and whispers in my ear. Chills go down my spine, and our eyes briefly connect before he hurries away. I've never seen him so glassy eyed. He's been turned into a Human Subordinate. Ryan follows him from the room, knowing that something is amiss. Not wanting to draw attention to the incident, I stay seated. The Brothers are all nearby, and I'm safe. I pick up the paper gingerly and open it. It's a heavy and luxurious cardstock. Written in a delicate script—no doubt from an expensive fountain pen—is a message:

Never forget, you cannot change destiny any more than your legacy. The Brotherhood may have won you over, but they won't with the Second Luminary. We already have.
Stavros

The room feels like it's getting smaller, and my chest is constricting. They have found the Second Luminary. I look around the room in desperation while everyone is rapt with Maximos' speech. It feels like forever until Maximos returns. The main course is now starting.

"What did you think?" Maximos asks, flushed with the joyous giving of the evening. "What's wrong?" he asks, now alarmed after he's absorbed my distress. I hand him the note. My hand is trembling. He reads it quickly, and his jaw clenches in response. "Let's go."

Maximos helps me from my seat as we subtly excuse ourselves. Luckily, a side exit isn't far. We head back up to Maximos' room, and he takes out his phone to call Aristos and Evander. Once we are behind closed doors, there is a torrent of discussion about the note and the Dark Coven. We learn Ryan followed Charles, who saw that he was being pursued. In a bizarre turn, Charles took a powerful cyanide pill, then promptly seized and died on the lobby floor. Charles may have betrayed me, but I never wanted him to become the pawn he did. The Dark Coven used him just to rattle me.

Once Maximos is off the phone, he lets out a series of curses in Greek. At this point, there is nothing we can do. We have no leads. I walk over to him, the tulle of my dress rustling against the plush carpet.

"We'll find her," I tell him. "You found me." He rakes his fingers through his hair and throws his phone on the desk in disgust.

"This never ends," he says in frustration. Maximos takes a seat on the edge of the bed.

"It will one day . . . and it will be a happy ending. We have to believe that," I say. All this time, Maximos has been the voice of assurance. But now, I'm the one who needs to offer it to him. I've never seen him deflated—until now. He stares at me with obvious pain in his eyes.

"Do you know I've been doing this for over two thousand years, matia mou?" Maximos says. I'm struck by the hollowness of his voice combined with the endearment I never thought I'd hear again. "And all this time I've been alone. I've had Aristos and Evander, and even the Brothers. But do you want to know something?"

"What?" I ask softly as I sit down next to him and kick off my heels.

"It's never bothered me, until now. For the first time, I want to be selfish. I want to tell the Brotherhood and the Dark Coven to go fuck themselves. I want to just live a life—for once. And I want to do that with you."

The dam of emotion I didn't know I had in my heart has just been torn apart. Happiness and sadness, all at the same time, come flooding out, along with my tears. I didn't cry at Raad's funeral, but now all of a sudden the tears are unstoppable.

"But why can't we, Maximos? Don't we deserve happiness too?"

"I don't know," he says uncertainly. "I don't want to hurt you. I don't want to compromise everything that we are trying to achieve."

"You cannot change destiny any more than your legacy," I say, echoing Stavros' words. "If that's the truth, my destiny is with you, and I don't want to change it. I'll fight for the Brotherhood, but I'm done fighting what is between us. The prophecy says I will have to make a sacrifice. And I'll do it—whatever it is. But right now, that sacrifice doesn't mean us. We've been brought together in the most unusual circumstance . . . but what's between us is real."

"I know it is," he says as his hand reaches to cup my chin.

"Then let's stop this game of pretend," I urge, letting myself speak freely without worrying about the impact and how he'll respond. But his response couldn't be sweeter . . .

"Agreed," Maximos replies.

And then, like a man who has just been unfettered from living a life in chains, he pulls me to him. It's not gentle or innocent—it's voracious. He tips me back onto the bed, and in the sea of tulle that is my dress our bodies press together—reaching to entwine every limb and ounce of exposed flesh. But it's not enough. There is too much fabric between us and not enough skin. My hands reach eagerly for the buttons on his tuxedo shirt, and his hands reach for the zipper on my dress.

Hands move at lightning speed, unfastening, unbuttoning, and unzipping. As if we've been starved, our hunger for each other has finally been unleashed. I need to be satiated. Our fangs are exposed, and I can feel my blood humming in arousal. I've never wanted anyone like this before. Finally, we're free of the constricting clothes, and I can appreciate Maximos in all his glory as I crawl my way up his body, brushing my skin against his.

I remember touching and tasting him the night of the Turn—how could I ever forget? But now, without the chaos of my hormones clouding my actions, I can appreciate the muscular planes of him and even the curl of hair on his chest all that much more. I explore his body with my hands, feeling the hardness of him everywhere. Where I've considered myself to be in shape and firm, Maximos is like rock . . . in more places than just his arms and abs.

"I've wanted this for so long, agapi mou," he groans between a kiss with his hand wrapped tightly in my hair.

"Me too," I whisper. My body is arching under his touch that seems to create electricity wherever his fingers follow.

"Your scent has been calling to me. I never knew the smell of honey and lily could be this . . . delicious." The tips of his fangs graze my neck, releasing some beads of blood. Rather than hurting, it feels amazing. He takes his time and licks. But I want more, I want to feel him inside me and to drink from me the way I want to from him. "By the goddesses, this is true ambrosia," he says.

I look into his eyes that are now glowing. He called me agapi mou, or "my love." Before, it's always been matia mou, or "my eyes" or "my dear." Now is as good a time as ever to tell him . . .

"I love you, Maximos," I whisper. He breathes in deeply and exhales. I can't tell if it's relief or regret he's feeling. Fear flutters in my chest. I wait for him to say something. He then closes his eyes, as if he's searching for what to say.

"I need to do something," he answers. What? What can he possibly need to do right now? I can't think of anything to say. But surely my expression of dismay is enough. "Just stay here. Don't move. I promise I'll be back in a few minutes," he says quickly as he pulls on a pair of boxers and nothing else. The next thing I know, he's gone. He shifted away.

I'm puzzled and more than just a little hurt. I thought we agreed we could be together? Did he get scared? I pull the sheet, now rumpled and twisted from our frantic encounter, over my body that is still radiating waves of heat. I'm not sure what I should do—ease my sorrow with a drink from the mini bar or watch television. What are you supposed to do when a guy leaves you right before you're about to make love?

I lay there for several minutes pondering my predicament. If he can leave, then so can I! My emotions have swung from hurt to anger. I throw the sheet off and retrieve my dress from the floor and begin to put it on. I'm so angry I end up ripping the zipper right off the dress. Damn it. With one hand closed around the dress to keep it from falling off, I search under the bed to find one of my heels that is now missing.

"What are you doing, Ari?" I hear Maximos ask. He's back.

"Leaving!" I whirl around to face the shirtless Greek god standing before me. "You do it so well; I thought I'd take my cue from you," I snap. Fear transfixes his face.

"You misunderstand . . . I didn't leave you because I didn't want to be with you. I left because I want to be with you." Now I'm only more confused.

"I don't understand this cryptic speak. Here in the twenty-first century, men don't leave their women right before they are about to have sex."

He lets out an exasperated sigh. "I was hoping to do this in somewhat of a charming manner, but then again I wasn't expecting you to fly off the handle in the ten minutes that I left you." He then starts to laugh. I'm about to start arguing with him, but he gets down on one knee. He actually gets down on one knee.

"I know it's the twenty-first century, Arianna Elizabeth Parker. But in my day, we believed in doing this." He then pulls out a small box that he had tucked into the back band of his boxers. He opens it to reveal a vintage-looking oval cushion-cut sapphire, hugged by two half-moon diamond side stones.

"I want you to be my wife. To be my partner and my friend. I want you to be my lover. The fact is I love you too. And I realized that I couldn't tell you that or go another moment without asking for your hand. Will you marry me, Ari?"

I'm shell-shocked. We've known each other for less than three months . . . I was hoping that Maximos might tell me he loved me. But to ask me to be his wife. It wasn't even in the consideration set. But the reality is, this is right.

"Yes!" I say. I think it comes out more as a squeal of delight. He then slides the sparkling ring on my finger. I pull him from his knee into my arms and give him a smoldering kiss.

"Maximos, I'm the happiest I've ever been," I tell him as I frame his face in my hands. "You've given me everything I could ever want: love and a family."

"What a relief, because you didn't seem too happy when I came back."

It's now my turn to laugh. "I suppose I do have a flair for the dramatic."

"The stones were my mother's," he says as he reaches down for my hand now laden with the stunning ring. "I had them recut and set many years ago—for what I didn't know until today."

"It's beautiful. You know you are going to spoil me rotten if you keep this up."

"I'll happily spoil you for the rest of our lives together. You know, before he died, I promised Raad I would protect you and help you find love. And I will give that to you, as long as I'm alive."

"Well I intend for us to live very long lives."

"Good," says Maximos with his devilish grin. "You should also know when I went to get the ring from the safe on Ambrosine, I asked Aristos for his permission. You should have seen his face when I showed up in his room like this."

"What did he say?" I ask nervously.

"He said, 'It is about time.'" We both break out in laughter, and I jump into his arms with my dress hanging down at a precarious angle. "I suppose I'm going to have to remove this dress from you again, my love."

"Good. I thought you were going to insist on waiting until our wedding night," I say, relieved.

"Well I did just promise to make an honest woman out of you, and I always keep my promises. So we'll do whatever you want to," he says mischievously. "Tonight is about us. Our duty can wait until tomorrow."

THE END